The Secret Language of Women

The Secret Language of Women

Nina Romano

TURNER

Turner Publishing Company
424 Church Street • Suite 2240 • Nashville, Tennessee 37219
445 Park Avenue • 9th Floor • New York, New York 10022

www.turnerpublishing.com

The Secret Language of Women

Cover design: Kristen Ingebretson and Maddie Cothren
Book design: Kym Whitley

Library of Congress Cataloging-in-Publication Data

Romano, Nina, 1942-
 The secret language of women / Nina Romano.
     pages cm
1. Nü shu--Fiction. 2. Women--Fiction. 3. China--History--19th century-
-Fiction. I. Title.
 PS3568.O549S43 2015
 813'.6--dc23
                                            2015009479

Printed in the United States of America
14 15 16 17 18 19 0 9 8 7 6 5 4 3 2 1

To Felipe

for a lifetime of love
and the priceless gift of world travel

Author's Note:

Pinyin instead of Wade-Giles is used for the sake of clarity, except for the capital city Beijing, written *Peking*, and also the old city of Tientsin .

Prologue

THE THINGS THAT TEST YOU and are vanquished bring everlasting joy. The differences between traditional written Chinese and *Nüshu,* the secret language of women, made it difficult for me to learn it. My mother and grandmother could not write Chinese and learned *Nüshu* when they were young and wanted me to grasp it too. I cannot say they harped on me or were tyrannical, but I will say they were insistent, and for this I am eternally indebted.

My mother said it challenged me because I wrote like a man and didn't have to rely solely on *Nüshu,* the way they did to communicate with other women. The ideograms of Chinese correspond to a word or part of one, whereas each of the seven hundred characters of *Nüshu* represent a syllable—women's language is phonetic, in *Chéngguān* dialect 城关土话, adaptable and pliant for singing, poetry, and writing with such delicate strokes they appear as lines of feathers.

Though learning was problematical, I mastered it, like I do all things I set my mind to conquer. At the time, I resented the study of it, yet I knew innately one day I would be grateful to possess the knowledge and skill of this secret language, which would offer me strength and solace for a lifetime. And although I was writing in *Nüshu,* for some reason, I signed with flourish in Chinese: Wǒ Lián.

I am Lian. 我连

The Great moderate Way has no gate;
There are a thousand paths to it.
If you pass through the barrier,
You walk the universe alone.

~Wu-Men

The Secret Language of Women

Chapter 1

Anjilika
安吉莉卡
Angelica

PEKING, 1895
YIHEYUAN, THE SUMMER PALACE

NOTHING HAPPENS BY ACCIDENT.

I finished assisting my father in a successful operation, and while washing my hands, realized how much I loved the art of healing and desired nothing more than to practice it. My father, Gianluca Brasolin, a Swiss doctor proficient in both Western and Eastern medicine, kept an inexpensive garret southwest of Tiananmen Square in the eighth alleyway in the Dashilan area of Xuanwu District in southern Peking. This was the capital's garish and tawdry red-light district, but Father chose it because he could do the most good there.

The surgery took place in a *qinglou,* a brothel built some decades prior that adjoins our humble residence, its decorated brick eaves touching ours. My Baba, as I called him, when not referring to him as Doctor in front of patients, saved a thirteen-year-old girl from dying of a self-induced abortion, but she will never have babies. He stopped her from bleeding to death by administering a hypodermic injection of snake poison to staunch the hemorrhage.

Fluent in both Mandarin and Italian, my father had been called to work as the doctor for the Italian Consulate; we had been in China's capital city of Peking for six months, but soon would return to our home in Guilin, where my mother's mother resided. Baba was bored with dignitaries and the artifice of court life and suffered from a heart that was weak and failing. Even more than these things, he was frightened by the brewing animosity toward foreigners and growing political strife that had seized parts of the country, especially in the north. Peasants known as Boxers sought to drive all foreigners from China—my Baba included. They belonged to a secret society known as *I-ho ch'üan,* Righteous and Harmonious Fists, in north China but spreading. They practiced boxing and calisthenics, which they believed would give them supernatural powers and make them impervious to bullets. In the south the situation was calmer, and Father said we would be safer there. I, however, feared the return to Guilin because I knew my grandmother, Wai Po,had arranged a marriage that would take place almost immediately. Lu was a simple man, a farmer, whom she felt confident would provide for me.

LATER THAT SAME EVENING, BABA smoked a pipe on our covered terrace overlooking a row of jagged houses while I gazed at an heirloom brooch with a picture of my mother on a porcelain oval. After finishing his training in his native Switzerland, Father had become fascinated by the Eastern arts and medicine. He traveled throughout the Orient where he met and fell in love with my beautiful mother. Only memories of her sustained me now. On the brooch her face looked so serene. I remembered the day she gave it to me seven years ago, on my tenth birthday, when she was dying. I took her fan out of the coffin before it was nailed shut. Baba was so bereaved he didn't even scold me. Grandmother kept Mother's diary, written in *Nüshu,* the secret language of women Mother had taught me. Wai Po promised to give it to me for my wedding.

I put the brooch away when there was a loud knocking on our door. Court messengers. At first, I was afraid that something untoward was in store for my father, but they had come merely to summon him to assist the Italian ambassador who had taken ill at a banquet while speaking with Cixi, our empress dowager. Baba was to tend to the sick man at the Summer Palace, fifteen kilometers northwest of Peking.

I stood behind the door left ajar, watching everything, remaining concealed. The messengers were stout men and wore a kind of armor and metal hat. I wondered how they sat a horse. They had brought Father a scroll, which he looked over and nodded his head. He told the two messengers to await him downstairs in our humble courtyard.

Baba opened the door, handed me the scroll, and said, "Don't take time to read it now, Lian. Hurry and ready yourself. You're coming with me to the Summer Palace. Get my bag and make sure it's in perfect order."

Had I heard him correctly? I had been training in medicine secretly with Father ever since my mother died and had always helped him in our neighborhood but never, ever at court. In my night attire, my hair loose about my shoulders, I looked down at my bare feet, toes curling with excitement and fear. My feet had not been bound so I did not possess the golden lilies wrought by pain to produce the exquisite, tiny feet all Chinese men sought.

We set out in the depths of a summer evening in the palanquin sent by the royal court and passed Zengh Yi Lu, site of the walled foreign legations. My father was dressed in Western attire, black tails and white tie, while I wore my most stunning Manchu banner dress, knowing that no matter how I dressed, I would be seen by the courtiers as an outcast of mixed blood. I trembled, thinking of their stares. I passed for Chinese with my dark hair and face, my willow-shaped eyebrows, but the instant anyone looked closely and saw my green eyes, they knew I came from a mix, a mongrel with foreign blood coursing through my veins.

Seeing the frightened look on my face, Baba said, "If you're planning on being a doctor, get over this nonsense of worrying what people think of you."

I nodded, but knew exactly how dangerous this was—the audacity of appearing in public as his assistant. Chinese women worked at matchmaking, as midwives, sometimes as herbalists, but never as doctors.

As the palanquin traveled through the summer night, the air sweet with lavender blossoms, I studied the scroll. The message stated that an ambassador had taken ill and the situation was urgent. I tried to appear unconcerned. "That's it?" I asked. "Nothing more, except he's sick? Plague perhaps? Maybe cholera?"

"We'll find out," Baba said. His philosophy of treating patients was never to speculate before an examination. I was barely listening, wondering about the type and gravity of the illness and the reasons my father had been sought out.

"Yes," I agreed, "even smelling his breath will tell us something."

We drove through a park dotted with gingko trees, an ancient pagoda on one side and opposite, a huge Buddha. Through a seedier part of town, we passed many brick buildings, some with overhanging portals, wooden bridges, or decorated arches in disrepair. Garbage littered the streets. The great city's commerce seemed to be crumbling. It was pathetic to bear witness to such degradation. Stores and shops were dilapidated, some looted. When I pointed, Father told me foreigners were commonly blamed, but the assaults were made by Boxers egged on in secret by our empress, who was fearful of the influence the foreign legions had and wished to see them expelled. Meanwhile she turned away from the suffering of her people and this disgrace of her own doing, claiming certain anti-foreign squads were responsible. From my mother I had been taught to revere our empress and our native land, China, *Zhongguo,* center of the universe or the Middle Kingdom, while my father had taught me to believe in the power of science and the universal progress of mankind.

As if echoing my thoughts, he said, "From squalor and filth comes pestilence and disease," his voice as grave as a mourner.

The city may have been just as poor as our own Guilin, but it seemed worse here because of the great population and the appalling overcrowding. Noises from brothels and the twanging music of the *pipa* and *yangqin* came toward us, buoyed on billows of smoke pungent from cookstoves, outdoor kitchens, and the opium pipes Father did not think I recognized. The things and places I loved were the *hutongs,* the narrow alleyways and lanes that enclosed *siheyuans,* the courtyard houses so typical of Peking. I felt most at home walking among these.

We passed a huge cemetery on the outskirts, and I tried holding my breath so the ghosts housed there would not know I was alive and come after me, but Father asked me something I had to answer. As soon as I did, I held my breath again. When he noticed, he tickled my ribs to make me laugh and breathe. After a big smile, he chided me for having Chinese superstitions just like my mother's. "There are no such things as ghosts. Only kind spirits of the dead. Look at all those graves. Some of them are works of art."

"All seem to be aboveground, making it easier to get out," I said. We fell into silence, but the air surrounding us was lively with our thoughts.

After passing the cemetery, we switched from the palanquin to a horse-drawn carriage. Weary from the ride, I fell asleep, my head on

Father's shoulder. As we approached the palace grounds, Baba woke me. The enormous palace, he explained, had been rebuilt after the huge fire of 1860. It consisted of Longevity Hill and Kunming Lake. "There are close to three hundred hectares—most of it water—and at least three thousand structures."

Soon I saw pavilions and towers, covered corridors and bridges, expanses of gardens and attached buildings with sprawling staircases, huge in the shadows of lit torches. The night lent brilliance with a bright, full-faced, fat moon beaming down and a sky draped with candle-lit stars. "I must have needed to rest in order for my eyes to behold such riches," I said. After all the poverty and derelict housing, this opulence was at once magnificent to behold yet nauseating. If the empress dowager truly was a god, why didn't she and her court assist the poor and sick?

We entered the East Palace Gate and descended from the carriage into an inner courtyard. A tall man in a gray tunic dress greeted us and then escorted us past the Hall of Virtue and Harmony, where our empress usually entertained, to the Renshoudian, the Hall of Benevolence and Longevity. When my father inquired why we were being shown here, the man made a curt bow.

"Please follow," he said. Then with disdain on his face, he added, "She stays."

The escort stared at my feet, an intense glare of disgust. In that instant, I felt ugly and unwanted, my confidence shrinking. I could have cursed Father for bringing me into the world with all his free thinking and not allowing Mother to bind my feet like hers. Even my father, a foreigner, fell in love with a woman with bound feet. I could not help wondering if he would have loved her without them. I knew in my heart the answer was yes because he loved me, didn't he? Still, in Chinese eyes unbound feet degraded a woman's value. Grandmother said so herself when she announced my engagement to Lu. The matchmaker had struggled to find a man willing to take a half-breed like me, and the dowry price, Grandmother made sure I knew, was exceptionally high.

Father met the man's gaze when he looked up, and with an assured manner said, "She's my assistant; without her, I do not proceed."

His turned-down mouth displayed the man's distaste and hatred of foreigners. He'd all but pointed to my feet. Though he certainly considered me polluted, he acquiesced and let me pass.

We followed him at a fast pace down an elegant, open gallery. A profusion of colors reminded me of a field of flowers—red and green columns, ceilings of purple and gold, and arches of a variety of cutout woodwork motifs. A light breeze flurried the silk coverings at some of the apertures, and from somewhere in the distance came a cry announcing the first trine, the hour of the rat. This *shichen,* or large-hour, lasted two hours from midnight. A most fortuitous hour, I thought, full of energy and unpredictability, and I speculated what this would mean for my father and me.

The escort ushered us through more hallways and galleries, filled with treasures, each more glorious than the last, and brought us finally to a small room with curtained walls of sea-foam Shantung silk. Once more, the man bowed. "Please wait," he said, as he disappeared though a doorway. Unlike the opulent chambers we had seen, this room was sparsely furnished. There was a small ebony table, a mirror in a gilded frame, a vase of bamboo on a high planter of ebony to match the table, and a carved seat.

Father lovingly slid a finger across the table and whispered to me, "Antique. Qing Dynasty." But then he began to pace. He stopped, fidgeted with his pocket watch, anxious to get to his patient. "Why do they always make you wait?"

Finally the attendant returned to escort us into an adjoining chamber where the patient awaited us. At the door, a hideously small servant tried to bar my way. Again, Father explained I was his assistant and bade me enter with him. I followed him across the room to a couch by the wall where a middle-aged man lay moaning.

"Signor Ambaciatore," Baba said with a quick bow. *"Io sono il Dottore Brasolin."*

The ambassador answered with a grimace and waved his hand, groaning and moving from side to side, holding his head. He was dressed in an elegant evening frock with tails like a penguin, but his tie and shirtfront were undone, his stomach bulging as if he wanted to give birth to a winter melon. He was unkempt—hair tousled, sweat pouring out of him as he lay propped up on brocade pillows—a porcelain basin on the floor next to him.

Baba asked him some questions in Italian, the language we used between us. But he changed to Mandarin when he addressed me, and

I knew he didn't want the patient to understand. The ambassador, Baba said, appeared to have overindulged in eating, but he would conduct a thorough examination to make sure. I asked him why the ambassador didn't speak Chinese. "It's a difficult language and the man is new to foreign service," Baba said.

Father bade me to come close and watch carefully as he examined the ambassador, touching a hand to his brow. The man complained of a bad headache; I assumed from drinking too much champagne. He began to quake from chills and appeared feverish. Father tapped the man's belly, smelled his breath, pulled his eyelids back and listened to the beat of his heart. He questioned the patient some more, then asked me what I'd do.

I said, "Take his pulses and look at his tongue."

"Go ahead," Baba said, and so I did.

"His pulses are fast and thready," I reported. Father agreed and said he was going to submit the man to an emetic, thus disgorging all *Signor* Ambassador had eaten.

The ambassador tried to sit up, and pointing to me, said, "Who is that woman?"

In Italian, I answered, "His nurse."

The man, confused by my knowledge of his language, flopped down on his pallet.

I felt disappointed that *il dottore* would not slice open the ambassador's bloated stomach and empty out the apparent suckling pig he'd swallowed whole. But then Baba turned pale and said he wanted to check something else but didn't have a good feeling about it. "You'd better leave, daughter," he said, his voice anxious.

I returned to the small antechamber where we had waited before. I wandered into a hallway where curiosity pulled me to have a look at all the paintings and *objects d'arte* in an ebony and ivory inlaid curio cabinet. There were carved ivory and jade figurines, some of them in what Father called compromising positions. I'd never even been kissed, but I certainly understood the functions of gender parts that Baba had explained. But that was not the whole of it, for sure, because I remembered once seeing my parents kiss, not a Chinese custom, and only yesterday I had practiced in the mirror what it would be like to kiss a man's mouth.

Soon Father came out of the patient's room and called to me. He looked worried, his brow knitted. My father said, sotto voce, that he needed to contemplate what he should do next. "It appears to be typhus. Be scrupulous. Wash your hands often," he said, and slapped his hand to his neck at a pesky mosquito. With that we both retired to a nearby courtyard with a fountain where we washed our hands.

The attendant found us there. Baba explained that the symptoms were grave and could be of epidemic proportions. "Or perhaps we will be spared and this will be just an isolated case. Typhus is most likely caused by a flea on a cat." The attendant bowed and exited the courtyard to make his report to the empress.

Baba turned to me and said, "There's some swelling of the lymph glands."

"What herb will you use?" I asked.

My father tossed my words right back. "What herb?"

"Anjilika?" I said, a note of hesitation in my voice.

"Why?"

"Angelica is an anti-inflammatory herb, the root of which can be made into a tea."

My father nodded and smiled. Then he did that European thing he did and pinched my cheek. He was pleased.

We were on our way back to the patient's room when a huge man dressed in black silk accosted us. "A eunuch," Father confided to me in a whisper. The eunuch gave Baba a purse, which he accepted with a bow.

Then to our surprise, the eunuch added, "The empress will see you now." The eunuch pressed a hand over a round jade medallion on a long silver chain.

My father bowed, even more deeply this time. "A truly unexpected honor, which we gratefully accept. However, I must finish attending to my patient. A doctor should never neglect his duty."

The eunuch accompanied us as we backtracked to the ambassador's chamber, where Father gave instructions to the servant to administer angelica tea. Assured that the ambassador rested comfortably, he turned to the eunuch and said we were ready for the audience.

"Why does the empress want to see us?" I murmured.

Father marched ahead of me down the magnificently decorated hallways as if he knew the answer but wasn't saying anything more in front of the eunuch. Did Baba suspect that the eunuch understood Italian? Or did Father think it was inappropriate to say too much in front of a person so entrenched with the empress? My heart pounded hard in my chest. It never dawned on me that I would come face-to-face with the empress—a goddess if ever any walked the earth. What could I say? I was terrified and at the same moment proud to actually meet this amazing force—this dynamic personage, a woman, no less, though I had heard her stature was much shorter than my own. I looked at my father—calm and collected while every one of my bones shook inside my skin. But of course, Baba was Western, scientific, democratic, and revered no man or woman on earth.

Then he spoke to me. "The empress must fear the threat of an epidemic. Worried, no doubt, as she should be."

At last the eunuch led us to the hall where the empress presided. We entered the room at the back, where he bade us to wait.

In my dreams, perhaps, I had seen such a place, but never on this mortal earth. We had come to the room where the banquet had taken place, an enormous table in the center holding the remains of the demolished dinner. Screens of semiprecious stones, enormous planters, wall hangings of painted silks, and huge lacquer side tables holding gilded platters of pyramids of fruit decorated the room. The smoke of candles and cigars swirled through the air. Seated in various poses of relaxation or standing huddled in small conversational groups were Chinese statesmen in lively colored brocades and silks and foreign dignitaries, each in the costume of his native land. Among the foreigners, there were many men, but only a few women, each one ornately dressed by Western standards. The guests whispered behind a gloved hand or pretended to cough, bending over and saying something to a companion. In one corner stood six men in Italian naval uniforms rigid at attention. To my great horror, one of them was looking right at me. Luckily I had Mother's fan with me, which I immediately opened to cover my face. I knew I was blushing. His dark looks were so easy on my eyes, so different from Lu's sallow complexion.

Father's eyes roamed the room, and he said to me, "The entire Italian delegation is here. If it is typhus epidemic, then many lives may be lost due to poor sanitary conditions."

At last my eyes took in the empress, a tiny lady, ornately coiffed and dressed, seated at the far end of the room on a large platform in her dragon-in-clouds throne carved in rosewood. The footstool alone would have made a lovely seat and valuable house ornament. Behind the throne rose fans of peacock feathers, porcelain vases taller than a man, a screen bordered by sandalwood, and a censer I thought resembled a hideous monster.

Taking my clue from one of the whispering dignitaries, I leaned toward Father. "What's the screen for?"

He cleared his throat, which made me realize he was good at this game and had some experience. "She usually holds court behind it. We're lucky to see her face-to-face."

A court elder approached and said he would translate for the Italian delegation. While I waited, two eunuchs escorted my father to the throne. How small he looked between the eunuch with a queue as long as my arm, and another eunuch, if one could go by his outfit, minus the medallion, but with the same queue and demeanor. Father had told me of the horrible way in which these once-men castrated themselves in order to serve the court, saving their cut off members—penis, testicles, and scrotum—by preserving them in alcohol. These body parts, genteelly referred to as *bǎo,* or precious treasure, were buried with them at the time of death, in order to be once again whole in the life to come.

The empress beckoned my father forward. I raised my head slightly in order to peek over my fan to see what was happening. Baba bowed ceremoniously from the waist, and then he kowtowed, kneeling down, bending forward, and touching his forehead to the floor. I wondered where he'd learned such gracious behavior. Everyone fell silent. There was a resounding echo in the room, and the empress's high-pitched voice squeaked around my ears till I wanted to cover them. Nevertheless, I dared not. In great detail, she questioned my father about the ambassador's illness. It was difficult to hear how my father answered the empress, and I wished he would use his professional booming voice with her the way he did with me when he wanted my full attention. The empress leaned forward and said something to my father that I did not hear. Finally the audience appeared to be over. Father did not turn around to walk back to where I stood, but instead backed up like some awkward turtle.

I was about to back out of the room when Father said, "Wait one second, she wants a word with you."

"Me?" I asked, my palms already beginning to moist over.

"Hush." He was perspiring.

But before I could even think, the two colossi escorted both of us before the empress.

I bowed, like I saw my father do, realized this was wrong, for it was male courtly behavior, and so I curtsied, which was laughable due to my tight skirt. The empress looked at me as though I had just sprouted a third eye. I quickly kowtowed as I had seen my father do, only I smacked my forehead too hard on the floor, wanting to yelp, "Ouch," but restrained myself.

She bade me to rise. "I understand you assist your father in his medical duties," the empress said. Protocol demanded that I put the fan away in the bodice of my dress, and I had nothing to screen me from the dragon-lady's gaze. "You are very strange to want to aid your father in such lurid work. What kind of girl are you? How old are you?"

"Seventeen, Your Imperial Highness. I desire one day to be a healer like my father," I said, the words eking out as though I had a money toad stuck in my throat, and it wanted to spit out the coin.

The empress appeared taken aback at my willingness to speak the truth. "And what of your mother? Is this what she wants for you—this lowly, squalid touching of sick bodies?"

"My mother is dead, your Highness."

"Better dead than to see you the way you are." The empress's eyes traveled to my feet, returning to my face with a look of contempt. "Such a shame. In other circumstances one might have even considered you beautiful." She turned and whispered behind her fan to the interpreter at her side, then looked back at me. "I understand you speak the language of the foreign devils."

I was unhappy to hear my beautiful Italian referred to that way but nodded.

"I could use a girl like you at court. Unafraid to speak her mind, fluent in the ways of the West. More trustworthy, perhaps," she added with a pointed look at the translator, "than those who claim to serve me best." Her eyes narrowed. "Where does your heart lie, girl? Are you loyal to your empress? Do you hold your mother's Chinese heritage above all else? Or have you been polluted by foreign ways?"

Where did my heart lie? I had never been forced before to choose between my father and my mother. Dismay must have shown on my face. My thoughts galloped and physically I had all to do to keep my balance and poise. A sideward glance toward Baba revealed his face expressing fright. He would die if I left him, he'd said so every day of my life since my mother died.

"Have you no tongue, girl?" the empress squawked.

Diplomacy was a thing I lacked, and so I just blurted out the truth. "I could never leave my father, Your Highness, unless you absolutely commanded me to. He is aged and infirm himself. I am his hands and eyes. My mother would be proud that I'm schooled in my filial duties."

She raised an eyebrow. Who was I really? I'd committed not just a gaffe, but an outrage against the court. Instead of ordering my head chopped off and put on a stake beyond the palace walls, she sniggered. With a gesture of dismissal, she flicked her left hand, her nails long and curved, the tips covered with pointy gold-fitted filigree tassels at the end. What a waste of riches to keep her clad in this manner, while the sick and poor begged at the Forbidden City's gates and the eunuchs could not have a proper operation to dismember their private parts and constantly leaked because of it.

"Leave. Now." Once again her eyes gazed at my feet. "I have no more time to waste on a girl of such monstrous appearance."

I bowed with my arms crossed in front of me inside wide sleeves. Still, I had one question to ask the empress—what she intended to do now that typhus had been discovered at the palace. I raised my eyes to her.

Astounded at this outrage, the empress shouted, "You wish to address me again?"

I started to say, "Your Supreme Royal Highness—"

My father interrupted. "Only to thank you, Oh Celestial Great One, for your kind decision to leave her at my side when she really would rather be at court. She has pity for me as I am widowed."

"Ah. Then done," she said, and repeated, *"jié shù."*

My father tugged my sleeve for we were to kneel down. I remembered to tuck my *qipao,* my banner dress, beneath me for the kowtow as we knelt. This was no easy feat as the long skirt, according to the Manchu Dynasty custom, was narrow and formfitting. When I'd managed the kneeling position, I followed Father's example, touching my forehead lightly to the floor, but again my touchdown resounded, and I said, "Ay," quickly coughing to muffle the sound.

Father, fuming, took my arm and led me to the back of the hall. The entire Italian contingency stared at us with open amazement, including one of the elder statesmen, whose chest displayed enough decorations to topple him over from the weight. Baba nodded to him.

"Brasolin," the man said, "I've never seen anyone so young dare defy the empress before." I listened, amazed as Baba explained that I was a girl of high moral standards who preferred a meaningful life like her father's rather than courtly life. *Nicely put,* I thought, smothering a giggle, covering my mouth with a hand.

The gentleman smiled at me and said he agreed.

But I was curious about the Italians who served as an honor guard—especially the handsome one who had looked at me. Why, I asked, were sailors on duty in the Summer Palace?

"Times are dangerous," the dignitary confided in a whisper, "even at the Palace. The sailors have been brought here to provide the Italian legation as added security. They will remain until they can be relieved."

I thanked him, then tugged up my skirt and beat a breeze with my fan, racing to keep up with my father. We exited the banquet hall, where the Italian sailors were now standing as an honor guard. As we passed by them, the same sailor noticed me again. He had a Roman nose, was clean-shaven, and quite intent on looking every bit on duty. How fortunate to see him full-face in radiant candlelight. I started a slight bow, wondering if I had a red splotch on my forehead, but came up straight as he winked at me—a kind of salute to my spunkiness with the empress, I thought. I almost tripped, not believing it, and glanced over my shoulder to glimpse his handsome face once more. Sure enough, another wink. On purpose.

Outside the eunuch was waiting to escort us to our carriage. His scent made me slow my step, and Father's words came back to me how these *castrati* often concealed their body odors with perfume. We followed him to a huge red portal, where my father ordered me to stop. The eunuch leading the way turned, walked a courteous distance ahead, and stopped also. How attuned he was to every human situation. Baba joined him and conferred briefly. Then he returned to me. "Your behavior was atrocious, but it's my fault for never having given you proper instruction."

I wanted to tell him about the sailor who had winked at me, but his fury was unleashed and I dared not.

He said, "With all you have read, I thought you'd know. Our woe isn't over yet." He blew out a huge breath of air. "You'll be escorted to a garden to wait for me. The eunuch will take you. I have to make sure the ambassador will be fully cared for and that the proper precautions are followed so the disease does not spread. The empress has demanded he be removed immediately from the Palace and is having him transported back to the Italian legation. She has made it clear she will not suffer any repercussions or scandal from this ordeal. She detests foreign devils, me included." His anger softened, and he gave me a small smile. "Though she's curious as to why a Chinese woman married one. Try to behave like a lady and don't speak to anyone for any reason."

I nodded. Following the eunuch, we walked along for what seemed like a *li*, passing through what I dubbed the Hall of Dragons for I saw many etched or painted everywhere. "If the empress hates us so much," I said to my Baba, "why did she bring you here?"

"Obvious isn't it? I make myself understood to all parties concerned and am a doctor who understands medicine of two worlds."

I mouthed the words: *European and Asian.* "But there's something more, correct?" I tried to keep in step with his long stride.

"The empress dowager cannot afford culpability if something happened under the auspices of the court. Typhus can spread in unexpected ways. There are many lives at stake here." He gave me a meaningful look. "Including Chinese."

The eunuch led us to a small garden where a fountain emptied into a small pond. Father bowed to me. As I returned his bow, he left me. The eunuch indicated a black lacquer bench where I sat down.

"Much cooler here," the eunuch said. "I will bring tea." He asked me if I required anything else.

I wanted to say, "Yes, a pallet to sleep on, and may I dunk my feet into the pool?" But I held my tongue, adhering to Father's admonition.

As he disappeared through a gate in the wall, I stood and wandered to the fountain. I sat down on the edge, away from the splashing water, and began to trail my hand in between lotus leaves. The garden smelled of jasmine. I took in a deep breath and decided that the empress wasn't really all that much. Wouldn't a goddess be more like Kwan Yin, the Goddess of Mercy my mother had taught me to revere? Aiding the sick, now that was a meaningful life, and exciting because so many things could go wrong that you didn't bargain for, no matter how carefully you tried. There was nothing in the world like the intricacies of the human heart, mind, body, and soul. This I had been taught by my father, and this I believed.

The carp frolicked in the light of flickering lanterns. "Hungry little fishies? Me too."

A servant appeared, set before me a tray of tea and some deep-fried bean curd with a light soy sauce, bowed and left, backing up as if I were royalty. At his gesture, I smiled but that faded fast. One of the honor guard sailors appeared in the alcove and beckoned me. Not only was I astonished to see a man here, but this particular man with the large brown eyes was the very one who'd winked at me—ah, for certain, this was the hour of the impulsive rat.

He called to me in Italian in a soft, strong voice. Had he followed me here? How did he know I understood him? He must have overheard me talking to Father. I stood, a little shaky on my feet. He was a god, tall past the lowest willow branch that canopied the space between us, so handsome in a European way, like my father, and his smile illuminated his face—round eyes the size of chestnuts held mirth and youth. I stopped quaking and began to walk with a steady gait. I never once looked down. His gaze held me until I stood in front of him, looking up into his smooth-cheeked face. He no longer smiled. A cloud covered the sickle of moon.

His serious expression conveyed a question, but I couldn't fathom its meaning. And then he spoke, saying, *"Sei la pür bella ragazza che ho visto mai."*

The way he said that I was the most beautiful girl he'd ever seen sounded to my ears like music from a piper, and I wanted to follow him anywhere, this man, who saw past my ungainly, big feet and ugliness straight to the center of my soul. Though how could I believe him, a much-traveled sailor? He stood at parade rest—an expression Father had told me was a more relaxed one than that of attention, though it looked rigid to me. I moved closer. Nothing of his body shifted as he held a bayoneted rifle in front of him. Only his eyes moved. They simply made me step into the space that embraced him, as he leaned down and placed his warm, soft mouth upon mine. A kiss I'd only dreamed of until now.

I thought I would faint from terror and pleasure. My mind begged permanence, but how could it when that was wholly irrational? When he pulled his lips away and straightened, I inhaled deeply his sandalwood cologne and tobacco. He whispered, *"Non dimenticarmi mai."*

I repeated like a child, learning a lesson by rote, *"Mai, e poi mai."*

He flipped his rifle to his shoulder, saluted, and at the sound of footfalls on the parquet floor, did an about-face. As he walked away, I wondered if I'd ever learn his name.

I touched my lips, again murmuring in Mandarin, "Never. Never will I forget."

Chapter 2

Huangqin
黃芩
Skullcap

THE EXTENSIVE HONOR GUARD HAD been recalled from the Palace—Giacomo Scimenti returning to the Italian legation with Captain Morante, Lieutenant Rinaldi, and the rest of the sailors assigned to the Peking security detail. Chief steward and cook aboard the gunship *Leopardo*, Giacomo preferred life at sea and had been sorry to be ordered to Peking. At least he could still cook. When the deputy ambassador heard he had a real Sicilian cook on the premises, he'd thrown out the Chinese coolie who usually prepared the Legation's meals and put Giacomo in charge of the kitchen. Meanwhile the *Leopardo* remained docked in Tientsin, some one hundred and sixty kilometers away.

At dawn, the morning after he'd met the girl in the garden, Giacomo stood in the kitchen preparing hot tea. He brought the tea and sweet biscuits to the deputy ambassador's office where the deputy was deep in conversation with Rinaldi and the captain. Giacomo put down the tray and stepped into the garden in the inner courtyard of the legation. In the garden, the shadow play of dawn did acrobatic stunts from trees to plants as light filtered down; even the weightless, keen air tumbled among the bushes till they shook and then fell still. He paced the garden two times, back and forth, and then returned for the tray, but the men hadn't even touched it yet. He shook his head and left the room.

Breakfast still needed to be prepared. He had already baked a *crostata* and a coffee cake, but Giacomo was in no hurry. He walked outside the legation and slipped past the wall to the street where the city was just beginning to stir. At the nearby market, merchants were setting up their stalls. Soon they would be squawking their wares to the music of pigs oinking and donkeys braying. Giacomo didn't understand a word of Chinese, but he loved to listen to the bargaining for ducks, fruits, and vegetables. Gestures and expressions were the same in any language, and watching the interplay of merchants and customers, he sometimes felt as if he were back in the market in his hometown of Carini in Sicily watching the hawkers sell their wares, and women, like his mother, bargain for zucchini and eggplant.

For now, peace hung in the air. Across the street Chinese houses huddled in the dim light beside the post office that served the foreign legations. The major powers of the world had assembled here—Russian, German, British, Japanese, American, and French, along with his own Italians—as a part of China's Relief Expedition Force, a multinational endeavor to rescue civilians from the violence of the rebellion. Movement drew his eyes to Ha Ta Men Street where lit lanterns were swinging just before daylight. It made a poignant sight, reminding him of a ship's storm lamp swaying with a sweep of rolling sea. How he missed the sea.

What would it be like to sail free of orders and visit the inlets, bays, and gulfs? At Tientsin, skinny fishermen with cone-shaped straw hats and long pigtails mended nets on the docks while cook fires burned on flimsy crafts afloat in the port. Amazing how the Chinese could eat at any time of the day—they loved vegetables as much as Sicilians. He remembered a few weeks ago he had hustled to the side of the *ponte di commando,* the vessel's bridge house to look out at men onshore engaged in an elaborate ritual of calisthenics. Word was they were Boxers, rebelling peasants stirring up trouble. They were strong and physically in good shape. He made a decision to exercise more. He had been in a hurry to return to the galley, so he slid down the metal rails of the steep staircase until he came to what he thought of as *his* deck.

He sighed and headed back into the legation. The men would want their breakfast. It was time to get to work and prepare a fresh *macedonia* of fruits.

At the legation late last night, there had been quite a commotion as an Italian state dignitary had been surreptitiously brought in and tended to by a Swiss doctor and a Eurasian girl, acting as his nurse. At least, according to his best buddy Bulldog, that was the scuttlebutt. Giacomo hoped it was the man and the girl he'd seen at the Palace, which meant that the girl was most probably his daughter, not his concubine. Giacomo shook his head, thinking of the liberty he'd taken with her, and yet he'd do it again. He'd chance anything for the feel of her lips, her scent.

He was enthralled with China. He loved the beer, the food, and above all, the women. When Giacomo wasn't drinking, playing cards, or carousing with his shipmates, he was fighting, not Chinese, but Frenchmen. He had a knack for getting drawn into brawls, his or anyone else's. It made no difference at all who was right or wrong. If one of his shipmates was involved, Giacomo stepped up to help.

Any member of the French Navy in clubbing distance would be attacked mercilessly, and Giacomo and his comrades expected no quarter from the French. He supposed his hatred had something to do with the Norman's dominion of his native Sicily for centuries. In the past year, he and his compatriots had beaten and battered more Frenchmen than Chinese. He'd had his share of whoring, too, mostly women in brothels, faceless girls that dissolved one into another. But the girl in the garden was different. He'd told her not to forget him—but she was the one he couldn't shake from his mind. He stood cutting up fresh fruit when Bulldog appeared at the kitchen door.

"What's wrong, Scimenti?" He slapped Giacomo affectionately on the head. "You're mooning around like a man in love."

"Forget it, Bulldog." Giacomo gave him a friendly shove back. "You know me better than that."

Seaman Shona Rotari, a short, stocky, half-African Neapolitan, called himself a mongrel mix, his father Italian, his mother Libyan. The nickname suited him. Bulldog had a fierce face but a gentle nature, and to Giacomo the name meant *faithful friend.*

Giacomo said, "Never heard the name Shona before. What's it mean?"

"Arabic for 'beloved.'"

"And you're telling me I'm a man in love. What was your father thinking? No wonder you want to be called Bulldog," Giacomo said, suppressing a laugh.

"Shut the door on it, mate. Trap sealed, or you'll find out how rabid a bite this dog has."

LATER THAT MORNING, JUST AS Giacomo finished the pasta sauce with pancetta, mushrooms, onions, and peas for lunch, Lieutenant Rinaldi stopped by the kitchen and said, "Scimenti, get up to the sick man's room—you'll find him in his chambers upstairs. They need you to prepare some special concoction for him."

"Who is it, Lieutenant, sir? The Italian ambassador who was sick at the Palace last night?"

Rinaldi nodded. "Get to it, Scimenti."

"Should I bring Messman Pillari, sir?"

"No. You go. On the double."

As Giacomo entered the ambassador's chambers, he heard the doctor who had been at the Summer Palace the night before, giving orders. Giacomo's heart wanted to bound out of his chest, knowing the girl was there too.

The doctor turned to the medic, Chief Petty Officer Donatello Lambrusco, on duty. "Strip the patient and burn his clothing—this should have already been done last night. Scrub him down with this solution." He scribbled a recipe on a piece of paper. "Before applying this, shave him completely."

The sick man was delirious and didn't put up a fuss.

The medic said, "Shave him everywhere?"

"That's what I said." The doctor opened his hand and waved it over the patient. "Everywhere."

Giacomo said, "Excuse me, but the Lieutenant said you needed something from the kitchen, sir." He extended his hand to the doctor. "I'm Chief Steward and Cook Giacomo Scimenti, sir." He leaned a little to the left and saw the pretty girl from the garden standing behind the doctor. She resembled her father. A vision in a pale-green dress.

She was diminutive in stature—a doll whose cheeks seemed splashed by milk and honey, her head crowned with raven hair. Her eyes slanted slightly and her nose, too perfect, was a chiseled piece of artwork. She had high cheekbones and long, graceful fingers. But her eyes. With a slight intake of breath, he saw they were green. He hadn't noticed that in the garden. He thought about the women he'd been with here in China—temporary elixirs for sexual relief. It was all he thought he wanted until a fleeting kiss in a garden from this girl.

The doctor handed Giacomo the paper with the recipe. "Here. Mix everything together. Show my daughter to the kitchen so she can bring it to me."

Giacomo looked at the paper. The solution was equal parts of olive oil, kerosene, and warmed vinegar. "Yes, sir. Will she be able to carry three liters, sir?"

"Lian is strong enough, but the steps are steep. Give her the mixture one liter at a time."

"I'll bring the whole batch up to you, sir," Giacomo said, thinking, *Now I have a name to go with her exotic face.*

"Fine. The deputy ambassador is arranging a room for us. We'll take tea after we finish here. It's been a long night and we haven't slept."

"Yes, sir, I'll have the messman bring it around." He could have kicked himself for that. He didn't want to lose any opportunity of seeing her again. "In fact, I'll bring it myself."

Giacomo saw the faint glimmer of a smile on the girl's face as she stepped from behind her father to follow him to the kitchen. As they walked down the stairs, all Giacomo could think was: *che fortuna! Luck's with me, and Bulldog won't believe this.* When they reached the bottom of the steep stairwell, Giacomo said, "In truth, I never thought I'd see you again. I must apologize for—"

She turned to face him squarely and without hesitation said, "I knew we'd meet again."

He was taken aback by her directness. He'd never been around a girl like her before; the women he usually chased were coy and dissembling. As they hurried along the corridor to the kitchen, he felt flustered. While he readied the liquid, he glimpsed her from time to time, but could think of nothing to say. When had a woman made him into such a fool?

"We will also need *huangqin,*" Lian said.

Giacomo asked for a translation, and she said, "Chinese skullcap. The root of a mint-like plant effective against many bacteria. The ambassador has welts and red blotches on his skin. The *huangqin* will inhibit growth. He's to drink it as a tea, but also we must pat some on the affected lesions. Can you procure some?"

Giacomo nodded. "You know so much. I'm impressed."

She blushed. "I am still in training, but one day I hope to be a healer like my father."

"It seems to me you already are."

When the pot was ready, Lian reached for it.

"I'll carry it. Too heavy, and I know the way, Lian," he said, thrilled to speak her name. He was already thinking of ways to sequester her for a long conversation, to learn more.

LATER, GIACOMO BROUGHT THE TEA tray to the doctor's quarters. The deputy ambassador had put Dr. Brasolin and Lian in a small room that once had served as a storage area. "Your tea, sir," Giacomo said when the doctor answered the door. Behind him stood a writing desk beneath a small window with a bunk bed on either side. These were made up with clean sheets, a gray woolen blanket folded at the foot of each.

"Take the tray," the doctor said to his daughter, who was seated on a small wooden bench. She had slipped off her cotton shoes and was stretching out her legs and wiggling her stockinged feet. She looked up at Giacomo and quickly donned her shoes, then took the tray from him, her hand grazing his. She inclined her head and raised her eyes to his. Giacomo watched her set the tray on the ledge that housed some books above the desk. He knew he was staring but couldn't help himself.

"I'll be in the kitchen if you need anything else, sir—"

The doctor ran his hands through his hair. "Wait. I realize it wouldn't be appropriate for my daughter to have a room of her own, but can you arrange some cord and sheeting to serve as a partition for some privacy to separate our bunks?"

"I'll see what I can do, sir," Giacomo said, and closing the door winked at Lian, pleased to see confusion color her face.

When he returned and knocked on the door, Lian opened it.

"I've brought cloth and rope to rig your partition, sir."

"Very well," the doctor said, standing.

Giacomo dropped the cloth, and to a high round wall hook opposite the door, tied a buntline hitch and strung the rope to another hook ten centimeters to the right inside the door. He looped the rope through and tied a clove hitch. Then he arranged the cloth over the line and pushed it back like a curtain.

"That'll do nicely."

"Will you take your meals with the staff, sir?"

The doctor, who was already seated and writing at the desk, didn't bother to turn. "Yes, the captain has asked us to join him at his table."

"If that will be all, sir," Giacomo said, and with no acknowledgment from the doctor, closed the door ever so slowly. He'd prepare a sweet and have it sent to her table at dinner. As for Captain Morante—what would he say if he knew Giacomo had kissed the doctor's daughter? Fraternizing with native women was strictly prohibited, although no one said anything when the sailors frequented the brothels.

THAT EVENING, ONCE DINNER WAS over and his duties in the kitchen were finished, he walked into the garden and saw Lian standing in a gazebo. "Beautiful night. Would you care to take a short walk?" he asked.

Lian turned to face him. "Unchaperoned?"

"We won't go far."

"I'll have to tell my father."

"We'll be back before you're missed. Promise."

"Isn't is dangerous for you to leave without permission?"

Giacomo shrugged. "In life we must risk to get what we want most."

They strolled along the street that passed the French legation and the customshouse, toward Chang'an Avenue, or Eternal Peace Avenue, known to the foreigners of the legations as Big Street. Their shoulders occasionally brushed, each of them making a quick sideward retreat as if it had happened quite accidentally. The wind jostled the leaves in the trees as they walked past, and the sweet symphony of it reminded Giacomo of Sicily.

"The moon is bright like mid-autumn at festival time," Lian said. "When I was little, I remember my mother making moon cakes."

Some rowdy, drunken men passed by, but not close enough to be considered a threat. Still Giacomo used the excuse to draw closer to Lian, his hand taking hold of her arm. She asked him if he ever listened to the moon. Giacomo shook his head.

"Listen harder," she said, stepping in between shadows and light, the play of moonlight on the ancient gates. Peering skyward, she said, "The moon seems to be saying something. Look. There's a painting—an invisible ventriloquist moving his man-moon mouth. Ah, but it's not the moon speaking. Not in Mandarin. Not in Cantonese. Not even in my precious *Nüshu*."

"*Nüshu?*" Giacomo said. "Another Chinese dialect?"

"No. Another language. Women's language. When it is written, some of it vaguely resembles Chinese characters. Women write on everything—fans, dried leaves, stolen rice paper, cloth, anything. My mother taught it to me. We practiced writing in the sand with sticks so it erased quickly. We even sewed and embroidered it onto handkerchiefs and on the hems and insides of other garments."

"Tell me more about the moon."

She continued, "Certainly the moon is not speaking Italian. It's my inner voice telling me what the painting in the moon is all about. Life, death, and in between, if you're lucky, love."

Giacomo took her hand and tried to kiss it, but she pulled back. "What makes you ponder so?" Knowing she was blushing, he said, "Don't be afraid of me." He took her hand again, and this time he did kiss it.

She drew it back, and rubbed her other thumb over the kissed spot. "I feel the earth has shifted and I'm a little off course, aren't you?"

Could she mean she was falling in love with him?

"When can I see you again? Alone," Giacomo asked.

"We come from different worlds. I'm Chinese. We have many taboos . . ."

"You're a girl and I'm a man and we speak the same language. We're not so different."

She bowed, looked up at him, and said, "Oh, but we are."

A pair of sailors strolled by, heading no doubt to the nearest brothel. Watching them, Giacomo knew Lian was right. He was different. He would never want another woman again. Only her. He longed for something binding with the girl he'd met in the garden, a union of souls.

Giacomo called out, *"Buona notte e sogni d'oro,"* as she stepped through the side portal of the legation. "Tomorrow evening?"

Chapter 3

Yín Qiáo Săn
银翘散
Honeysuckle and forsythia powder

AT THE LEGATION ONE AFTERNOON, two days after our convalescent showed some slight improvement, my father left me in charge of the patient. Word that Father, a skilled surgeon, was in the foreign compound had spread. He had been requested by the British ambassador to help with some soldiers who had been injured during an anti-foreign demonstration that turned into a skirmish. He would be gone at least several days, perhaps more. I was worried about caring for the patient alone, but Baba assured me that I had the necessary training and the medic to call on for help. For days now I had been concerned about my father, who appeared tired and drawn. "All the more reason to return as quickly as possible to Guilin," he said to me and smiled. "I will finally be done with my courtly duties and can rest." But I was in no hurry to return to Guilin, the place where I would be wed to Lu.

I looked at the neatly stacked medicines in a small white cabinet. The patient's fever was due to insufficient yin, and so I administered *yín qiáo săn*, fever powder, to release the patient's wind-heat. Soon he began to speak, complaining of a headache. Instead of covering him, or using Chinese water therapy to induce sweats, which was the usual treatment for a high temperature so the patient could "release bad humors," I took off his blanket and opened the window of the sick room, knowing the herb I administered along with the fresh air would alleviate his headache. Before I pushed his pajamas up his legs, I recalled that Baba said this was quite contradictory to Chinese beliefs, but he found that it worked better for the patient.

The patient recoiled at my touch. "Please," I said in earnest. "I know what I'm doing." I bathed him with cool water. Then I removed his jacket and sponged him down some more. He began to shake. I dried him and covered him with a light sheet only. "You must be cool." I gave him a *bai li*, a Chinese white pear, to eat followed by a glass of cool water.

"Why are you feeding me? I'm going to die anyway."

"Of course you're not."

"This is a miasma. Tell me the truth."

"No. Your condition is due to a scratched insect bite, which caused the feces of the animal to infect your open lesion."

The patient's mouth opened wide. "I thought all you Chinese girls were brought up to be pleasant. How can you speak so rudely?"

"You mean candidly, don't you?"

"I mean you are vulgar and bold and should learn some respect."

"Really? There's nothing rude about the truth or what your symptoms are. You were either unhealthy in your hygienic habits or wore unclean clothes—or perhaps you were in close contact with someone else who was dirty. A singsong girl from a brothel? That's all there is to say. If you don't like speaking to a woman, you can tell my father. But be cautious with him, he doesn't appreciate his patients being impolite to his daughter. Anyway, it seems you certainly didn't mind my ministrations while you were unconscious, babbling and messing yourself."

His face flushed. I was pleased that I'd silenced the old, blustering windbag.

"I'll leave the door open somewhat so you'll have more fresh air. There's a lovely breeze this time of evening." *And just maybe,* I thought, *it'll also whisk away your pompousness.*

As I attended the patient, my mind carved woodcuts from the past. My thoughts, dark as ink, formed the face of Yi Xiao Lu. Lu, my grandmother said when she announced our engagement, was a man of serious disposition. My father permitted the match to go ahead because he'd promised my mother to see me settled, even though Lu was not to his liking. He never admitted that to me, but a girl knows her father's heart. There weren't many available men who would marry the daughter of a foreigner with revolting, big feet. And though I knew that Lu despised that part of me—his glance betrayed him—he desired me the way I desired Giacomo.

My bedeviled mind scratched out Yi Xiao Lu's face, replacing it with Giacomo's strong and beautiful profile. Lately we spent more and more time together, stealing every moment we could. Just that morning, while the ambassador slept, I snuck into the kitchen where Giacomo gave me some freshly laundered clothes and a cap from one of the coolies. Thus in my new disguise, not calling attention to myself, I could stay with him in the kitchen all morning while he prepared lunch for the legation staff.

"You look pretty even dressed like a boy," Giacomo said.

We talked about the fish he was going to bake Sicilian style with tomatoes, capers, and black olives. He told me about the herbs he was using and why he loved Chinese cooking because it was full of vegetables, spices, and herbs like his island home.

"When you go back to Sicily, will you be a cook?"

"Heaven's no, but whatever I do, I try my best at it. We have vast land holdings and my father rents out his vineyards, almond, olive, and lemon groves. We have a grape called *zebibbo*—long, pale green, and sweet—it's from the Arab word *zebib*, raisin. We bring these to a winemaker in Partinico . . ." In that instant Giacomo's eyes hooded over as if he were seeing something I could not. I was about to ask him why he looked so mysterious, when his expression changed back again, and he said, "My grandfathers were fishermen and merchants. Horse traders too. Do you like horses?"

"My father taught me to ride. I first sat a horse when I was five years old."

"We could ride into the hills and picnic overlooking the Conca D'Oro—or ride into the surf at dusk when the sun is setting." He stopped chopping olives and looked at me, his arm waving in a huge arc. "Every evening there's a wide, silvery path that leads from shore to the orange ball of fire at the end of the world. Do you think you could live there?"

"I doubt I would fit in among your people—"

"They'd love you. And you can heal people there just as well as here."

"But I don't look Sicilian. I'm Chinese. Would people trust a physician who looks like me?"

"Why not? Every Sicilian's different. You haven't seen many—we have blondes with blue eyes from the Norman French, and descendents from the Bourbons, dark-skinned people like Bulldog, whose people come from Libya. Arabs. Nomads with high cheekbones and almond eyes." He pointed at her eyes. "We're a mixed breed."

So am I, I thought. "Are you asking me to go with you when you leave China?"

"I am asking you to go with me anywhere."

"How could I leave my father?" I bit into a flavorful olive.

"It's natural that he'll leave you someday." Giacomo sprinkled salt and hot pepper over the fish. "Yesterday at dawn your father came for tea. He's wonderful to talk to. He knows everything about the ocean and tides."

I was pleased that Giacomo had spoken with Baba but hated to think about losing him, although my heart knew it was true. Was Giacomo serious? Did he love me the way I felt myself falling in love with him?

❦

THAT EVENING WE SLIPPED AWAY from the legation for a short walk, even though I sensed Peking was getting more and more dangerous. Giacomo had started carrying a billy club with him. When I asked him why, he told me there had been a scuffle between two of his buddies, Bulldog and Pillari, and some peasants, calling themselves Boxer sympathizers. Somehow this news didn't disturb or frighten me on our walks, as I felt safe with him. I lost my reserve and was no longer concerned that our hand-holding would be observed by passersby. Still from time to time he lapsed into silence, and I sensed there was a darker part to his soul.

As we walked together, I wondered: Was I willing to give myself to Giacomo despite all taboo, without remorse or anguish? Only a lovesick fool could even contemplate it, for despite his dreams and promises, he was a sailor, and I worried he would leave me and I would no longer be intact for Lu. Fear gripped my insides and I wanted to heave up bile, but I forced it down. One day soon he would be recalled to his ship, and I would never see Giacomo again. Yet how could I live with myself knowing I could be his even for this fleeting moment of time in this vast universe? I remembered what he had said the first time we left the legation together: *"In life we must risk to get what we want most."* Did I not owe that to myself—the memory of a great love for the rest of my life? Like my parents' love.

AFTER WE RETURNED TO THE legation, I looked in on the ambassador, then went to get my book that I'd left in my room so I could make some notes for myself in *Nüshu*. I was an avid diarist, as was my father. I came out of the sick man's room and there stood Giacomo waiting for me.

"Meet me later," he pleaded. "When you've finished. Please," he persisted, "I beg you to come to the kitchen when all is quiet and everyone is asleep. I must see you."

"Hush," I said, putting my finger over his soft mouth. He nipped my finger gently, and I started to giggle but squelched my laughter, cupping a hand over my mouth. "In two hours." I looked at the moon and stars to judge the time.

"Two hours, then."

He kissed my finger.

I CAME TO HIM IN A white shift. Threshed by the wind's velocity, I felt a ghost accompany me in the gossamer folds. I knocked lightly on the kitchen door. It opened and I jumped back. Two strong hands grasped my wrists and pulled me into an embrace. I had no time to think. I was wrapped in his arms and sprang on my tiptoes, flinging my arms around his neck. He sat me on the kitchen counter and removed my cotton slippers.

"My heart's caroming in my chest like I just took a flight of stairs two at a time," he said.

"What do you mean?"

He took my hand and placed it over his fast-beating heart. Then he took my naked feet in his hands, caressing them. I tried to pull my ugly feet away but he said, "Your feet are lovely, sculptured—perfect enough for a marble statue." He kissed the tops of my feet and I felt woozy with thrills.

"How can you think that?"

But he didn't answer and instead kissed my forehead and lifted me so my bare feet rested on his. He, too, was barefoot. For the first time in my life, I was not embarrassed by my unbound feet as they steadied me. We swayed and danced as if music was playing. His mouth slid from my forehead down my nose, and then his kiss engulfed me and I was lost, lost, lost as if a boat's gentle rocking made it seem as though I were floating.

If there was a clatter of pots and pans, it was somewhere else. All I knew was that in one swift movement Giacomo had swept everything from the long table, a symphony of crashing cymbals. He set me down, a toy doll, and his hand brushed my throat upward and he tilted my neck back. A patch of moonlight in a long stream covered me as his hands slid from my neck to caress each breast, his thumbs stroking my erect nipples.

Abruptly, he ceased all movement. My eyes were riveted on him as he pulled his tunic over his head and rolled it up, placing it in back of me. Then, ever so gently, he pushed my shoulders back—the tunic pillowed underneath my head. I felt the indentation of the wood beneath me and realized this wasn't a table but a large chopping block. How appropriate if I were to be taken. Could I object?

He took hold of my raiment, folding and folding it upward from my feet, until it became a silken scarf at my neck. He unbuttoned his trousers, letting them fall to the floor, never taking his eyes from my body, and stepping out of them, came closer into the shaft of light, bending over me to wash my body with his tongue, turning me this way and that, kissing me all over till I wanted to shriek with pain and pleasure.

When he entered me and we were united, the electricity of our thoughts made us one being, one desire, one heart, one soul. His arms surrounding me were like a walled fortress and made me feel protected. I desired nothing more than the comfort of those arms.

BABA HAD SENT WORD HE would be away for three more nights. Enchanted nights I would be with Giacomo. Later, I thought back to that first night. I realized the pain was due to inexperience but also to desire, but thence onward, we shared a oneness, a union of identifying love.

The second of these precious days, after lunch while my patient slept and Giacomo had finished his chores in the kitchen, we took a long walk. On one of the side streets, we came near to a hawker selling his wares. Giacomo stopped and said, "Look, it's a walking stick. How this reminds me of my youth." He picked up the cane with its silver-handled dragon head and marveled at it, twisting it this way and that to catch the fading light.

"What will you do with it?"

"Not for me—for my father."

The breeze carried the scent of a mixture of flowers and fried food. I looked a little further on, and sure enough, a man was cooking on a small brazier, releasing succulent scents enough to make my mouth water.

I had taught Giacomo some Chinese expressions, and he asked the cane seller, *"Duōshǎo qián?"*

And I thought, *Asking how much the cane costs is no way to start the bargaining.* So I strolled back and faced Giacomo.

"You do not want this—it is an unworthy stick, far too ugly for your father," I said, thinking, *How can I feel so certain of my feelings for him? Will he stay with me when this uprising is over? I cannot lose him. Ever.*

He looked at me surprised, but then a flicker of understanding crept into his eyes.

"True enough—this is worthless compared to the one we saw on the way here."

The hawker lowered his price and began raising his voice, speaking in staccato half-phrases about the wood, the quality of the silver used for the dragon. On and on he went.

When he took a breath, I said, "Calm down. You cannot possibly expect us to pay such a high price for a secondhand gift."

Again the hawker lowered his price as I laid the cane down on his blanket and took hold of Giacomo's arm, which took him off guard as we never touched in public. With slow and purposeful steps, we walked away. The vendor tapped me on the shoulder with the cane, and said, "Last price?"

I took an embroidered purse from my bodice for some coins and tossed them on the blanket. "Take this—only to keep you from pestering me any longer." And with that I seized the cane, and retrieving Giacomo's arm once more, walked away, only this time at a brisk pace. A little farther down the lane, I dropped his arm when I heard laughter near an unlighted streetlamp. Giacomo reached into his pocket and tried to pay me back in Mexican silver coins, but I refused, saying, "A gift from me for my lover's father."

He took the cane and stroked it, as if conjuring his father's presence.

◆━━◇✕◇━━◆

LOVERS WILL ALWAYS FIND A way to be together. That night, he stood waiting for me in the garden. He turned and I ran to him, springing up and flinging myself onto him like a she-tiger, and he grasped me fiercely as I ensnared him with my legs, arms locked around his neck. He held me with one arm, and with his free hand unbuttoned his pants and took me there, leaning against a stone wall. Fear rocked me, but I was too enthralled to make him stop. Then he carried me to the patio and helped me to a lying position behind some huge plants. We made delicious, quiet, unhurried, gentle love till almost dawn; he whispered things in my ear that my heart wanted and needed to hear. Close to dawn when I slipped away to my room, the import of his words dissipated into the smoke of pipe dreams.

◆━━◇✕◇━━◆

ON THE THIRD NIGHT OF what I was now considering my honeymoon, he greeted me with hungry kisses and a passionate embrace that suddenly frightened me. We sat on a wooden bench some distance away from the building but secluded by huge plants and bushes. He laid me down, a rolled apron under my head.

"Slowly," I said in Mandarin, then repeated, *"Piano,"* in Italian, and I realized I was talking to myself more than him.

"Relax," he said. "I'll never hurt you."

With one arm clutched around Giacomo's neck, I ran the fingers of my other hand over his cheek. I kissed his lips with the gentleness of a butterfly on the wing . It seemed to me that my voice hummed a soft and melodious tune as I leaned into him. I murmured something seemingly faint and far away. My raspy voice caught his name in my throat, repeating over, and over sotto voce, "Giacomo, Giacomo, Giacomo." His name, a quiet mantra. Then my voice subsided into silence. I felt his skin burnishing, brushing against me; my breasts were like light strokes of a willow branch ruffling his hairy chest. My fingers skimmed piano scales across his cheek, around his ear, down the side of his neck, traversing his shoulder, kneading it, down to his muscled biceps. I grabbed his upper arm and pulled it so that his arm encircled and supported my arched back. He stroked my neck with his lips. I took his face in both my hands and kissed each eye—a movement so physical, yet soulful in a sensual way, as if I'd never been with him before this moment. With one swift movement he lifted me up and laid me next to him. I looked into his eyes and said, "I trust you. I never dreamed I would ever say that to a man. I never knew there existed such tenderness and passion. How I wish this day would never end."

THE NEXT MORNING VERY EARLY, expecting Baba's return, I saw Giacomo in an alcove by a storage room. The first thing he did was pull me to him and hold me, whispering in my ear, "This seems impossible but somehow we'll be together. You're the only one for me. Believe me."

In an instant his hands crawled from my waist, opening the frogs on my *qipao*, but I broke away after a final kiss, knowing I did not want to love this man but could not help myself. He was a rake, complicated and foreign though we spoke the same language. How did my mother fall in love with and marry Father? But Father was serious, not the seafaring, wandering man Giacomo was.

The ambassador had finally recovered and Father and I had to leave. I told Giacomo I would see him later in the day to say good-bye, adjusting my blouse, remembering the first time we had stood face-to-face, breath to breath before his lips claimed mine. Little did I know how that kiss would bind.

"I will come back to you. I must try to convince my father to break my forced engagement. Will you wait for me?"

"Engagement?"

"To a farmer. In Guilin. Three years ago. I barely know him."

"You were only fourteen—how is that possible?"

"This is China."

"I'll see you, my treasure, when I get back from the market."

By mid-afternoon Baba had returned from his duties and looking exhausted and grey, told me about three other legations where he had worked: French, German, and Spanish. He spoke German and French and could get by with Spanish easily as it was similar to Italian. Despite his protests I examined him, diagnosing typhus. Seeing how weak he was, I begged the ambassador to allow me to care for him at the legation. But the ambassador refused, saying he had no responsibility for Swiss citizens, or—with a harsh look at me—their half-breed daughters. His fever had finally broken and he would return to duty—without, apparently, a shred of gratitude for the nursing Father and I had given him. I tried to explain that it wasn't contagious, although Baba had caught it from the same pest that had bitten him. He tossed me a purse in payment for our services and concluded by ordering us to leave the legation at once.

I hurried to get the rest of Baba's belongings and stacked them with mine outside our room. I searched for Giacomo to say farewell, but he was nowhere to be found. Then I remembered that he'd told me earlier he would be gone all day, obtaining provisions for the legation with Pillari.

Before leaving, I told Bulldog my address but in case he did not remember it, I thought it was better to write it for him. I dashed off a note to Giacomo, saying: *Please come to me as quickly as possible*, giving him our Peking address.

At the bottom of the drive, I hired a rickshaw, as Father was too tired to walk, to take us to a palanquin that would bring us back to our garret.

A DAY LATER, GIACOMO CAME to me. Surely heaven was smiling upon us because Bulldog had remembered my address and my father had just left on a two-day journey. This meant I would be able to spend two more glorious days with the love my life. He was hungry so I asked him, "Have you ever had fire pot?"

"If it's hot, it's for me."

WE WALKED EAST FOR SEVERAL minutes and then turned south. Twenty minutes later we were in a red room with nine golden dragons painted on the walls. A four-part carved, lacquered divider screen of a dragon scene, detailed in agate, jade, and mother-of-pearl, separated them from the rest of the diners, some of whom were in evening dress and tails.

"Are you embarrassed? We can go someplace else, shall we?" Giacomo asked.

"Hush. The kind waiter adjusted the partition. We are completely private here."

We sat at a low table covered in green baize.

"Looks like a gaming parlor," Giacomo said.

I ordered. While waiting for the food to arrive, I told him about her childhood in Guilin, and he of his home in Carini, and how he played the *maranzzano,* a twangy Jew's harp.

"I heard it called a *scacciapensieri,* a thought squelcher," I said.

"That too, but I think it was brought to Sicily from Spain by Marrano Jews."

"I'd love to hear you play it."

A waiter came and set down a tin-lined copper bowl above a fire stand in the center of the table. In the shark broth mingled with ginger root and scallions floated a white chrysanthemum. The waiter bowed. Another waiter placed platters all around the hot pot. One held *pidan,* thousand-year-old eggs preserved for one hundred days, which wobbled in a dish as the waiter placed them down near a plate of prawns. Other dishes soon began to encircle the fire pot. Carp, pork liver, tripe, duck gizzards, spinach leaves, squid, sliced chicken breast, strips of roast pork, dried bean vermicelli, ham, and fried egg noodles. A bowl of beaten eggs was set before each of them, and in close proximity also a tiny ramekin of dark sauce.

I waited until all the servers had disappeared and then deftly picked up the chrysanthemum in my chopsticks.

"We must wait till the broth bubbles," I shredded the flower, slowly like a child's daisy game. "He loves me, he loves me not," I said, as petals of long filaments, like falling feathers from angel's wings, fell from my fingers. I selected the first ingredient, a prawn, and plunged it into the consommé until it was lightly poached. Then I dipped the cooked prawn into the egg and then the sauce. When it was thoroughly coated, I fed it to Giacomo. When the meal was about finished, we supped on the noodles flavored by the rich soup.

I wiped the corners of Giacomo's mouth and repeated the gesture for myself. "As a girl, whenever we ate this, my father would conclude with: 'We gnaw the chiliad gifts, we shall never again thirst nor hunger, tasting a thousand years—this dense and concentrated dollop on a spoon we lift to our mouths, mouths crammed with this predator and essence of the sea, graced and spangled chrysanthemum.'"

"Quite a poet." He leaned forward to kiss me and I kissed him back.

<hr />

WHEN MY FATHER RETURNED, HE became so weak, and the days turned into weeks as I struggled to save Baba's life. Each day I waited for the knock on the door telling me Giacomo was there. Had I been wrong to trust Giacomo's love? Yet I could in no way fault him for taking me, I was so eager. I cursed myself for falling in love with a sailor—known for their wandering ways.

One morning I sat with my back resting on a yellow silk pillow propped against a trellis, writing in my diary, studying the effects of *bai zi ren*. This ripe kernel could help my father sleep and strengthen his heart. I left my journaling and walked through the back-entrance moon gate in the wall to the garden. On the far side of the roof-tiled wall were red pillars, shrubs of various heights, scattered rocks. On the inside were bamboo and plum trees, signifying man and wife. The enclosure made one feel as though entering a secret garden.

I walked back and went to check on Baba, who was resting. "You look so pale. You haven't been sleeping. Why not take some *bai zi ren?*"

He tapped his heart and said, "There are just so many beats left in this organ. The herb may help me sleep, but the damage is irreparable, I'm afraid. It's not just my heart. The typhus is strong, and I am too weak to recover."

That night, as I tried to ease Baba's fever with cool cloths, he put his hand on mine. "Sit, daughter." I sat on the raised platform of my parent's marriage bed as he began to speak.

"We have so little time, and there are things I must say to you. Your grandmother is old, and you won't have anyone to turn to. You must rely on your own strength to maintain equanimity in all things. Promise me you will return immediately to Guilin and marry Lu."

I protested that surely he would recover and that we would go to

Guilin together, but he dismissed me with a wave of his hand.

"Listen to me, child. A year ago in Guilin, Lu came to me for treatment—he said the wound was an accident with a farming tool—but I knew it was a powder burn from gunshot. I discovered later he was a dissenter taking orders from *tufei*—bandits with Boxer sentiments. He was responsible for inciting trouble among foreigners at the train station not six months ago. This doesn't bode well for you, my beloved child, for you are part European. Although he seems genuinely fond of you, but watch he doesn't turn on you someday."

"I can't marry Lu," I said, and I cried.

"You must," Baba said. "There is no other choice. When Lu first came to me, he was full of vindictiveness, influenced by other radicals. Your future husband doesn't have your keen insights, intuition, or intelligence. You will suffer because of this, unless you find a way to keep your mind and talents busy. I need to know you will be all right once you're ensconced in the Yi household. You'll be giving up much, my dear. But remember, above all else, you have a gift for healing. It will see you through."

"I love another," I blurted out. At that moment I told him about Giacomo—everything—except that I had given him not just my heart and soul but all of me. "What can I do under the circumstances?"

"You haven't a choice. Your grandmother has made a promise to the Yi family. Her honor—and the honor of your mother's memory— depend on fulfilling it. Lu has the dowry—you must accept him. Tell him the truth but beware—jealousy is a green beast and can eat one alive and turn love to hate."

"Are you saying he's the kind who'll hurl a stone and hide the hand?"

Baba was fading and didn't answer. "You must try to forget me and forget the sailor," he said, and finally, "I see now that I was wrong to have given you so much freedom. Forget the West. This is China. Your life is here. Remember your mother and give yourself over to the Eastern way."

Although I doubted it, I could try, but I could never forget my Baba. "Can you ever forgive me?" I reached my hand toward his and he took hold of it.

"I'm your father. My love is without restrictions. Learn to forgive yourself."

The next day Baba died. My dearest father, who had been suffering with a failing heart, died of typhus and left to find my mother in the world of spirits. I had his body taken to be cremated and returned with his ashes. The night before I had dreamed of teeth and snow, so I was not surprised when I set the urn by his desk and saw the last thing he had been working on before that fateful day we were called to the Summer Palace. He had been writing me a note about ginseng. It read: "Astragalus strengthens *wei chi,* or defensive energy, our immune system. This potent tonic is effective as an antibacterial . . ." Here his words stopped, and his quill skittered across the page, the tail of a spent comet.

I sat down, overcome with dizziness and nausea. For a moment I thought I must have caught typhus, too, but remembered what Father had said. "Person to person caring for a typhus victim should not mean contagion. The night at the Palace, I slapped an infected insect on my neck, not a mosquito." He had made me look at his neck, and there at the base of his hairline was the mark. I had no marks anywhere.

So full of grief at times, I wished I had contracted the disease and would die too. Then I pictured Giacomo. It had been over two weeks since I had last seen him, and I knew I wanted to live to see him because I was certain that the bile in my throat was nausea, but not from typhus. I was carrying his child.

THE NEXT DAY, I WENT to the legation, seeking Giacomo, but my search was in vain. He was out and the sailors of the *Leopardo* had been recalled to Tientsin and were packing up to leave. I was informed that the Italian minister of war in Roma had sent Bersaglieri soldiers to replace them as security guards in Peking.

Chapter 4

Niutouquan
牛头犬
Bulldog

GIACOMO RETURNED TO THE LEGATION after purchasing the provisions needed with Pillari. Whistling an old Italian love song, he started to organize his food stock. He was pleased with himself because he'd found skinny eggplants and would take them to Lian, who said how much she liked them with hot pepper and garlic. Somehow he would find a way to weave their lives together forever. As he hung the braid of garlic near one of the stoves, Lieutenant Rinaldi came into the kitchen.

"New orders, Scimenti. We move out tomorrow. Get packed and ready to go."

Giacomo looked puzzled. "Back to the ship?"

"Where else, sailor? Get a move on."

"What about this food?"

"Later."

He had to find Lian. What would he say to her? He'd tell her to wait for him—that somehow he'd come back for her. He went to her quarters but she wasn't there. He peered in one of the windows, but it seemed the rooms were empty.

He searched her grounds and gardens and then all over the neighborhood, but no one could tell him about Lian.

Finally he went back to the legation and met Bulldog coming downstairs.

"Where were you?"

"Looking for Lian. Her house is empty."

Bulldog told him he thought something happened to her father.

"Where did she go?" Giacomo wiped his forehead with a handkerchief.

"I don't know. It all happened so fast."

Giacomo started for the door nearest the French Legation.

"Where are you going?" Bulldog asked.

"To the Palace. They'll know how to find her."

"Yiheyuan, the Summer Palace? Crazy bastard. Way too far. Hold up—" Bulldog yelled.

"No. The Imperial Palace. The empress is back and that means her retinue will be also. I'm still on a pass."

"I'm coming," Bulldog said.

Giacomo saluted the guard at the gates and left, Bulldog following. "Hey, slow down a minute, Moon Eyes. What makes you think they'll tell you, even if they do know where she is?"

"We'll head toward *Chang'an*—Big Street—it's a busy thoroughfare, always a line of rickshaws," Giacomo said. "Maybe she left a message for me."

"Are you out of your mind? Seriously?" Bulldog whistled to hail a rickshaw. "Take that hangdog expression off your face. Who's cooking?"

"The prep work's all done. Pillari can handle it."

Bulldog hailed another driver and they mounted their rides.

"For me, it's worth a try," Giacomo said. He knew the words for the Imperial Palace and said them to the coolie.

As they wove through traffic together, Bulldog shook his head and said , *"Pazzo."*

"Right. I am crazy. For Lian." They arrived at the gates and were ushered into a small building with a red tiled roof, the corners curled upward. Two Foo dogs with menacing faces were at the entrance. Giacomo paced the waiting room, stopping every so often to peer out the window. Mendicants of all kinds were turned away. Soldiers on horseback rode through the gates in pairs, and several sedan chairs were ushered in past the building where he waited. It took over an hour before a translator clerk came to Giacomo's assistance.

He paid him and the clerk left, returning with a big eunuch. Giacomo thought it might be the one he'd seen at the Summer Palace but wasn't sure. He asked anyway, and when the eunuch answered the clerk gruffly, Giacomo recognized the medallion, certain it was the same man. He felt that the clerk softened the eunuch's responses and told the clerk that he'd pay more if the translation were accurate. "Otherwise, I'm only guessing."

The clerk stepped in front of Giacomo. Facing him, in a calm, low voice, the clerk said, "If you make a threat or touch the eunuch, you will be imprisoned and no one will ever find your body. He says he does not do the bidding of bleached-out foreigners. He does not know where the doctor or his half-breed daughter live. This meeting is over."

The eunuch bowed slightly and left. Bulldog restrained Giacomo, and the clerk said, "It's best to leave now while you still have legs to carry you." He bowed. Giacomo handed him some Mexican silver. The man looked at the coins in his hand. "He is lying. He knows where the girl lives but will not say. Your days in China are numbered." He bowed again and left.

Giacomo and Bulldog returned to the legation. Bulldog packed up his gear, but Giacomo sat sullenly on a bench, staring out into the garden. Bulldog walked up to him and said, "Get your gear. My knapsack's already packed."

Gicaomo looked up as if he hadn't heard.

Bulldog said, *"Va bene.* If you can keep your temper under control, I'll tell you what happened before you returned from the market."

"What're you holding back from me?"

Bulldog told him Lian had come looking for him. "She wanted to leave you a note—"

"Where is it?" Giacomo asked.

"I didn't tell you before—look at you—you're pathetic."

"You're going to look even more pathetic if you don't tell me what she said."

"She tried to give it to me, but Captain Morante snatched it from her. She jumped back like his cat does when surprised."

Bulldog put his hand on Giacomo's shoulder, but he nudged it off. Bulldog said, "If I were you, I wouldn't ask the captain about it."

"But you aren't me," Giacomo said, pushing himself off the bench to stand.

Bulldog grabbed his arm, "Keep a stone face, like playing *briscola,* hothead."

Giacomo blew out and pushed a lock of hair out of his eyes. "Guess I'll have to wait."

"Guess you'll have to do just that. Now go pack it up." Bulldog's words were barely out of this mouth, and Giacomo was in motion.

"Pack, my ass, I'm going to look for that *bastardo."* He walked toward the library. A few men played cards. The captain sat smoking a cigar, speaking to Lambrusco, surrounded by easy chairs, some vacant. There was bustling in the anterooms as men were trudging their kits and paraphernalia down stairs.

Giacomo felt his hands clench and forced himself to relax as he approached the captain. Giacomo saluted and asked for permission to speak. Lieutenant Rinaldi, seated at a desk, folded a map while Di Louise, Pillari, and Melle were placing papers into a box.

When Giacomo was acknowledged, he asked about Lian's note, noticing Bulldog had stepped inside the room behind him.

"Yes, come to think of it, the girl who assisted Doctor Brasolin left it for you. I forgot," the captain said, and coughed. He cleared his throat. "You know the rule about fraternizing with the natives—"

"Forgot? It was only this morning, sir."

"It must have gotten lost."

Giacomo's expression changed to a glower. "How could it have been lost?" he said, gritting his teeth.

"Watch your tone, Scimenti. Unimportant—didn't remember until you mentioned it now—"

"Which is it, lost or forgotten," Giacomo said, adding a hissed, "sir?"

The captain stood, and the room went quiet. "Are you calling me a liar?"

Giacomo saluted without another word and started to do an about-face without being dismissed when he balled his hand into a fist and heaved a punch at the captain, who ducked.

Bulldog came up behind Giacomo and grabbed his arms. Even with pinioned arms, Giacomo fought for freedom and lunged once more. Two shipmates, Melle and Di Louise came to restrain him.

"Keep this man under guard until morning, and I want him in irons until we return to the ship where he will be placed in the brig," the captain said, cleared his throat, and inclined his head toward Lieutenant Rinaldi, who, shaking his head, said, "Yes, sir."

TEN DAYS LATER, THE SHIP stopped at the provincial capital of Hunan, Changsha, meaning "long sandbank," on the historic Xiang River. Giacomo had finally been released from the brig. Those first days out of confinement, he steered clear of the brass and even avoided talking to Bulldog, whom he'd not forgiven for restraining him from attacking the captain.

That night he leaned on the guardrail; anger bombarded him from all directions. It gushed up again and he leaned over and spat into the water. What did he feel? What use was it to waste anger on something already past? He could do nothing, and if he did, he could end up with a court martial for insubordination and striking an officer; the judgment could end with execution and get him hanged. After all, this was a war zone. He thought about jumping ship. With what means could he travel, and how would he make himself understood? He had only a handful of Chinese words at his disposition. He didn't even know where Lian was. Bulldog had said her father was ill. Was she still in Peking caring for him? Or had she gone to Guilin to marry the man she mentioned? He rubbed his temples. A drum whacked and thrummed inside his head. He went to the galley to make himself an espresso, thinking the caffeine would clear his rumbling mind.

Bulldog came into the galley. "Got any for me?"

"I should throw the pot in your face. You call yourself a friend?"

"If your wild, stupid punch had connected with that blowhard's chin, you'd still be under lock and key with the key thrown overboard. *Strunzo.* When will you ever learn to control your temper? That's why I didn't want to tell you about her note in the first place."

"How will I find her? What if her father dies? What will happen to her?" Giacomo poured another cup of coffee and handed it to Bulldog.

"You're not going AWOL—*assentarsi senza permesso.* I'll lock you up myself."

"I swear to God I'll never give up hope of finding her."

"Hope is a thing for saints, a wild bird on the wing—give it up, whoremonger—"

"Not anymore. You don't understand. Each day without her is torment—thorns in my eyes blinding me. When I think of how helpless I am, pain in my gut doubles me over."

Bulldog opened his hands. "Good God. What did she do to you? She looks so innocent, how could she be such a *strega*?

"You're right, I'm bewitched."

Bulldog shrugged and shook his head. "What's it like?"

"I want to be with her, protect her, share things with her, feed her, look at her when I speak her name to see pleasure brighten her face, and to see her shy smile when she says mine, as if she's hoarding the unlimited sky from angels in flight."

"You're a poet, Giacomo."

"No, I'm not. I wish I were and had the words to express how much more I feel, but I'm thinking of going AWOL."

"Like hell, you will. Over half the crew and my body."

THE XIANG RIVER FLOWED NORTH into the Dongting Lake, which immediately poured into the Yangtze River. The gunboat *Leopardo* was marshalling the area as many peasant rebellions were taking place. Changsha had been inhabited for three thousand years but was now an intricate mix of modern European buildings and ancient Chinese structures. Pagodas, Taoist and Buddhist temples, and statuaries stood regally among leafy trees and were spectacular. Giacomo's mood improved when he saw them.

Giacomo bought the local loach, a kind of carp, which he fried and served with hot, spicy frogs' legs. After dinner on the third night in port, when the crew was advised that the uprisings had been stopped, the group of four men—Giacomo, Bulldog, Pillari, and Lambrusco—walked into a small residential area where a lantern shone its light on the wet, shiny cobblestones. For some reason the candescence of it made Giacomo think of the richness of Zhōngguó or "central nation," the Middle Kingdom as the Chinese referred to China. And the Italians were making inroads here, but for what? Greed?

To the south of Changsha in Hunan, he learned that women wrote each other letters in their secretive language—the language Lian used—on rice paper. Late-summer rain trailed down the dark rooftops of shadowed houses, creating a lonesome atmosphere. If Lian were in Guilin, she would be fairly near, only five hundred kilometers from here. He imagined he could feel her closeness. They stayed a week in Changsha and then worked their way backwards toward the ocean and then south to Hong Kong.

◈

THE SHIP REACHED HONG KONG and had been docked in the raucous and overcrowded port for several days when on a moonless night, Giacomo and Bulldog had leave and headed for the pleasure quarter—a district of small houses and businesses. They walked along a crooked brick lane toward the house of red lanterns. Upon finding the right house, they remained an hour. Bulldog was busy upstairs while Giacomo drank a beer with some of the men at the bar. A willowy girl dressed in yellow with a matching flower in her hair sidled up to Giacomo and asked in a mix of Chinese and pidgin English if he wanted to go topside. How could he when the material of the girl's dress reminded him of the frock Lian had worn when he last saw her? He declined, and one of the sailors at the bar said, "Hey, Scimenti, you must rate—that little flower's a virgin and doesn't offer her services to just anyone. She has to get consent from the madam. If it's a matter of money, hell, we'll take up a collection for you."

Giacomo shook his head, thinking of the precious girl he had possessed for so little time.

As Bulldog and Giacomo exited the establishment, the madam of the house thanked them in Italian. She bowed and Giacomo followed suit. Before they left through the back door, the madam said, "Next time you take virgin flower? Here, she give memento for you."

Giacomo took the delicately embroidered handkerchief from the madam, who said, "This means she wait for you. Not Chinese. *Nüshu.* She not from here."

Nüshu. Lian had told him about it. He hadn't given it importance then. He handed back the hanky, shook his head, and said in Cantonese, *"M'goi."*

Giacomo had no taste for other women, determined to stay celibate until he found Lian again. Bulldog teased him at every instant, but

Giacomo understood his longing for the girl was something special, though he wondered if his celibacy could last.

THE NEXT DAY, GIACOMO GAZED out over the starboard railing of the middle deck and watched the fog roll out across the bay on a blustery wind. It swept across the harbor so that his field of vision became uncluttered. The less chaotic view beguiled him. He followed a sampan with red sails as pretty as a sunrise. His eyes lingered on junks floating by in single file as if each were propelled, pushed from behind by huge unseen hands. He was mesmerized, reminded again of how much he loved China, just as he loved Lian, even as he feared his time with her would one day be nothing more than fleeting memories.

He walked to the aft side and saw that travelers' trunks littered the ground near a big ship. Passengers milled around waiting for someone to take charge of them, like a group of schoolchildren given freedom at recess. A Brit he'd met the other night drinking said he'd seen local unrest some distance from the harbor. Giacomo asked him what he'd meant by "unrest," and he answered a massacre of white Protestant social workers a few kilometers from here. He told Giacomo the raid was led by Boxers who referred to all white men as "barbarians." It wasn't the first time Giacomo had heard rumors of atrocities such as this one. They were becoming more and more frequent.

How could Lian want to heal these people whose injuries were caused by their cruel natures? Although, wasn't his own culture filled with violent history?

THAT AFTERNOON, GIACOMO LEFT THE ship to go to the post office in town. Hong Kong in late summer was hot and muggy, reminding him of his dream of his hometown, Carini. On a day like this in his dream he rode his horse to the beach for a delicious, refreshing swim. He strengthened his horse's ankles by cantering along the beach at the *riva*—the water's edge, where the sand was harder packed, heavier and wet. After the horseback ride, he awoke from the dream with an image of himself holding a snake in his arms. A dog sat watching him. What did it mean? He'd heard that a snake dream meant transformation and positive change in your life. Where had he heard that? Lian?

He didn't know for sure, but maybe it meant dogs were faithful creatures and trustworthy like his friend Bulldog, whom he had finally forgiven. Bulldog would always cover his back. He shook himself back to the present where he was in Hong Kong and held a green and white stamp with a fierce dragon in the middle, and the word *Candarin* across the bottom and a tiny number "1" in the bottom-right corner. *China* was stamped across the top.

Bulldog met him outside the post office. "Why buy a stamp?" he asked. "You should've put the letter on the Lieutenant's desk, and he'd mail it with all the rest going back to Italy."

"This goes inside the letter, not on the envelope. It's for my mother." And with the thought of a letter, Giacomo extracted from his pocket what he believed was a love letter from Lian in *Nüshu*. She'd given it to him the last time he saw her. He didn't understand one feathery scrawl of it but felt sure it was an important key to her true feelings for him. He wondered if the girl in the brothel would translate it for him. He kissed the writing and put the paper back in his pocket. Would he ever see her again? He had to believe he would. He could bring her back to Sicily with him. What a feeling of lightness it gave him. But would she feel alienated there?

The breeze picked up as the two men started to walk toward Stanley Main Street to look for an Italian restaurant. They passed the marketplace filled with cheap ornaments, silks, toys, souvenirs, and dresses. The sound of snapping material caught Giacomo's attention, and he looked up at a Quing Dynasty flag unfurling on the corner of a low-slung building in the dazzling brightness of the day. The flag was a shock of color—the lower diagonal a yellow-cloth background held a red sun at the top left corner along with a blue dragon painted with a white spiked horny back all the way from its tail to white ears. The dragon's gaze regarded the sun as if to devour it or anything else on earth or in the universe. The dragon's eyes and tongue flamed red, green spurs at his hind legs. The top diagonal of the flag was dazzling white, pure as a wedding dress.

After they had found a restaurant and eaten spaghetti made with tomato sauce, Giacomo said, "Even though Chinese invented noodles, and they're not bad, nothing's as good as pasta."

Bulldog signaled the waitress to bring another beer.

"After lunch we could go swimming," Giacomo said.

"What for? There's a brothel just a few doors down."

"Not for me." Giacomo toyed with a red carnation in a small vase.

"Still longing for your little beauty from the Summer Palace, your royal highness?"

"Till I find her—the right one for me—I'm not interested in anyone else."

"We'll see how long that lasts." Bulldog tossed the napkin on the table.

"She has the most incredible green eyes."

"Thought you said a cloud passed over the moon—wasn't it dark in the garden? Hey, are you sure you even kissed her? Maybe you did more than kiss her when she was at the legation?"

"Don't you wish you knew."

"Old and boring, friend. I've heard it all before. Your virtue can't last forever. Too much of a ladies' man—"

"Yeah, I do like women—if only I'd gotten her note before we left Pechino. For now, let me hold on to the delusion I can be faithful."

"Maybe you can be, with the right lady—but now you're young, alone, a sailor in China. Who the hell are you fooling?"

"Can we drop this now and get going?"

Bulldog and Giacomo parted to the west of Stanley Main Street. Past the amphitheater in Stanley Plaza stood the Tin Hau Temple or the Temple of the Queen of Heaven. Giacomo stopped and tried to make out the inscription on a small plaque. A boy about thirteen approached him and said in broken Italian, "This built Cheung Po Tsai in 1767. Oldest temple Hong Kong."

He held out his palm and Giacomo shook it, saying, "How would a little industrious fellow like yourself like to come and work aboard a bad foreign ship?"

The boy's face lit by a sly grin, and he said, "I want tip." He made a sweeping motion, almost a bow, and held out his hand.

Giacomo laughed. "I made you a better offer. What do you say?" Giacomo talked to the boy at length in a bastard Italian pidgin, noticing facial expressions to determine how shrewd he was. The boy's lively eyes lit up when he laughed. His ears lay flat against his head, and he wore his long hair in a queue. Giacomo surmised that when the boy told an untruth, his nostrils flared slightly. The boy said something odd when Giacomo asked him what he dreamed of.

"Dreams," the boy said, "big pomegranates, many seeds, leather skins, red silk kites, summer sunset, plump persimmons." He looked up and smirked. "Dreams fat stones in persimmons—each secret—hide other."

Giacomo told him about the snake dream and asked what it meant. The boy said he thought it meant the blessing of a child with many gifts.

Giacomo learned the child, Shen, was an orphan from poor circumstances, living by his wits. He was from inland China but had a good grasp of Cantonese. Along with a smattering of Italian, he was clearly intelligent. Such a boy could be useful. They walked to the ship, where Giacomo asked the lieutenant if he could take him aboard and give him over to the head coolie, Chang, or use him as an assistant cook. After Giacomo chewed his ear off as to the boy's many qualities and usefulness, the lieutenant secured the captain's permission while Giacomo showed Shen around the ship.

THAT NIGHT, AFTER SETTLING SHEN onto the ship, Giacomo found himself following Bulldog to a brothel. Giacomo woke the next morning in his bunk with a vicious hangover. He couldn't remember the face of the prostitute he'd slept with, and for a moment, in a great state of panic, he couldn't recall Lian's. He felt guilt and shame, the remorse making him feel queasy. He touched the letter she had given him to steady himself and behind closed eyelids, her smiling face bloomed. He had to hold on to the belief they'd be reunited one day. Not just for her— for him too. He swore he wouldn't go back to being the drifter he once had been. Lian had believed in him. Holding on to her, meant holding on to a better sense of himself too.

Chapter 5

Nüshu
女书
Women's Script

QUING DYNASTY
GUILIN, CHINA

BECAUSE GIACOMO WAS NOT AT the legation, I intended to give a note to Bulldog, who was standing guard at the gate, but just as I approached him, the captain appeared.

"Something I can help you with, Miss Brasolin?"

My hand went to my throat and toyed with a frog. "I wish to leave a written message for Scimenti."

"Why, certainly."

I turned to face Bulldog, but as I handed him the note, the captain grabbed it and pocketed it with an air of condescension that gave me little hope. He cared nothing for me.

Humility be damned, I pleaded, "Please, sir, be so kind as to give it to him as soon as he returns."

I nodded to Bulldog, his face fuming, and bowed to the captain. I said a little prayer that Bulldog would tell Giacomo I had come looking for him.

I returned home and sat in the living room with Baba's blessed ashes on his desk and wondered: *What should I do now?* I ate some cold rice and browsed through one of his notebooks. I set down my chopsticks, washed my dish, and then prepared a small cloth bag with some necessary items in it. I would travel to Tientsin. Father thought I would be safer with Lu, but I knew my destiny was with Giacomo. I would leave now to get a head start and meet Giacomo at his ship.

The trip of one hundred and sixty kilometers was arduous and took me over a week by railway, steamer, and buffalo-drawn cart, but I finally reached my destination. I went to the port and walked up and down the quay asking questions of foreigners and fishermen alike until I finally located the mooring place where the *Leopardo* had been docked, but my heart splintered because in the slip was another ship, flying a British standard and my country's visiting flag.

I learned that the ship was not expected back for a long time—whatever that meant. A kindly dockworker said it was usually months before a ship returned.

Chinese porters, some of whom had been practicing Boxer calisthenics, made fun of me, jeering and taunting. I walked along faster, but they yelled obscenities and I became anxious. Even from a distance, they began to throw things, heckling and harassing me, calling me a foreign she-devil. One of them followed me, screaming something about my evil-spirit green eyes. He gained on me and when he was close enough, spat on me. I ran quicker due to my unbound feet, which must have surprised him, because he did not pursue.

I heard the word *whore* reverberate behind me. How could my own countrymen be so foul and vicious? I hurried away. It was not safe for me here, but to my great horror, worse than this mocking, was the feeling of warm blood—in my crotch. I must do as I promised my father and go to Guilin, but first I must tend to the child I carried, making sure I did not miscarry.

"All in Heaven, hear me," I prayed. "Do not let me lose this child." I repeated the words over and over until I happened upon a small infirmary with an Italian name written above the Chinese. I knocked, opened the door, and collapsed into a nun's arms. When I awakened, the kindly Chinese nun with a rotund face knew of my condition. I asked for the herbs I needed, and she kept me for the night. In the morning, the spotting had ceased, and I felt it was safe to travel without causing harm to the baby I carried, if I was to stop and rest more frequently.

I returned to Peking by the same grueling means of travel. I packed our meager belongings and gave the keys back to the landlord. While readying myself for the trip to Guilin, I had one thought: Giacomo and our child. I closed the door, but before taking a step toward the palanquin, I placed my hand beneath my breasts and made a promise that one day Giacomo and I would be reunited. Until then, I would do all in this world to protect our baby.

I wished Baba a happy reuniting with my mother. Although instead of bidding him a fond farewell, I took his ashes with me and begged him to shadow and protect me.

❧

AFTER ANOTHER DIFFICULT JOURNEY OF weeks, traveling by cart and partly by unfinished railway, I arrived in Guilin and considered myself fortunate I'd had no more bleeding. A journey of discovery. I learned I was capable of making up my mind. I decided no matter what, I would not marry Lu, for in my heart I carried Giacomo, in my womb his child, and in my mind a strong will that bespoke of seeing him again; and this idea would help me keep my resolve.

In Guilin, I reunited with grandmother, whose expression on seeing me changed from shock and disbelief to one of contentment. I literally threw myself on Grandmother's neck, weeping to see her again.

Grandmother stood bent and small and seemed one muted shade of gray—face and hair. Wai Po did not possess my mother's warmth, but maintained an aura of kindliness and integrity, which reminded me more of Baba than Mother. Relieved to be home again in familiar surroundings that comforted me, I showed her the urn, but Wai Po had already guessed. She said, "Your Baba is now with the ancients."

Sadness veiled her expression at the news of his death. "Then we will go together and bury his ashes with your mother. I can see in your eyes you are exhausted from the journey. You must rest a few days until you are strong enough in body and spirit."

I knew I had to tell Wai Po of my pregnancy and how much I wanted to break off the engagement to Lu. But not now. It would be a crushing blow for Wai Po to hear and accept this.

"Mama loved this house and garden," I said, seeing the carved wooden characters for love, happiness, and prosperity hanging on the wall beneath the curved roof near Baba's office.

"Your father and his bride took me, not very willingly at the time, to Guilin before you were born. I couldn't be parted from my daughter—she was all I had in the world."

How well I understood this.

Wai Po told me the story of how my parents had been guests in this house with which Mama had fallen in love, so Baba purchased it, paying an exorbitant price as it had not been for sale. Baba had adored everything about Guilin, which is situated a little west of Hunan Province, where my mother's people were from.

While Wai Po went to make tea, I strolled into the garden. I opened my diary. As soon as I made the first threadlike stroke in the secret language of women, my mind was drawn back to a more idyllic time; I wandered through a portal filled with radiance and flowers.

I put down my pointed quill and recalled how I had learned *Nüshu* with Mother and Grandmother right here beneath a radiant sun and splendid clear, cerulean sky. Grandmother, Mama, and I walked in the garden when we stopped for a rest in the summerhouse. My mother and grandmother still kept ties with women friends, writing letters and messages in *Nüshu*. My mother had a *lao tong*, a lifelong female companion, an avowed sister, a connection made through a matchmaker when she was a little girl. Neither Grandmother nor Mother wrote Chinese, although my womenfolk wanted me to learn *Nüshu* and taught it to me. I hated to practice writing it because it seemed a waste of time, already knowing Chinese characters.

At the time of the lesson, Grandmother had taken a cushion from a bench trunk and sat on it. "Old bones need padding."

"Wai Po, why does Mama have a *lao tong* and not me?"

"You have no need for an 'old same'—times are changing."

"Then why do I have to practice these feathery syllables—with no *lao tong* to write to?"

Mama cut a few climbing roses and some camellias and put them in a basket. She laid them on a small rosewood table. "One day you will be glad you have our women's writing. Not everyone is schooled in it. Who knows what joy or comfort it may bring you?"

"Mama, how can you say that? It's sheer torture. Like not having bound feet. Why wouldn't you bind them?"

Grandmother clucked her tongue like a chicken. "You have no idea of the amount of torture involved in breaking the bones and binding feet."

"You know quite well, my child, because—" Mother began in her sweet voice.

"Yes, yes. Because my father would not permit it."

"But think why." Mother snipped a Buddha's Hand citrus and held it up to me. "The peel will make candied fruit."

Father drummed his fingers on the studio window that faced the garden enclosure and we all looked up. He pointed to his watch. Mother would bring him tea now.

I CAME OUT OF THAT reverie with a sorrow-laden heart. Mother never lived long enough to give me the *Sanchaoshu,* the Three-Day Missive, a cloth-covered book containing poems and sundry writings in our women's language a mother gives her daughter, upon marriage.

Then I remembered Ma speaking of another booklet, not for marriage, a *Jiejiaoshu* comprised of the commitments made by sworn sisters, whose vows in front of gods are recorded, their pledges written on red paper. I decided then that Giacomo would be my *lao tong.*

Wai Po returned with tea, and when we finished, she said she would go to bed, knowing I was tired too. I went to my old room, my hand trailing a brush, comb, and mirror set on my dresser, which had belonged to my mother and that Baba had given me when she died. Tired though I was, I couldn't quiet my mind enough for sleep.

Indeed Giacomo would be the companion I'd write to. I was aggrieved; I couldn't send him missives because I didn't know where he was. Instead, I'll write in the diary for him, imagining reading entries to him when we were together again. This diary would stoke fires of hope and make me close to him. I sat at my old school desk and picked up my brush and inkstone and began to write about myself and where I came from:

> On a soft, rainy night at vernal equinox, the Year of the Dog, I was born Zhou Bin Lian—Lian meaning lotus flower—in Guilin, China, a painter's paradise. My life revealed itself to me as in spatial colors. I began to understand much. After my mother died, I hoped my father would love again and remarry, but he never did.

One would think because Baba was Swiss, he was stiff and proper, but at times we laughed at silly things, and once we danced without music. He taught me to waltz. I remember the beats of 1-2-3, 1-2-3, and his soft humming voice and the way he held me. He had a serious side but generally was a good-natured healer with a keen wit, a practitioner who believed there was no higher calling for a human being than to help others. He taught me about the human body, acupuncture, and herbal cures. He had a skeleton in his office in Guilin, where I studied the bones. While we were in Peking, he had bought a monkey, and we dissected it—I learned the muscles and the ligaments and where they attached, all the systems of the body: circulatory, reproduction, digestive, respiratory, etc., and all the internal organs and their functions. I'd also dissected a cat, but a monkey is closer to the human body. He had promised me that when we returned to Guilin, he would purchase a cadaver for me to dissect. Will I ever get to study more anatomy on specimens now?

I assisted Baba with a patient by noting the necessary observations. First I would ask their chief complaint. Next I'd examine a person's tongue and consider the coating color, the shape, how it moved, and the quality. I would inquire about their emotions, energy, sleep patterns, pain, appetite, and digestion. I'd ask questions about chills, thirst, perspiration, and in the case of a woman, her menses. One old woman had a breathing problem, and I took her left pulse palpitation: cun, guan, chi, and then her right. Father had approved. Sometimes it was necessary for a patient to present Baba with urine or stool samples. This was unpleasant work, but important, and I never shirked from my position.

Before the end of my apprenticeship, I learned formula and dosage amounts for many ailments. I memorized the thirty manipulations of tui na, and the twenty-nine therapies, and many other things. At the end of my training period, Baba died, as if he'd waited until his teaching me had concluded. The ambassador recovered and Father died, though not before he saw all the changes beginning to take place in China. Rebels burned and looted and started to persecute foreign missionaries in the hills and mountain villages.

ONE AFTERNOON, SEVERAL DAYS LATER, I was sitting in the garden, thinking about Giacomo. I felt strong enough now and resolved to tell Wai Po the truth. I couldn't put it off longer, and I needed to enlist Grandmother's help to break off the engagement. When the dowry money was returned, I'd use it to set myself up in Guilin as a healer, supporting myself, the child, and Wai Po until I found Giacomo. I was about to stand and go to her, but just then, she entered the garden.

At first I was delighted, but then froze, for she was followed by Madam Yi, her son Lu, and the matchmaker. Wai Po smiled. Of course she would not expect rebellion on my part. Doubt engulfed me, knowing Grandmother would not be pleased. Why hadn't I confided sooner? My eyes met hers, challenging, and she shivered.

I bowed, extending my arm toward chairs, and we all sat in the garden. According to protocol, we made the usual chitchat. Ignored like a block of wood, I sat still while my thoughts raced. *What to do now?* My eyes swept over them in their silken finery: Lu, broad and stocky, Lady Yi, lean and tight-lipped, and the cunning broker, plump and well-endowed.

How could they know I detested this man even though he had always been civil and polite to me? Clouds formed overhead, and the realization that we would have to make "clouds and rain" revolted me. How could I lay with Lu after I had been with Giacomo? Lu couldn't possibly love or desire me—we hadn't seen each other for three years. I stood at once and made an excuse, lowering my voice as if saying something of dire consequence, which nobody really heard but Lu, whom I asked to accompany me on a walk, a bold move with the sole purpose of getting him alone. We walked into the deepest part of the shaded garden, and I stopped stone-still and blurted out to Lu I could not marry him, confessing I carried another man's child. His horrified look frightened me. What I'd expected, maybe even hoped for, was a heartbroken reaction, but his look held hate and his anger flared. He said, "How dare you speak these words?" He punched one fist into an open palm, constraining himself not to strike me as he might a whore in a brothel. He walked ahead of me, and we returned to the others in the garden.

Lu didn't tell his mother or the broker of the quick, hushed, fractious argument or that I was with child. His tone was deadly calm, masking his true sentiments, when he said that I wanted to break off relations with him due to my great grief of losing Baba.

Madame Yi jumped up. "We refuse to give back the dowry."

I thought she had every right to keep it and was about to say so when Wai Po, my old, sharp grandmother, voiced her opinion. "If there is to be no marriage, then the dowry must be returned, although, there will be reconciliation when my granddaughter has had time to grieve."

Thinking the matter resolved and noticing Wai Po tottering a bit, her unsteady gait due to her fragility and lotus walk, I took the lacquer tray from her hands. Wai Po flung me a look, bowed to Madame Yi, the broker, and Lu, grabbed the tray back, and carried it away, embarrassing me and a fawning serving girl standing by the door.

Unguarded and unprotected, I overheard them speak among themselves as if I were a piece of the wooden fence. When Wai Po came back, the atmosphere in the garden had changed.

Lu bowed and said, seemingly quite sincerely despite my change of heart, which he understood was due to the loss of my father, he had every intention of keeping his part of the bargain, the dowry, and making me honor my promise to marry him, with Wai Po's permission of course. And as soon as possible. In other words, I counted for naught in this arrangement.

How mollified and delighted Grandmother was. I had never before given importance to money but now understood how it keeps one not just from poverty and starvation, but from independence. I remembered Lu's father had a reputation for gambling, and it dawned on me the Yi family might not have the dowry money to return. Cool air, an almost imperceptible breath at the back of my head. My impulse was to smooth the hair on my neck from the slight breeze, but when I turned, it was an odious stare from Lu; I could never make retribution.

Naturally, he felt betrayed. What could he be thinking, feeling? Did this man consider himself in love with me? Or was this rage and fury because he was forced by his mother into this marriage despite himself? Would it change things if I told my future spouse that the man who impregnated me was not Chinese? Would Lu relent and let me go? My thoughts ran wild like an untethered horse in a field. Could I run again?

I recalled how I'd almost lost the baby when I'd run after Giacomo to Tientsin. No, I must be clear-headed. I haven't a choice but to throw my lot in with Lu to save my lover's baby. I must forget finding Giacomo and begin thinking of him only as my *lao tong,* my trusted and dearest friend on earth. I felt faint with misery.

❦

STILL PRAYING TO GODS UNFEELING and unseen, I wrote Giacomo once more in care of the embassy, as if he or those aloof deities could come to rescue me. Days passed swiftly and then wedding preparations were concluded. Wai Po and I traveled to the Yi compound where the ceremony was to take place. On the way, I finally told Wai Po about my love affair and pregnancy. Once she calmed herself, she advised me to follow through with the wedding plans rapidly, saying to forget the sailor. She asked one question. Had I told Lu? I nodded. She patted my hand, saying, " My honest, foolish child." Another rent in the fabric of possible dreams.

It was not the auspicious affair I'd hoped for: At dawn on my wedding day, the rain began to fall softly like the day I was born. I bathed in water infused with pumelo, a variety of grapefruit. This Chinese custom was to cleanse away evil influences, but the Western side of me knew it was a skin softener. I donned new underclothes and sat before lit dragon and phoenix candles. Wai Po paid an exorbitant price for a good-luck woman to attend preparations for my wedding. With propitious words she prattled, dressing my hair as a married woman. Had my father been alive, he'd have teased me for such foolishness. But I was alone and unsure.

The wedding took place quickly and was a small affair—the only guests I knew were Doctor Han, an old colleague of Father's, Wai Po, my dear friend Ping, and the bride, the girl who faced me in the mirror. Just the immediate Yi family attended. *Shame or lack of funds?* Did I even care to know? On the actual wedding day there were no firecrackers, no ribbons, and no confetti. Not a single lantern festooned the entrance from the garden. Only two drummers, not six, played the drums and gongs, and four stout family men, not hired, carried me in the *huajiao*— wedding sedan chair.

Not all of these bad omens could I attribute to my mother-in-law. Instead of the festive red for luck, I foolishly wore a blue silk bridal jacket, embroidered with nine dragons by my great-grandmother's hands, copied from an antique Ming design. I can only blame myself, for Wai Po had cautioned me against it. Headstrong, I thought familial loyalty was more important than the auspicious red, thinking the red veil covering my face and the sedan chair would be enough for good fortune and happiness. Another miscalculation of the generosity of the gods—for one can never have too much luck.

At the celebration, my husband gave me a red handkerchief and wished me luck, but no mandarin ducks were embroidered on it. I had no handkerchief to exchange with him, and stunned into silence by my stupidity, I never wished him luck. How could I hope for an image of ducks when I'd only married him because I had lost my true love through no fault of his own?

On a table in the garden laid with food, there was far more to drink than to eat. Unaccustomed to alcohol, I drank a little too much wine, and my husband grew disgusted with my intolerance. We walked with a small entourage back to the house I now viewed as my prison. While I undressed to prepare myself for the wedding night, I was alone long enough to make an entry into my chronicle.

> *To rob me of what little luck I possessed, my bridal pallet was desecrated. When I saw the pillowslip, red for good luck, my heart began to soar, but on closer look I noticed a long gray hair snaking across it. If it had not been gray, I would have thought my husband had already begun to cuckold me, but it belonged to my mother-in-law, who had lain upon it, defiling it, murdering my dreams even before they were conceived, let alone born. This has but one solitary meaning: Lu has told Madame Yi, now my sworn enemy for life, that I carry another man's child. What kind of man did I espouse?*

Lu stormed in just as I hid my book in my *piccolo corredo*, if it could be called a trousseau at all. He ordered me to my bed. I wanted to say, "Ha! My bed? You mean your mother's?" But I kept still, despising the creature I had become since my father's death. With an inconsolable heart, cold and intractable as uncut jade, I sank into my marriage bed, a pregnant woman in need of a warm caress and a practiced hand to coax my heart into an awakening into womanhood, but I was alone. I drifted to sleep contemplating growing a suit of armor, becoming impervious to sleights, ceasing feelings of self-pity, and moving mentally to a position of power.

My slumber brought dreams filled with things my father had warned me of, and of a kiss in a garden several months ago. Why had my sailor kissed me? To taste Chinese lips? I awoke wondering if I'd ever see Giacomo again. If I didn't have him, at least I would have the best of him in the child within me, and I patted my belly.

◀━━▶◆◀━━▶

THOSE "HONEYMOON" DAYS HAD NOTHING honey about them under the moon. Lu and I had broken many of the formal traditions of marriage. I spent my initial nuptial days embroidering stitches on handmade shoes, painting on fans, and pretending I didn't understand the meaning of the poetry recited by an old blind man to my sisters-in-law and me as we did these tasks.

To comfort myself and keep alive the memory of Giacomo, whenever I could, I escaped to "rest" but in reality wrote in my *Nüshu* diary, which I believed was safe as no one in the Yi family read. I walked in the garden and learned to cook and to arrange flowers.

On the fourth night, while the Yi household slept, I pushed back my sleeve and began to write by the light of the moon streaming into the kitchen, but soon put down the brush and closed the box with my ink stone, my mind reeling back in time to that fateful event, my wedding.

Days after the wedding, I had been writing in my chronicle. I found in a much younger hand in the corner of the binding the character for *yung*. A flood of memories overtook me. At my father's insistence, I learned calligraphy—a sport, my mother had said, not appropriate for a girl, and she argued with Baba that a left-handed girl like me could never manage the brush. How I practiced that *yung* character after Mother died for it was a good test for a calligrapher and her art. My teacher explained that it makes use of all the fundamental strokes. I traced that character, recalling Giacomo's lips on mine because it means, "forever," or "eternity," and I knew I could love no other man for all my life and beyond. I brushed my thumb across the spot on the cover and then brought my thumb to my lips.

◀━━▶✕◀━━▶

DOUBLE SORROW VISITED ME WITHIN three weeks' time. News reached me that Wai Po was unwell. I made several entreaties to visit her but was kept waiting for three days. Wai Po was very ill. Another week passed and finally I was allowed to go to her with one of my sisters-in-law as chaperone. Fate had numbered the days for Grandmother when she and I met at the cemetery.

"Death is coming for me," she had said, "but I intend on meeting it on my own terms."

We left my sister-in-law waiting outside the cemetery gate, and Wai Po took me, in spite of her feebleness, to visit the graves of our ancestors, where we left bowls of rice. Mourning doves nested in a banyan tree. A feather glided toward us and she caught it. She handed it to me. "They mate for life, but not all marriages succeed. This I bequeath you, be true to yourself."

She began coughing up blood and I took her home. If Fate were to deem it possible for me to be together with Giacomo, would our love be like my mother's for my father, or be as noble, sure, and proud as this bent, old woman, who had once made me practice *Nüshu*? I am forever thankful, knowing my mother's words about *Nüshu being a comfort to me* had been prophetic. How had she known?

Wai Po died in her sleep shortly after that visit. I was bereft at losing my only relative and uncomforted, knowing I'd never be able to keep anything of hers or from my father's house. To make matters worse, Lu finally sealed the marriage by taking me that night.

I begged for one or two of Baba's pharmaceutical objects or ledgers. My request was denied. Madame Yi sold our house and the furnishings went to auction, every last book, cylinder, Bunsen burner, beaker, funnel, including the calligraphic scroll *anjilika* I'd made for Baba. I held on to my father's notebooks and medicine bag, but even these Madame Yi snatched from me. She left with an entourage of workers and Baba's textbooks to sell them privately, saying she'd return soon, leaving me with buyers clamoring to disperse my inheritance.

The last piece of furniture was my father's desk, with locks of bats with outstretched wings, emblematic of longevity and happiness. As it was being removed, I cried.

A commotion erupted with the clattering of horse's hooves in the courtyard. The arrival of a court messenger distracted me. The messenger handed me a missive from the empress dowager: *Your father no longer needs you as his hands and eyes. The court awaits you.*

Where could I hide? Where could I run? What could I do?

I yelled, "Stop" to the coolies carrying my father's desk, and they set it down. I took paper, quill, and ink from the desk and wrote my current circumstance to the empress in hopes she would let me fade into the obscure life of a farmer's wife. I handed this to the messenger.

Even then, my father had been looking out for me. Why else would Lady Yi have been absent, giving me an opportunity to write the empress?

MADAME YI, KNOWING I WAS pregnant, had lied to the family, saying the baby I carried was her son's. She must have convinced Lu not to rupture our betrothal, realizing she would soon be in control of my worldly goods, not just my dowry, with the death of Wai Po. Or had he thought of that on his own? Father had stipulated in his will that my inheritance would pass to the Yi Family after Wai Po passed, which was expected. With Grandmother gone to the spirit world with my parents, I was completely alone except for the baby I carried.

I had awakened from the tossed and tumbled nuptials into a family that despised me. Over the next few months, as my body grew, I survived with cunning and wit, obsequiousness to Lu's mother, and certainly by the ironic winds of Fate. Lu was the second son, and though it was important for his family to produce a son, it was more important for his elder brother's wife to have a son first. Not only did she succeed in this, she had borne three sons in succession. The last came before I entered my last trimester.

With my pregnancy well-advanced, I worried about giving birth. What a shock it would be when the truth of parenthood was known. My child. Three quarters of the baby's blood and features would be European—how many unwanted babies were murdered in infancy in China? What if I had a girl? So many of them disappeared without a trace, and somehow I felt it would be a girl, but even a son with white skin would be gotten rid of for certain. That was my preoccupation—all I could think of on the day the midwife came to discuss the birthing of the baby. She demanded part payment in advance on a Sunday evening after dinner. Seated in the kitchen sipping tea, I overheard Madame Yi tell the midwife to make sure to prepare the bathwater for the infant. Her words made my blood congeal around my heart. She had said, "You do understand what I mean about the bucket of water, don't you?"

And without hesitation, the woman answered, "A girl child will be immersed in cold water before breath, a boy child will be bathed in warm water." The conversation stayed with me after everyone had retired.

I was not merely fretting—I was petrified of what Madame Yi was capable of doing and would do if it was not a male child. I went to the kitchen and found a cord, a sharp knife, clean rags, and one of the pails used for slops to feed the pigs. I scrubbed this with a bristle brush and disinfected it with boiling water. I placed all of the kitchen items in the pail and took it with me to hide in the garden far from the house. I would have to deliver my baby alone.

Two days later, fortune smiled on me. When the contractions started, I forced myself to ride my bicycle, the prepared pail dangling from the handle bars, to the factory where my best friend Ping worked. I found her on her lunch hour, which terminated in my delivery. It was a girl. News about the baby spread quickly, and now there could be no "accidental" death.

After she was born, I kept Ya Chen with me every moment, making her suckle until the milk she needed came forth. I had disgraced my husband by being delivered of a worthless female, fruit of another man's loins, but I had foiled Madame Yi's intention to do away with my infant. I implored my husband to allow me to keep her. Mercifully, he did. Perhaps this was because I had been a dutiful wife; perhaps because he was growing fond of me.

After six months, my child's light hazel eyes never changed, and her features were more Occidental than mine. The child of a foreign devil and a half-breed. Everyone suspected, but no one spoke of it, save Lu, whose feelings turned icy with wanting to find and kill my lover. He badgered me with questions, but I never answered about Giacomo or his ship.

The men had gone out. Rebels had set fire to village stores, had robbed whatever wasn't anchored to floors, and had started to persecute foreign missionaries in the hills and mountain villages. Rumors spread and came bouncing back of Lu practicing callisthenic rituals with Boxers.

Father had been right. My husband was one of them, and I feared not only for the child's life but also my own.

Chapter 6

Tianshi
天使
Angel

THE *LEOPARDO* SAILED ITS WAY from Hong Kong to Macau where they took on provisions.

The protected light cruiser, the *SMS Irene,* had been in Hong Kong at the same time having its engine refitted, and had followed the *Leopardo* toward Macau.

Susequent to a two-week stay in Macau, the *Leopardo* headed north to Shanghai, and from there toward Wuhan along the Yangtze. The Italian ship wasn't the only gunboat controlling the waterways for demonstrations, outbreaks of unrest, or signs of revolution. They were in a convoy with a German ship, the small cruiser *SMS Cormoran,* also patrolling the river.

The ships parted ways when the *Leopardo* stopped for a few days at Hangkow and the next day set underway again. The trip was leisurely, passing many towns and villages, stopping at places with interesting names like Fengdu, the City of Ghosts. Giacomo toured the temples, the statues so lifelike in their resemblance of the dead that it gave him pause. Lieutenant Rinaldi had been here before and told Giacomo not to fret because as the legend went, the dead go to Fengdu, but the devil goes to hell.

After Fengdu, the ship meandered, maneuvering beneath the high cliffs and luscious, verdant hills. Giacomo couldn't imagine warlords were causing an upheaval a few days from here upriver. The spectacular scenic views of these imposing ravines and canyons made Giacomo feel insignificant. The steep rock precipices bordered the Qutang and Wu Gorges, where lofty crests and crags were mist-covered, making them seem otherworldly. Overhangs and rock canyons jutted out far over the water, as if to give each other a handshake. Others hung back, awaiting some supercilious god to push them into the chasm below. The valleys and ravines were speckled with pagodas. The silence at sunrise made Giacomo feel at one with nature and the God of all things, and he thought of his beloved Lian. *Breathtaking* was the only word that came to his mind as he ducked into the galley to prepare the morning's meal.

After an hour's exercise on top deck, Lieutenant Rinaldi made the announcement, "When we arrive at Wuhan, those not recruited to negotiate with the warlords, or assigned to some duty onboard, may disembark and take the skiff to see the Little Three Gorges. I guarantee you've never in your life seen anything as splendid. Don't sleep your time away—get cracking."

When the 'peace negotiators' returned to the ship, it was late. Scuttlebutt had it that Captain Morante bribed two warlords with money and munitions in two different meetings. Ensign Bartolo confirmed it that evening over coffee, cigarettes and *briscola,* but of course someone had laced his coffee with *choujiu,* a rice wine, or he'd never have been so talkative, or capable of divulging this information.

Giacomo wondered if any other of the foreign nations represented in China would hand over ammunition to the supposed enemy to obtain safe passage in their waters. In the morning, they would pass on to more hospitable waterways, but first they had hired one hundred trackers to file past the risky shoals, hauling the *Leopardo* with tie lines. Two days later they reached the "golden channel" and arrived at Wuhan, capital of Hubei Province.

◆━◆◆◆━◆

ONE AFTERNOON GIACOMO WALKED OUT of the galley storeroom with an armload of fresh produce for the evening meal. He set down the foodstuffs on the chopping block, running a hand over it with remembrances of Lian. He picked up a sack of cashew nuts for the chicken and set them near the vegetables. Lian had given him this recipe—now one of the crew's favorites.

After all the preparations were set out in order, he stepped out onto the deck to have a look at the water and the sky. Leaning on the guardrail, he breathed in the scents of people cooking on the backs of their sampans. A young girl, scrubbing clothes, looked up at his sailing ship. It must have seemed an immense monstrosity to her. He smiled at her, but she looked down immediately, and for a fleeting moment, he wondered if it could have been Lian. His girl in the garden. Would he ever think of her as anything but that? He patted the shirt pocket above his heart—a girl who wrote to him in a secret tongue. If he closed his eyes, he could conjure her—hear her hesitant step as she came toward him; see her small, nimble body approach. He inhaled deeply and the scent of her freshly washed hair filled his nostrils; his lips quivered with wanting to taste her kiss again—a spasm of longing rippled through his loins. He relived the night of their first lovemaking and wished he'd taken the girl of his dreams over and over. What chance was there of ever seeing her again now that he was so far from the capital, traveling the rivers of China? If he ever saw her again, he would protect her with his life.

There was something his mother used to say about wanting and wishing. We make our own destinies, and if we desire a thing a great deal, it can become a reality. "How can that be," he'd asked. His mother had answered, "Because God in His infinite mercy can read our thoughts and hearts and takes pity on us when we beg, plead, and pray"—Such faith.

He sat on the deck steps and thought about Lian with the surprised look on her face, her startled, shimmering eyes, green as wet magnolia leaves in spring.

"I'm praying, Lord, I'm pleading, begging to find her. Next time, I'll never let her go," he said to the rising westward wind. Giacomo knew he needed faith along with the words, but wasn't sure if God existed, though he believed in the faith his mother possessed. So lost in thought was he that he didn't hear Lieutenant Rinaldi until the officer was at the stairs, hand on the banister.

"Sorry, sir," Giacomo said, leaping to his feet and saluting.

"Daydreaming, Scimenti? Know what they say about people who talk to themselves? Shouldn't you be in mess or the galley?"

"No, sir, I have some slack time."

"Make better use of it."

"Yes, sir, on the double."

The lieutenant dashed up the steps, and Giacomo sat down again and pulled a pocketknife and a small piece of wood he'd been whittling since yesterday. He smiled insolently and showed wood and knife to the officer who'd turned to look back. But Rinaldi let it go with a laugh. Giacomo thought the hard ass wasn't half-bad after all. He began to carve. His thoughts went from wood to the chopping block. And to Lian.

THE NEXT DAY WHILE THEY cruised, Giacomo prepared dinner. Bulldog stopped by the galley and said, "Hey, what about a story? I'm bored."

Giacomo hesitated as he chopped and cooked. Every glance at the chopping block was like a punch in his gut, and sometimes he had trouble concentrating or speaking.

"How about a story later? I'm running late." Giacomo untied his apron.

"What for?"

"Come with me. Shen's teaching me *Wing Chun*." Giacomo tossed the apron on the chopping block.

"A flavorful dish, I hope," Bulldog stepped aside for Giacomo to exit the galley.

"No. It's body defense—your centerline must always point toward your opponent. Like this." Giacomo took the stance. "Small movements timed right can kill a man. Energetic jabs of the elbow—come try it." Giacomo explained that the sessions would teach relaxed, close range engagements that would be fast, powerful, and practical.

"I'm in," Bulldog said, taking the steps two at a time following Giacomo.

The lesson was comprised of learning the six forms and practicing *lat sao,* a sparring exercise, and *chi sao,* a sensitivity training for the arms. They would repeat the lessons once a week for the following months, practicing in-between.

When the lesson was over, Giacomo took a huge wooden plank and set it over one of the sinks. "Shen, get me a chicken from a cage," Giacomo said in a soft voice. He was growing fond of the boy and pleased at how well he worked and was willing to learn. Giacomo showed Shen how to wring its neck. He cut off the head and feet to use for a gelatinous broth and pulled the feathers and, burning over live coals, the remaining quills, whose nibs didn't wrench free with a swift yank. Then he gutted it, saving liver, gizzard, heart, and ovaries. That's what he needed—fierceness and savagery to wipe away all memory of the altar he'd created for her. He nicked his middle finger with the knife, the blood reminding him of Lian's virginal bloodletting and how he'd washed the insides of her thighs and ministered to her. If only he could tend to her again. His mother would have said that cutting the middle finger meant a letter would arrive soon. Before Giacomo asked, the boy had cleaned the cutting surface.

The ship pulled into a broad swath of canal. From the galley doorway, he saw monks in saffron robes, ringing bells along the shore pathway. They swirled round noisemakers, a call to prayer. In the distance, Giacomo saw a temple and decided to ask his all-knowing assistant about the monks and their beliefs. He wondered how different theirs were from his own, and decided not to judge, lest he be judged—a lesson in tolerance. He noticed Shen and one of the Chinese crew who spoke pidgin watching him as he looked at the monks. Shen told him the monks had housed him for a time and he learned some of their ways. He explained as best he could that Buddhists believed in karma, cause-and-effect, which Giacomo had heard of often enough. The other crew members made clear that they also believed in Maya, the illusory nature of the world; Samsara, the cycle of reincarnation; and the ultimate life goal to achieve "enlightenment." Giacomo questioned them further about the meaning of *enlighten*. Shen said something in Chinese to the other boy who translated that as far as they knew, Buddhists lived a middle way, not luxurious indulgence or self-mortification, but he thought that the monks were stricter. He struggled to explain, and finally said, it meant awakening, insight, truth.

That night when he finished work in the galley, he stepped outside. A clear, crisp night. Unable to sweep the image of Lian's face from his mind, he scrutinized a sky sprinkled with mica, like the sand on the beach. Funny how the mind works—one moment concentrating on Lian's face and next seeing earth matter in the sky.

THE FOLLOWING DAY THEY THREW anchor in a deep bay. Giacomo and Bulldog got a ride ashore on a tender that hosted Lieutenant Rinaldi and Chief Petty Officer Lambrusco, escorted by Ensign Bartolo, Sartori, and Di Louise. This party would deal with another of the warlords to negotiate safe passage for the ship. Giacomo and Bulldog entered a deserted-looking cottage bar. The shades were drawn on the windows to give a semblance of night. A game of cards was going on in a rear corner. A dartboard was set up near the front. Candlelight from a glass lantern cast light on the green baize of a gaming table. Toward the middle of the dingy bar was a space occupied by three small tables, and each table had four rattan chairs. They sat down at one of them and ordered rice with clams in black bean sauce.

Bulldog said, "What I wouldn't do for some *bruschetta* smothered in green-gold virgin olive oil."

"I haven't thought about that for a long time," he said, thinking, *but I sure do remember my virgin.* After one drink, they went back to the ship and headed for the mess hall. Giacomo brought out a bottle of anisette and fresh-baked almond cookies.

"Did I ever tell you the story of when I was fourteen years old and got home from the caves where I'd met Ciccio, a thug who worked for my father?"

"We've got the night, no women, and a bottle of booze, so how can I refuse to hear it?" Bulldog said.

Giacomo began his story in a low voice.

I went to Le Grotte to pick *fighi d'india.* The ripe prickly pears were bountiful all over the abundant cacti. The October evening turned cool. I untied the hand-knit sweater Mother made for me fastened around my waist and pulled it over my head. I scaled the top ridge of the cave, scraping my knees on shale and rocks to reach the thickest cactus, and put the fruit in a knapsack.

"Ai," I yipped as I took hold of one of the prickly pears. *"Cristo!"* I blasphemed at the spines, immediately crossing myself, asking the Lord's forgiveness. I was an altar boy back then.

The cloud-filled sky darkened. I'd been long on my foray and began my descent—part run, part slide down the cliff to the cave.

I reached the mouth of the grotto just as the heavens opened up and sheets of rain pummeled the parched earth. In front of the cave the troth was filled to overflowing, and around it were scattered lemon peels for the sheep. A shadow crept into the dimly lit cave, and a man stood dark and ominous before me. He was a flesh and bone mafioso, whom I'd seen in the piazza. The tall man held a tether in his hand. His black cape fluttered in the wind and he wore a beret on his head. He made me think of a hawk just landing on his perch, pulling in his wings. Over the man's shoulder was slung a *lupara*. The hair on the back of my neck prickled because I knew the rifle was loaded. I met the dark rider's eyes. He asked, *"Che stai facenno ca?"*

"Picking fruit when the rains came—I took refuge here. You're Salvatore aren't you?"

"Not the good Salvatore. His brother Ciccio. Where are your manners?"

"I am Stefano Scimenti's son. My name's Giacomo. Sir."

"Beh, that's better."

"You're one of the men who stand in the cold early morning to look for work." I shifted weight from one leg to the other and cracked the knuckles of my left hand, startled by their echoing sound. I shoved my hands deep inside my pockets.

"Yes, but now your father has leased me this land. The lemons will be fat and juicy when we harvest, and the almonds will fall soon. They're plentiful."

Ciccio slid his soggy beret off and wrung it out. "This rain. I smelled it in the air this morning, so I didn't set out the nets to catch the nuts. I'll lose much of the crop." His huge hands spread the beret on a rock. "I'll make a fire for Don Stefano's son. Sit," Ciccio said, in a menacing way and pointed to another flatter rock, worn to a seat by many who had tended this land.

"I must get back. My mother will be worried," I said.

"Sit down. Wait until the storm lets up." He spat out a wad of tobacco. Ciccio hunched down to light the fire and smiled a mouthful of blackened teeth. He took a small package from his pocket, the size of a box of wooden matches. From it, he withdrew a piece of a brown substance with a slight musty odor like clothes hung in the back of a closet for many seasons. I imagined its woody flavor. He popped it in his mouth and chewed.

Something distracted me. I looked back again and heard the crinkling of a wrapper, reminding me of Christmas, but then saw Ciccio toss it into the fire. As the fire blazed, I thought back to last night's fire burning bright when I felt safe at home. Even though the fire warmed, cold wrapped around my heart. I distrusted and disliked this man, though I had no right to; I didn't even know him—how could I judge him? I'd heard he was a killer.

Ciccio stood up and threw back his cape. My eyes caught the black bandolier of shells crisscrossing his gaunt chest. I'd miscalculated his size and strength because of the cape. Ciccio's eyes were shiny, his voice slick as oil being poured into a demijohn.

He took off his cape, laid it on the ground, and sat cross-legged on it. He took a Jew's harp out of his shirt pocket and placed it in his mouth. He cupped a hand in front and began to pluck. The twanging emitted a mournful sound, like the bagpipes at Christmastime when shepherds come down from the hills. Ciccio stopped playing, snapped the small harp against his hand several times, and put it away. We sat in silence, broken only by wind and rain.

By the time I reached home, dinner was ready. The large chestnut table was covered with a white linen cloth and earthenware dishes filled with the remains of lunch—roasted wild boar with a mixture of early fall vegetables, what Mamma called a medley of broccoli and cauliflower. A salad of chicory and dandelion sat in the middle of the table flanked by flagons of oil and vinegar, a carafe of water and one of red wine. Pecorino cheese abounded, alongside a platter of *bruschetta* dripping with first-press olive oil from our *orto,* and radishes big as apples.

I flung down my satchel and rushed to the water pump, splashing my face and arms. Seated at the table, the family prayed. My father lowered his head. After the prayer, Babbo raised his head and tucked a huge linen napkin into his shirt collar.

"Why are you late?" he asked me.

"I was caught at Le Grotte in the storm." I cut into the meat and dropped the knife.

"Why were you there?"

"A huge squall came up from the gulf. Didn't it rain here?" I felt a lurch in my stomach as my father set down his fork. I looked down to avoid his glare.

The candles on the table flickered, and the wind rushed through branches that scratched against the windows.

"Answer me. Why were you there?"

"I went to pick fruit."

"How long did you stay?" he asked.

"An hour. I met Ciccio." I pictured the workers saluting Babbo with respect.

"You're forbidden to talk to that man."

"I shielded myself in the cave from the rain when he rode up."

Mamma looked at me, pleading with me to do something, but what? "Eat, child."

"Let the boy finish speaking," my father snapped.

I pushed away the plate. *"Basta.* Enough, Mamma."

"Continue," my father said.

"I thought it was his brother, Salvatore. At first Ciccio frightened me. Then he talked about you and the land he rents. He played the Jew's harp like me and said it calms the sheep." I took a bite of toasted bread smothered in olive oil and garlic.

"Never mind. What did he say about the *latifondo?* His words about the land, son."

A piece of crusty *bruschetta* stuck in my throat, I coughed and sputtered. My father offered me some wine. I wanted to leave the table but by the tone of his voice knew it was better not to ask. Taking the carafe in my left hand, I started to pour.

My father stopped me. "Don't ever pour with your left. It's the sign of a traitor," he said, and motioned me to continue speaking.

I switched hands. "Ciccio said the rain would cause him to lose much of the almond and lemon harvest. I was cold and he was soaked, so he built a fire to warm us. He seemed afraid— always listening for something. His eyes are like a fox, looking here and there—on guard. He carried a *lupara* with a bandolier loaded with bullets."

"Do not disobey me. Never speak to that man again. Have I ever struck you? I promise I will break my cane across your back if you do. Now go to your room."

Why was he angry? It was accidental. No one ever told me to avoid Ciccio's company, and I hadn't sought him out. Why ever would I?

"Let the child have some fruit, Don Stefano," my mother said. "Then he'll go straight to bed after supper." To me, she said, "Don't eat too many prickly pears."

"Remember the last time? They make you sick," scolded Father. But my child's brain already reserved the fattest fruits to soften his harshness. I indicated the ones I wanted. Mamma peeled them deftly. It amazed me how fast she could do it, never pinching her fingers with the spines. I watched her pick up a pear by thumb and pointer finger, gripping it in a vice of fingernails. She sliced off each end, then drew the knife lengthwise—a perfect dissection. My mother held the fruit by its ends, she flattened the open skin and rolled out luscious red meat of what I knew to be God's wild bounty for the poor and rich alike.

After I'd eaten the fruit, Mamma touched my forehead and neck. "You're a shade lighter than the tablecloth, but maybe the candlelight makes you seem paler still. Up to bed now."

She came to check on me, and I stifled a moan, clutching my stomach, so she moved closer. "Why did you eat more when your father warned you? I should've known you'd eaten some earlier at Le Grotte. Let's see your hands, you little piglet."

"Oh, Mammina." I groaned again.

"I'll heat olive oil to rub on your belly, you glutton, but next time, listen to your father."

Mamma covered me with her crocheted shawl, brushed back hair from my forehead, and pressed her lips to my skin. "Warm and clammy," she said. "Say your prayers. Sleep."

I imagined Mamma moving so as not to disturb Don Stefano, kneeling by the fireplace, a rosary dangling in his hands. She came back and placed a small copper pot into the smoldering coals of the brazier near my bed. After it heated, she set it on the night table with a cloth under it. She poured Brioschi crystals into a glass of water, stirred, and then handed me the effervescent drink. "Swallow it all."

She made me sit up and rubbed my back until I burped. I felt like a baby, but relieved.

"There now." She puffed up my pillows and made me recline.

She raised my nightshirt, and I winced as she spread warm oil on my bare belly. She covered my stomach with old, clean woolen cuttings.

"I'll never again be so foolish. Who is this shepherd who tends father's flock and land?"

"A person to be wary of, my son. He's from Partinico." Looking out the window past the courtyard into the orchard shrouded by nightfall, she hummed a *ninna nanna*, although the night before I'd told her I was too old for such things. Lights, like stars, flickered in the distance.

"Mamma, you're an angel."

She turned her shoulder and pointed to her back. "See? No wings. Not an angel. Hush now and think of the vineyards and plump grapes ready for picking—vintage time is close. November will usher in the harvest and on the feast of Saint Martin you'll be stomping and crushing grapes, but only if you're well and strong. Sleep."

She kissed my forehead. "Cool." She pulled up the coverlet, woven on her loom. "A gift from God is what you are," she said.

And Giacomo, thinking of his angel girl Lian, a healer, just like his mother, repeated to Bulldog, "A gift from God."

Chapter 7

Shenxin; xinling
身心心灵
Mind, body, and spirit

AFTER TWO YEARS LU AND I had no other child except for my bright and beautiful baby girl, Ya Chen, Precious Pearl, whom I nicknamed Zin-Zin. The child was quick-witted and advanced for her age—some of her inquisitiveness and questions reminded me of Baba. My husband desperately wanted a male heir. I, on the other hand, knew I would never get to raise a boy myself. My in-laws would take over, as they had already done with Zin-Zin. I would have adored raising children, just as I would have loved to work as an herbalist, or practice the medicine I'd learned with my father. But Lu's family would not tolerate this. With all my dreams squelched, they made me work in the small factory where Ping worked, owned by a man my father-in-law was indebted to, and my earnings paid his gambling debts. Anything left over helped feed the family coffer. Unusual, indeed, but I was the one with big feet.

Luckily I liked my position in the factory making cloisonné. It kept me away from my poisonous mother-in-law, and I discovered I had a talent for painting. Luckiest of all, I could write and read *Nüshu*, women's secret writing, which neither Madame Yi nor any of the women in the Yi household could. This meant even if my journal were discovered, it would be gibberish to them and if shown to the men, they would not be able to read it. I did suspect one sister-in-law of knowing it as she was from Changsha, but I felt she wouldn't betray me. She was married to the third brother, adored Ya Chen, but had no children of her own.

My other secret talent was that I could read and write Mandarin, though Lu's family did not know this—they considered this men's writing. I had held onto Baba's notebooks, but on the day my father's things were auctioned, my mother-in-law took them from me, saying they were good only to start a fire, and since I couldn't read anyway, why should I keep them? She left before the court messenger arrived. What would she have said if she'd seen me write to the empress? My father's words resounded in my ears: *"When you marry Lu, you may have to give up your love of books, calligraphy, and maybe even a part of your very soul, my child, but never lose hope of one day practicing medicine."*

ON A LATE AUTUMN MORNING, by the Western calendar 1897, I sat with dear Ping, the sister of my heart, in the tearoom during our factory break and wondered what Destiny's winds hoarded in its cache for my little girl and for me.

Ping passed me my cup. I blew on the tea and then sipped.

"I am not a participant in our bed encounters but rather a used vessel, a receptacle into which Lu pours his essence along with his frustrations. It wasn't always like this. At first it seemed like passion. I'm nauseous every day. My body betrays me," I said.

"You're so pale, are you telling me you're pregnant?" Ping asked, setting aside her cup.

"I'm tired, and my cycle is late." I sipped from my tea once more and then put the cup aside. "I feel downtrodden. My mother-in-law, dearest Madame Yi, found my *Nüshu* writing to you on a linen handkerchief I was painting—"

"Where were you?"

"She came up behind me—Sunday in the kitchen. All was in order and put away. I thought the women napped after teaching the younger girls how to walk like ladies with their newly broken feet. Madame Yi slithered from the alcove into the kitchen—she must have been watching me, but I was unaware of it. She snatched hold of my artwork with some *Nüshu* and looked at it intently. She didn't understand it, but I pictured her showing it to an acquaintance that could. Instead the skies opened and blessed sun shined upon me because she tossed it into the fire. The sparks shot up and the embers remained to console me."

"Do you respect your husband's parents as Confiucious decreed?" Ping asked.

"Don't I have to? I dread the servitude. I detest the idea of a steady diet of rural life and fieldwork. Painting, I choose colors that give vent to a captured spirit." I painted *Lung,* our Water Dragon, often, but my ideas, gossamer as butterfly wings, were fantasy harbingers.

Of late, I designed butterflies broken forth from their cocoons—they nested on the cloisonné pieces as if alive. My grandmother told me during the reign of the Emperor Jing Tai, craftsmen discovered a dark-blue glazed material to make handicrafts, hence its name, *Jing tai lan,* or cloisonné. Blue was my favorite color. Magical imaginings fluttered—swallowtails sketched onto decorative crockery—gliding me to Giacomo's arms.

"All I can do is think how Lu's unborn child will subjugate me further to all I despise. My love of learning, my regard for books, all have been taken from me." I handed Ping my cup. "I'll break under Lu's family yoke. My mother-in-law berates me now for everything; can you imagine what another child will do? At least now I'm free to paint." In her words with my imitating voice sharp, I said, "'You call your painting work? You are exhausted? Clean the wok and cook our vegetables. After you eat, pull out those coarse stitches from the shoes you made my son.'"

"It's like that in every family. Give them a male child and things will change. You haven't told Lu, have you?" Ping looked into my cup, and reading the tea leaves, said, "You carry a boy." She rinsed and stowed our cups on a shelf. "This is your chance to make it better."

"If the child were intelligent, he would not be able to study but would have to toil the fields. He would have no chance to learn the classics, poetry, or calligraphy, and would never be able to take the state exams."

The end-of-break whistle sounded.

"This is our way, these are our traditions. Can you fight them?"

"I'm too independent. I must prevent this birth, but how can I and still be true to myself and conserve my integrity as woman, wife, and mother?" We stood from our squatting positions. "Can I count on you?"

"Are you sure this is what you want?"

My look implored her.

"Do you have a name and address?" she asked.

"You know the herbalist who has a shop outside of town?"

Ping nodded.

"He has the information I need." I recalled with a bitter heart when I first married and wanted to work with the herbalist, but Lu forbade me. What a change of heart when his father's debts began to encroach upon the family, and the old man had begun to sell off his property. Then, under my chameleon husband's terms, it was fine for me to work outside the home.

Ping and I held hands, silent till I reached the doorway of my workroom. She was the sister my parents couldn't give me. I'd faced other problems, but not like this. Knowing she stood by me made my heart soar like the butterflies I painted. "After work?" Ping agreed, saying she would get permission from our leader Chen for us to leave an unheard-of half hour early. If anyone could do it, Ping could—for as my Baba used to say, she could charm the saints off the wall.

AFTER WORK WE GOT OUR bicycles from the stand. As Ping rode alongside on her "bone shaker" that my grandmother had called "fast foot," I thought of the day Lu carted my old wooden velocipede with a carved griffin's head and burlwood handgrips to the city, where he sold it to a foreign collector "quite by accident." He bought me a used modern one with metal wire spokes and solid rubber tires. I missed the old one.

Ping began to harangue me about how wrong it was not to tell Lu and how dangerous it was to wash the baby out of my body. "You could die," she yelled, pedaling furiously.

"I could die," I said, "but we all die anyway."

It began to rain. Ping and I rode faster, passing occasional outcroppings of shanties beyond Guilin's city limits. A crooked wooden fence had good intentions, trying to maintain an orderly distinction of roadway. But the unpaved road abounded with dead and dying leaves: yellow, gold, orange, red, brown, and a smattering of green—fallen heaps of autumn leaves between huge trees, dark as charcoal in the distance lining the pathway, trunks wider than outstretched arms if I'd encircled one in front of me. The leaves made my bicycle tires skitter, riding through bunches wet and slick. The scent of burning leaves reached me, and I saw smoke ahead.

The burning leaves added to the poignancy of the moment. We pedaled at a steady pace. My melancholy mood piqued and on the verge of tears, I reprimanded myself, for what good is it to feel pity for oneself? Actions alone prove a person's worth. I'm not a coward, merely afraid.

I'd wanted Ping to buy the potion for me, but she declined. Instead, she accompanied me partway to the place where I could purchase it. I was hurt Ping refused but understood her reticence. When we parted, my heart began to race.

In that instant, I understood what it meant to be an orphan. I mourned my sweet blood relatives, but most of all I missed Giacomo, who had been gone from me for so long, I feared he could be dead. The cure for this malady was to act with confidence—a strong face masks the shaking soul.

The rain abated. I walked my bicycle into an alleyway strewn with animal dung. The bicycle clattered on some large, flat stones. A young boy kicked a ball, a little girl rolled a thin wooden wheel she commandeered with a baton-like stick, and a man smoking a cheroot looked on. An older girl squatted as she washed cabbage under the rusty spigot of a water fountain. I took the paper with the address on it from my quilted vest and read it aloud. The washer girl didn't understand as her dialect was strange. The man motioned me over and I showed him the paper, knowing he would understand the characters, if not my accent. He pointed me in the right direction.

The herbalist's open wooden door was adorned with dried, coiled snakes of variegated colors, ranging in size. On a wall behind the door were upended deer antlers, turtle shells, and what looked like dragon's bone, *long gu.* Shelves intermingled with cages of all manner of small animals, the noisiest of which were chattering monkeys.

I murmured the three classifications: the four energies, the five tastes, and the movement of herbs. Before me, clusters of herbs and roots hung on nails and hooks: dried peppers, red sage, yellow dock, ginger, and skullcap, which induced menstruation, and bark of magnolia, *huo po,* fruit from the tree of heaven, to increase menstrual flow. Fenugreek seeds spilled out from a small hemp pouch, Chinese rhubarb and *ru shen*—ginseng root. A shelf of oils, ointments, powders, and unguents. A kaleidoscope of roots, stalks, bark, leaves, seeds, fruit—one was *wu wei zi,* dried fruit from the schisandra, containing the five tastes: sour, sweet, salty, hot, bitter. Stems, flowers such as *hong hua*—safflower—emitted a profusion of odors, and pungent, bitter, salty, cold *mang xiao,* which Baba had called Glauber's salt. My eyes grazed over animals and minerals: cicada husks, oyster shells, gypsum, and even poison aconites: *fu zu;* I half expected to see Baba—if only he had lived to have set me up as an herbalist, and if, and if, and if.

The man was clothed in black. Skeletal hands with curved, inky nails extended from the wide sleeves of his robe. It was him—a man I'd met once with Baba. I felt repulsed yet resolved. I bargained with the bird-boned, jaundiced man, his face, sparse of whiskers, sprouting a rat-tail beard and a thin queue to his waist. Fascination seized me as I observed him prepare the potion for which I paid the exorbitant price of three coppers. Though I lied and said it was for my older sister, the wily creature understood my desperation. I secured the bottle into my deep pocket and bowed.

I peddled my bicycle at a fast pace, passing through a stand of cassia trees, then underneath arbor after arbor of arching trees back to Guilin, my mind sorting excuses for the lapsed time. As I rode, I felt the bottle slip and almost flip out of my pocket. I stopped, leaned the handlebars against a tree, and took hold of the medicine. It fell from my hand as if knocked aside by a ghost. I watched the bottle drop—the shock of it more horrific than the foul smell of star jelly that permeated the air, leaking from the cork—but it hadn't shattered, landing on a pile of leaves. I placed it in my tote in the basket attached to the handgrips. My father called star jelly pond scum whipped by a whirlwind, the odor especially strong when collecting it.

THE NEXT DAY PING AND I were in the lavatory of open urinals. I reached into my smock pocket for a yellowed piece of *South China Morning Post* newsprint, left by a British tourist. I had to use that as I had no cup to fill with water in order to rinse myself clean. At the sink, Ping let me use a tiny bar of soap she'd gotten from a friend who worked at a hotel nearby.

I glanced up at the curtain bar. "Do you think they'll ever replace the curtain?"

Ping dried her hands on her apron. "We could use the bar to do chin ups."

After I washed my hands and dried them with my smock, I patted the soap and she pocketed it.

"Maybe almost dropping the bottle yesterday was a sign for you not to take it, and wait instead to catch the baby," Ping said.

"I am not sure I will even be able to swallow it, but I want the choice."

"Wishing your way around Chinese tradition—to have your baby and still continue working in the city—is not going to make it come true," Ping said, her tone exasperated.

Then she added, "Women rid themselves of babies all the time." She tugged at her earlobe, meaning her thoughts were revving up, a child about to run with a kite to fly.

"You mean smother or drown a live child? Or like the infant I found dumped in a garbage bin? Better to kill myself." I ran a broken comb through my hair.

She shook her head. "You could give the child up to a guardian for prostitution."

I opened the squeaky door to leave. "How could I manage that? What if it's male?" As I stepped out, a young girl jostled me and the smell of fried pork from her cook pot gave my stomach a jolt .

Ping looked at me, rolling her eyes. "It is a boy. I told you. You can give him away."

"Sure, to the opera company, to make him into a fine girl, a lovely concubine."

We walked to the break room where we drank tea.

"What if I decide to have the baby?" I asked.

"Will Lu's family force you to quit your job to work beside him and eke out a living from the land for the rest of your miserable coolie life?" she asked.

I looked at my big, repulsive, unbound feet. "None of the Yi women work the fields; that lot is left to me, sometimes, but a steady diet of it would render my hands so rough I'd never paint again or sift the dust of powdered herbs either. He scares me—always tries to bend me to his will—an indentured servant."

"This is the way to ensure your factory job. Besides, you'd never get to see the newborn raised by your in-laws, would you, slave?"

Before the whistle blew, Chen, our division head, told us free time was over and marched past us in the corridor.

Ping rinsed our cups and stacked them on a shelf. "You could somehow get to Hong Kong—leave Lu and Zin-Zin."

"Never Zin-Zin."

The whistle blared. I closed the door behind us. "I could adapt, but Lu would never sacrifice family, heritage, and China for me." I broke my own train of thought, "Although in Hong Kong I could become a healer."

That evening I played with Zin-Zin, who resembled her father so much it hurt me to look at her. I fed and bathed her and put her down for the night under my mother's quilt. I told her a story, weaving in my horoscope. "My sign is the dog, always ready for action, has soft ears, and is steadfast with inner strength. A dog sits on hind legs, prepared to spring. Now, Zin-Zin, I must cook and serve the men. Later while you skip in dreams, I'll sew your rag doll."

"Give her yellow hair like the sun foreigner you told me came to the factory. Give her blue eyes like summer sky. Not muddy like Baba's." She yawned and closed her eyes. Chinese do not show affection like Europeans—my father did with me —but I kissed her forehead.

EARLY SATURDAY MORNING, ON MY way to bring slops for the neighbor's pigs—such a lowly task—I wondered at how, even in my misfortune, I was fortunate to have married a farmer, rather than the poor, abominable butcher next door. On my way out, Lu's grandmother chastened me, saying, "Skin over bones. Nothing more. Girl, you are so thin I see the wall through you. You are a scarecrow." She pointed and all but hissed, "A belly like Buddha in our entrance, but nobody gives you flowers."

I bowed to the wizened woman who also bowed slightly. With a flip of her gray braid over her shoulder, she picked up the straw broom, kicked a feed bucket toward me, and walked outside. As little as I knew my own grandmother, I was certain she would never have checked to see if all the women in the house had gotten their periods. Smugness tightened my lips. I'd fooled her, faking the last two times with rabbit blood from the kitchen. I was elated, uplifted by my thoughts till the bitter recall that the old one had noticed the tiny swell of my belly.

The thought of rabbit blood brought to mind the cherry plant. How many times had this old one scolded me about the winter cherry outside the door, tumbling its way toward Buddha's crossed legs? She called me useless because I forgot to water the ornamental whose blossoms were lanterns of red. Blood. Had I fooled her? Or had she noticed I'd skipped my monthly visitation? She knew my cycle better than I. What if I'd waited too long? Taking the herbs was dangerous and could cause a hemorrhage. My thoughts scurried like field mice in a dung heap.

Later, I smiled with the awareness the old woman didn't know all the happenings in the house. Lu had gathered a windflower and camellia bouquet for me in the evening when we'd walked among the taro. Surprised at his gesture—he had never done things to make me think our marriage stood a chance—I gave the flowers to Zin-Zin, as soon as the old one went to the women's room at the far end of the house. I cherished this brief respite without the old woman when, after my chores, I played alone with my daughter. I went to bed, knowing that Lu was off gambling and drinking with his father. He came home smelling of cheap perfume. Pretending to sleep, I watched him toss his clothes in a heap when he came back from carousing.

On Monday morning, I couldn't eat a morsel, but rather sipped green tea and recounted my money to buy temple offerings. The sum was short so I took some from my husband's pants while he slept. At least he hadn't squandered it all. I'd never taken anything before without asking, and for a moment I stood frozen, crinkled notes in my hand. I stuffed them back into his pocket and took some change, hoping he wouldn't remember the exact amount. I grabbed my linen bag. This catchall carrier held my blue work smock wrapped around the Guilin beer bottle with the soy-colored liquid that smelled like the fetid oozing of a dead dog decaying in summer heat. I kept the brown bottle and my diary in my satchel with me for fear of being found out. I used this as a pillow until I could put both of them in my safe place, the ramshackle factory locker I shared with Ping. I moved toward the door, stepping over Zin-Zin's pallet and my husband, still sleeping off a hangover from rice wine, huddled in bedclothes in a stupor of alcohol.

I strode rapidly alongside my bicycle on the dried-mud walkway—a thief evading capture. I waved to Ping as she came into sight at the appointed place where bamboo rafts were moored for a jaunt around Diecai Hill. She straddled her derelict bicycle, awaiting my arrival. After a quick greeting, I took the bottle from my bag and uncorked it. I brought it to my nose to sniff but jerked it away because its odor brought a rancid taste from my stomach to the back of my throat. I fought the urge to vomit.

"I can't believe I have to drink this," I said, looking at the malevolent, dark medicine. I let her smell it, and she pulled a face. I recorked it and placed it back in my bag.

"You don't have to take it. Why didn't you leave it home?" she asked, dismounting.

"To have the old one discover it?" I held the handlebars and began to walk.

"Rank dung and horse piss are perfume in comparison," she said.

On our way to work, I explained to Ping that if the herbs didn't start the impulse to expel the fetus, then the old method would have to be used.

"Solved," she said, "in the way women have taken care of this situation for centuries." Her words remained scorched in my brain long after the conversation ended. Women have always done this, risking all since time immemorial. What made me think I was any different? I was naught but a speck of dust in the universe.

But I was also young, with the positive outlook of youth, and though there were no guarantees the herb mixture would work, I felt they would. I could have mixed them myself if I'd had them at my disposition—I was versed in their potencies, classes, meridians, and indications. If the roots of rue concoction didn't work, I'd have to rely on the operation. A possibility, but how remote? If this were to be the case, I hoped I'd come out of it without repercussions. After all, it was as Ping said, "A simple matter." *Simple.* I thought of needles, cups, and instruments Father had used in the brothel beside our home in Peking—that girl had lost her baby but would never get pregnant again—and in Yangshuo when Baba was called upon to give assistance.

During Monday's factory lunch break, Ping was busy so I walked alone a city block to the huge banyan tree. At the lake's edge, old men gathered to do *ch'i kung* ritual exercises and shadowboxing. Men, ageless as the tree itself—each muscle, every sinew, etched like Chinese characters painted on fibrous rice paper. I marveled that famous artists came to Guilin to paint the hill peaks, the violet-mottled sky at dawn, the river, but not these men. I saw the city's history depicted in their movements. For eight centuries men had pushed lean, supple legs, completely stretched against the gnarled tree that stood on the road by the lake forever. Men. What can they know of a woman's longing for children and a man to hold them?

I walked to the temple in the weak autumn sun trying to peep through vaporous fog. When I reached the enclosure gates, I sighed and clutched, then cradled my abdomen with two hands. A quickening? Impossible. Too early, but life, through a commingling, was in me. The seed of my tormentor. "The Lord of heaven sees me," escaped my lips as I thought of Lu discovering my intent. He must never know. Not only would he never forgive me, but he might do me bodily harm, or even murder me.

Entering the temple, I slipped off my cloth shoes, feeling nauseated by the perfume of mandarin peel mingled with the scent of burning incense. I pushed my long hair back and bowed to the Buddhist monk in his saffron robe, thinking him fortuitous because he traveled a spiritual path. How attached to the world was I? To my Zin-Zin? Could I ever withdraw? The monk shuffled barefoot behind a wood table scarred with burns and gouges.

I reached into my pocket. Stolen coppers from Lu for an offering? Nothing deterred me. "Joss sticks, incense, and gold leaf," I pushed Lu's coppers toward the bald priest, who was sipping tea through teeth brown as the tea itself. Steam made his face glow an eerie mustard color.

I padded along the cold floor and glanced at a rock garden through a window's iron fretwork where mist covered a massive stone. To the right, tall bamboo, haloed by circling rooks, swayed. I tugged myself away, reached the benign jade Buddha, knelt in front, and put down the incense and brown-paper-wrapped gold leaf. I lit the joss, jabbing them into a sandbox. Then I rattled small sticks I'd taken from my bag and tossed them to the ground after a plea for help for my predicament. Three times I bowed with my hands clasped in front of my mouth. But the scattered sticks lay in a way that had two meanings. A forked road.

It seemed to me that prayers and promises to be good and to serve were futile. What did the future hold? Hadn't Lord Buddha just granted me a favor—my wonderful baby Zin-Zin? I prayed, *Forgive me, Lord, for the life I destroy. Curse my husband's loyalty to his family.*

Closing my eyes, I saw my daughter at play around the windmill near Lu's sampan on the river. How I'd fretted when she fell overboard this past summer. I screamed, "Zin-Zin" again and again as Lu dived into the water, fishing her out like a bass on a hook. Afterward, I begged him to teach Zin-Zin and me to swim. But after a few brief dunks in the water, he gave up. I can still hear his voice: *"Lian,"* he'd call, *"keep your face in the water. Now turn sideward, breathe through your mouth, and exhale through your mouth into the water. Arms pulling, legs kicking. Together now."* I never learned how to breathe properly, but I could drink with my face in the water. I learned to dog paddle and float on my back. *"At least you won't drown,"* he had said. A smile swallowed his eyes. But he never had the time or patience to teach Zin-zin.

What joy if I could have this child and make Lu a father. A real father. A conundrum: make Lu a father for this baby, but not me its mother. Or if there were only another way I could lose it. A tumor, influenza, anything but to have to do away with an unborn wonder that would never know his life. Aloud I said, "I only pray when I need some favor. Every day from now on, Lord Buddha, you will be with me. Just grant me this. Take the baby." In the end, choice remains a godly thing. *Do I give up? Live a feudalistic life under my in-laws? Or lose my husband or my life if he discovers that I am capable of this abomination?*

I covered my face with my hands, my shame so great not even this statue should see it. *What choice, Buddha, does this humble servant have?*

I rose, picked up the sticks, and placed them in a lacquer box in my handbag. Lacquer workers cover the boxes with pig's blood as a base. Everything seemed to remind me of tainted blood—life source that would wash away this unborn.

Placing incense in a ceramic stand, I unwrapped the gold leaf. I peeled the foil from the paper and plastered it on one of the smaller Buddhas, amongst gold peelings from other mendicants, beseechers, offenders.

The incense assailed me, and a buzz in my ears made me dizzy. The weakness came from the fact that I'd not yet broken my fast. I should have eaten with Lu's grandmother.

I patted Buddha's belly, my hand sliding along his crossed legs. Then I stood still a moment, bowed, and turned. On the way out, passing Kuan Yin, benign and beautiful Goddess of Mercy, I dropped a coin in the offering box and left the temple. I stepped down onto the last concrete step and slipped into my shoes.

On my way back from the temple to the factory, I crossed the open-air market where I stopped to buy a sesame cake with the last of my funds. As I ate it, I meandered past an antique vendor's stall where I pressed my forehead against the cool glass of a curio cabinet, which reminded me of the one in the Summer Palace when I'd met Giacomo. A small blue and white snuff bottle caught my eye. Sweat beads formed on my upper lip, and I wiped them with my jacket sleeve. I squinted to focus on the bottle. It had a small chip at its lip. Blemished forever. Scarred. Ruined. Like me, never the same if I terminated this little life inside me.

Along winding cobble streets, dust lifted in gusts and tiny squalls. Something blew into my eye, calling to mind my meeting Lu. I took a handkerchief from my pocket to dislodge it. Was there no other way than to dislodge this child I carried? A wrestling proverb: man's schemes are inferior to those made by heaven.

A month ago, the fortune-teller dentist who cleans teeth at the Sunday Bird Market had told Lu that he would impregnate a woman if he had not already. Later, Lu told his father, and I dropped and spilled the wicker steamer of *cha sui ba*. On the clay floor, barbequed pork buns oozed. "So hot, forgive my clumsiness," I said, bowing.

Lu inclined his head, but my father-in-law, short of patience, reached for and would have laid the switch across my back if Lu hadn't cajoled and distracted him.

My head and shoulders bent in preparation for the blows, awaited the sting that never came. A day without a beating. A thousand thanks, my husband. Lu motioned me to back away. Back away, girl, who once rode on the back of a bicycle, hair flying wild, and tearing through a paper dragon at a New Year's parade. So many New Years since then . . . so many wishes for good wishes, for dreams to become realities. Wishes and dreams—fantasy harbingers, heralding what? For me there's no other existence unless I change, unless I make it so. How, sweet balmy breeze, do I do it?

"Better so," I heard Lu say to his father, "we are saved burning our mouths, and now have slops to fatten our neighbor's pigs."

His father laughed. Lu poured tea, saying, "Let me serve you something worthwhile for your palate." He settled the teakettle on a straw mat and took his father's bowl, ladling out bird's nest soup. When his father slurped the dregs, Lu placed a thousand year-old egg on a blue and white porcelain plate, saying, "How fortunate we are to taste of grandmother's cooking."

Times like these that reminded me of his gentler side, though I saw it seldom.

◄━━►≫≪◄━━►

THAT NIGHT, THERE WAS A violent storm, so Lu cancelled our walk in the fields after he decided not to go to the drinking house. I didn't mind because I finished sewing the doll for Zin-Zin. I had no private opportunity to speak to him until we went to bed. I groped for courage, fearing if I delayed for the perfect moment, I'd lose it. "Will you not reconsider a move to Hong Kong?" I whispered hastily, "To anywhere?"

His voice, muffled under the covers, brimmed with annoyance. "Live in squalor among strangers?"

"No worse than this. No privacy. You call this cattle arrangement *living?*"

He tensed. Why hadn't I waited until he was sexually sated? He wanted to strike me, but he couldn't swing with my arms intertwined with his. Instead, he silenced me with harsh kisses grinding his mouth into mine. I snapped my head backward so fast it smacked the floor. I rubbed it hard but was determined to have my say. I put my mouth to his ear. "We could live in the country then, work on a farm," I said, knowing the sacrifice it would mean for me. "Why won't you agree with me?"

"Will you not give me peace?" he said, his voice metallic.

"I'll have peace enough when I'm dead, and I'm dying here. We could have a better life, and many children. And I could practice medicine," my voice bolder.

"Foreign devil's medicine. And what of my parents and grandparents?" he asked. "End it."

This was his stock finish to the argument. So I gave him mine. "We can send for them later."

His family would always come before me. I could never trust him with my guarded secret. The rustle of bedclothes. He was determined to conduct the business of our bed that might finally ensure his male heir. Little did he know his desire had been granted by the gods he prayed so little to. He pinioned my arms, as though I would defy or oppose him.

How could I resist when he asserted his conjugal rights, knowing this act sprang neither from love nor longing, but proof of his mastery and my submission? I lay still while his lascivious rage made him brutish. If I fought him, he would beat me. He could possess my body, but I'd never surrender my soul. Maybe I deserved punishment. I hoped it destroyed the life within me. Even if it did, Lu could make me pregnant again, molesting me. I could take a passenger train north to Henyang, then south, maybe by freight to Guangzhou. If there were a border inspection at Shenzhen before riding into Hong Kong, I'd have to hide in a bathroom ceiling, like I'd heard my cousin Liang did, or sneak across the border on foot. Risky. Others had succeeded, but I would have Zin-Zin with me. However, I could never chance it with an infant. The only other way was to swim. I pictured myself dog-paddling all the way across the channel. I would exercise like the supple men I watched daily and pull my own weight up onto the crossbar in the lavatory, where once hung a heavy curtain.

ON SUNDAY, MY DAY OFF from city work, I toiled in the fields—the only woman in Lu's family. I had freedom of movement and agility—the women and the men I worked alongside despised me. The women wanted me to bind Zin-Zin's feet. I promised her arches would make her feet the perfect-sized golden lilies, if she waited another two years. They'd cripple her. She was too young. I relished every one of her running steps, though their echo warned time was passing. Could I subject her to the suffering of unbound feet in this society? Once I had wished for them.

I brushed straight bangs from my forehead and stretched, a fistful of muddy shoots in my hand. I looked up over manure heaps and their unseen host of spirits, hovering in rising steam, past the arbor of willows that edged the Li River, toward the mauve cliffs that surrounded Guilin, into rain that would camouflage a face full of tears. Except for the salt taste when I licked my lips, I hadn't realized I was crying. I had almost finished the bone-wrenching planting of tender shoots in the rice paddies and stopped to massage my back with the shriveled pads of my fingertips. I hated Sundays now that I tired easily because of the pregnancy.

Gazing at the rain-slicked, glistening lotus leaves in the adjacent field, I shivered like they did in departing typhoon winds. Each green plant reminded me of flowing silk head coverings and the flowers of Lu's sister's upcoming nuptials. Because I was pregnant, I couldn't be a member of the wedding party. Superstition forbade it; though the wedding members were unaware of my situation, I believed it. If I couldn't purge my body of this burden quickly, what excuse could I give for not being a member of the wedding? I rolled up my sleeves and bent to push the last seedling through the murky water into its clump of mud. The summer season had lasted from April until August, and September was mild. Now the rice harvest would be at the end of November. Again I looked at the sky. If the herbs worked, at this hour tomorrow I would be treading the South Ronghu Road toward the factory, no longer a remnant leaf in an ill-guided storm. With an image of an infant's hand reaching for my finger, my impulse was to throw the vile liquid onto the manure pile to mate its likeness, but my problems would end by drinking it tonight when the planting and supper were over. I had to take it on a full stomach after the evening meal. What if the dose was too strong? I could bleed to death. Who would care for Zin-Zin, Giacomo's baby? Lu would marry again. Would the new stepmother be harsh to the extra mouth to feed? Who would brush back the hair from her eyes and wipe her tears? What cowardly flaw in me would risk death rather than flight?

AFTER DINNER, THE SERVANT WOMEN cleared the table while the men talked, occasionally eating lychee, persimmon, and pomegranate. They smoked cheroot, the strong odor bringing on a bout of nausea for me, but how could they know? And even if they did? At the door, I threw the dirty dishwater onto the earth. I thought of Hong Kong's streets, the garbage splaying filth toward the rat-infested gutters Baba had spoken of with disgust. Maybe Lu was right, there were better places.

I welcomed the cool night breeze. Lu said he was leaving to attend a farmer's meeting, though I suspected it was to go to a teahouse. Before he left, he furtively handed me a letter. He could not read and didn't want the others in the house to know that I could. Whenever there was a letter for the family, Lu's father would take it to one of the elders and pay to have it read. The postmark read Hong Kong, and the return address was Piero Milano's, a friend of my father's whom I'd written to weeks before for an apothecary position, in hopes I could convince Lu to move there with me. I was thankful the letter had not been opened because it was from an assistant and written in Chinese, not Italian.

When I finished my kitchen chores, I went to the back of the house and lit a tallow. I read that the apothecary had gotten my letter and the post was available. Instead of being happy, I worried what I would say to Lu when he demanded to know the letter's contents. Though his mother was unaware, he knew I understood Chinese characters. I decided to burn it. If he took the letter to the elder in the village to read, he would beat me for sure.

I left the house to feed three skinny tramp dogs some meager scraps. The animals recognized me by scent way before they caught sight of me, and their contented yaps comforted me. They nuzzled me at my approach.

Even though minutes ago, I wanted to throw the poison away, drinking it was my only recourse. In truth, I wanted another of Giacomo's children to be sister or brother to my Zin-Zin. I crept beyond the range of the skulking vision of those in the house and stood hidden between schima and camphor trees as I reached under my quilted vest for the bottle. Uncapping it, I envisioned Giacomo and uttered lines from *The Book of Odes:* "Are you thinking of me? Your love I cannot see." I gulped and fought to keep the liquid down as it struck the back of my throat. I drank again and finished it, wiping my hand across my mouth, and then threw the bottle out into the field. By the closing whistle tomorrow evening, I would be free of the affliction threatening to ruin my life. Even my beloved schima and camphor trees mocked me with overwhelming fall fragrance. I clutched my stomach and sprinted away to dogs barking.

The commotion alerted Lu's grandmother and she called, "Who's there? Who disturbs our peace?" I gained control of my body.

"It is Lian, who asks pardon, venerable one, for attending to night soil." How far had I fallen? Thank heavens my father was in the spirit world.

I returned to the house and waited until Lu walked in the door tipsy and laughing, making certain he saw me hold the letter to the lit cook flame. His father stumbled off to bed.

Lu grabbed me by the shoulders and shook me, but I yelped, and he let go. I said, "It was nothing important, an old friend of my father's."

"Why did you burn it?" he asked, peeved.

"I didn't want to displease you more than I had by receiving it."

He shoved me toward our sleeping pallet. I took my time undressing, and when I undid the last button on my chemise and took hold of my nightshift, he was snoring under the bedcovers.

THE NEXT MORNING I ATE hot congee, washing it down with black tea. Feeling queasy, I vowed not to trifle again with Nature. I admired Zin-Zin while she slept in sheer abandon outside the covers, legs and arms akimbo, and carried her image with me as I rode my bicycle along the rutted path. Rain washed my face. Nature cleanses and absolves, but could I forgive myself, or carry the stigma the rest of my life? Was reparation in store for me?

On the road near the factory, men dressed as Boxers were having a rally, waving flags, shouting slogans and marching in colorful array. I pulled my bicycle into a narrow alley and waited toward the back until they passed. I reached the factory when the sky turned to slate except for the intrusion of lightning to the east. A small brick lean-to with a tin corrugated roof was situated in the rear of a narrow alley. It was nestled among several of the factory's buildings. I entered and inclined my head slightly. "May I join you?" A group of four women squatted around a potbelly stove on top of which was a dented teakettle. The workers drank tea and laughed about Saturday's customer who thought he was clever, but was merely tight-fisted.

"I'm glad Chen didn't sell my blue amphora to him. I'd hate to think it held his cheap ancestor's ashes," a stout woman said.

I went to the cabinet where I now kept my chronicle, writing materials, and wedding jacket hidden from the eyes of the women in the household. If they found my book in *Nüshu,* they'd burn it. On break or lunch hour, or even sometimes early in the morning, I wrote apologies to the unborn child, and to Giacomo, begging him to forgive me for getting pregnant. As for the jacket with the magnificently embroidered dragons, I feared Lu's mother might sell it. My mother told me that the jacket had been in our family for generations. I caressed the fastened parcel and took out my yellow porcelain cup. Removing the lid, I looked closer and noticed for the first time that tiny red flowers in the decoration were winter cherries. A blood omen? As I poured boiling water into the cup, some spilled onto my hand. I bit my lip but relished the burn as something to focus on as I swished the water around and threw it to the ground. Prying the lid from the tin, I scooped and poured out tea leaves, but the jasmine scent made me turn my head.

A small woman who worked on painting the insides of tiny bottles looked up at me. I furrowed my brow and she gestured for me to step closer. I went nearer. The precision painter took the cup from my shaky hand and said, "Sit, girl, your actions falter. You'll spill the tea, or crash your pretty cup."

"Thank you," I said. I tried to smile.

The woman put the cup on a small wooden workbench. I wanted to squat with the rest but was unsteady. The woman saw me stagger and took my cup off the bench—her own cup on the floor next to it. She patted the bench for me to sit. I settled myself on the stool. Then she handed back my tea, which I took trembling. The woman inclined her head. I did likewise.

The herbalist had told me the medicine might take awhile to work, and, perhaps, would make my "elder sister" feel quite sick. I could still see his smirk.

Ping opened the door. She yelled, "Good day, ten minutes to the whistle." Her eyes held mine. Her steadfast gaze informed me she could not help me for I had begun a journey where she could not reach me.

As the twitching of my limbs began, I heard through a cave the old woman who had taken my cup say, "She's convulsing. Put something under her head. Give me the dish rag to put in between her teeth."

Time diminished—like watching Lu's grandmother's labored breathing as she negotiated the steep climb of Fubo Hill above the river. Fire from tiny sparks hypnotized me. Rabid dogs raced, snarled, bit, and chewed my lower abdomen. A sound like a door closing and a picture of Ping appeared, her facial features falling into place one by one. I slid down Elephant Hill into the river, disintegrating like time, but the fall brought me somehow, ever so slowly, limb by limb, joint by joint, to the floor. Everything swam like free-floating tadpoles with weights keeping them back as they fought to move forward.

A scream fractured the air. It seemed to be coming from outside the building to awaken me from a place beyond. Seconds split to thousandths. My teeth, a vice, clamped the woman's finger. My jaw was forced open; my eyes took in the room to the tempo of feathers floating groundward.

I moaned, clutching my pulsating stomach. Cramps, waves of bile in my throat and nostrils, and a feeling of disembowelment engulfed me.

A thunderclap ruptured from off in the distance as white light snuffed to gray, and outside the high window, raindrops plopped upon the roof.

"She's so ill," someone said in a voice like Ping's. "At least the convulsions stopped."

"She could have swallowed her tongue. Make her sip the tea," the master painter said.

"Still too hot," Ping said. But hadn't she already left the room?

Someone complained that her finger hurt. Was that me?

I tried to shake my head, to hold open my eyes. They refused to focus but gradually caught sight of a piece of fabric, a length of hair, a section of profile. I looked from one woman to another. The quaking in my body slowed but did not stop as I attempted to stand, my feet unhinging at the ankles. Unresponsive. From the floor, I grasped at the teacup dancing by me as soon as I felt the distance shorten. Once again a contraction in my lower belly pitched me forward, drew me back. The painter sprang up from her squat, dove midair, and knelt at my side—faster than a fisherman's tied cormorant trained to catch fish along the river. Somehow the cup lay shattered on the gray cement floor. Again my head lolled around my shoulders, then fell backward. And the world spun itself into a black spider web with lightning bugs and hills engulfed by nightfall. No moon. Not a star in the sky.

I swooned, trying to break my fall with a stiff arm. My wrist hurt. Sunspots—broken pieces of retina floated under my eyelids the way they did when looking at the sun from the river shallows in summer. *Retina,* a word my father used. I couldn't say it in Mandarin.

Someone said, "The warning whistle already blew."

"But what about this girl?" another asked.

"She must have some kind of influenza," said the painter.

Ping said, "I'll get Chen."

"Where does the sick one work?" someone asked, and put a freckled hand like Ping's on my head to smooth back my wild hair.

"Her name's Lian," the painter said. "I see her when I pass number fifteen to go to the toilet. She sits by the window and once gave me a paper napkin. I asked her what for and she said, 'There's never any to wipe your hands.'"

"I think she works on ornamentals," said a woman, whose voice I didn't know.

Before Chen bounced into the ill-lit room, warmed by the stove and where the sweet smell of jasmine and the stench of human feces pervaded, Ping whispered in my ear, "So sorry, little sister. I didn't know you'd be this sick."

Chen said to Ping, "There's a cot in the keeper's shed. Can you get her there?"

"Assist me with her," Ping said. Both women got me to my feet. My unsteady gait brought my jerking shoulder close against the stove. I singed my sleeve and my arm. The acrid smell of burned cloth and flesh made me skittish.

"Give me your arm," Chen said. "Careful. You have a slight burn. I'm strong. Lean on me." The rain had ceased, but I looked at Ping and Chen through eyes wet with rain. I reached the cot and must have fainted. When I came around, Ping washed and patted my face and put a salve on my arm. I lapsed into spasm.

Ping was nearly out the door when I said, "I'll be docked."

"Chen will cover for you. She'll say you're with customers out front."

"Did you wash me? So wet, so cold—"

"You messed yourself. I had to clean you."

I fell into a deep slumber, waking occasionally to my own soft moans, pulsating groin, and need to urinate.

I heard voices outside in the courtyard after the lunch whistle with its long shrill. The morning had slipped by with the swiftness of a bicycle thief. Opening my crust-laden eyes, I saw blurry figures. Superintendent Chen stood next to Ping and a little behind them was the woman who painted bottles.

Ping sat down on the unclean pallet and bent to tell me things would be all right. The looks on their faces shamed me. Chen and the painter knew what was happening.

Pain subsided. The wracking of my body had ceased. I coughed, spit up, and then began to urinate, squeezing my legs tight to stay the flow, only it wasn't urine.

"Help me, Ping." I said and grunted. My body no longer belonged to me—it pushed and writhed in a series of contractions and expulsions. Where were my quilted pants? Ping put her arms around my shoulders and lifted me into a crouched position with my knees bent.

When it was over, I rolled onto my side, and Ping gathered the bloody rags and newspapers beneath me. Chen helped settle me once again on the soiled pallet, bringing me a cloth to use as a pad, helping me pull on my damp pants. The woman who painted bottles said she had cleaned the mess in our tea–break room, but I did not have the energy to thank her. Instead I stuck my tongue out at Ping. "Is it purple?"

"Very dark," she said.

I took my pulses—one was wiry, the other a little more choppy. All I could dwell on was my own stupidity for not buying *shi-xiao-san* at the herbalist's. In my mind's eye the ideograms for it appeared: 失笑散— only six grams of "sudden smile powder" added to some vinegar or white wine would have triggered the blood flow to change and coagulate in order to harmonize the stomach and thus relieve pain.

Too cheerfully, Chen said, "Take tomorrow off. What's a day's pay to a girl like you? You'll be back at your bench the day after tomorrow, mixing sands and cloisonné colors. We won't speak any more of this terrible flux."

But I knew I couldn't afford to miss the next day's work, much less complain about my discomfort. Lu's grandmother must not suspect. And what if Lu wanted to possess my body to prove another domineering point? I bore the pain and shame from those unions, but tonight I would die of a hemorrhage. I couldn't go home. Not to Lu's home.

I sketched a mental picture of myself washing away guilt, easing my aching body into the Li River. Ping was back and gave me a cup of strong black tea. It tasted oddly sweet, not the way black tea tasted at all. It was wonderful. "What did you do to the tea?"

Ping smiled. "It's laced with osmanthus wine and honey and probably could bring back my venerable great-grandfather from the grave."

Chen left the room.

Ping whispered, "Chen said you'll be ill for hours. Like poisoning from bad fish. She has more experience than I do—my knowledge is secondhand. Drink more tea."

I wept silent tears. Grief and relief. I wanted to banish from my brain the consequences of this abortion. I lay back. Now I'd remain a factory worker yet still the farmer's wife, and the unborn wouldn't be raised by my in-laws and would never feel the inert kitchen switch alive across his back. What would Lu do to me if he knew I did this? Oh, Buddha, he will be lost to me forever. To be scorned would be a living death. How had I done this?

Ping cradled my head in her lap. "Come home with me after work."

"How I wish, but I must return to my husband's house and tell him I miscarried." I knew if I didn't play the obedient dog, inventing a sin to be pardoned for just for his delectation, then I'd have no chance of getting my Zin-Zin. I began to tell Ping about my plans to leave China.

"Am I not my father as well as my mother's stock—didn't he pick up a smashed life, glue it together with spit, and begin again after mother died?"

"But Lu's alive, what of him?"

"My grandmother taught me that love with love is paid. Lu has given me the gift to understand not all love is repaid."

"We'll talk when you're stronger," Ping crooned as if it were a lullaby.

"There's nothing more to say," I said. "Except . . . I bleed."

"Hush." Ping laid my wedding jacket across my chest.

"No one can staunch the flow that washed away my baby."

My forehead was wet with perspiration, and Ping dried it, feather-fanning it, and then she left. As the door shut, a blast of air rushed at me. I shivered. I heard the cooing of doves. My tears stopped.

Looking out the window, I saw it had begun to rain again.

Chapter 8

Baiziren

柏子仁

Oriental arborvitae seed

LULLED TO SLEEP QUICKLY FROM the day's toil and the slight sway of the boat, Giacomo slept fitfully and traveled in and out of a dream state. He saw his folks dressed in funeral finery, sitting in a cabriolet making a right turn onto a wide boulevard in Palermo, but his father erred and the carriage went up on the sidewalk and almost careened into Lian walking toward him. Lian's father, sitting in the foreground, was haloed in a haze. Giacomo had a bad feeling. What if something had happened to her father and she was ill and alone? Somehow Giacomo knew the doctor was dead. But when? How long? It had been years since he had seen her. Would Lian still be in Pechino or married to the farmer in Guilin?

He rose from his bunk, neither rested nor refreshed, and feeling anxious. He washed, dressed, and reported to the galley. Chang had already sent Shen to prepare scrambled eggs with chives and congee made with tangerine peels and chicken stock.

Giacomo came in and said, "How about some of those deep-fried devils?"

The thin boy's straight black hair was tied back in a long braid, and a folded bandana across his forehead was knotted in the back. He nodded and reached for salt, alum, baking soda, and ammonium bicarbonate on a top shelf. He ladled out two cups of water from a bucket and scooped flour from a huge canister, measuring four cups.

Shen poured about twelve cups of peanut oil into a large, deep wok that had seen happier days. The boy was quick and once he watched the preparation and assisted Giacomo hands on, he had a recipe down pat. Giacomo tossed all the ingredients into a bowl and stirred with chopsticks. When the mixture was smooth, he poured it out onto a flour-dusted large board and began to knead, from time to time, sprinkling in some more flour. When the dough was elastic enough, he cut it into pieces for frying in the sizzling oil.

Giacomo said something in the pidgin he'd picked up over the years he'd been in China, some taught to him by the older crew, a contact language made up on the spot along with a sprinkling of Mandarin. He had an awakening and finally knew he needed to speak the boy's language, had to learn Lian's native tongue. If he wanted to be understood and accepted in this world still so foreign to him, it was about time he learned in earnest—a fistful of words carried no weight. Wouldn't Giacomo expect this boy to learn his language after so much time in his country? It was his only chance to find Lian. What had he been thinking picking up barroom and brothel expressions, terms to buy fresh produce in the market or flesh in a whorehouse? He knew phrases to instill fear in the coolies, but he needed to learn words of love and how to speak and communicate on a human level.

That night in his bunk, Giacomo began to study in earnest, wanting a complete lexicon of words to communicate. He studied a translated text of the poems of Wu-Men and tried memorizing one, mumbling the words, trying for the *err* sound in the back of the throat and the five tones. The boy could get by with Cantonese, whereas Mandarin was his language—Lian's language. Giacomo wondered why and how the boy ended up in Hong Kong, and what had taken him so long to ask?

The following day when slicing scallions, Giacomo thought about Lian and his time with her while she was tending to the Italian dignitary. How could he still call up the vision of her face, the hesitancy in her step, her voice? He had to put her out of his mind. How could she possibly want him after the bloody brawls in bars and all the singsong girls he'd lain with?

Instead he tried to focus on the poem he was reading, speaking the lines out loud, grossly mispronouncing the words. He'd found truth in what he had read: "One instant is eternity, eternity is now, when you see through this one instant, you see through the one who sees." When Giacomo finished saying this, he realized the verse paraphrased his thoughts when he'd been with Lian. He stopped himself, reliving moments he'd had with her. Is this how you banish her from your thoughts?

With the cleaver poised in air, Giacomo repeated the last line.

"Wu-Men," the boy said. He wore an inquisitive look.

Giacomo hadn't seen the boy standing in the doorway. "What?"

"Our poet. You understand words—your heart Chinese."

Giacomo smiled, having grasped the Mandarin the boy spoke.

"Say poem more. My pleasure. I say first, you say."

The boy spoke rhythmically, and Giacomo echoed the poem, his accent much improved. The boy smiled a crooked smile and shook his head, delighted yet puzzled. Shen repeated the poem and Giacomo followed suit and resumed cutting.

The men of the first shift piled into the mess hall; all of them still sleepy and grumbling.

Giacomo said, "Shen, what's your surname?"

"Yi Shen."

How apt a name, Giacomo thought, repeating to himself in Italian the boy's name, Cheerful Soul.

Giacomo passed the plates to him and watched Yi Shen set them on the tables.

"Thank you, Yi Shen."

"You welcome, Giacomo."

Giacomo wheeled around, surprised and pleased—*the boy knew my name all the while, yet called me Boss until today.* Giacomo patted Shen's shoulder.

Some of the men bristled at being served congee for the fifth day in a row.

"Compliments to me, gents. Complaints to Rinaldi."

Just then Rinaldi opened the mess door, and gunner Samuele Di Luise said to Giacomo, "Shall I do that now, Scimenti?"

But Giacomo called his bluff, stood over him, and said in a low voice, "As you like. I don't spend money on supplies not sanctioned by the Lieutenant."

Bulldog called out, "Officer on deck." The men stood and saluted.

Rinaldi said, "Be seated and finish eating, men."

Di Luise couldn't keep his mouth chewing and spewed out venomously, "I was told you ordered these slops, Lieutenant, sir?"

The Lieutenant stared Di Luise down. "Are you calling yourself a pig? Since supplies are low, we've had some monotonous and repetitious meals. No fault of the cook, to be sure."

"Point well taken, sir," Bulldog said, earning a poisonous glance from Di Luise.

AT A BREAK GIACOMO TRIED to nap because he hadn't slept fitfully due to the blustery and rainy weather. He awoke uncovered and shivered. He'd dreamt that he was on maneuvers, climbing over rails and ropes, getting out hoses, mounting and loading 15 mm guns on the top deck, and then jumping from deck to lower platform, encouraging his mates to move rapidly as the officers on the bridge watched them. The ship pulled into the southern harbor of Guangzhou, teeming with junks, fishing skiffs, and modest sellers peddling their wares along the wharf dotted with European factories. Giacomo knew if he kept busy all day, the time would close in fast and soon he'd get a pass for the evening. He scrubbed the galley in the afternoon, trying to dissolve the unease he felt after his siesta. Soon there was quiet onboard for many of the men had already gone on shore leave.

Standing at the rail, he looked above him, where a hushed canopy dark as coal dust was ignited by a smattering of twinkling stars. What if galaxies lay beneath our feet? Maybe there were other stars on their way to us, undiscovered, unhurried, and all the more beautiful for their uncaring aloofness. *I'm as heretical as Galileo.*

At the beach when Giacomo was a child, he thought he could dig to China. Here he was, a grown man, wondering how much dirt he'd need to unearth for a glimpse of his mother's eyes. He didn't want to think of her or become maudlin. He wanted to go ashore, play hard, and come back exhausted and mellow enough from drink to fall into a deep, inconsequential sleep with nothing important to consider. He asked the heavens to give him a dreamless night, a lost, profound sleep in a haven of pitch—only without star glitter that somehow made him feel unmoored and adrift.

Yi Shen approached and handed him a small packet wrapped in rice paper. "You take, you sleep."

"What is it, and how do you now I'm not sleeping?"

Yi Shen rubbed his forefingers underneath his eyes. "Black." Then touched his heart with the flat of his palm and tapped it rapidly. Name—*bai zi ren*. You"—he moved a finger across his eyes—"two takes."

Giacomo opened the packet of seeds and guessed about twenty grams in weight. How he wished the healer's hand giving him the medicine had been Lian's.

Yi Shen held up two fingers.

"Thanks," Giacomo said and consulted his herb book. By the time he found what he was looking for, he'd waited too long to approach the lieutenant for a pass. He finished the galley jobs and didn't bother to fight it, merely hunkered down in his bunk and let his mind travel after he'd taken one half of Yi Shen's seeds along with several swigs of sake from the storage room.

He awoke refreshed and thirsty the next day. After breakfast, he was sent on a commerce detail he knew he'd relish. From the north shore of the British Shamian Island, Giacomo and Yi Shen crossed a bridge to the Quingping Free Market and assessed all the turtles, possums, dogs, cats, and other species of rather-large live animals. Without much cold storage, Giacomo figured, if it was breathing, it must be fresh. He at least had an icebox onboard.

They bought the vegetables and other items necessary for a two-day pass that Giacomo was permitted to take to escort Lieutenant Rinaldi, leaving Di Luise and Yi Shen to do the cooking for the skeleton crew left aboard.

After lunch and before dinner preparations, Giacomo mentioned his orders to take a boat tour of the Pearl River. The two mates remaining at the table by the window laughed, especially Bulldog. "You mean you're taking a busman's holiday? A sailor taking a river tour. Sweet."

"I like water, *scemo.*"

❦

GIACOMO RETURNED FROM HIS RIVER trip and resumed his duties. He'd secured a special five-day pass at the end of the week for a bicycle expedition with Bulldog to reconnoiter the landscape for any upheavals or Boxer-led skirmishes. Their orders were to investigate a Christian settlement and an area colonized by Europeans, mostly British, on the way to Guilin. This was Giacomo's chance to do what he'd longed to for the last three years. Search for Lian.

A breeze fluttered the squat, gauzy curtain by a window in the mess. The sea and all the soiling elements of men upon it came in with the breeze. Dead fish, frying oil, and a sweet smell like caramelized sugar.

Giacomo closed the window and pulled the curtain. "You done with that rice, Yi Shen?"

Bulldog said, "Let's go gambling tonight. Heard there's an inn called Garden of Awakened Orchids or something like that."

"I'd like to awaken an orchid or two," Di Luise said.

"Have you ever been to a teahouse, Di Luise?" Giacomo asked. "That's where I'm heading. Come along, mate. You might see something incredible that'll last your whole life."

"Only one thing fills that description—singsong girls," Di Luise said.

"And there's a tea ceremony that'll take the breath from your body," Giacomo said.

"Our poet means," Bulldog said, rolling his eyes, "it's as good as being with a woman."

"I didn't get a pass for tonight," Di Luise said. "Who cares anyway? Sex is sex, not the suggestion of it with tea."

The ship was moored in Guangzhou for repairs for at least three weeks, and at last Giacomo was going to Guilin to look for Lian, ostensibly to see Karst Basin. He'd heard from some of the crew how beautiful the cliffs were. Rinaldi chose Giacomo for his understanding of the language and the boy as translator and guide for his innocent looks. Shen had begged to go along, saying he had relatives in Guilin, although nobody believed him. Bulldog would serve as bodyguard. The ride to Guilin from Guangzhou would be a five-day trip by bicycle to evaluate dangers and assess damage. They dressed in local garb and Yi Shen negotiated a price for the bicycles.

They squirreled away packs loaded with foodstuffs, rain gear, canteens, and anything else they figured they needed or might come in handy for their expedition and left at first light.

On the way north out of town, they stopped at a guesthouse where Giacomo met Fritz Munchnick, an Austrian officer and aquaintance, enjoying drinks with a young girl, who appeared to be from the country. Giacomo peered over her shoulder as she doodled on a napkin, and he wondered if the characters were *Nüshu*. A country girl would not know how to write Chinese characters. They had one more round of drinks and turned in for the night. They set out once more at daybreak toward Guilin and Lian. On their way they would detour to survey the landmarks on the map prepared by Lieutenant Rinaldi.

Giacomo had written a note to remember every possible detail Lian had told him of her house and its location. This he explained carefully to Yi Shen as they pedaled along a narrow pathway that led to a wider expanse of a packed-earth road, Bulldog teasing mercilessly. Giacomo checked his compass often, and each time whispered a prayer he was getting closer to her; hopefully, by some miracle of God, he'd find her.

They slept in a rural hostelry outside of Guilin. There was an herbal depot nearby and Giacomo was intent on looking around. Shen asked directions of the gaunt herbalist. After Giacomo satisfied his curiosity, they left for the short ride to South Ronghu Road.

"We're close. I know it," Giacomo said, his eagerness obvious, but to be sure they stopped once more at a factory to ask where the foreign doctor lived. Their next stop was at the house that Giacomo recognized from Lian's description.

Shen, the designated knocker, hit a lion ring against the door three times, and a servant girl opened up almost instantaneously. Shen bowed and asked to speak to the doctor, and the servant told them to enter and please wait in the entranceway while she went to call her master.

Gaicomo couldn't cease pacing, his heart racing and his eyes trying to behold everything at once, while inhaling deeply as if he could catch Lian's scent on the air.

Bulldog sat down on a quilt-covered bench. "What if it's the wrong house?"

Giacomo wheeled around and almost ploughed into him. "It's not, I'm telling you, but they must have moved the scroll she told me about."

A distinguished gentleman with a serious demeanor entered and bowed. "I am Doctor Zhang Wei, you wished to speak with me?" His eyes swept all three of them.

Giacomo's chin fell, and he started to stutter something rather inaudible when Shen bowed, tugging both sailors by the sleeve to make them bow also. Shen introduced himself and his two companions and asked about the foreign doctor who used to live here.

The doctor shook his head and replied, "Forsooth, the man has died." He expressed sorrow to be the one who was giving this sad news.

Shen asked, "And what of his daughter, Zhou Bin Lian?"

Doctor Zhang thought a moment, placing his hands in his sleeves, and then answered that she had lived with her old grandmother but then married Yi Lu, a farmer who lived in a compound not far from here. He added that, sorry to say, the grandmother passed away shortly after the marriage, and he purchased the house.

As the doctor continued to speak, Giacomo noticed that Shen began to squirm and fidget something awful, stammering his questions to the doctor, finally translating for Giacomo and Bulldog, "Bad thing."

Giacomo asked, "What is it, Shen?"

"Grandmother die too."

"Where is Lian now?" Giacomo prodded, seeing discomfort rise in Shen's wary look.

"Lian. She marry farmer."

Giacomo swayed a little as if he were tipsy and sat down heavily on a cushioned stool.

Doctor Zhang picked up a tiny bell from a high lacquered credenza and rang it. The same servant girl came in and bowed, and as the doctor gave her some orders, Shen said, "More worse."

"More worse?" Bulldog said, echoing Shen.

The girl returned quickly carrying a tray with a pitcher of water and some cups, which she distributed.

The doctor apologized for giving such shocking news as to make the sailors feel unwell.

"Dear God, what could be worse?" Bulldog bellowed.

"She have baby, cousin family I run away," Shen blurted out, looking at his feet.

"What? She married your cousin?" Giacomo said, his voice incredulous.

"My name Yi Shen, he Yi Lu."

AFTER LEAVING THE KIND DOCTOR, they went to Bridge Tavern. Giacomo was inconsolable, but he swore he would not leave Guilin without seeing Lian once more. Shen told him he was frightened. He knew exactly where the Yi compound was located but begged Giacomo to leave him out of this search. He explained to Giacomo and Bulldog where they had to go, but warned not to expect a warm reception, saying that Yi Lu, normally volatile, when drinking became a warrior capable of murder.

Bulldog couldn't imagine what one man could do against the two of them, so they left Shen and headed out. But Shen ran after them, mounted his bicycle, and said he would follow at a distance and remain hidden while they confronted his cousin.

When they arrived at one of the back fields, Shen pointed out his cousin and was about to go into hiding in a grove of trees beyond a meadow, but said he had a change of heart because he knew Giacomo needed him to translate, and hoped that Lu wouldn't recognize him as he had grown so much and had been a mere child when he left.

The sun hung low in the sky. Four field hands with farm tools on their shoulders departed the upturned field and walked off, leaving Lu alone. When Shen approached him and began asking questions, Lu's face changed; he had a moment of realization as to why this boy and these two men were looking for Lian. He spat out in a barrage of hateful language that he had kicked her and the child out, and she was probably prostituting herself. Then he picked up an animal's horn and used it as a trumpet to sound some sort of signal. At the call of alarm, the men who had been walking in the opposite direction did an about-face and came running full tilt to aid Lu. A huge fight ensued, but Giacomo, Bulldog, and Shen used the *Wing Chun* skills and economized their movements in the close combat that Shen had taught them. They fought using striking action drives by advancing and retreating, grappling their opponents to the ground.

Their speedy thrusts to vulnerable parts of the body: throat, groin, eyes, and stomach were intentionally brutal. Lu and his Boxer companions were left strewn on the field, quite bloodied but not dead, as the two sailors and young martial artist who had taught them escaped, mounting their bicycles and riding hell-bent back the way they came.

As they rode through town, they passed the factory where they had sought information earlier, and a girl straddling her bicycle blocked their path, waving furiously at them to stop. She ranted that her name was Ping, and she had heard about them coming to ask directions so she waited for them because she was Lian's best friend. Speaking so fast, Shen had to stop her several times to ask her to repeat herself.

"Lian left Yi Lu with her foreign child of a sailor," Ping concluded breathlessly.

Shen translated.

"Where? Where did Lian go? Shen, ask her where?" Giacomo shouted.

Ping answered, "To Hong Kong with her little girl, Ya Chen."

Bulldog glanced at Giacomo, who for once remained speechless.

Chapter 9

Taifeng
台风
Typhoon

I STOPPED CALLING MY DAUGHTER Zin-Zin for I would soon rob her of her childhood and wanted her to get used to it. Leaving for Hong Kong, I intended to take a few things with me: my little Ya Chen, my chronicle, ink, brushes, my wedding jacket, onto which I had fastened a pin, and my new teacup—a gift from the women at work. Four integral parts to the puzzle that was me—one for each of the seasons.

In a few weeks, feeling stronger, I would escape my husband's home. But not without repercussions, for the gods mete out justice in cruel ways.

LATE SPRING OF 1898, MY daughter and I made our escape to Hong Kong. Ping helped me pack the little basket on my bicycle. I removed the jade pendant I had received from Lu's family and consigned it to the place where it belonged: a kitchen wok, wondering how the family would settle up Lu's father's gambling debt. Ya Chen took her doll and we walked out of the house before dawn, a calculated operation. I knew the women were in the back part of the house training the young with new bound feet, and the men were already in the fields.

I picked up my baby girl and sat her in the bicycle basket on top of my chronicle, packet of brushes, ink stone block, and wedding jacket. I tucked the teacup in her lap.

"Where are we going, Ma?" she asked.

"To see a man at the train station."

"What man, Ma?"

"The man who is going to buy this bicycle."

"But if you sell it, how will you get to work?"

"We will take the train, and I will work in a place far from here."

"Does my Baba know?"

"Not yet. It's our secret."

IN THE FIVE DAYS OF our escape, we were bedraggled, tired and hungry, as we traveled by almost every means of transportation. Hong Kong was under British domination, and it was not easy to travel without proper papers. After our train ride, we went by cart with the servant brother of a young woman whom I knew from the factory, along the route to freedom together. He had made this trip before and had family nearby. Ya Chen and I were fortunate to find lodgings and food with thm. He did not ask us for cash, as I tended a wound he had sustained running to catch the train. He also was staying in Hong Kong., Hiang-Kiang, place of sweet lagoons. Ya Chen and I arrived safely with him. Freedom came at a price. We stayed in the worst possible neighborhood, a dwelling that housed many overcrowded families. We did not intend to stay long with him, only until I found my cousin Liang.

Our garret, lodged near a marketplace, was fenced in by poverty rather than geography. A giant mountebank hawked his wares, selling trinkets, showing off, telling fictions, and beguiling all, especially Ya Chen and me. He stood higher than a horse and would grab an onlooker to hoist on his hulking shoulders and trot around the audience arena.

For two weeks I went to the docks and looked for my lover's ship. I recognized Italian seamen by their uniforms, the same uniform that Giacomo wore. I stopped to ask them questions about *Il Leopardo,* but soon realized my behavior could only bring me grief. These men did not want to help me find another sailor, each of them wanted to be *my* sailor. Some were gruff, others offered money, most were too drunk to understand me. I scoured the waterfront until my feet were raw and bleeding. I could not continue searching for a phantom sailor.

❦

EARLY MORNING OF THE DRAGON Races, clouds splintered the sky and sun dawned in a distilled light. We walked along the promenade to the pier of the Star Ferry. I still had money from the bicycle sale, so I treated my little girl to tickets. Excitement was in the air. While we were queuing up, it seemed we kept getting pushed back by the wind's muscle. We finally boarded, holding onto the rail of the gangway. I pointed out into the harbor where cargo ships were anchored. It was a pleasant morning, promising a perfect afternoon. We took the Star Ferry from Tsim Sha Tusi on Kowloon to Hong Kong Island. The ferry transported us across Victoria Harbor. Ya Chen shrieked over the wind every time she saw something interesting from the open window. In order to get a better look, we climbed the stairs to the upper deck. The movement of the vessel in the water brought with it thoughts of Giacomo. In all the vast water of China, where could he be? Sampans and fishing boats lined up in triple file in the crowded harbor, teeming with life. Wailing babies, peddler's cries, catcalls, hoots and whistles from sailors on foreign riverboats passing by, and the insistent roar of life exuded from every passing boatman or toothless granny offering vegetables. Ya Chen's eyes filled with anticipation. The trip over was an hour from Kowloon, *Gau Lung*, or Nine Dragons, a suburb of Victoria.

Before the races began, I cautioned Ya Chen to stick close to me as though she were a sticky bun, but I couldn't keep her still. Soon our boat was swamped and my little Ya Chen fell into the lagoon. There was a crush of boaters and oars flying. They restrained me from jumping in after her. "Ya Chen!" I screamed. "Ya Chen!" Her arms flailed. "My daughter. Help me, someone." A man had wrenched my shoulders back, and I fought to glimpse the frothing water. Where was she? My heart skidded to a stop.

Someone yelled, "Don't worry we'll get your girl!" With all the confusion, and through my tears, I couldn't see which boat had rescued her, and it seemed her rescuers sailed in the opposite direction. Onshore I searched for her in every party.

"Have you seen the little girl who fell into the water at the beginning of the race?"

"No. No."

I walked from fire encampment to fire, "Ya Chen!" I called, repeatedly, my voice hoarse.

A youth with a fishing pole slung over his back said he thought a group of jugglers had picked her up. I tried to question him more, struggling with Cantonese, but he hurried off, casting a glance behind him as if I understood his meaning. One old, tarnished hag, her gray braid encircling her head, surrounded by a brood of grandbabies, said, "How could we know her? There are so many children who fit that description, and so many dropped into the water."

Exhausted, I begged a cup of water from a man selling nuts, but he had none. I trudged onward, weary, afraid and unforgiving of my carelessness with so precious a cargo. I came upon a company of artists and an opera group. I sat on the ground, watching some pantomime. There she was or if it was not her, her ghost, for surely at this point I thought she had been drowned. For the first time since I left Guilin, I was overcome with remorse and realized how badly I'd betrayed Lu.

Her skinny frame outlined by the clothes sticking to her, her hair a riot of snake coils. She was damp with sweat and unkempt, and from what I could make out, the camp's darling. Could anyone imagine my happiness at seeing that drenched and scruffy child learning acrobatic stunts from revelers? When she glanced in my direction, she stopped her practicing and ran into my waiting arms, and I all but smothered her. Her arms were bruised and I wished I had some salve to apply to them, but I would have to wait until we returned to our room.

A WEEK OF HUNTING, MISLEADS and misinformation passed until I finally contacted my cousin. We thanked the people who housed us for that time, packed our meager belongings, and were on our way. The only payment I had given them was my ability to clean and cook, which I did with love and gratitude. I had with me a small jade pin finished in gold—a wedding gift from Ping. It broke my heart to part with it, but I left it on the pillow of the pallet Ya Chen and I shared, recalling the tainted beginning of my marriage.

At my cousin's, after I scraped together a little money and time, I purchased a stamp and stationery, and with my fine brush and ink block wrote a letter to Ping. Her answer shocked rather than surprised me. In the first sentence she begged forgiveness for telling Lu where I was, but he threatened to have her fired. How could he possibly? It didn't matter; the damage had been done. The rest was a dictated letter from him because he could not write. In it he entreated me to come home and promised me that all would be forgiven. At the conclusion, there was a postscript in *Nüshu* in Ping's hand, saying there was nothing to fear as he would not follow me to Hong Kong. How little Ping understood the nature of my estranged husband, or my indentured situation in his family. Or perhaps Lu had dictated that too. I wondered if he had the courage to break in to the family coffer for a wayward imp and her daughter.

BY THE BEGINNING OF THE next week, Lu was seated at my cousin's humble table, voicing his entreaties in person. After dinner he played rough-and-tumble with Ya Chen, a thing he so rarely did anymore, and her face was bright with enthusiasm for his attention. He enfolded her in his arms and carried her to her pallet perched on his shoulders.

I was thinking of a way to get Lu outside so I could talk to him, and was about to suggest a walk when my cousin and his wife absented themselves with precisely that excuse. The awkward silence was deafening. Leaving us alone to discuss our separation frightened me. If I opened my mouth, he'd yell that I'd become a harlot, so I waited till he breeched the gulf between us. He did it simply. He backhanded me across the mouth. When he finally finished berating me between blows, he ordered me to pack and go back with him to our home. I crooked my finger, the way I sometimes did to get the attention of Ya Chen, and when he drew close, I whispered, "Never," recalling a time when I'd said that word before, but it had meant something so different, so special with my sailor. As if he read my mind about my sailor, he slammed me hard against the wall, saying my sailor lover had come to Guilin looking for me, but that he murdered him with four other Boxers and they desecrated his body. While he screamed, I wiggled out of his grasp.

"How will you survive?" he screamed, pushing the table behind which I'd positioned myself.

I could barely breathe thinking of Giacomo dead, yet somehow I answered him. "I'm going to work in an apothecary starting in two days."

"You need me. You can't care for Ya Chen without me."

"I will have to—for Ya Chen will be fatherless once more." I waited for the effect of this, but it was slow in coming. For him this was a hidden conspiracy of words. So I said, "You can be here with us too." Clear enough, but how could I say this and mean it when he just caromed his fist off my belly? I could not help but utter his name like a prayer, "Giacomo." A second blow glanced off my defiant arm to protect my face, and I knew I must be mad to want this man in my life.

Lu answered me with the same argument about his parents. His fist poised again for smashing, I sensed it coming, stood from my crouched position, and blocked his arm. "You can beat me to death like your ox, but I will never return to the house of your parents."

My cousin, who as I'd suspected had not gone anywhere, lingered behind the door. I heard muffled sounds on the threshold. Were they, I hoped, pretending to come back from their walk? Liang must have understood. They had heard the scuffle of chairs and feet, our raised, strained voices. Cousin knocked at the door; I imagined him showing restraint by not banging it down. Liang came inside, did not bow, but in a low voice asked Lu to leave his home, pointing to my disheveled appearance and the coloring welts as testimony for further lack of hospitality.

AFTER THE INCIDENT WITH LU, I left Ya Chen in the care of Liang's kind wife as usual and went to work. I walked into the pharmacy, passed jars of belladonna, tenders for other drugs, oil of cassia, cinnamon, chemicals, sundries, wine, spirits, stimulants, books, pipes, beakers, mortars, pestles, and ledgers. I reached the back of the shop where I took a smock from a nail and put it on. Of course I was crushed at the idea of merely being a stock girl, but he paid me generously.

I paid heavily with regret for aborting in Guilin. I had duped myself, thinking father's friend the pharmacist in Hong Kong would allow me to work beside him in the front of the store where he kept ginseng, mandrake, and myrrh or *bissabol,* an ingredient in joss sticks, used in our temples.

While restocking the shelves in the apothecary, I slipped from a small step stool and fell. *What a clumsy fool,* I thought just before hitting my head. I injured much more than my head. The pharmacist told me later that he found me soaked in my own blood but not from my head. I hemorrhaged due to internal bleeding from Lu's beating. The chemist carried me to a rickshaw that took us to the hospital.

Recovering at Liang's, I learned that Lu had departed, and thanking the heavens, I decided two days was sufficient to heal. More than the need to fill our rice bowls, I needed to occupy my mind. Liang's wife, Changchang, meaning Flourishing, insisted I remain abed, but I could not, even though my sweet companion, Ya Chen, sat cutting out paper dolls from old newspapers for hours on end at the foot of my pallet.

I thought of how I'd begged Lu to come here with me to eke out a life like these people, but I could not stay with him. Lu was always reluctant to find joy even in lovely things. Somehow he always needed to grapple enchantment to its knees. I should have seen that in him before I married, but I was alone, desparate without a choice, an alien with large feet in my own homeland.

How could I keep working in the apothecary, leaving my Ya Chen to fend for herself all day long? I needed a more permanent settlement and work that would enable me to keep a watch on my little girl. I inquired about working in a hospital and serving as a nurse. Though I spoke foreign languages and knew European medicine, the minute anyone looked at me—apart from the color of my eyes—they always asked if I had my husband's permission. I thought of the Italian priests who ran a school in Hong Kong. There would be work for a person with my linguistic abilities. Work in the apothecary was too many hours, and I didn't want factory work—who would care for my child?

It was a holiday time and I couldn't even look for work, so instead I dressed in white for mourning with respect for my lost unborn one and took Ya Chen to Victoria Harbor. I wanted to take Ya Chen to the harbor waters north of Lantau where the wild pink dolphins frolic, but I had no extra money for that activity. Instead we went to hear over one hundred guns firing salutes. I met an Italian couple who stood on the quay with us. The well-dressed gentleman explained they had steamed here from Shanghai, "Over a thousand kilometers—swimming distance to Victoria," he said, and laughed at his little joke.

"Shanghai has a small population, many European," the stylishly dressed lady said.

"No, really?" I asked, although her high-pitched didactic tone was irksome.

I translated for my daughter, and she said, "The lady talks like Wai Po to you."

So the little minx had noticed. I couldn't help but ask, "She screeches?"

Ya Chen shrugged her shoulders. "You mean like an owl?"

"Do you miss your Baba and your Wai Po?"

"Baba likes only boys. And I never please Wai Po. Like you."

The Italian man, astonished I could speak his language flawlessly, interrupted and asked, "Did you know, *cara mia,* Hong Kong stretches only four meters along the coast, and its breadth varies from—"

Before I had the chance to hear what he was saying, another gunboat fired and whatever he said was lost. After the last report, he continued with his geography lesson. I gazed at the Praya, or esplanade, given to shipping.

His wife turned to me and said, "Now he'll explain how the Praya Reclamation Scheme provided for a land-frontage protection in all states of tide."

"Even typhoon?" I asked.

She hesitated for the moment, and since I'd just heard her explanation, I had no wish to listen again. I looked down at Ya Chen and asked if she minded my speaking Italian, and told her how the lady had committed to memory such dull information to please her husband.

My little one smiled.

The gentleman began, "The main commercial street runs parallel with the Praya and on each side lie the Chinese quarters."

I crossed my fingers behind my back as my father had taught me and hoped beyond all possible hope that the Italian's next sentence would not be about the overcrowded population of those quarters. I detested the way he pronounced *Chinese,* as if we were intruders in his country.

But instead he said that he and his *gentile signora* had been invited to the Government House, a ten-minute climb up the side of the island.

At this point, Ya Chen let go my hand and quite peevishly said, "Tell the foreign devils to speak Cantonese."

Stunned by her expression, and annoyed by her display of bad manners, I wanted to shake her. Later, of course, I'd be awash in guilt for considering to discipline my child.

"There are lovely gardens," the lady said, and he added, "Solid roads with luxurious semitropical flowers and fauna. Why not join us?"

"Thank you, but my daughter is anxious to ride the cable tramway to the peak."

"Our friends have a bungalow there," the man said.

"My father told me the well-to-do go there to summer at the health resorts."

"Will you join us for lunch tomorrow?" he asked, adjusting his cravat.

I smiled and then shook my head. "I am pleased to have had this opportunity of speaking my father's tongue and appreciate your kind offer, but tomorrow we leave for Lantao."

"At least take my card. Oh, and here," he took out a reservoir pen. "Let me write the name of a priest friend and the mission where he resides. In case you ever need to contact someone who speaks Italian. You seem to be traveling alone, that is, I beg your pardon, but without your husband." He blew on the script, waved the card, and handed it to me. I gave him no explanation but took hold of the card. Dottore Antonio Castellano. I turned it over. He had written, Don Alberico Crescitelli, Yangbinguan, Sichuan.

"You're a doctor?"

He smiled.

"So was my father—he taught me a great deal about Western medicine, but he also practiced our Chinese cures."

"How admirable, my dear," he said again in that grave timbre. "Don Crescitelli is in need of a good nurse. Consider it. But you've heard of the things happening inside China, eh? There are rebellious hellions rabble-rousing against strangers in their country and deliberately provoking incidents against white intruders, like us. Their arms, for the time being, are rudimentary, but they are dangerous, and some reports say the empress sanctions their disturbances." He deliberately looked at me, and I immediately felt my own foreignness. *Because of my eyes? The fact that I speak Italian?* Why was he warning me?

He thought I was from Canton. How little he understood accents and dress codes. I wanted to ask if he were in need of a nurse, but he was only vacationing here.

With a broad sweep of his hand, he said, "You've noticed the amount of foreign ships in the harbor? They're here at the behest of foreign ambassadors. There have been peasant riots, and foreign missionaries have been assaulted. And," he continued with an arched eyebrow, "looting of churches."

"An exaggeration. China has always suffered rebellions."

"This is different from the Tai Pings. Do be judicious—it's not all hearsay. Things here in Hong Kong are getting worse by the minute—and here there's British rule. Maybe you'd be safer on the mainland," he said, a note of sincerity in his words.

I bowed, tugging Ya Chen's little hand, and she made a most courteous bow, knowing our discussion was finished. She insisted on knowing what he'd said, and I told her. She planted her feet and put her hands on her hips, saying with a defiance I recognized as Lu's, "I'll never leave Hong Kong."

Why didn't I assure her that we wouldn't? She sounded so wise, so sure. And how prophetic her words were, as a fortnight would show. Two short weeks. Fourteen little days.

❦

YA CHEN AND I WERE on the beach one afternoon after a miserable morning of searching for work. As I gazed out to sea, I thought how cruel a fate that Giacomo did not even have a burial in the waters he loved. Did he have a burial at all?

We'd been collecting shells by the bay and were about to quit the shore. A sudden calm reigned over the water, and then long swells rushed forward, soaking my legs and thighs. We ran up a sandy embankment, cloth shoes in hand, to the top of a cliff. The sky went from overcast to the color of a child's slate, turning from a luminous dove-gray to the color of soot.

Then I noticed it. A wall of seawater began to draw back. We started to retrace our steps, but a fisherman yelled, "Inside! Here!" He pointed to a lean-to shelter. Rain came in torrents. Brutal typhoon winds raged in a matter of minutes. The man, Ya Chen, and I got inside, and he bolted the door. I thought how strange to see the water tugged and gulped backward; fish left behind to flounder on the dark, wet ocean floor.

"Ma, what is it?" cried Ya Chen.

"Hush, my little love, it's nothing."

We settled ourselves on overturned wooden crates.

"It's an underwater disturbance, a volcano eruption," I said, thinking the term, *tsunami*.

"Like those boats in the harbor sounding their guns?" Ya Chen asked.

I wanted to say *tidal wave*, but knew I'd have to explain more, and merely said, "Yes, a type of explosion."

The fisherman's shack whistled as the winds began to blow harder. The temperature had dropped, and now hail along with rain beat upon the shack.

"*Tai fung,*" he said in Cantonese.

"*Tai feng,*" I repeated, in Mandarin, matter-of-factly, nodding in agreement.

"Where are you from?" he asked.

"Guilin."

A little woman came from behind a curtain in front of a board structure that must have been their bedroom/kitchen. She offered me tea. I took it, my hands shaking, while a gale force grew in intensity, and through the apertures of the lean-to we saw trees uprooted and building roof tiles hurled about like birds in air currents. Ya Chen began to whimper, never having seen a tempest like this before. I set my cup down on the small table, gathered her onto my lap, and tried to soothe her, crooning softly in her ear.

Boards flew off our shelter and the stocky fisherman and his wife said they had never seen anything as fierce as this in many, many years. But we couldn't move for fear of being trounced by the wind or borne upward like tree branches and oars sailing through the air.

Banging and knocking sounds shook the building. Slats tore away. I clutched Ya Chen as a gush of water was thrust upon us as part of the roof ripped off. We were soaked through and shivering, and the fisherwoman's frightened eyes sought mine. Then she shook her head as if to acquiesce to the winds of Fate.

I buried my head into Ya Chen's little body when an angry noise eerily pierced the air. When I looked up, the little fisherwoman was nowhere in sight. Cups, table, lantern, fishing nets, and tackle all had been sucked and shoved outdoors, and the tiny shelter was being torn asunder. The howling wind had competition from the desperate man, crawling around looking for his wife as though she were a mouse hidden under planking.

My daughter and I had been flung against the wall, or what was left of it. My voice and words were taken by the roar of the wind. With my mouth close to her ear, I yelled to Ya Chen, "It isn't safe here!"—thinking we must brave the elements or be shred apart like old clothes.

She nodded her head, her eyes rimmed red from salt water, tears, and fear. I grabbed her hand and we dashed for the only other building still standing erect on the shore. The water's waves, the color of gray molding clay, beat the shore and jetty. The water that had been taken back was engorged with fury, racing to a shore that no longer existed. We ran toward a structure that stood closer to the bay's waters, which were surging into a monster sea. The building appeared to be a lighthouse, though bent, hobbled, and unsure of itself.

The pounding surf now became a swirling cone, a vortex, beset on swallowing my legs like a mad fiend, desperate to drag me down. A rope lashed out like a whip. I snatched at it, but it snaked around my waist. What was it tied to? I was being yanked under. "Take a breath!" I screamed to Ya Chen, as we were thrust, unbalanced, and heaved below the water. We never made it to the lighthouse. I reached for the rudder of a beached sampan embedded in heavy, wet sand, the rope ensnaring both Ya Chen and me—a whiplash now floating away in a riptide of swells. I clung to the rudder, my daughter's twig-like arms and legs wrapped around me as if she were my own limbs, fending off the lashing wind and water. Another surge knocked me down, and I felt her body slide off mine as she was snatched from my grasp and, arms outstretched, ripped away by vicious currents into the raging sea.

I hurled myself in after her; gasping and sputtering, I dove repeatedly, thrashed and beaten with every intake and gulp of air, screaming her name over and over till all was black.

My karma, unhappily, was not hers.

I AWAKENED DISORIENTED IN A makeshift hospital room to the lilting sounds of Italian. It was Dottore Castellano in a white coat, speaking softly as he held my wrist, taking my pulse.

"How are you feeling, *mia cara?*" he asked in a sweet, hushed voice.

I felt cold all over, but my face was burning. I closed my eyes. My lids were so heavy. My teeth chattered and I stuttered. "Ah, Ya Chen, there you are. Talk to me."

"Still feverish," the doctor whispered. "Your child is not here."

"Where is she?"

He did not respond and I tried to get up. He gently pushed my shoulders back on the pillow and continued to talk about my condition and my health, but he avoided my eyes, which could not properly focus on his face.

"You are just awakening from a great shock," he said.

A nurse walked by and beckoned him, but he answered her harshly, "Not now." Then he turned to me again and bent close. "Do you know your name?"

I nodded and thought, *What an absurd question,* but I could not answer, somehow knowing I would have to learn an awful, inevitable truth. I closed my hot eyes and there she was, my little girl wading at the river's edge, wanting to swim with Lu.

The doctor stood straight and interrupted my vision with his chatter. "You are in the hospital. Do you remember what happened, Lian?"

Surging water. Cold and wet. A storm on the beach. I held her tight against me, but she was ripped away. I begged her to swim, only she couldn't and flailed her skinny arms, drifting away from me. "Swim! Swim!" I screamed.

"Hush now. You're still shaking," he said as he covered me with another blanket. "Do you remember now? You were carried here by a fisherman. I'm afraid he died of exhaustion, but not before telling us of your loss. I am so deeply sorry. My sincerest condolences for your little girl."

"My Ya Chen. My daughter." My head was swimming, and all I could think of was maybe if Lu had taught her to swim she would be with me now. I turned my face to the white wall. White, the color of mourning, the absence of color like this day, like all my forever days to come.

He touched my shoulder and squeezed gently.

I listened to his retreating steps down the corridor and brought my arm up to muffle the sobs in the bend of my elbow. When I stopped crying, the bleakness and desolation, the conscious moments of my breath rising and falling in my chest, alerted me that I'd survived the events of my daughter's loss; the shards and wreckage constructing those instances taught me nothing more than a brief insight—my own inadequacy—we are nothing, nothing at all in this cosmos.

AFTER I WAS RELEASED FROM the hospital, I recalled that at the temple in Guilin, I had prayed to Buddha to take the baby, but I never stipulated which one, and so he took them both. "If there ever is a next time," I muttered under my breath, "I will make restitution karmically." I thought of the proverb: "Quiet thoughts mend the body."

I knew I must leave Hong Kong. But before my departure, I went to the shore and wrote a sorrowful farewell note to Ya Chen, and as the waves washed away my words, I realized that not only could my little Zin-Zin not read *Nüshu*—she couldn't read at all. Would she learn in the afterlife?

I took my rapid departure from Liang and his wife, but it was the kind doctor who paid my train fare. I still had four things with me: my teacup, my wedding jacket, my chronicle, and Ya Chen's stuffed doll, but the most precious of all was lost to me. I was a walking dead, a hungry ghost with no ancestral home to return to—a healer who could not heal herself, knowing grief was causing my energy to disperse—I still had to go.

Chapter 10

Suixinsuoyu
随心所欲
Listen to your heart

BEREFT AFTER NOT FINDING LIAN in Guilin, Giacomo consoled himself with the thought that at least she had left her husband. He wondered when his ship would ever sail for Hong Kong again. He reached shore in the skiff and set off for the Inn of the Shadow of Seven Swallows, so long a name that the men shortened it to Seven Swallows. Giacomo hoped for sunny weather. He sniffed the air. Rain. He held up a moist finger to determine wind direction. He walked a kilometer, and then the rain began in earnest, and as he looked at the sky, he knew there wouldn't be any surcease from it. Was this an omen? Hell, China invaded his existence, and he was beginning to think like a native.

After repairs to the boiler room, Giacomo's ship docked in the port of Guangzhou, a hub port in South China, preparing to cruise, control, and police the Pearl River Delta. Lieutenant Rinaldi spoke to the men of the Hundred Days' Reform, which was to have a huge effect on national, cultural, political, and educational reform movements. Rinaldi had the crew spend their days onboard drilling for a battle they were yet to have a hint of; then came the news of a coup d'état, known as "The Coup of 1898," commanded by formidable traditionalist adversaries of the Empress Dowager Cixi.

Waiting for news of a possible confrontation with the Chinese,

Giacomo received a three-day leave, rather than the usual forty-eight hours. Bulldog had already left with some buddies, but Giacomo had to be sure Yi Shen knew exactly how to prepare meals for the captain, Lieutenant, and the skeleton crew elected to stay onboard ship.

When Shen was settled, Giacomo went below deck where he took out his frustration and distress at never finding Lian by pummeling a sack of rice till his hands were bloody and he was soaked in sweat. He cleaned up, signed out, and walked for a long time. Water pooled and puddled. The wind picked up and he made a dash through alleyways and crowded streets, vendors and hawkers selling their wares, and customers haggling over prices, pointing and gesturing to other cuts, bigger pieces. Passing a barbershop, he watched the barber deftly shave the forehead and top of a coolie's head. A cacophony of sounds assaulted his ears and cooking smells made his mouth water. He hadn't eaten since the morning's hot congee. The combined pungent smells of pork, sizzling green onions, garlic, ginger simmering in woks, and other usually delicious foods— things he loved—were not appealing to him.

He hadn't been eating with any appetite and was becoming increasingly more obsessed by one thought: *the girl with the green eyes.* Lian wanted to be a healer—she was certainly the only cure for his ailment. He had searched for her in Guilin, but all he found was that *Guilin* means cassia tree forest. Like searching for a scent on the breeze. Now with three days to fill, he wondered how this lovesick feeling for a girl he'd never see again could possess him to this degree? And the child? Surely the girl was his. Every time he stepped into the galley and traced his hands across the chopping table, the length of three Chinese archery arrows, his thoughts eloped back to the embassy, and he knew she'd been real. Feeling low, he wanted some excitement, which usually involved women. He'd heard the women here were lovely, but he wasn't interested. He hadn't gone whoring or picked a fight for the hell of it in such a long time; he must be lovesick. How in God's name had he ever found a girl who spoke his language in this huge country? When would he ever get back to Hong Kong now that the coup had transpired? And if he did, could he find her? Her father had worked for the Peking Italian consulate. But Giacomo had already tried to get information there, and that was so long ago.

He passed a wizened-looking old man in a quilted jacket, a coolie hat covering half his prune face. He smiled, exposing a toothless mouth. Giacomo pointed and the old one scooped out a handful of rice with a bamboo spoon and plopped it on a leaf. He rolled it and dunked it in a sauce and handed it over. Giacomo shoved it in his mouth so quickly the old seller cackled. He nudged the sailor's arm to have more. Instead Giacomo pointed to a sticky bun.

The man said, "What do you think of this?"

"Mmm," Giacomo said, and wiped his mouth with his sleeve.

The rain abated a little as he reached inside his peacoat for a coin.

"*Tse, tse.*" Giacomo was sure now China permeated his skin and almost laughed at himself, knowing to use Mandarin instead of Cantonese. The vendor bowed deeper with serious intent. He raised an eyebrow that Giacomo understood meant a foreigner with manners.

Giacomo returned the bow. A few stalls down from the parchment-skinned man, a woman sold spiced pumpkin seeds. Giacomo bought some and the woman rolled them in a cone of paper, reminding him of the street vendors in Carini roasting chestnuts at this time of year.

Turning a corner, the unfamiliar street's offering was one of magic and melancholy, of light and shadow. Giacomo saw in a window red material like a fancy scroll with calligraphy on it. It couldn't be *Nüshu*, that wouldn't be in a store window. Giacomo knew at that precise moment, surely as he breathed, that he would find Lian and his mood lifted. He did an about-face and headed back to his ship. Of what use to seek release when the only pleasure he wanted and needed were her thin arms around his neck, her scent filling his nostrils?

When he got back to the ship, a card game was in progress.

"What's the celebration for?" Giacomo asked no one in particular.

"Guess you don't know everything aboard, eh, Chief?" Bulldog asked.

"You're back early, Bulldog," Giacomo said.

"Yi Shen birthday," Yi Shen piped up.

"Ah then, come to the galley and I'll give you a sweet." Giacomo crooked his finger.

Yi Shen followed Giacomo down the hall. In the galley, he pulled three hard candies from his pocket and handed them to the boy with the cone of pumpkin seeds.

"Why here? You had in pocket?"

"Only part of your gift. Here's the rest." Giacomo handed Yi Shen a paper. Giacomo had scratched out in Chinese characters a poem from Wu-Men, which Yi Shen read hesitantly.

Ten thousand flowers in spring,
The moon in autumn,
A cool breeze in summer
Snow in winter.
This is the best season of your life.

Yi Shen's eyes sparkled. "Double sweet. Double happiness."

Giacomo pulled Yi Shen's pigtail twice like tugging a cord to ring a bell. "You're a jackanapes at times, aren't you?"

The boy smiled a gap-toothed grin. "I keep?"

"As long as you don't show anyone and don't get sweet on me."

"Ha! I save for woman."

"Are you ready for one?

Nodding his head vigorously, Shen said, "Yes. Take me shore find?"

"No. And take that hangdog expression off your face. I don't—I can't take responsibility for your young soul. Ask Bulldog to take you, or your boss man, King of the Coolies."

"Why you say this?"

"Because he gambles away his pay instead of sending it home to his family. That, my little friend, is also a vice—just like womanizing is, but he won't admit it."

"You have woman Sicily?" he asked, trying his best at pronouncing the words.

They sat down at a galley table, and Shen brought a teapot and two cups.

"I'll tell you about the little girl I fell in love with at school."

Shen's expression was alert as if his head had grown another pair of ears.

"I had one particular advantage over the other boys at school, Shen. None of them were interested in girls. But I was. Sure as sunshine."

Giacomo stopped speaking for a moment. Emotion had him gripped in its jaws, and his memory filled with a bright greenness, the color of Lian's eyes.

The sweet smell of green roasting peppers Giacomo had put on the brazier wafted on a breeze and stirred his thoughts to other sweet things, of other coal fires.

GIACOMO HAD VISITED LIAN ONCE immediately after she'd left the embassy. She'd sent word for him to come to her as her father would be away for two days. He wangled a pass from Rinaldi and found her little abode, knocking on the door. Three taps, stop. Three taps, stop. Three taps. The door sailed open and she flew into his arms. He slammed shut the door and dropped his knapsack on the floor.

She had prepared a small dinner and afterward he was sitting on the floor, his back against the fireplace wall. Sliding down, wanting to be next to him, falling into him, she said, "I have done this so many times in dreams." He bent forward to kiss her bare thigh as the white silken robe she wore opened. Lian leaned across his back caressing him in both arms, her cheek on his upper back. In a while Giacomo released himself from her grasp, looked in her eyes and saw sadness. "What's wrong?"

"I was just thinking how much of life I've missed until you."

"Ah, so the meal has not yet satiated you. You hunger for me as I do you."

He removed her shawl and untied her hair, shaking it free. He loosened her robe and watched it fall to her shoulders, taking the cloth from her arms to pull it back, kissing the hollow of her neck. His mouth traced her collarbones as the robe fell off of her, revealing white breasts and pink areolas, her nipples erect. His face traveled her chest, shifting from space to space till he had glided over every curve. Lian's head was thrown back in ardor and ecstasy. Giacomo's tongue washed her neck, chin. He found her mouth, which he devoured.

Moonlight jetted like a stream and poured in through a narrow window, reminding him of their first time together in the embassy kitchen. There was a small rush mat in front of the fireplace, which her robe now blanketed. Firelight, hypnotic and dreamlike, brightened the room, while coals burned like sea coral in the hearth. The heat from the dying coals and embers heated their sides closest to it. On the dining table tapers burned down, and they extinguished each other's flames until sleep overtook them in a tangle of arms in a net of dreams.

GIACOMO SHOOK HIS SHOULDERS, WAKING from the memory. He looked at Shen and could tell by the brightness in Shen's eyes that he wanted the story because he wanted or had a little girlfriend somewhere. Before he could ask, Shen said, "Me," he pointed a thumb at his chest, "No girl, get girl now."

Giacomo smiled and said, "Always listen to your heart."

"*Suixinsuoyu,* always listen to your heart." Shen repeated.

Giacomo sat at the table until everyone had left the mess hall. A candle sputtered. Perhaps it was those initial feelings that opened Giacomo up to understand his feelings for Lian were genuine. He never wanted anyone so badly in all his life. His life without Lian was impoverished. Yearning made each day a struggle. Young love. Hadn't he told Shen to listen to his heart? Was Giacomo finally listening to his?

Chapter 11

Yongeng de ai
永恒的爱
Love eternal

YANGBINGUAN, SICHUAN 1898

FOR MANY WEEKS, I WANDERED like a ghost, numb and blind, my grief like sand sifting in an overturned hourglass, until I found myself in Yangbinguan, Sichuan. The inside of the missionary compound consisted of many buildings and seemed like a garrisoned village, mostly self-sufficient with high surrounding walls—a work shed, a gate beyond the shed, a row of hedges on the opposite side that fenced a vegetable garden. And beyond that, free-roaming chickens and penned-in pigs.

I met the mission priest, Don Alberico, and told him my story and gave him the letter from Doctor Castellano. The priest said I was like John the Baptist and asked if he could feed me wild honey, teasing me as there were no plump locusts to offer. He conducted me to my new quarters, a room with a bed, a desk and a chair, a crucifix on the wall.

My journey here had been waylaid by magical incidents, others tragic. I was taken in by German nuns, Buddhist nuns, and a family of weavers; each time questioning myself every place I stopped. Where does one begin to stop blaming herself for all the mistakes, accepting self-forgiveness for errors, for egotistical maneuvers? What made me dare to want more of my life? How would I ever find a sense of contentment again? Time was a healer of wounds, but as time passed, the idea of never reuniting with Giacomo in this life pitched me into a deep depression. And the gravity of leaving Lu and taking my daughter with me seemed to magnify. I still had not written Ping to pass on the news to Lu. Heartbreaking to think that Ya Chen's blood father never even knew she had walked this earth, and she never saw the beauty of his smile. Would he have forgiven me for losing Ya Chen?

I should have made the shorter, more direct trip from Hong Kong and gone northwest on my journey, but instead I went northeast past Shanghai, and made my way to Shandong. That was where I met the German Catholic missionaries. I blessed the Italian doctor more times than I could count for giving me the means to travel. Ah, but the heart has a mind and destiny of its own. I should never have gone there— why was I meant to meet them? Only days after I left, these nuns were murdered. That would have been my fate too—why was I saved and the sweet nuns brutalized by my own people? It seemed there were insurgents everywhere, ready to take up arms against the innocent merely because they are foreign. Resentment and hate are brothers.

I went to Shanghai right after that only to become embroiled in Germany's understandable umbrage at the incident. Germany reacted by seizing and occupying Qingdao, which seemed like pure insanity—a foreign power's excuse to invade.

In Shanghai I found work as a maid in a German doctor's home. I learned of the terrible floods in Shandong, immediately chased by severe drought. These natural disasters were ascribed to the intervention of the devils who spoke foreign tongues, whose terribly lofty churches hid and diminished our skies. But more horrible than this news was reading about the massacre of those sweet nuns in a German newspaper in Shanghai. Everyone must die, but torture was the evil invention of sick minds.

I couldn't stay in Shanghai, despite the generosity of the Frau and Herr Doktor Deutsch, and I scrambled away, taking the travel route I originally intended and finally arriving here, asking myself why I was made to see all these horrors. *Why did I suffer all of these losses? My penance?* I unpacked and immediately began writing in *Nüshu*.

Why do I document? I record to analyze, to help me fathom the dark tunnel from which I am still extricating myself—crawling out of a thin eggshell like a baby dragon, though haphazard emotions hinder progress. There must be more to my life. There has to be laughter and love and greenfields at the other side, hope, too, and life renewed, perhaps even the thrill of excitement in knowing I may play an unexpected role in our changing society. Though, not for a bracelet of jade, can I think what it could possibly be. My moods vacillate. The extreme highs border on hysteria, and my lows are the basest loss of human hope.

Why chronicle this life? I write this history for so many reasons, but now one of the most important is to communicate with my Ya Chen in the afterworld, and to set my thoughts on paper for Giacomo. So strong in my wanting him, I feel Destiny will grant me this. I cannot believe he is dead. My heart pounds when I think of him. Lu lied to me. How did Giacomo get to Guilin?

I want to leave a testament, for anyone who cares to read it at the end of my wretched life. I write now, a silent amanuensis, as if my Ya Chen's spirit whispers in my ear. Had she but lived awhile longer, I would have taught her this women's script and perhaps to draw.

My thoughts are of my eternal love for Ya Chen and Giacomo, sorrow for my unborn baby, but they are also concentrating on this dragon that I draw. I give him the nine characteristics he should possess—a camel's head, horns like a deer, eyes of a hare, ears of a bull, an iguana's neck, a frog's belly, the scales of a carp, a tiger's paws, and eagle's claws, capturing perfectly the large canine teeth in his upper jaw, the trailing, vine-like whiskers, which extend from both sides of his mouth. My mind's eye sees him use these as feelers in the bottom of muddy ponds. I paint the short and longer spines along his back and his twisting tail greenish gold. This long, this mighty dragon, has wings at the sides to walk on water—if only my little one had had this ability, I would be teaching her drawing instead of weeping over it.

I am a sleepwalker across time. My body moves me to the unknown, this mission place, comprised of outbuildings, a spirit screen, a school, a church, a garret on top of a storehouse, a dormitory, a nurse's lodgings, a kitchen, a laundry, all housed under skies the color of my father's eyes—but grief is a wily cur strapped to my back. At the spirit screen, I resign myself to my fate.

At first the monastery reminded me of a school I had attended in Guilin with the nuns of the Sacred Heart—high gray walls, summerhouses dotting the landscape, a lake with a statue of Saint Michael the Archangel in the center. I felt as though I was stepping back in time. It had been my father's choice, naturally. I had known safety there and have the same feeling here.

Yesterday, an unseasonable rain reminded me of the typhoon in Hong Kong. Afterward, the stars came out, and in a pool of collected water in the path, reflected from up on high, I saw my history mapped out as a tiny constellation—would that I could see the future.

Then last night I dreamed of a mandala. Ya Chen centered it, holding a mass of bloody rags I recognized as the ones on the cot at the factory. I awoke shaking and thought of the old man who tends the pigs here, Yang Zhugong, because the mission people say he's somewhat of a sage and interprets dreams. The thought of dealing with someone as unclean as a pig-keeper, a butcher, a slayer of animals, repulsed me, but am I any better, a slaughterer of children?

The pig-keeper's hut at the back of the compound faced the cookhouse, covered with bluish purple wisteria. I stumbled on some of the wisteria roots toward the unclean one, and thought of turning back, but something drew me to him. I found him napping in the shade of a lavender crepe myrtle's wide canopy near a wayfarer tree with its green leaves and ripe purple berries mixed with red—colors I will use to paint another dragon. I wondered how the crepe tree would look in the fall when the leaves range in color from yellow to orange and red. And then I thought of the large clusters appearing on the tips of new branches beginning in early summer, continuing into fall. After the flowers fade and fall from the tree, fruit remains in the form of small brown capsules. These fruits last throughout the winter. Will I still be here then?

With my mind jumping like a frog, I glanced at Yang Zhugong sleeping in a chair, his open mouth, a net for flies. The pig-keeper's view on the other side of the quadrangle that included the outer buildings was a lush garden of magnolia, azalea, dogwood, and walnut. I wanted to sketch this vegetation that envelops the mission, so serene, a peaceful haven from everyday life, or perhaps a promise of the afterlife.

He awoke as I approached, even though I walked as if on goose down.

"I was only thinking with my eyes closed," he said, his wizened face benign.

I bowed and after pleasantries to show respect for his age, I told him my dream.

"Red is significant and auspicious, is it not?" I asked.

"Seeing a mandala in your dream," he said, squinting his eyes against a ray of sun filtered through lacy flowers, "means positive changes are occurring, a waking life."

"Can you tell me more?"

I watched him stifle a yawn. "A mandala symbolizes wholeness, unity and healing—" he started to wheeze and then coughed. He spat in the grass. When he regained his composure, he continued, "Also spirituality and harmony." From a pail at his feet, he scooped water into the hollow of his hand and drank. "Sorrow and death, the affliction of ill health— the common denominators of life—levelers that make men equal. You suffer a loss and must heal from it. The mandala is one way. There are others, like *qigong*, which you must know."

I nodded, knowing the ancient art. Before I dropped a coin into his aproned lap, he said, "Yet another powerful way to seek heaven's forgiveness is the path of humility. You have taken a big step coming to see me. Fear not for your daughter accompanies the unborn one's spirit."

An image bolted though my brain—my little girl holding bloody rags. Surprised by his keen awareness, the coin slipped from my hand.

He bit the coin and slipped it into his pocket. "Snuff is the stuff of the mandarin. Opium suits my pipe." He patted his pocket. His hooded eyes drooped with age. He smiled then, as if we shared a secret, opening the orbs so I could see yellow liver spots and what seemed like an opaque film. The smile touched my heart, and I saw him as a young man, virile and full of wiles.

I sat in silence with him awhile. His lusterless gaze reminded me of the blind woman who taught me the art of massage. My father asked her to instruct me because she was renowned for her soft strength. She never went too deep or too far, muscles sang to the tune of her touch, and so recalling, I offered my services to this bent old man. When I touched his skin to work his gnarled and twisted sinews and tendons, I controlled the urge to wince and closed my eyes, the way I was taught. We set up another appointment in a few days. I was pleased to think I'd humbled myself enough to touch an unclean one.

Who am I to judge this old man after all I had done? Who can say what reduced him and brought him to this low station? How much of life has his body known? Thinking thus, I bowed to him.

He must have read my thoughts for he said, "I was not always a keeper of pigs."

I walked away yearning for something sweet like lychee, and at the thought of its white meat, my stomach groaned. The farther I got from the old one, the more desirous of sweet—unlike this bitter, lonely existence without love. A vacant compartment in my heart ached for Giacomo to complete me. I wanted us to be like my parents, a world unto themselves.

◆➤⋇◄◆

LATER THAT EVENING THE WEATHER turned cool and gray. Arriving at my empty garret, I lit a lantern. And then another. A timbre to the brightness, a seemingly different glow, flickered disquietingly like my heart, hungering for something steadfast, someone to love. Sitting down heavily at my desk near the opened window, I looked toward the foothills and above them the mountains sheathed in snow. After a while, I closed the window and gazed about. Now at night, with lamps glowing, this sad, little house became a heavenly vision, a wayfarer's dream of respite. What better way to celebrate this night in the safe comfort proffered by the light than to drink a cup of *cha*. Yet I felt strangely anxious. Instead of green tea, I decided to make some *pai mu tan*, white tea leaves, knowing their peaceful effect. I took a spoonful of the leaves that had been dried in the sun, not the usual process for teas, especially green. I steeped these in the kettle of boiling water on the wood-burning stove, watching the steam rise above my cup and wishing for a genie to emerge on top of it; all I got was its fragrant bouquet, and this alone calmed my agitation. The steam caused me to picture early-morning mists in Fujian Province, where coolies pluck the leaves from the *chaicha* bushes, also known as narcissus.

My elusive thoughts ran along forest edges and were hard to grasp, but here and there traces of me could be seen. *I am like the seasons. In time I hope to bloom here during this spring, loll through the languid summer heat that will transmute chill into autumn, soon cobbling space for winter, each season ceding place.* The still night air, tinged honeysuckle, hinted at change. The tea was insipid and by now cold, so I tossed it out the window. How easy that was—I wish all troubles and woes could be thrown to the winds.

THE NEXT NIGHT WARM WINDS blew sweet caresses. I listened at the open window to a chorus—a steady buzz of cicadas and cricket chirps—reminding me of Guilin and my walks in the woods, though the man holding my hand was not Lu, but Giacomo. How the mind is a monkey, always grasping.

I prepared a pot of hot tea—this time I used jasmine, so richly perfumed, I wanted to eat it with a spoon. I poured my cup half full, watched the steam's swirl above the cup until I was almost hypnotized, and the tea no longer hot. In the leaves, I saw five moons, and each held a dragon. What did it mean? When a jewel-wet pre-summer day ends and the night sky's moon voice can be heard, it tells me things I want to hear, but seldom believe. I closed the window and slept till early morning.

I brought unguents and clean sheets with me to visit the pig-keeper. When I began to manipulate the deep tissue of the old man, I was surprised at the strength and suppleness his muscles still possessed. We didn't talk; between us there was a vibrant communication. After half an hour he raised his hand. "Enough torture for one day. Come again next week, and I will speak to you of all your heart needs know."

That afternoon I returned from a place adjacent to the lake called Quail Hollow, but should be called Duck Hollow, as there are many in all seasons. There was a mamma mandarin with a brood of ducklings tramping with vengeance the damp earth of the river's shore. How I'd love to carry off a brace but can't bear the idea of depriving her. They are primarily herbivores, though occasionally they eat worms and snails. My father told me in captivity they eat acorns.

We had been sitting by the Li River one day after rain upon the high grass made a summer sigh, when my father and I saw the dabbling ducks, as he called them.

"What does 'dabbling' mean?" I asked.

In his reflective tone, he said, "They feed by upending themselves to reach water plants with their bills. The mandarin duck is the only species that cannot interbreed with other ducks due to a different number of chromosomes." He explained all the articles he'd read about this. "My friend Walther Flemming studied genetics observing salamander larvae."

My father had a photographic memory and lest he give me the entire text, I asked him, "Do ducks mate for life?"

His smile was impossibly sad. "If the partners are still alive through a second season of mating, they will choose each other again, rather than seek new ones. If the mate dies, the remaining duck will wander far and wide in search of the other."

Thoughts of my father filled my mind all day until early-evening shadows stole into the courtyard and I once again picked up my inkstone and brush.

> *I paint the dragon the colors of the carp and set him down to head my chronicle in hopes of better understanding myself. My people, Long Tik De Chuan Ren, are descendants of the dragon, divine mythical creature that carries by nature: ultimate abundance, prosperity, and good fortune.*
>
> *I am Chinese, and therefore essence of dragon, for I, too, possess some of his traits, though sadly not all. Here, I name his characteristics: power and excellence, valiancy and boldness, heroism and perseverance, nobility and divinity. I am not noble, nor divine, but human with frailties, yet I, like the dragon, fight to vanquish obstacles until I succeed. And not unlike him, I am energetic, decisive, optimistic, intelligent, and ambitious. I know this because I am like my father, who was not born Chinese, though he owned our spirit.*
>
> *I chose a difficult path when I left my husband, one that brings unimaginable sorrows. I suffer now from guilt washing over me like the waters that drowned my daughter and cannot shake my splendid obsession, Giacomo. How different my life would be if only I had been able to see him, to tell him that I carried his child.*

His followers called the saintly priest, Don Alberico Crescitelli, by his Chinese name, Guo Xide. He sat with me outside the kitchen one day. I broke down this name for him so that he could fully understand it. *Guo* meant eaves, the roof structure of a house. A common name. *Xi* meant west and *de,* morality. Under the roof the Western morality, in his case Catholicism. It took me awhile before I could refer to him as Guo Xide.

The man tried, and continued to try to succor me; I felt like a lost soul for certain. Where was the optimism of my youth?

He lit a pipe and asked me about my beliefs. I told him my faith in a higher power, my Buddha, wavers like flickering candlelight about to be extinguished. Indeed a lost, dark soul. His answer was, "Pray, child, and I'll also pray."

"In my own way, I do pray."

"You speak excellent Italian," he said.

Once again, I bask in the musicality of Italian. "My father used Latin words to speak of drugs and Western medicines and taught me his beautiful tongue."

"Where was he from?"

"Chiasso," I said.

"Ah, so he wasn't Italian as I presumed."

"Swiss. Canton Ticino."

Sometimes just hearing the priest speak was a balm to this sinner's soul. He bade me good day, and I watched him walk away in his flowing black gown. He moved with a great deal of energy in his cassock and skullcap, and middle years would not be upon him for a long time. I noted he had new facial hair like a Mandarin. He stopped, stood in an oblique position to a little girl, shadowing her as he leaned toward her—a tall, leafless man-tree blotting out the sun.

I HAD NOW ASSUMED THE duties of teacher, a role I enjoyed. I sometimes did the shopping. The cook or one of my students would accompany and help me, but not today. I was grateful for the buzz and hum of the market—the criers bartering, mountebanks screeching, children crying, animals aflutter, squeaking, squawking, howling, barking, yipping. Dizzy but enthralled to be caught up in the melee—how alive and frenzied it all made me feel. At the market, there were all manner of things my purse did not open for, but just seeing them reassured me maybe I was still meant for a purpose; though I couldn't think what at present. My eyes feasted on sesame, fish, snakes, turtles, dogs, peanuts, plum and black bean sauce, orange peel, shrimp paste, tea, *jiang*—soy, and fragrant things such as garlic and ginger and pretty things like flowers, even bonsais.

ONE DAY WHEN I CAME back from shopping, I met Don Gabriele, Guo Xide's assistant, who told me Guo Xide had gone to speak with several of the chief imperial civil service Mandarins nearby.

"What about?" I asked, but received no answer. My arms ached with the weight of the two baskets I carried, filled to overflowing with fresh vegetables—scallions, leeks, taro root, tiny aubergines, snow peas, water chestnuts, bamboo shoots, *mu-erh,* wood ear mushrooms, ginger, puffy watercress, star anise, bean sprouts, cabbage, lotus root, and tofu. Gabriele took the baskets and deposited them in the kitchen. The cook needed all of these items for *pengtiao*—cooking. All the mission's meals were based on the belief of *pan-cai. Pan*—grains such as rice, staples, starches, and *cai*—meat and vegetables. *When did this need to dissect words begin?*

Light disappeared and evening drew close. Although I should have felt cosseted and comforted by the sights and smells, I was ill at ease. Nearly being run over a dozen times by bratty boys, ringing their chorus of bells as they darted by on bicycles, made me feel hunted. The mission village bustled with activity—I had to weave in and out between rickshaws, horses, and carts. In that frantic place, I stopped myself from the urge to pitch my body in front of a swift-moving vehicle. I wanted to die but didn't wish to remain a burdensome invalid needing care. One minute I was in the world so vibrant around me, and the next I wanted to be a spirit on the other side.

THE COOK AND I PUT the food staples in the cookhouse, and now unburdened, I told Gabriele I decided to take another stroll. I had just passed the spirit screen and saw Guo Xide had returned from his discussions with the Mandarin. He was across the inner courtyard, coming out of the chapel. He must have been in there talking to his passionate Christ. Guo Xide is often on his knees. I've even seen him prostrate with his arms out like the crucifixion tree, a tree with a bar on top, his body mimicking the cross on the chapel. Christ and cruciform.

He has told me there is forgiveness for all because Christ suffered and died for everyone. Ah, if this priest could absolve me for the life I am about to take. No one would miss me, but would I be forgiven? I am courting Death, which will bring me to the afterlife, but will my ghost wander earth forever? Shall I never know peace? I am already repenting my suicide, though still seeking a method in the wakeful hours before dawn.

When I asked Guo Xide if he was content to do God's bidding, if he felt this was where he should be, he was fond of saying, "My heart tells me I am where I belong, where God wants me, and I am happy." Such a blessed man. So lucky. To be sure, to feel positive, like my father—the priest knew that his work had value in this little microcosm, and was important in this dragon country, this gigantic world. What must it be like to be certain of everything?

❦

THE OTHER DAY DOTTORE CASTELLANO'S warning of peasant uprisings rang in my ears. There had been fighting in the park near the marketplace. He mentioned it again in his letter of thanks for the money I'd sent to repay him for his loan. He wrote to tell me he'd mail my letter to Ping so she could tell Lu of our loss, but at the same time, Ping wouldn't be able to reveal my whereabouts. Castellano reiterated that these incidents of revolution were occurring more frequently—animosity toward foreign missionaries was prevalent, but now was directed toward foreigners. I thought of the German nuns. Here in the mission, nothing troublesome had happened . . . yet. The doctor noted clashes in cities on his travels outside of Hong Kong were intensifying, and he didn't like to travel unless he was escorted in the company of someone Chinese.

Until now these brutalities had remained outside our compound. Peasant uprising had increased and there had been fighting in the park near the marketplace, only about one *li* from here. Closer. They seem to be getting closer, I told Guo Xide, but he merely smiled, living up to his ever-growing inscrutable nature, his Chineseness.

Yesterday, a group of rowdy children pelted him with rotten vegetables in a side street off the market. The good priest unhitched some tethered ducks on the point of strangulation. The children didn't see it this way of course. I found out later. They told Cook their parents had left them in charge of the animals and cautioned them not to let them wander off lest they be lost. Guo Xide's interference was not such a grievous event, but harsh feelings against him seemed to be sprouting up here and there. Instigators said our missionaries were rapists and fornicators. I'd seen none of this, but was alert. My people are a violent lot. It's the nature of the dragon. Even though some Chinese had accepted Christianity, others were not receptive to Guo Xide's teachings and were indifferent, even hostile to him and the other missionaries' efforts to convert them. Nevertheless he continued catechizing, giving aid, teaching agriculture, and buying land for the poor and the mission, but for how long, I wondered.

I want to practice medicine, yet all I am is a lowly schoolteacher, who on occasion shops for groceries. What good am I here to these children, to myself? I might as well not exist. At times, in wakeful daydreams, I trip backward into a well, falling, falling, but never reaching bottom.

Chapter 12

Ma
马
Horse

DAWN, JANUARY 3, 1898

GIACOMO HAD JUST BROUGHT TEA up to the bridge for Lieutenant Rinaldi, Ensign Bartolo, and Bulldog and a bowl of milk to the cat, the ship's mascot. Giacomo peeked over Bulldog's shoulder as he wrote in the log: *Niúzhuāng*. He asked Giacomo to write in the Chinese name. Copying from a book, Giacomo wrote 牛庄. Bulldog finished the entry. Ship's location: northwestern segment of the Liaodong Penninsula. Left bank of Daliao River. To the west, Liaodong Bay on the Bohai Gulf of the Yellow Sea. He closed the log.

"The cat's nervous," Bulldog whispered to Giacomo. It may have been superstition, but the cat's weather forecast, always right according to Bulldog, predicted major warning signs, almost as good as the ship's barometer and anemometer. Bulldog reported to Lieutenant Rinaldi.

"If we become locked in by heavy weather, sir, the ship could not make way—we'd be engulfed in an ice storm." Bulldog turned aside and sneezed. "Excuse me, sir, I'm allergic to the cat," he said, and waited.

Rinaldi agreed they should get underway before getting blocked in a freeze but had to consult the captain. He picked up the cat and headed out the door.

The weather came upon the ship early and though Bulldog had predicted it, the brass dragged out discussion time instead of prevailing upon the warning.

A half hour later, Captain Morante, nervous and jumpy, walked in barking inconsistent orders and left. The men, perplexed, looked at Lieutenant Rinaldi, who said, "Relax, men. The captain is under some stress and unused to these situations. Carry on. Bartolo, come with me."

As soon as they left, Giacomo told Bulldog that the lieutenant, an academy man out of Livorno, had practical experience, more than the captain, and was also familiar with the Orient. Heading to the galley, Giacomo said, "Many Italians aspire to the *Academia Navale,* but even testing for acceptance has to come from a political nomination."

"I heard entrance as a plebe was like sucking a raw egg though a pinhole," Bulldog said.

"Cadet Rinaldi was fortunate a senator recommended him to the Academy. Rinaldi's father was straddled with another debt of gratitude that could ruin a man with debt."

"If the upper echelon doesn't know how to cope under the frigid circumstances, then how are we, brother Giacomo?" Bulldog said.

"Non lo so, I don't know. I've never felt such intense cold."

"But we have common sense. Let's compile a list of tasks to manage with the situation." Bulldog took hold of a loose sheaf of paper and wrote. He was the most-traveled and seasoned sailor, handy at dealing with improbable situations. His greatest fear was that this ice storm might not be the only one, and perhaps the ship could be marooned here for the rest of winter.

Before the storm hit the *Leopardo,* Bulldog began to prepare himself and warned Giacomo what the frigidness would mean, telling him of an intercepted message between a German freighter and a Russian trawler; both ships were apprised of the extreme conditions in arrival, and therefore were heading south. Lieutenant Rinaldi set up a rendezvous with the Russians. They stopped long enough to exchange three bottles of vodka for five kilos of potatoes, a liter of wine, and one of olive oil. The Germans dashed off after they relayed the message.

Later, Bulldog accompanied Shen and Giacomo to shore to lay out the supplies needed to offer warmth: French cognac, rice wine, and Tsingtao Chinese beer. They bought all kinds of dried foodstuffs to last: beans, fruits, nuts, bean curd, rice noodles, vegetables, dog ear and other mushrooms, and hot peppers. Plus staples like salted fish and dried duck gizzards.

By midmorning, Giacomo had bought three pigs, slaughtered them, and told Shen to coarse-grind meat for sausage. Giacomo used the pig intestine as sausage casing, remembering how his mother made it with fennel seed, and dried the links over clotheslines placed close to the furnaces. Task finished, he and Shen baked several loaves of bread, some left warm and cooling, others toasted for a kind of hardtack.

Giacomo and Bulldog managed to get hold of a good quantity of food that wouldn't spoil and put it in a storage closet, a room near the captain's quarters. They traded goods with neighboring ships heading for Macao: bullion, covered teacups, and extra drinking water to which they added a small quantity of Eau de Javel, a weak solution of sodium hypochlorite bleach to sterilize it. Giacomo took Shen into the bunk quarters below deck, which was totally against regulation—fraternizing of sailors with the Chinese had to be sanctioned by the officers.

Giacomo strung a third bunk between theirs—a hammock for the boy, currently sleeping on the floor among the Chinese aboard—while Bulldog and the two stalwart sailors, Di Luise and Manetti, retrieved the stores from the tenders and organized and laid in extra gear: matches, coffee, tea, water jugs, blankets, wood piled under the sailors' bunks.

Giacomo realized there would be insurrection, and perhaps even desperate measures taken by the men if any remained without provisions. He hid two handguns and bullets in the wood encasement flooring underneath his bunk. Giacomo talked of probabilities with some of the other men, including rather than excluding them. He handed out lists of things Bulldog said they'd need and told them to do it quickly, even if it meant using their own pay.

Giacomo hammered on extra Dutch stable locks, to which he held the keys to all three: the pantry supply, the stock room, and the galley. Next, Rinaldi called the carpenter on the horn radio speaker from the bridge and had him install another door in front of all these facilities with the addition of other locks. When the doors and locks were in place, he handed over an extra set of keys. Rinaldi fondled the keys, shook his head, saluted, and dismissed Giacomo, muttering his thanks.

"Where'd you get the locks?" Bulldog asked Giacomo, walking away from the bridge.

"In an open air market in Pechino. Never dreamed I'd have to use them onboard." Suddenly Giacomo was awash in memories of shopping with Lian. On one of their early-evening walks, they had passed a street peddler and Lian had bargained with him to purchase these locks for a pittance.

Bulldog jabbed Giacomo. "Eh, wake up—where are you?"

"In Pechino."

"With her?"

"No one else for me."

"No time for this now, *fratello.* I'll spread the word among our bunkmates to store extra blankets, clothes, food, burners, wood, and anything else they might need to live throughout several possible weeks—"

"Perhaps even a month. I'll find Shen."

Shen, fleet of feet, refused no order and complied with every request. Besides all of the things he was asked for, he thought of a few more important rations and supplies and stockpiled them also. Shen told Giacomo that like the Chinese, each man should have his own chopsticks, plate, and cup and be in charge of keeping these utensils clean.

Lieutenant Rinaldi stopped Giacomo and told him to see the medic before going ashore. Giacomo finished putting away tools from the galley and skipped downstairs to speak to the medic, who wrote a list of medicinal supplies, including opium. Giacomo gave this to Bulldog and Shen, waiting by the skiff to go ashore.

Giacomo realized the captain was stunned into a stupor, a kind of dormancy, when Giacomo suggested other ideas to his superiors—some of which they didn't see the need for. Therefore Giacomo went over the commander's head, on the brink of mutiny, adding extra things they needed to do for the safety of the men and ship. He recognized the captain's torpor, so Giacomo approached Ensign Bartolo, enlisting his help.

Ensign Bartolo agreed with Giacomo and gave the order to have the men strip their bunks and wash the soiled sheets at once to hang in the boiler room to dry. This would be done in shifts—the same for showers and haircuts. Bartolo recruited two men who grudgingly went to assist in the laundry and two more for the galley.

Giacomo held out two aprons to Di Luise and Manetti. As chief chef, Giacomo intended to make a number of baked and cooked foods with a design to last—pickled eggs, pickled pigs feet, foods stored under vinegar or spirits. When he saw the look of desperation in their eyes, he gave them each a swig of port to sweeten the work detail.

The afternoon darkened, the temperature hovering above zero degrees Celsius, not cold enough for snow or freezing rain. A constant drizzle made the overcast sky bleak and dreary.

With Bartolo's authorization, Shen, Manetti, and Pillari manned the galley to make huge pots of soup so that Giacomo, Di Luise, and Bulldog could make another shore trip. The skiff moved slowly in the churning waters, whipped by wind and now a sudden rainsquall. They docked, made their acquisitions and returned to the skiff, loaded and took off. By now the temperature dropped, the rain turned to heavy, wet snow. Within minutes of shoving off, the men felt the frigid air accost them; now dense snow whirled about, settling heavily, covering them and the equipment under tarps.

"Not letting up all night," Di Luise said.

Bulldog answered, "Not if the temp keeps falling—"

"Can't wait till we see the ship. With the extra weight we're moving like snails!" Giacomo yelled above the motor noise and the howling wind.

Bulldog said, "Me too, my hands are ice."

"Switch places with me," Giacomo said. "I'll take the rudder—you stand. Put your hands under your armpits. Do knee bends. Move up and down—don't rock too much or we'll tip over." As they switched positions, winds beat the water till it sloshed into the boat.

"*Merda,*" they all said at the same time, and laughed.

"Hey, Giacomo, light up ahead, see it?" Bulldog said, doing knee bends.

"Where?" Giacomo squinted.

"10 o'clock. Ha! We made it to *casa Leopardo,*" Bulldog said.

"Hate to disappoint you. Flag's German." Di Luise lowered his binoculars.

After a while Giacomo and Bulldog switched places again, trying to follow the coastline, until they came into sight of their ship along with the bay's waters. They pulled the skiff over, starting to offload heating supplies, kerosene, alcohol, and matches, logs, and tinder materials for the two wood-burning stoves purchased that week. Close to suffering hypothermia, they left the gear and skiff in the hands of Chief Petty Officer Bigo and Manetti, who Giacomo acknowledged with a pat on the shoulder. Lieutenant Rinaldi told the three of them to report to sickbay and barked orders at Bigo and Manetti to secure the tender and get the gear.

They stripped and wrapped themselves in blankets. The medic gave each man a tub of cold water to soak their hands and feet in, and when their hands had thawed sufficiently, the doctor checked for frostbite. The medic gave them hot coffee. Shen said he had some strong medicinal Chinese herbs to put in their drinks. As he poured from a small flask, he winked at Giacomo, who understood before he tasted that the coffee had been laced with brandy.

"Nothing like Chinese herbs to warm you. *Bravo,* Shen. *Cin-cin, mates.*"

THE BIG FREEZE OCCURRED DURING that night when the men fell into their bunks exhausted, and early the next morning, the captain decided to get underway but had delayed too long, thinking the weather would soften—it was early for this kind of cold, but now they were ice prisoners. He had miscalculated the fickleness of weather.

The captain had Bulldog try to contact a Russian trawler in the vicinity, in hopes they'd be able to break up the ice. But the Russian "scout-about" had left the area, heading south.

The long days of captivity gave the men excuses for fights. They bored easily and weren't used to so much free time. A ruckus broke out at a table of men playing cards. When the argument ceased, someone called out, "Hey, where are you going, Scimenti? Want to ante up some of your stash?"

"Another time. I'm in no mood for a fight," he said, and beat a retreat for his bunk.

ON A NIGHT WHEN GIACOMO felt that a distraction was necessary so there wouldn't be a series of mishaps and arguments, he decided to entertain some of the crew with more of his life's story before China. He always thought of himself from a long line of *cantastorie,* oral storytellers and ballad singers.

A few men gathered in the mess hall and the galley was shut tight. Pillari, Manetti, Shen, Bulldog, and Lieutenant Rinaldi sat with their tea, and Giacomo continued the story that Shen had begged to hear. Soon some of the other men drifted in, cold and bored.

Shen went from the mess to the galley to make tea for the new arrivals, asking Giacomo to speak louder till he could get back to the table.

"*Va bene,* Shen," Giacomo said. "I will."

The men hushed and Giacomo couldn't help but think what kind of adolescence Lian had before he spoke of his own.

He looked around and then began his story again.

Six months after the new teacher arrived, I began to understand the difficulty of adolescent years, endured yet often not understood. As my gangly arms shot past my sleeves, I suffered embarrassment and self-consciousness whenever in the presence of adults, but most especially my father.

Don Stefano, unwell, became more intolerant of my fidgeting. One Sunday as I stood in front of him tugging at my sleeves, hoping they'd stretch to cover this new growth, my father's cane flew through the air with a swish that ended in a whack. The cracking sound of wood upon my knuckles made me flinch, but even if my face contorted with pain, I stifled the cry. The garbled sound pained me more than the whack. Pointing with his black ebony cane to the fuzz on my upper lip, my father said, "What's this?" I hated his goading. Maybe I even hated him.

Giacomo stopped talking and looked around the room. On many of the men's faces, there was a look of understanding.

Shen grew impatient. "Please more."

Giacomo looked at the group and began again.

I despised my brother Neddu for having given the ivory-handled ebony cane to our father . I couldn't master the feelings of guilt that accompanied the intense dislike I felt at times. But I never confessed, not to my priest, not a whisper to God.

The sturdy cane separated into three parts. The swivel silver handle, the embodiment of Don Stefano himself, was a lion head displaying fierceness in its open mouth. The top of the head lifted to serve as a snuffbox. If the whole head was extracted, it became the hilt of a deadly stiletto. The second section, divided by a thin gold band, unscrewed to reveal a hollow to conceal a rolled document. The cane had been the property of an Italian dignitary in the court of Vittorio Emmanuele I, *Rei di Sardegna,* during the early part of the nineteenth century. It had been an anonymous gift to Don Stefano and delivered to our house by a Mafia *sotto capo.* My father used this cane on Sundays and holidays, to receive formally, or to pay a call. All of Carini and the surrounding towns respected him.

I wonder if one day I'll treasure his cane, not for its elegant beauty, but as a reminder of where I've come from. My father had been in an accident on one of the trips he made to Palermo. He was thrown by his horse and walked with a limp from then on and always used the cane. Don Stefano, an excellent horseman, never spoke of what happened or why he had been thrown, but I knew that my father did not fault the steed, or he would have shot him with his *lupara.* His horse had to be re-shod by Enrico Mancuso, Father's friend, a man I worshiped.

The following afternoon Mamma said, "It's getting cold. Come away from the window. I feel the humidity in my bones."

"It's going to rain, neh?"

"Ah!" Mamma said. "When I was a girl, I'd walk in rain. Here, I've something for you."

I opened the package. Two new shirts. It wasn't even my birthday. I thanked her and we sat by the fireplace. She closed her eyes as if to hear better the fat raindrops pelt the green leaves of her garden and her youth.

She pointed out the window. "I picked wild *finocchio* for my mother beyond that knoll. It's that pungent herb scattered along hillocks; we use it for *pasta con le sarde,* your father's favorite. It tastes like *licorizzia.* I leave the stalk and roots, nipping only the tender shoots."

She looked at her hands. "Some days my fingers are green from gleaning so much."

Without warning dark clouds gathered and the heavens erupted, splattering the windows.

"Rainy days when I was young, I'd whisk up my gatherings and dash to the olive trees."

"Did you get soaked?"

"Sometimes it'd turn so cold so fast, I'd run out from underneath the trees' cover to the trough where the sheep drank. There's a nearby cave, not unlike Le Grotte, where the shepherds took cover with their sheep—from what they called *tempo dei lupi*, wolf weather."

I remembered my struggle, negotiating the mud path to the cave at Le Grotte.

"Several times," my mother said, her voice sounding young, "the shepherds would build a fire, or give me bread and wine—"

"Weren't you afraid?" I pictured that night Ciccio had lit a fire for me.

"They were men of honor, indebted to my father."

I stared silently, watching the rain beat the green olive leaves, the shimmery undersides silvered with wet. "When the rain let up, you'd go home?"

"The weather's tricky, sometimes the sun shone while it poured rain—the old ones say that's when the devil's daughter is marrying. Occasionally it'd turn so cold, *grandine* would fall heavily."

"Hailstones?"

"They crystallized over the whole area—a blanket of frozen bubbles."

"Cat's eyes. Like marbles. I didn't know you loved hail, too, Mamma."

"Funny, I knew you did. I also know you snuck out last night to go to Enrico's. Don't make that face. I couldn't sleep until you came back. Do you know what time it was? This is not child's play—it's dangerous to meddle in things you don't understand."

"I risked a punishment for a friend whose life is in jeopardy. Babbo says he's a marked man. I had to warn him."

"God forbid you saw something you weren't meant to see. You'd be hunted and killed for it. You've gambled your life and may be in great peril."

A log crackled, and another crumbled, splintering into coals. Mamma threw another piece of wood on the fire. She sat down again. "I'll tell you a story about your father. You do believe your father is a brave man, don't you?"

I nodded in agreement.

"One day when you were about six, he was coming out of the *pasticceria* near church. A man yelled to him, 'Don Stefano Croce, this affair doesn't concern you.'"

Mamma took a deep breath and sat up straighter. "Shots rang out, so your father, brave but not stupid, covered his face with his hat and crossed the church steps, never once looking in the direction of the massacre that took place in the piazza by the fountain. When he was questioned by the *maresciallo,* he answered truthfully: 'I saw nothing.'"

My mouth fell open.

"Now tell me exactly what you did."

"I went to Enrico Mancuso's stable, but his house was dark. I banged on the door and then went around to his window. It was open. I climbed in."

Mamma gasped. *"Mio Dio."*

"Enrico wasn't in his room or anywhere in the place. I didn't light any lamps but waited till my eyes accustomed themselves to the dark. I waited a long time and must have fallen asleep. I awoke with a start at a scurrying mouse. No one saw me come or go. I'm sure."

"You cannot be certain, foolish child."

My mother's voice was dead calm, worse than if she'd raised it in anger.

After a small silence, she said, "The walls have eyes as well as ears. That house was surely watched during the night. I could tell your father of this incident, but I choose not to because you, my son, will tell him yourself the minute he walks through that door." She indicated the living room door with her chin and gathered her wool shawl about her.

Later I confessed to my father; I shuddered at the news he gave me.

"Sit down, son," my father said. "Two days ago Enrico's mule was shot out from under him returning from Partinico. He's not dead, but this was to scare him. Someone wants to warn him. *Mi capisci?"*

My brain wouldn't work, so I shook my head.

"An attempt was made on Enrico's life today. Someone tampered with a cart axle he was fixing. As he pushed the wheel in place, the axle rod gave way and crashed. He saw it coming and jumped out of the way in time. A warning, sure as a kiss of death, but unheeded. We make our own destinies. Enrico is a marked man. You're forbidden to go with him anymore on his forays away from Carini. Understand?"

I nodded but decided not to tell Enrico I could no longer ride with him. Instead I promised myself I'd learn to shoot. I couldn't ask my father or my uncle to teach me, so the logical person was Enrico.

"Vendetta," I said to Enrico. "Someone's seeking revenge on my loved one." He would keep silent, although he assumed it was my father; so began my shooting lessons. I became accurate but not fast.

Days afterward, my father returned from the fair at Salemi. He came upstairs to find me reading and said, "Clean out the farthest stall. An animal is being delivered today. Get to it."

Delighted with my father's return, and even more at the prospect of a new animal, I was less pleased with my chore, but obeyed. This new responsibility was a notch in my maturity belt.

I pulled on a warm lamb's wool sweater carded from my uncle's sheep. I opened the stable door, stamped my feet, and heard mice scrambling. When the daylight hit the rump of a magnificent saddled Arabian in the last stall, I swallowed hard. A lump rose in my throat. I yelped for joy.

Walking over to the horse, I spoke gently to him and stroked his neck and breathed soft words in his ear. I led the beauty out of his stall with a halter and lead line and then bridled him. I patted his mane, mounted him, and with a wild hoot, cantered down the road and out of sight of my parents, who stood watching their son's antics from the living-room balcony.

I returned in twenty minutes, ashamed I hadn't thanked my father. Flying up the stairs, I reasoned, the horse may not even be mine, but it must be, dear God, it is! It has to be!

Once more at the dining table, I threw myself at my father

who laughed. I didn't thank him, and he never said the horse was mine. We separated from the embrace, he with pride in his eyes, and me with constrained love I'd learned from him. Then my father recounted how at the fair, he'd bargained well. The Arabian stallion and saddle brought over from Libya.

From that day on, the horse received the finest care and regard of any horse in all of Sicily. I brushed and combed him once a day and gave him exercise, fresh water, hay, and oats. Sometimes I'd bring the horse a special treat such as an apple, or a carrot, or a sugar cube.

I never let the horse, Liberty, graze when I took him out for a ride, only rarely on the way back home. I was determined to be a good disciplinarian as well as trainer and believed I possessed a combination of both qualities—heart, and awe of nature and animals.

Summertime, I rode bareback, but for long distances I'd saddle the horse, taking a small, rolled blanket and a shepherd's cape, which I tied in front of the pommel. How I loved this horse and spent hours honeying him with sweet talk, currycombing his coat till it shone. The small Arabian, alert and quick, had tiny ears that indicated danger by pointing upward.

In order to strengthen the horse's ankles, I rode him on the beach and in the surf. At dawn or at dusk I would leave the saddle, blanket, cape, and horsehair wine pouch filled with fresh water on the beach, strip myself, and ride him into the surf. I loved to watch the sunset, silvering the ocean with a wide streak of dying, reflected light. Some days, I felt I could walk across that path to the end of the world and see God.

At fourteen, I no longer stood in awe of my father as a god but realized he was a man, quite fallible, and capable of making grave errors. I learned to respect him as head of the household and family because of his honorable nature. My growth was not just physical; I underwent emotional development as well. Adoration and fear blended into admiration and trust. My love was reciprocated, and I began to understand Don Stefano was incapable of demonstrating outward affection.

The night before my sixteenth birthday, I dreamt of Enrico

and realized it had been two years since his pet *assino* had been killed. During breakfast, I asked my father if someone would wait that long for revenge, and he answered there are men who wait a whole lifetime for the sweet taste of revenge.

That last day in May when school let out for vacation was the end of my formal schooling. I was tired of the taunting from boys, ridiculing me because of my height, a head taller than the tallest boy in my class. I'd been in more fights and lost all my battles. I handled myself awkwardly. My schoolmates considered me a weakling. I was thin, carried the girls' books, and was even guilty of being an excellent student. Now my gangly arms and shoulders showed signs of flesh and muscle. I was proud to know Babbo had procured me a job with the *pannetiere,* which would begin in a month's time.

After school I had to face a heckler who pestered me. "Fag can't fight, eh, coward?" Words I hated. Someone lunged at me. No escape. I defended myself, but was thrown off balance by a rash, uncoordinated swing and miss. I lay on the dusty ground. It wasn't the smash, or crunch-of-hand's punch that made me wince with pain and brought angry tears, but the feeling of impotence in self-defense and a year's worth of pent-up frustration. I tasted blood mixed with the salt of tears. Blinded for a moment, fear of losing sight made me react, and I was at my stunned opponent who flailed backward as I heaved him off me.

I knew I'd caught him by surprise and relished every punch I laid into his bloody face. The boy, pinioned with me on top of him now, screamed for mercy, but my ears were deaf. I gave no quarter, and the boy's pleas and cries went unheeded.

Victory and a sense of power surged through me. I could have killed him by cutting off his windpipe and was about to beat him senseless when three boys dragged me off. No longer would I suffer the torments of hecklers. The boys hauled me from my victim. One sat astride me and held my arms to stop any possible further damage to my enemy. They now understood I could fight. I swung and kicked with determination. Finally they quieted me and I stayed on the ground in exhausted pleasure and relief. I'd gained the respect of every boy in attendance. A freckled-faced kid helped me with my books, patted me on the back, dusted me off, and asked if I wanted company walking home. Not one of my peers from Carini or anywhere else from that day onward ever dared call me a name, least of all a coward.

Giacomo stopped his story for a minute as he glanced around the room and heard some of the men mumbling. He knew they'd lived similar experiences and his victory in the fight was a triumph for all of them. He continued.

I was black and blue and bruised when I walked through the kitchen door. The housemaid's hand flew to her mouth, and she stifled a scream when I warned her to hush by putting a finger over my sore mouth. I recoiled and fell into a chair.

Anna winced as if she, too, were in pain and then moved to the sink. She wrung out a towel. How comely—slender waist and breasts the size of *tarocchi* blood oranges.

Bulldog cleared his throat. "Uh oh, here comes the mushy love stuff. I don't think the men can take it, Giacomo—why not tell us instead why you joined up?"

Giacomo looked around the room, thinking about how horny some of these guys were and said, "You're right."

Only Shen disagreed, but he was overruled.

Before Giacomo continued speaking to the men, he was awash in memories. As he cleared the table of cups, he recalled how he'd sulked for weeks until the day when he was deflowered, losing his virginity to the family maid. He remembered how glorious it felt to be a warrior, come home battered from a fight, and conquer a lover in the same day. He had long awaited the moment to hold a woman in his arms as he'd often fantasized in his dreams. Before dinner Anna took the wash out in back of the house, sheltered by a thick grape arbor. There, helping her with the laundry, they ended up in a tangle of sheets, and he declared himself a man.

And now all he desired was Lian. Lian. Lian. He wanted her the same way his lungs sought air to breathe. He wanted her the way she was for the time they were together—her innocence and beguiling ways enthralled him.

He deliberately forced his thoughts in another direction, came back to the table, and said in a dreamy voice, "Enrico's story . . ."

My father's horse had to be re-shod by my friend. I loved Enrico more than my father. Every day I walked passed his livery stable and cart workshop. Sometimes I helped brush the horses or did some odd jobs for him. He owned a new *assino* who constantly nibbled on something. Enrico often frolicked with the donkey, demonstrating what the animal was capable of doing in the right hands.

I had seen Enrico's brute force and vigor exhibited many times. Once I saw him, single-handedly and with outstretched arms, hoist up the wheel of a *carretto* and place it on its axle rod.

I remembered my father saying, a man with such power is said to have been born with a *coda*. A tail. The men of Carini swore Enrico had such a tail. My father's words came back to me. *"His super-human strength is ox-like, due to his tail."*

How does someone grow a tail?

I held my breath until Enrico finished securing the wheel. The scent of horses and smoke from searing metal mixed in my nostrils. When I stood near Enrico, human sweat commingled with the other odors, vile but virile. I closed my eyes and listened. The hammering became louder, the blows intensified. A lifetime from now, I knew as I lived and breathed, that sound would conjure up the memory of that morning. And I was right.

That day, against my father's wishes, I rode to Partinico with Enrico. He ordered wine to be hauled to his home from his uncle, a Mafioso big in stature and position. When the deal was concluded, Enrico strapped two raffia-covered bottles over the hilt of his saddle, saluted his *Zio*, and mounted. I did the same.

When we climbed down from the hills and were outside of town, Enrico unhitched a bottle, uncorked it, and took a swig.

"Mmmm," he said, "here, taste some. It's a nice, aged Muscatel." He passed me the bottle. I sipped gingerly, sputtered and coughed, and gave it back to him.

"Ha! I forgot to tell you, it's close to eighteen percent alcohol. Good, eh? Tomorrow you lunch with me, and I have some biscotti you can dunk in the *vino."*

We crossed a stone bridge over a swift-moving brook. Enrico pointed. "My uncle's son hung himself from this bridge."

I felt a chill. "Not a very happy place. Why did he kill himself?"

"He was my cousin and a good friend." He looked over the side.

My horse started to pull at some grass. I yanked up his head.

"He couldn't be the man his father wanted him to be."

"You mean like him?"

"Una vera disgrazia. A disgrace. Be your own man, Giacomo, no matter what."

After a while, I looked back over my shoulder as if I knew by instinct this place would hold more significance. As we rode, I remembered the story of what I'd overheard two years prior in the piazza in front of the bar.

It had been inclement weather, so the men gathered inside to play *briscola.* Coming out of the bar, after a particularly lively win, my father and his brother Luca discussed the game. They stopped in the middle of their laughter, their mirth interrupted by a small man hurling insults on none other than Enrico, the *carrettiere.*

Don Stefano turned to his *compare* Enrico and whispered that the man was obviously drunk or out of his mind and not worth spit. Enrico could squish life from this insignificant worm, who tried to block Enrico's step. The giant brushed him aside with one swat—a careless gesture at an annoying fly. But the slap proved too much of a blow, knocking the screeching creature off balance, and he hurtled to the ground. Now the horsefly was enraged, his insults and the thudding sound of his fall hung in the air. A wary onlooker, a stone's throw from Don Stefano, appraised the situation, walked quickly past Enrico, pretending to accidentally brush into him, proffering him a weapon. The practiced movement didn't escape my father. The man muttered in a hoarse voice audible to Don Stefano, "Kill him, you fool."

With that Don Stefano raised his chin toward the barman, grabbed his brother Luca by the arm, and steered him back inside and told the owner to turn out the lights.

But Enrico couldn't hurt God's tiniest creature and was incapable of snuffing out this miserable one's life. *"Meschinu,"* Enrico said. *Meschinu.* Wretch. An insult men killed over. Enrico laughed his hearty, good-natured laugh, flashing a boyish grin. He tossed the weapon to the ground next to the vile, pitiable being. "Take it or be gone, pest."

My father and Uncle Luca continued to talk in hushed tones in the library. Within earshot of the closed door, I dawdled as if about to re-enter on the pretense of a forgotten book, when I stopped stone-still, my hand on the doorknob.

"Too many witnesses," Don Stefano said to Luca.

"He signed his own death warrant, you know that, don't you, Stefano?" Luca said.

I leapt back from the door at the cruel words, but who? I envisioned this beloved but fool-hearty friend lying in a pool of his own red blood. That night I'd snuck out to warn Enrico.

Enrico couldn't hide the truth from his trusted friend Don Stefano. They discussed it into the early hours of dawn, in the upper sitting room of the Scimenti household, and Don Stefano learned what no other man knew. Except me, who'd listened through the room's fireplace flue. Enrico confided he was a condemned man, yet no vengeance could be extracted on his assassin, and this he resented more than his own demise. Who was this insulting little bug, or who had sent him? Enrico didn't know for sure.

Then nothing for months. Exactly twenty-four of them.

Continuing on our way back to Carini, somewhere after getting the wine in Partinico, and somewhere near the fateful bridge where Enrico's cousin had hanged himself, I dropped my knapsack and called to Enrico, "I'll ride back a little to find my sack."

"Va bene."

"Wait up for me." I turned Liberty around.

"Meet you at the next turn," he yelled over his shoulder, never stopping.

I looked back, but he was gone from sight. I rode on till I saw my sack and stopped to pick it up when I heard a crack rend the air, and I looked skyward—a hunter? But then another, and there were no birds in air nor thunder.

By the time I wielded the horse around and reached Enrico, he was dead.

"It's late, gents," Giacomo said. "Time for more another night. Or maybe someone else would like a turn at spinning yarns."

Everyone cleared out except for Bulldog. When the door closed, he said, "Convenient place to stop, my friend."

"You know?" Giacomo asked.

"I can guess, but I'd rather hear it from you."

The first shot killed his *assino,* but the second blast tore through his back and killed him. The murderer must have been hiding ahead behind some umbrella pines fairly close by. He must have thought that Enrico was alone or I'd be just as dead.

I jumped off my horse as I approached Enrico's corpse. He'd never had time to pull his *lupara* from its sheath, but I did. Dropping the sack, I mounted and galloped Liberty into a sweat. I didn't have time to think. I sighted his killer, riding breakneck speed toward Partinico. The rifle was in my hand. I raced after Enrico's killer. I slowed from a gallop to a canter and then to a trot. I hopped off the horse, dropped on one knee, and took aim. Too far. I mounted again and rode like fury. Way past the bridge now, just before the horseshoe turn toward the hill, I was about to overtake the man. I yelled *"Aiuto! Aiuto!* A man's been attacked and killed, can you help me?"

"What? Where?" Ciccio turned to face me. He looked at my face, trying to place me.

"Here, you fucking coward." I raised my loaded *lupara* from the hip, and with those words sent him to hell as I blew away his face with two blasts.

My horse reared, but I gained control and though I was shaken, I never stopped moving back toward where Enrico lay dead in his own blood. Breathless, I tossed the rifle down, slid off my horse, and went into the brook. Cupping my hands, I drank in huge gulps until I choked. I cleaned the rifle, reloaded and placed it back in Enrico's sheath. I cut a leafy branch from a bush and swept away any prints Liberty and I had made. The horse stood in the brook, drinking.

I kissed my friend's forehead. *"Addio, amico mio."* Walking backward, I swept away the marks. I entered the water, stood on a rock, and mounted Liberty. We rode in the creek for a few kilometers, slowly, lest the horse go lame. At some point, we came out and trekked home.

Father and I were in the same room where Enrico had called himself a dead man. Now he really was, and my father told me he'd heard that Enrico's donkey was shot from under him; he knew death was pending. What did Ciccio have against him? Was he just a hired killer? Whatever Enrico's secret was, it was his now, forever.

"Why and who?" Don Stefano asked. "I'll never know. Some farmhands discovered his body, his face distorted with pain."

What I wanted to know was why there was no news of the other murder. Who knew about it? Who had covered it over?

"The second shot blasted him in the back," my father said, standing by the fireplace.

"It's rumored he didn't even receive *un colpo di grazia*. Laborers found him in a field of poppies near a bridge on the road from Carini to Partinico. He was probably on his way to see his uncle." But I knew better—it was on the way back from Partinico. He was going home.

My father's face was grim. He poured himself a drink and gave me one, and I thought, *How ironic*—the same Muscatel Enrico had given me to taste.

"I've been impotent trying to save Enrico's life. God forgive me," Don Stefano said.

I felt the same hopelessness. I had relaxed my vigil, and Enrico's wariness had made him careless. I drank the wine, looking into the flames remembering what my father didn't know. I had been a witness to Enrico's death.

"Nothing anyone could do. Enrico was alone. A target," my father said.

I stared at the sparks in the hearth, but my eyes were like stones, unflinching and lifeless, until a solitary tear escaped the rim of my right eye while my father patted my shoulder.

"Will they get the killer, you think?"

"Someone avenged Enrico. The police are investigating," my father said.

"You mean the assassin had a judge and jury?" My thoughts ran rampant. How long until someone discovers I'd been with Enrico? Climbing the stairs to my room, I wondered, *Was I a dead man if I stayed?*

The next day, I stood in front of the same bar in the piazza where Enrico's troubles began. Plastered on the wall was the death notice of my beloved friend. I traced the large white rectangular paper with its black border. Climbing chrysanthemums spiraled upward, curling around the entire edge. Chrysanthemums. There was a medallion at the top amid the floral pattern. The center picture was of Christ crowned with thorns. My eyes rested on the broad, black print letters of the message. So great was my disbelief, outrage, and confusion, I reread the notice:

AFTER A BRIEF ILLNESS ENRICO MANCUSO HAS BEEN TAKEN FROM THE AFFECTION OF HIS DEAR FRIENDS AND RELATIVES. THE FUNERAL SERVICE WILL TAKE PLACE ON THIS SATURDAY, THE EIGHTH, AT 10:30, LEAVING FROM HIS HOUSE IN VIA PALERMO TO THE PARISH CHURCH AND FINISHING AT THE LOCAL CEMETERY. SINCERE THANKS ARE EXTENDED IN ADVANCE TO ALL WHO PARTICIPATE.

On a crisp afternoon when leaves were gone from the persimmon and ripe fruit burdened the trees, and once lush, green fields had turned a dun color, Enrico was laid to rest.

Dreams haunted me. Every chore I did brought visions of that fateful day. News of the investigation of the assassin's death carried the rumor that there had been another rider with Enrico. I panicked. How long before some detail of my ride with Enrico leaked?

From Carini the sight of sea usually calmed me. I gazed despondently, knowing I had to leave. The distance to the ocean was twelve kilometers, and I rode the horse along the dirt roads where carts had made their grooves. The roads curved until the sea surfaced, almost touchable.

The day the newspaper quoted Enrico's uncle, saying he was sure another man from Carini was with him, I turned my horse toward Palermo. To the docks. To the naval office.

I'd always loved the sea and heard stories of my great-grandfather being a sailor. I decided that was the life for me. I wanted to see exotic places and travel the world. Since I was under age, I'd need Father's permission. There must be a way around that. I looked much older because of my height, so I chanced luck and entered the Navy's enlistment office.

The sailor in the office somehow believed I was old enough. He said, "Address?"

"What for?" I asked, looking around the room that needed a good painting.

"We can't take a chance of giving you these papers to take home. Forging papers is illegal, yet it happens all the time. We'll send them to your home. To your parents."

I was on the lookout for the official envelope and took it the day it arrived, filled it out, and sent it back. I picked up my uniform two days after that. I thought of all the sins I'd committed in the past two years: lies to my parents, the pretense of going to confession and then receiving Communion afterward. Ticking off my sins, including the forgery and the murder, I decided to cleanse my soul before going overseas. On the way home from Palermo with a parcel containing my new uniform under my arm, I went to church in Carini.

I confessed to Don Ruggeri, expecting him to be stern, even angry because of all I'd done. But the priest received me as a long-lost, repentant soul who'd now make reparation for his sins. In an odd way, he seemed pleased to know that Enrico's death had been avenged.

Don Ruggeri said, "Go, my son, and sin no more," and I asked if my secrets were safe.

"Remember I am first, last, and always a priest, bound by the seal of confession. You know what that means, my son?"

"You're obliged never to speak of what I told you."

"I'm glad you're enlisting. Are you sorry for these and all your past sins?"

"I am, Father." There seemed nothing I could do about them but ask forgiveness, though I knew in my heart it would be impossible not to sin again.

I made the sign of the cross in unison to the priest's blessing, "*Te absolvo, in nomini patris, et fili, et spiritu sacnto, amen.*"

Outside of the confessional, I invited him to dinner to break the news. My parents couldn't make a fuss with Don Ruggeri present.

How misguided I felt when my disclosure of enlistment blew up in my face. Don Stefano raised his cane and beat the table thunderously. The stemware shook. The china rattled. Neither my mother nor the priest could stop him when he raised it again over my head and cracked it in two. I was dumbfounded. Yet the good priest had not divulged the real reason for my departure. My mother succored me, but fury brought tears to my eyes and, for the first time ever, I left my father's table without permission.

In the predawn light, in my smart, new navy blues, I hugged and kissed my mother. She cried and begged me to ask Father's forgiveness before leaving for God knows how long.

"Maybe someday, Mamma, but not this day."

"He could die, never to have known you sought amends."

I shook my head.

"I could die—don't break my heart, Giacomo."

I felt my heart freeze in the doorway. "Mamma, I could die too—"

"God forbid!"

"It's part of living. It's got nothing to do with the fact I'm his son or he's my father."

"He loves you." She brushed back hair from my forehead.

"He's never voiced it to me, and I'm not sure I love him. Until now, he's always had my respect. Our future depends on his ability to bend, but not his cane over my head."

Mamma touched my head.

"Ouch," I said, when she rubbed the bump. "I've got to go, Mamma."

"For my sake, son, find it in your heart to forgive him. Where will you go?" She reached into her skirt pocket and pulled out some lire bills, but I bent her fingers over them. "Take it. You may need it," she said.

I couldn't see how much it was, but I knew my mother only had petty cash. "Where did you get this?"

"Never mind." She unclenched her hands.

"How did you get it? I don't want his money."

"Do this for your mother," she pleaded.

I closed her fists around the money, took her hands in mine, and kissed them. "Do this for your son."

"I can still see her look." Giacomo raked his open fingers up and down his forehead and then buried his face in his hands. After a while, he looked up again, glad to see only Bulldog.

"And after that?" Bulldog asked.

"I sailed around Europe and then I was on my way to the China Sea, and I'm still here to help quell the Boxer Uprising. But I sure can understand why the Chinese hate us. Who are we to come in here and tell them how to run the place?"

Chapter 13

She
蛇
Snake

I HAD BEEN DEPRESSED FOR a long time—ever since I left Lu and could not rid myself of the scenes of repeated defiling violation with him—and have been craving death, as someone desires a lover. The assault tainted and stained me forever. How would Giacomo ever be able to love me, touch me, if by some miracle ordained by the heavens we were to find each other again? I obsessed over it days upon days, long into the nights. Impure thoughts upbraided me for weeks and months now that I was alone to contemplate my inner being. I also dwelled on my failure as a mother, falling into a deep well of sadness that even Guo Xide could not pull me out of—and then I read in the paper of a suicide. When one wants to die, only a method is necessary. The afternoon wind had blustered and a storm raged. The evening grew frigid, and one always seeks the comfort of hot things on cold nights. The idea of simmering and stewing came to me, the thought of preparing soup soothing. There was a bouquet of large white chrysanthemums in a vase by the statue of the Immaculate Mary in a niche in the kitchen. I bowed to her, asked her permission, and then took one of her flowers to make a fire pot. Nothing happened, so I knew she was not angry. She is much like Kwan Yin.

I began to peel, to slice, to cut, to chop, to dice, and then I stopped, fascinated with the object I held. For when one wants to commit suicide, there's nothing stopping them, except means, and once it is found, one can succeed. I looked at the sharp paring knife; the glint of it in the candle glow seduced me. There have been stories of daughters adding their blood, even flesh, to broth to give strength to a dying mother, but never had I heard of a mother adding her blood to a pot to raise a child from eternal sleep. A frisson of terror and a rush of insane glee took hold of me.

As the blood spurted and then poured with steadiness from the gash, I watched it flow, catching some in a cup. I thought of my red wedding veil, which oddly reminded me of my blue bridal jacket, which should have been red. Perhaps that is why the marriage failed. How disingenuous of me to even think it. I heard a gasp and realized I was not alone. Wo, one of the students, had come in from the cold, holding her cup to ask for hot tea, and to see if she could assist me. There was a crash, and as I started to pick up the pieces of her cup, I knocked over the one catching my blood, splattering it on the wall and floor. She screamed and ran out the door. The freezing air blew in with ferocity. The door banged and banged against the whitewashed wall, now spattered scarlet. Stunned due to the loss of blood, I didn't have the presence of mind to either cut my other wrist or close the door. I tried to sit in a chair by the table but missed it and ended up on the floor.

Guo Xide's puzzled face seemed to glow above me, the light and steam circling a gold halo that spun round his head, like Mary's statue in the niche.

"Lian, Lian, oh, my dear God, Lian, what have you done?"

Nothing. Nothing at all. But my lips could not form the words.

I AM NOT DEAD, I repeated to myself over and over when a few hours later I awoke in my bed fully clothed, a bandage on my arm from elbow to wrist. A kindly, old doctor I recognized from town ministered to me like a clucking mother hen over a newly hatched chick. The room reeked, permeated by a thick odor of some healing herbs my mind was too foggy to recognize. When my eyes focused, I looked into the smiling face of the doctor, who was dressed in a gray robe with matching beard and who wore a black silk hat.

He placed his hands inside his wide sleeves and bowed quite formally.

"Doctor Wu, at your service. You fainted. At first when they told me, I thought you were expecting a child. But you were merely foolish with a knife."

"I . . . I . . ."

"Do not speak now. Time enough later when you explain yourself to the priest and his God. Here, drink this *xi hu long jing.*"

"Dragon well tea?"

"Just green tea, but you could use a bit of dragon." He held the cup for me.

I sipped. "I should have cut both—"

"What good? You went into spasms with only one cut; with two, you would have doubled the spasms, but that's all, pretty miss."

"But the blood loss—I could have died hemorrhaging if Wo had not come."

"Hush. You could have accomplished nothing. The blood flow slows down. The priest told me you are a nurse and must know there was no danger of your dying."

"Oh, why didn't I disembowel myself? Stab myself in the heart or slice my throat?"

He put the cup on the windowsill. "There can be only one embarrassing answer. Ah, I see by your tears you have guessed. You did not want to do away with yourself."

"Yes, of course I did, but I'm a coward. I have lost everyone I love. My child and her father. How then would I have dared end my life? Hang from a tree, a Judas to my daughter? Or drown myself? Too unworthy to die as she did."

"Your daughter? The child is gone?"

"*Wo de tian.*"

"My heaven, indeed."

"You cannot possibly understand. It was my fault she died. I want so much to die too."

"Oh, but I do understand. You are not a candidate for death . . . yet. In any case, if you were really serious you could have eaten raw opium like Mangen's mother."

"I considered it, but I could never—it's only for the brave of heart. You know Wang Mangen and his family? He's one of our best students. His mother's dead?"

"They moved to the country afterward. The father remarried. A harlot. Mangan is a child too smart for his own good. Rest now. Here, drink more tea. I've put in a draught I prepared. You will sleep."

Again he held the cup for me, but this time made me finish all of it.

"If you need me, send Mangen tomorrow. I pronounced his mother dead, so he knows my abode. But you, you will live, and once more will know the joy of carrying a child in your womb."

I was so sleepy I didn't argue with him, and I knew the tea had some morphia, made from the opium poppy. Opium. I must confess I'd shared a pipe or two with the pig-keeper. It gives you mental alertness, though it relaxes every bone, joint, and muscle in the body. My perception of ideas seemed flawless, and in this semieuphoric state I was not sad, nor did I see the need to take my life. It takes courage not to seek refuge often in the dream state that opium offers. After a while, though, I gave it up, afraid it would enslave me, and I have had enough enslavement for one lifetime. Gave it up, except for the slight lightness of being I received from smoke wafting from old Zhugong's pipe. However, I did continue to procure it for him, unbeknownst to Guo Xide.

◆━━◆◆━━◆

TWENTY-FOUR HOURS LATER, PROPPED up in bed, I read pages of my chronicle that I had written before the incident with the soup and knife.

> *I have always tried to pass for Chinese, though my eyes are as green as the lady slipper ferns Father pointed out to me in southern China. And when my green eyes turn emerald in surprise, anger, or rebellion, or with this great sorrow of my losses, there's never any doubt that I am the daughter of a foreign devil, my darling father. Often I wonder what shade my eyes were when my sailor kissed me in the garden, or when he took my maidenhead, or rather when I willingly surrendered my virginity. Where is his spirit now?*
>
> *I never discuss my true background with anyone for fear of ostracism and alienation. I want to be Chinese, after all I live in China. But Lu's mother knew the truth, and let me know that I could never be good enough, never pureblooded enough to satisfy her.*

Lu and I married and I thought perhaps good fortune was finally coming my way as I teetered on the brink of pregnant spinsterhood. There is an ancient saying, "Good luck seldom comes in pairs but bad things never walk alone."

I put down my book and closed my eyes, better to recall the events. When I had recuperated, I paid my respects to Doctor Wu, who had cared for me. When I returned, I was fearful Guo Xide would ask me to vacate the mission because of what I had done. I didn't know then how forgiving his nature was.

❦

FALL GAVE WAY TO WINTER, and I repented my attempt at suicide and even did penance. For weeks, I scrubbed floors on my knees. I cleaned urinals. I washed Guo Xide's bed linen and hung it across a cord line in the cold air. The smell of clean sheets was heaven-sent, but when the crisp wind beat upon them, they whipped themselves up into ghosts, fringes straggly as unkempt hair. One day, I took several steps backward, the crunch of hoarfrost on spikelets of dormant grass made me jump, for the steps seemed to be coming toward me. *Foolish girl,* I chided myself. Who could it possibly be? Trying to relax, I bent my head back and rubbed my neck and shoulders with my eyes closed. I felt as though I were stepping off the edge of the world and losing my balance. I opened my eyes to catch the whirl of eddying clouds form chariots and dragons in the sky. Dragons everywhere. What kind of divination was this?

That winter morning, I took down the wash with chilblained hands as blood oozed from the cracks of my skin. If I got blood on the sheets, my work would be for naught. I went to see what the cook had in his stores, and since he wasn't there to control my peeking around, I hunted in his herb cabinet and discovered black sesame seed oil, almond oil, rice bran oil, grape seed oil, evening primrose oil, corn oil, peanut oil, and fish oil. Last but not least and behind all the others was some camellia oil, and this I poured into the new cup Guo Xide had given me and mixed it with crushed juniper berries. I left without having disturbed anything, quite smug at having duped the old windbag cook.

Afterward, in my room, I ministered to my hands and bandaged them with light gauze, so that I could iron all the altar cloths. Yes, none other than my own sinful hands redressed the chapel. Yet no task distracted me. Nothing brought peace of mind because my mind could not still itself, and one thought nagged: *'unsuccessful' in my attempt to end my life.* The doctor was right. I yearned to live. Longed for health. Had I not proved this by taking care of my hands? Oh, wretch of a wretched, self-indulgent creature.

❦

LATE IN THE SPRING SEASON, I mourned my daughter and unborn child officially with the pig-keeper's help and with proper pomp and circumstance. Time flew backward, a butterfly flapped, a typhoon surged. I wept for the baby I'd washed away and wept because I would not be able to wash my Ya Chen's body nor dress her in a costly white dress, and though I could burn incense, it would not be near her bier. The worst part was to know that her ghost swam the waterways, sucked away in the thief typhoon . Maybe she will encounter her father as he sails in China. Hong Kong. How I despise that city, its name, its founders, its demography, Mount Victoria, Aberdeen, the bay—name anything about it, and I loathe and abhor it, am repulsed beyond measure. Who is responsible for dragging the child from her safe, natal home? How can I put my daughter to rest with hate in my heart? A daughter who never knew her real father. I will seize strength and cast these self-absorbing, negative thoughts aside and concentrate on small details. Step by step, I will walk a Calvary of my own invention.

It was almost night—a husky hour, neither a yell nor a whimper, but a backroom murmur like the Dragon and Tortoise Sailors' Club in Hong Kong where I'd looked for Giacomo when I'd heard that an Italian ship had docked. I washed and with each ablution, I cleansed my mind of odium, thinking only of her grace. I put on white silk pants, a hand-me-down gift from Wo's mother, and pictured my child's smile. I donned a white blouse—a buttonhole like the dimple in her cheek. Then I tied my hair with a white bandana—reminding me of her glossy hair whipping across her face as she ran toward me, her eyes shinning and full of glee. Full of love. Full of me. How will I go on without her? This has plagued me since I lost her. Forever lost.

I walked to the pig-keeper's hut and called out to him. He pushed back the beaded curtain that kept flies out. I took off my cotton shoes and entered. We knelt on a rush and mulberry mat in front of her picture—the one picture I had of her taken the day of the dragon races—such a shy smile and eyes like plump almonds. And so I lit candles and mourned my daughter. The pig-keeper had framed her picture for me, and he and I burned incense and joss sticks. I felt so grateful he was helping me grieve Ya Chen's passing at last. My thoughts were of Giacomo—if he had known of his baby girl, would he have forgiven me?

As I looked at her picture and attached paper money and gold leaf, the heavy scent of the incense assailed me. I concentrated on the soft lowing of the water buffalo nearby, the chorus of croaking katydids, the sultry breeze, scented night-blooming jasmine ruffling my hair through the open window, the glimmering candles, all making me drowsy except for the sharp taste of metal on my tongue. Was this metallic aftertaste when I swallowed grief for Ya Chen or fright for my own mortality? Yang Zhugong lit a fire in the stone-lined pit in the center of the hut, and I threw into it the doll I'd made for my Ya Chen, along with the only photograph of my daughter. In the blaze, my child's rag doll cried the torment I felt. I had nothing to burn of my unborn one, except the guilt I bore.

How many times did I say her name, adding "little pig" after it to hide her beauty from the gods, but they took her from me just the same. No matter. She will be with me always. As her picture burned I thought, *Have I not tucked the image of her face into the pocket of my heart? Who would dare remove it?* The heat spiraled with billowing smoke. I thought Yang Zhugong said, "Who would dare?" But it was only the hiss of the fire.

It was then I saw what was to happen. Through the flames I saw a vision of how I will cremate this dear, old man. I looked over at him once more, the tannic taste stronger in my mouth. Was it the tang of fear at having to let go of him too? In the curlicue of smoke above the fire, I watched myself mourn him also, yet without time to do so, touching his old bones, sharp sticks beneath the thin cloth of his garments, his skin papery and sheer, his veins showing through. He, content in death; me, miserable mourning him. I saw myself gather him into my arms grown strong from field labor, drag him to a funeral pyre, and heave him onto what would burn to become his shallow grave carved out with my bare hands. Covering him with the mulberry mat I have dragged from the wreckage of his hut—no time for ritual washing, no rites at all, nor even a quiet instant to bring him rice or mandarin oranges, or leave his pipe. *Where is his pipe?* I looked around to see, and through the wall, I found it smashed outside against the very hut we occupy now, crumbling like the pigpen. The loss of this venerable grandfather made me weep harder, giving vent to tears and grief now for both Ya Chen and him.

Then the smoke cleared and in the coals and ash I saw a future time beyond his death, the land surrounding the mission laid waste, but not by a host of scorpions or a plague of locusts, but scourged, burnt, and plundered by peasant revolt, an upheaval not of plowed earth ready for sowing, but of bloodshed and a carnage of human life.

The mission shivered like a falling horse in the dying flames. It was close to dawn. I decided to leave him at first light, but already he slept the sleep of babes, drunks, and old men—mouth open with an occasional snort—like one of his own pigs. Still. I will keep vigil for a while longer before returning to my empty room, save for the flitting hither and yon of ghosts.

❧

AT THE END OF TWO weeks mourning, I went back to teaching. I am suicidal no longer. Neither am I humble. One evening that spring after dinner Guo Xide and Father Gabriele, his faithful assistant, walked in the compound. The dusk light was a splendid array of pink and lilac and pearl-gray clouds interspersing a cornflower-blue palette of sky. Pointing to the sky, Guo Xide said that saints are somewhere up there, never to be seen.

"A word with you please, Guo Xide. Pardon us, Gabriele, won't you?" I asked.

Gabriele looked at him as if to say, *What does she want now?*

"Leave us, please, brother," Guo Xide said.

"Thank you," I said as Gabriele strode off, his gaunt frame a fleeting black crow.

I separated my feet and folded my arms, my actions slow and deliberate. I drawled out the words, "I know what I know and I know how to impart it, Guo Xide. Why won't you let me practice medicine?

Why must you call old Wu? What if there's a serious problem and you can't wait for Doctor Wu?"

"I can't. I'm sorry."

"Give me a chance," I entreated him. "You can't do it all. Look at you. The bags under your eyes are even empty of puff."

He smiled. "Are they?"

"Let me try. Please," I begged. How could he refuse?

His firm but gentle eyes said no.

"Then I must go. I'll leave tomorrow," I said, finality in my voice. "I serve no purpose here, and I cannot go on living off your charity."

"How can I replace you in a classroom?"

"That was my past life. This is a new incarnation. Believe me. *Believe in me.* Allow yourself to trust." I unfolded my arms and took a step closer. With clasped hands together, fingers pointing upward, I made a formal bow of obsequiousness.

His laughter filled the courtyard, but I had not won. "Oh, one thing before you go, Lian. Tomorrow we have a photographer coming, and he will take a picture of you and your class."

"Can I have a picture taken with Zhugong?"

"I must warn you about the pig-keeper. He is a louche individual, and full of guile."

I wanted to defend Yang Zhugong, but thought better of it because I was the one asking a favor.

"Lian? Did you hear me? You're not to spend much time with him. Are we clear?"

Without words of assent, I inclined my head. Clear, yes; compliant, no.

Ayii. I am like the pig-keeper, and had no intention whatsoever of giving him up. Guo Xide cannot read hearts. Though he said to me once, *"It is through the eye of the heart we have mystical sight for the presence of God."* I'd asked, *"The eye of my heart, or yours?"* I have more experience with people with the little I've lived than the priest. Not a conceit, but a truism.

In the evening I read passages from my writings. I wished to wrap myself inward for Giacomo, the words on the pages sympathizing with me, the familiar phrases comforting me, giving me relief from emotional pain.

❦

AT THE END OF THE summer of 1898, I finally received a new work status. I had taunted, teased, cajoled, begged, and promised Guo Xide till, exasperated, he finally gave in. *Vouchsafe,* a word I'd heard in his prayers, is the word he used to grant me what I'd wished for so long. Though I would not give up the chalk and pointer, I would minister to the sick. I made this chronicle entry:

> *Besides teacher and masseuse, I am now a nurse, a position I have longed for. And though I still pine for my Ya Chen, and love being around the little ones, it was the fixing of bodies that I longed to do. I instruct the children of mixed ages and classes in our small one-room school with a pot-bellied stove in the middle of it. There's a settle against the back wall. The children sit on it, and I store books and slates inside. The lessons comprise reading and writing in Mandarin—the children love things Chinese, are most open to studying these—lessons in mathematics and some geography—not just China, but also Japan, Russia, England, Austria, Germany, Switzerland, Italy, France, and the United States.*

Rumors were spreading and unrest among the peasants was becoming more frequent. There was a beheading in the public square near the market the evening before last. I had been there only moments before with two of my pupils yet missed it. To quell their unease, Guo Xide instructed them in religion, telling them Bible stories and somehow equating them to the lives these children and their families understood. He also taught them the holy Mass.

Today the children wanted gaiety, so I gave them a bit of a holiday. Don Gabriele met a sailor who had given him hard candies and said to distribute these among the schoolchildren. I wondered what kind of sailor and asked if he was Italian, but the priest thought he was German, well schooled because he spoke Italian. He was out of uniform and the priest didn't question him further, as he said he was going to see his sweetheart.

In this festive atmosphere, I decided to tell them the ancient fable, "The Cicada, the Praying Mantis, and the Sparrow." I began in a serious tone, "The prince of Wu wanted to attack the state of Cha ." Few Chinese girls were schooled so it was a pleasure to teach them. One little girl raised her hand and asked to sit on my lap. Could this mother's heart refuse?

Clapping my hands for attention, I continued, "A wise steward wanted to oppose the prince's decision, but he could not come out and say this to the prince. Instead he took a catapult and pellets and went into the courtyard where he meandered all around until he was wet with dew and became disheveled. He came back in the evening. The prince asked him why he was wet. He answered the prince, saying there was a tree in the garden and in the tree perched a cicada, and behind him was a praying mantis, and further back from his nest, the sparrow, never realizing there was a man with a catapult below and behind him, craned his neck to peck the praying mantis.

"The steward explained these small creatures are all so eager to benefit from what's in front of them that they fail to realize that the real danger lies behind them.

"The prince approved of what the steward said, and so the prince decided to relinquish his plan of invasion."

Why had I chosen this tale of precaution to recount on this day? Perhaps my subconscious mind was panicking at news of uprisings and beheadings.

Guo Xide brought a two-week-old Italian newspaper, *Corriere della Sera,* into the compound yesterday. I read conditions in China's big cities were frenzied and disorderly and lawlessness prevailed. Many had advocated change and new technology to enhance our resumption of Confucian tradition. Reformers argued in favor of Western science as well. There was a feeling of unrest among the farmers and peasants. I told Wang Mangen, who helps me tutor after school, about what I'd read in the paper. He was my best student, extremely intelligent, though he came from peasant stock. He sometimes demonstrated a haughty disposition, maybe because he'd never had a childhood and had severed every youthful instinct a human can possesses. It made sense when I recalled what the doctor had told me about his mother's suicide.

A few days after I gave him the newspaper, I had the opportunity to speak with him when his after-school lessons were finished. Wang Mangen. His name intrigued me. Of late, I analyzed everything. Words allured and fascinated me, and I discovered this need in me to learn more than just the superficial nature of things and names. Mangen had a common family name, Wang, meaning king, and being the youngest, was therefore Man, root of trees, male gender.

I admired his strength and, though he was lean, wiry, and tall, had a powerful mind and deceptively strong body. The children respected him, and sometimes when it was difficult for me to explain something, Mangen always had the perfect analogy, the exact expression, or the clearest metaphor to open a pupil's eyes, allowing understanding of a concept to flood in and water a kernel of knowledge.

Today I taught the class the proper divisions and nomenclature for the provinces of China. To help the children remember, Mangen took two strides with his lanky legs to the head of the classroom to lead them in a song, a mnemonic he'd devised. Afterward, he made a gesture with his head like a wiry colt, tossing back the hair from his eyes. He had deliberately cut his queue, letting the hair on his forehead grow out into long bangs. He created a poem for the class to memorize using Chinese characters representing a concept, an idea, or an object, as there is no alphabet in the Westerner's sense. Each province began a line of his verse. So clever, so much the dragon, though it broke my heart to see his contemptuous behavior with Guo Xide. Somehow I must find a way to convince the lad of the priest's goodness and pure intentions.

Mangen believed because Guo Xide was foreign and wore a cassock, he hid his true nature. I tried to dissuade him. On occasion when near him, I felt my heart totter on the verge of sadness, thinking my daughter might have been influenced by him and learned much had she lived.

When the schoolhouse emptied, I asked Mangen what he thought of the newspaper article I gave him. "Conditions in China are at an all-time low. Change is necessary," I said.

"Mmm," he said, gathering his thoughts. "I agree." He folded his arms and in some learned rhetoric he expounded a theory formulated by the bandits he'd been seen with. "We must borrow Western science and technology, but not the encroaching Westerners themselves, to supplement the revitalized Confucian tradition." He turned abruptly and began collecting papers from desktops and stacked them into neat piles on my desk.

"Reformers support demands for change by taking a pro-Confucian position," I said. His hooded eyes were difficult to read.

He gathered up some stray ink blocks and brushes from the floor and handed them to me.

"Defense of their demands isn't enough. Action counts." He scowled at me.

My thoughts took refuge in the pig-keeper, and I found myself wishing for opium.

Then Mangen continued with an edge to his voice sharpened by an unseen sorrow. "The arrogant behavior of foreigners stirs up hatred among many factions. There are Chinese splinter groups instigating unrest. This anti-foreign focus is directed at Christian missionaries' activities in the countryside. Soon there will be many groups—whole areas becoming anti-Christian."

"More like savage, you mean. I came from a mission where two innocent German nuns were killed, merely because their eyes didn't slant—"

"Neither do yours."

I threw some rubbish into the pot-belly stove, realizing he resented me as well. I closed the door and sat at my desk. "What about the educated Chinese?" I hoped to redirect his thoughts.

He leaned into his knuckles resting on my desk, his upper torso thrust forward, menacing. "Foreigners humiliate China and Chinese. Even the educated resent the condescending manner of the lowliest European clerk for he shows no deference, not even to our Mandarins. As we speak, northern peasants are galvanizing forces known to Westerners as 'Boxers' because its founders named themselves 'The Fists of Righteous Harmony.'"

"Insurrection?"

"Foreign powers are strong, but we gain in strength daily." He stood back from the desk but still faced me.

I thought, *Ah, and where is Gicaomo fighting now?* "Insurrection is a cultural happening in which people, like things, are increased or decreased." A bell rang, and I looked out the window toward the clanging.

He tried to gain control of his loud and pedantic voice, "History's timeline is a textural one, governed by people's behavior, their psychic strain, and the manner in which they live and die—a choice for valor to fight and defend, or for cowardice, to be lambs awaiting slaughter." He slammed the window shut. Was that his final punctuation to our discussion, which wasn't a discussion at all? He was giving me a lecture. His attitude irked me.

I shook my head. "You sound like a textbook—" I thought, *He's one of the difficult ones—the ones in need of the most love and tenderness, but unapproachable.*

"My own political perspective, Doctor," he said, disdain in his voice. "Maybe you need instruction in the ways of the world, instead of instructing these children the abacus and fairy tales. It would be wise for you and the priest to prepare for lean times and begin rationing."

"A threat? You speak as though we're about to be attacked, pillaged, and—" I cut myself short, seeing he was becoming incensed. I wanted to change the subject, but my mind recreated a scene from a few weeks ago when, charged with enthusiasm, Mangen had returned from a visit to his peasant father and stepmother in the north. Was he an insurgent, taking part of this growing animosity toward foreigners? I remembered my father reading me a passage from Dante's Inferno: "Abandon all hope ye who enter here." Was Mangen the devil's advocate?

"Do you think—" I started to say, but he broke in with fury, "Within months many secret societies will unite and this will no longer be a rumor, but fact. Economic hardship, anti-foreign feeling resulting from the activities of the Christian missionaries will increase atrocities."

"Or is this superstitious belief by the uneducated lower classes? Perhaps instigated by peasants?" I asked, anger escalating.

"Mark this word down in your notebook, teacher," he said, all venom and disrespect. Taking hold of the chalk, he scrawled the word *REBELLION* on the slate behind my desk.

"Rebellion?" He was an infiltrator who didn't support the mission.

"It's coming. Prepare for it. Instruct these children so they'll know how to conduct themselves. Don't pamper them because you're not doing them any favors."

I never dreamed asking this boy-man about an article in the paper would bring me such distress. But here I was, palms sweating, stomach tight. I stood to leave, hoping this would end the discussion, but he blocked my retreat. Stunned, I could only think of how well read he was and therefore had been such a great help to me up to this moment. He must have read the *shi*, poems from Shijing, the Book of Songs, from the Zhou Dynasty. From *A Soldier's Return*, "Picking Ferns," I began to recite,

"When away we marched
The weeping willow hung green
Now I return through mists and sleet, rain and sleet
Hungry, thirsty, with weeping in my heart
None can know my sorrow."

"War is no joy," I said. "There's no glory in blood and gore, dismemberment or suffering—only anguish burying brave or even foolish men."

Mangen's eyes could not meet mine. "Already our conservative dowager empress and other court officials are coaxing and encouraging the Boxers to attack foreign churches, and soon they will assault legations— take heed, teacher," he said his voice deep and low.

"Are you—"

He looked up. "Keep in mind a revolt spreading like pollen in springtime from Shandong across north China, to include—"

More like the sickness of pestilence, I thought, but asked, "Are you spouting the words of others? Is that why your tone is disrespectful and thunderous? Don't you want order for China, Mangen? To have a peaceful, good life?"

"China will never see peace again until the foreign devils who've disrupted our natural harmony have been eradicated—like this liquid you use to cancel out our ink scratchings." He picked up the bottle and hurled it, smashing it against the slate board.

If only the chlorine-based ink eradicator could cleanse this air. I breathed deeply. "No facile undertaking. It involves violence, bloodshed, death, and destruction. Let us not forget the fable of 'The Cicada, the Praying Mantis and the Sparrow.'"

He brushed past me, muttering, "You, too, big sister, are foreign."

Shock and disbelief did not make me feel relieved by his departure. I had been ill at ease the entire time, but hadn't understood how much until his slamming of the door. I unclenched my fists, nail imprints in my palms.

⊶≫⊷

THE NEXT DAY, I DID not see Mangen. Long after the end-of-school bell had rung, and late classes for slower learners were over, I still sat for a long time hoping he would come.

I wanted to ask Guo Xide to join me for a walk to the lake. There was a garden with a statue of Mary and three kneeling Chinese girls near a small pool of water. I thought of how in winter, scrims of ice would rim it, and that gave me a chill despite the warm air.

I walked past the pool, thinking of the pig-keeper, surely he would be able to divine my future if he watched my face as I looked into water. *I will ask the pig-keeper about scrying.* I remembered Lu's old grandmother and how she'd been able to scry into a bowl, or bucket of water, or even an upright glass mirror. Once, she'd read Lu's fortune in a puddle of spilled soup.

On the far side of this pool, I found Guo Xide hoeing in the small vegetable garden by the kitchen house.

"Would you care to join me now in a *passeggiata?*"

He looked up and smiled at me, a smile that read, *Now why would I want to do that and lose all this daylight?* He straightened, saying something like, "No, no. You go along now. A little solitude makes one introspective—it's good for the soul."

"It's not solitude I hunger for, but to pick some wild lavender to infuse in my honey." I wanted to inform him of yesterday's discussion with Mangen, but that would have to wait. One must pick and choose times for appropriate action. My father had this capability, and now I, too, needed to learn this. I had tried this tactic on Lu, but to no avail.

As I approached the spirit screen, I turned and called out to the bent priest, *"A più tarde. Ci vediamo.* We'll see each other later."

He stood and called out to me, "Until then, good luck, *zhu ni hao yun!*"

Odd that this man of the cloth should wish me luck in Mandarin, but this I pushed from my mind, not wanting to ruin the tranquility of the moment. I waved to him and took a winding pathway down to the lake. There were wild stargazer lilies that had been visited by musk deer, as there were tracks all around. And from what the deer left behind from their meal, gophers had gorged on. My father taught me that the lily exemplifies a large family of perennial herbs, including onion and yucca. These flowers were adornments for my wedding reception in my in-laws courtyard outside of Guilin. I should have anticipated bad luck with such an inauspicious beginning—I'd forgotten to remove the pistils and stamens, which gave off their pollen, staining my hands and Lu's coat vermilion.

A peasant in a straw hat squatted in the mud flats, his long bamboo fishing pole extended over the water reminded me of the last four lines of Wan Wei's poem, "Green Gully." He smiled a toothless smile at me and we exchanged pleasantries. I said his pose made me recall two things: an album leaf ink painting on rice paper entitled "Fisherman" and the artist who painted it, Gao Qipei from the Qing Dynasty. I told him I'd seen it in a picture book, and on the opposite page the lines of the poem, which I quoted to him:

> "My heart is free and at peace,
> As tranquil as this clear stream.
> Let me stay on some great rock
> And trail my fishing-hook forever!"

I asked him if he knew of the poem, and he said he might have heard it when he was young, that it sounded familiar, but perhaps it was a song he remembered, a similar verse that had been sung. But for certain, he'd never seen the painting.

He was a perfect picture. Oh, how I wished I could sketch him. And though he seemed pleased I'd spoken with him, his attitude among the freshwater marsh plants made me feel uneasy. I looked at the rushes, sedges, and tules. The verges of the marsh remained green until the seventh day of the seventh lunar month. Lover's Day. A quick slithering movement made me step back. I stood still, making sure no reptile lurked, then sought another path.

I walked beneath small willows—laden with catkins, drooping in clusters of flowers devoid of petals—wending my way past hibiscus, blueberry bushes, and the corkscrew unicorn rushes all along the water. They love water. Where was he now, my sailor, and upon which waterway? Blue and yellow flag iris, cattail millet, and water lilies surrounded me. I mulled over where I'd last seen these plants. In Guilin, of course, with Ya Chen.

Once I reached my destination, I stood behind a cherry tree. I found it difficult to breathe because the poignant vision shattered my sense of happiness, casting me into tiny frozen memories of Giacomo I was unprepared for, and fleeting thoughts I'd had of becoming his wife. When would pain diminish and memories fade like old photographs dimmed by summer light?

I straightened my shoulders and fought the urge to feel sorry for myself. How could I whimper at such grace, this gift of nature? Now that

I had mourned Ya Chen, I needed to finally mourn the loss of my old life, and find meaning once more. I peered through a natural trellis at what appeared to be a painting framed by a garland. The lake glimmered and beyond it stood a pagoda, and to the right of it, miniature people moved among a canopy of swaying trees. Other trees dotted the landscape in the distance small as buttercups and ferns. Many trees sprung up between a small cluster of peasant houses with thatched rooftops, smoke billowing out of them from unseen fires within, and all this encircled by delicate pink-blossomed branches I reached to touch. I inhaled a slight fragrance of redemption and relived a walk with Giacomo. Would I ever stop thinking of him?

I stepped away, tossing my gathering basket on the ground, and went rooting around with my stick in the higher brush, burdock, a tangle of weeds, and overgrowth. Ah! There. The sun began its descent, an orange ball falling into the lake, leaving a silver streak across it, where a cat's-paw ruffled the surface. I followed its line straight to a patch of lavender. With my knife, I slashed the stalks close to the base of the plant, and others I sliced at the top. I laid the pruned cuttings in my harvesting basket in a single layer, covering them with a cloth I'd embroidered with a crane and a pine tree—and the words *symbols of longevity in Nüshu.* I didn't want to crush the flowers, but keep their scent intact till I could use them later. With the flowers I would make lavender rice wine vinegar, use some for baking, and add a few to a salad.

I noticed a plant near the compound that my father had used to cure women's ailments. Its name was *sheng ma,* literally to ascend mother, but I had no use for it and kept to my path. I returned with the harvested flowers, made myself a cup of tea, and while it steeped, washed the lavender and set it to dry on rush mats. In a day I would heat some of the flowers and use them as an infusion, stirring them into honey. Then two weeks later I'd strain this. The rest of the flowers I'd set on cheesecloth above the honey pots and cover them with earthen lids. Each day I'd ruffle up the flowers and recover them until they were dried.

I drank my tea slowly and, when I finished, rinsed the cup in a bucket of water near the door. I dried and put away my cup and was about to go out, for the dinner hour was fast approaching, and I wanted to see what the cook had prepared with the fresh vegetables and some of the herbs I'd given him. Before I reached for the handle, there was a gruff barking voice on the other side of the door accompanied by loud banging.

Guo Xide called my name as I jerked open the door with alarm.

"Quickly—a child has been bitten by a snake."

I ran alongside him until we were past the pigpen and down the road a stretch where the road forked like a serpent's tongue. Before a decline, I saw it was Wo, who reminded me of my Precious Pearl. She sat, rocking back and forth holding her calf. In a harsh voice I told her to stop moving.

"Lay back. Rest on your elbows," I said. I ripped her pant leg to reveal the wound, red and swollen. "How long?" I asked Guo Xide.

"I was with her—I'm not sure—a matter of minutes for me to run and get you and to run back." He held his side from the exertion of the run.

"Sit down and extend your legs, Guo Xide."

I took a knife from my pocket, thankful I had not replaced it after I'd gotten back from my foraging. I remembered the plant I neglected to harvest, as I had had no need of its healing properties at the time. I wiped the knife on my quilt jacket and said to the girl, "Your name is so beautiful, Hang Wo. Are you brave, Wo?"

"No, Miss."

"How can I believe it? You helped me when I bled in the kitchen, did you not?"

"That was different, Miss."

"How so?"

"You were hurt, not me."

I smiled at her. "Then turn your head away, and sing Mangen's song out loud."

As she began to sing, I pressed the wound gently but decided not to cut the bite open, as the blood was running freely. I touched the area around the fang marks, and she winced.

"Sorry, Wo." I turned toward Guo Xide and whispered, "It could be just a dry bite."

"Which means?"

I continued in Italian. "It's painful and will swell. She may have some reactions, but not the severe complications of a venomous bite. I could suck the blood out, but the mouth is unclean and may cause more of a problem."

She cried and started to twitch.

I said to him, "This could be a sign of snake venom or just fright." Switching to Chinese, I said, "Do you know what kind? Did you see the snake?"

"No, but I heard its rattle," he said.

"Are you sure?" I looked up, confused. "She might go into shock. I must go to cut some of the roots of a plant I saw. Don't move her. Stay here and keep her still. Make sure her leg is below the level of her heart. Let her lean back on you."

A boy named Hua, not very bright for his age, but always willing to be of some help, stood by watching. I took him by the arm cajoling him to accompany me for an important task. Walking fast in the direction of where I'd seen the plant, I left the boy at the pig-keeper's with instructions to have the old man boil a pot of water for tea for me.

I crossed the courtyard at a brisk pace and found the black cohosh plant topped by a plume of white flowers. The large leaves, a pinnate compound and leaflets shaped with sawtooth edges, I brushed aside, and swung my knife to hack at the roots, cutting rhizomes and pocketing them. My hands were muddied and ruddled with blood from my many swings and misses.

After I washed my hands with the roots at the pig-keeper's, I cut away some bark and threw the pieces into the hot water. I took hold of the small pot with a corner of my jacket, thanked and bowed to the pig-keeper, and with the boy in tow, returned to the prostrate child and a stricken Guo Xide. The girl had vomited.

I shook my head.

"What?" Guo Xide asked.

"Not a good sign. It could be a panic, but if strong poison is racing though her small body—" I stopped from saying, *There's little hope.* "Give me your handkerchief."

I parceled up the pot with a wide hanky and handed it to the boy. "Blow on it, Hua," I said, indicating the decoction. I ripped another piece of the child's pant and dipped it in the liquid, which had darkened in color. I washed the wound and then used this as a compress. I kept looking at her, afraid she'd pass into unconsciousness. For a moment I thought she was going into paralysis as she stiffened, but she was just shifting her uncomfortable position. I took the pot from Hua and forced her to drink the hot liquid. She choked a little. I waited a bit and then poured more of the liquid into her mouth.

"Help her up," I snapped. Guo Xide supported her back while I held her neck and head in the crook of one arm as I tried to force her to drink, almost drowning her, poor darling, with the pot in my other hand. Her eyes rolled back in her head; her pupils looked dilated. I was losing ground with her and in an angry voice castigated the heavens and all the gods therein. "Are they never satiated? Must they gobble up all our children?"

"In nominee patris, et filii, et spiritus sancti . . ." the priest prayed, his mumbled Latin infuriating me to a pitch that made me want to strike him, push him from his kneeling attitude into the dusty road.

Instead I lashed out in his own tongue, "For the love of God, be still, man."

"What?"

"Help me pick her up and carry her." I threw the pot down and told the boy to help us, and off we went to the dispensary on the far side of the courtyard. Several boys and girls ran out and followed us, thinking this was some sort of game. Guo Xide shooed them away like so many squawking chickens.

Hua opened the door and we deposited her on a raised rush mat. She appeared feverish. I started to strip her, and Guo Xide blanched.

"Then get out," I said, "you and the boy, and send me one of the older girls. Do it fast. Bring cool well water and clean fresh rags."

The boy looked confused. He stood holding the pot like an offering for his ancestor.

When had he picked it up?

"Place it here." I patted a small table. He did so and bowed.

"Oh, and, little Hua, I humbly thank you for your help." I inclined my head, as I could not stand to bow, but he did, again, and then his child's face lit like a firecracker, as if I had given him a red purse filled with coins for New Year's.

I finished taking off the girl's clothing. Her leg had stopped bleeding. She was pallid. I felt her pulses at different spots. Her breath appeared to be shallow. The older girl arrived with the pail of water and fresh cloths. Without ceremony, I bathed the child and watched her shiver. When her body temperature had dropped and I was assured she was cool, I covered her with a light linen sheet. Only then did I thank the older child and give a slight bow to acknowledge hers.

When Wo was settled and resting, I asked the older child to watch over her while I went to speak with Guo Xide.

I found him in the chapel and motioned him to follow me outside where we could speak. In the atrium, he asked how Wo was doing.

"Fine. She'll live. Wo should not concern you now. We have a contagion spreading—"

"My Lord, do you think it's plague?"

"Heaven, Earth, and all the elements, no. It's the catechism of a peasant uprising. I think our dear Mangen is involved," I said, and added Wo was out of danger.

"What about Mangen?" He motioned me to sit on a small wooden bench.

"I had a discussion with him the other day and he is parroting propaganda. You and Don Gabriele may be in danger." I patted the space on the bench next to me and he sat.

"Nonsense. He's such an eager student."

"Yes, but a malcontent, one not willing to submit to foreign influence." I was beginning to sound like Mangen myself with my high-flown speech. "What I mean is—"

"I understand." He stroked his thatch of chin hair, the action making him look serene and contemplative, and almost Chinese.

"No, you don't. You should have seen the rage in his serpent's eyes."

"I've seen and heard similar things—enough to give concern to Don Gabriele. There's little we can do, except watch out for his subversive influence over the others."

"What do you know of his companions? What they discuss at lights out? There is no supervision in the dorm. He's in complete control. And he's very charismatic."

"I will have Don Gabriele keep guard from now on."

"They are not prisoners. Mere boys. Where does he get his information? Where does he go when he leaves the mission compound? He says to visit his parents, but I learned from Doctor Wu his mother killed herself and his father remarried a prostitute and Mangen hates her."

"I didn't know. Have you ever seen boys fight ferociously when they've been starved or mistreated, and want to escape tyrannies?" he said.

"Scrappers using tooth and nail. That, dear priest, is our Mangen."

TWO DAYS LATER, I MET with Guo Xide again in his office. "I've heard rumors Mangen's affiliated with the *I'ho t'uan,* but for now all we can do is watch and wait," he said in a hurry. "Have you also heard this?" He indicated a stool and I sat.

"Sounds familiar. I'll find out more tomorrow—if he comes after class."

"And yesterday?" He toyed with his beard.

"Absent. No explanation when he returned. And he now has a horse."

"Why wasn't I informed?" He jumped up as if he had just been stung by a wasp.

"I assumed you knew. Wo insisted I see her parents because they wanted to thank me for tending her. They made us a feast. We got back late. You were sleeping."

He sat. "Like Saint Peter, I should've been more vigilant. Where does he tether the horse?"

"Stabled with the pig-keeper."

"I'll see to it," he said, gathering his skirts.

"I would permit it, were I you."

He started like a horse out of a Hong Kong racing gate, and without stopping, he half-turned and shouted, "Be sure to let me know if you find out more."

"Let it be, Guo Xide," I called after him.

That night I dreamt of a white snake shedding its skin. There was a coterie of phantoms nearby watching in astonishment, while I understood it was the nature of the snake. My dream fragmented into colored mosaic bits. I awoke. I knew, of course, it was the power of suggestion because of what had occurred a few days prior. Still old customs die hard, and superstitions even harder. The snake was white, not a rattler. I decided to consult the pig-keeper once more before the start of school. I trotted over to Yang Zhugong's and found him tossing slops to his pigs.

I bowed. "Please. Spare me one moment?"

"Young, pretty, bothersome women never need more than a minute and then somehow the time flurries into hours." His sagging shoulders and the exasperation in his voice belied the enthusiasm for my request.

"Yang Zhugong, tomorrow marks my year anniversary at Yangbinguan, and I cannot help but contemplate my deeds here." I inclined my head. "I've had an ominous dream."

He threw the remaining food to the pigs and wiped his hands on a rag tied to a wooden pole of the pen. He opened the gate, came through, and said, "Is there time for a pipe?"

I shook my head, reading disappointment on his shriveled countenance.

"Then at least may we sit?" He motioned me to a tiny bench leaning on the shelter.

Without prelude, I began all in one breath, "I dreamed of a white snake and there were specters standing by not believing what was happening, though I myself—"

"Was there blood? Please do take a breath, girl, you are exhausting me."

With more control, I skipped the part about Giacomo, his head bloody, uniform torn and disheveled. "The snake slithered forward shedding—"

He put up his hand, revealing his wrinkled, hairless arm. "The significance?"

I nodded.

"Shrewdness."

This wasn't what I'd hoped for.

"You wanted more I suppose? Consider this lichen." He pointed to a rock.

"You tease me? When you know my heart?"

"After all that running, there is a word your heart will treasure more—"

"Which is?"

He cleared his throat. "Transformation."

"Oh, Yang Zhugong. *Tse-tse.* Thanks and a thousand blessings from your ancestors."

"Only one thousand?"

I bowed. Then I turned to go.

"Next time, come without asking a favor. We will watch the lichen to see it grow."

I blushed, and though he couldn't see my face reddening, he knew he had scored his victory, and without turning, I tossed out, "I'll come again and read to you."

"The lowly lichen secrets away tiny insects, but are they no less important to nature?"

I could not fathom what he was telling me, but broke into a run, dashing as fast as I could, trying to outrun the school's bell. It wasn't until later when the evening bell tolled the Vespers' chime that I understood that I was the lichen, growing slowly, harboring arcane intricacies, which had not yet been divulged, and elements significant to my being.

THE NEXT DAY I HAD such a productive session with Wo and her small group, that I'd almost forgotten completely about the unpleasantness with Mangen. School was out, and though he'd not attended, here he stood in front of me. He made that quick gesture with his head, his long hair flogging in air like uncoiled whips.

"Hello." I smiled at him, trying to convey how much I liked him.

He couldn't look me in the eye.

"I made progress with Wo today. A breakthrough. Did you hear of the snake scare?"

"I've come to tell you I'm leaving. I've decided to join the *tufei* outside the city."

"You've decided to join the bandits, or have you been commandeered?" I asked, my voice shrill. My mind broke down the word *tufei*—land robbers, local outlaws.

"It's my decision. These are merely local bands, but soon I expect to join the rebellion."

I couldn't help wondering about Giacomo and how he fared in all these uprisings. Where was his ship? What battle was he embroiled in? Had he seen much combat? Was he alive? I pulled myself together and faced Mangen. "Sure you're not just aping what you've heard others say and do? You have such a good brain, why are you influenced by subversive ideologies?"

"Why aren't you married, Miss?"

"The root of your beliefs sounds like puppet indoctrination."

He slammed his fist on my desk. "I will not have you slander our cause."

"What is this cause? Some warlord in need of mercenaries?"

"We will rid China of foreign devils." He paced the long slow strides of a stalking panther.

"Ah, so." My hands shook, so I folded them on my lap. The composure smudged over my face like artist's paint, but the sweat beading at my temples was not from greasepaint. "Please reconsider." I dabbed a handkerchief on my brow.

"I was born to lead, and lead I will."

"Even if it means leading your troops on a death march or yourself to the grave?"

"I am so sorry you feel this way, Miss. I only came to pay my respects." He bowed low.

When he raised his head, I held up my hand, a futile gesture to stop him from leaving. His hand was on the door handle. I jumped up and forced it closed. "Please, Mangen, do not go with bitterness in your heart. I feel it in the air between us. You will rue this day if you go now. You have mixed feelings about me, because I am not wholly Chinese."

"There's nothing more to say, and I feel no animosity between us."

"Then let me at least offer you tea, before you leave."

He nodded slower than usual, a drawn out yes.

Chapter 14

Bing
冰
Ice

AS THE FREEZE CONTINUED, THE men of the *Leopardo* were getting into shape every day by doing calisthenics with Di Luise. First the men swept the snow off the lower deck and then lined up for activity. Lines, spaces, rows, and one more hour of gymnastics. When Di Luise was called away, Bulldog would lead them. After the hour, the men were ready for lunch in the mess hall, usually followed by a nap.

In the afternoon they performed all manner of drills, but mostly manning stations. Giacomo often would run through a series of *Wing Chun* movements, and when he was done, word spread among some of the crew members that Giacomo would finally continue his story, but most preferred to play cards. Giacomo sat in the mess hall with the same audience, minus the brass. Before he began, his thoughts wandered to a moonlit night when a girl with her hair loose around her shoulders came to him in a white shift. Her rap on the door thudded through his brain, and he couldn't believe he'd departed without seeing her. Would the aching feeling of wanting her ever subside?

Giacomo began in a strong voice. "Here's the part of the story Shen wanted." But just then a siren went off and Bulldog yelled, "Man your stations!"

Men grabbed jackets and weapons and ran to their positions.

The poop deck, a superstructure at the stern of the ship that was a weather station deck, was on fire. Through gloomy air rife with gunpowder and smoke, Manetti, Di Luise, and Bigo fought the blaze. Bigo's arm had been singed, so Di Luise brought him to report to the medic. As Bigo was getting bandaged, Di Luise saw through a porthole that several of the junks had broken through the watery ice patches and surrounded the ship, throwing more lighted flares and torches onboard.

Di Luise dashed back to the captain to inform him of a rear attack. The captain ordered the hoses out to spray the junks, but the temperature was too cold for the water to pass through them. A waste of energy and time. A surprised captain turned to Rinaldi, who in turn yelled to Bulldog and Di Luise, the closest men to him, to shoot over the junks as a warning. They ran to their posts and started firing. Several of the junks and sampans retreated.

Men were dousing the fire above on the bulwark. From the forecastle cabin, Lieutenant Rinaldi yelled though a megaphone to men on the other side of the ship to shoot high above the junks. More fire incendiary lanterns were flung at the *Leopardo*. The men at the left gunner positions scrambled over the decks, heaving live torches back toward the junks. Several sails caught fire. Screaming Chinese and sampans started to disperse. But from the opposite side of the ship, other small craft with bowmen aboard were shooting lighted arrows.

Gicaomo stood next Bulldog. "What the hell am I doing here? I'm a cook for God's sake." Bulldog nudged him and whispered something. Giacomo picked up a rifle, looked at Di Luise, and the three men took aim and fired directly into the keels of two of the junks with the bowmen, hoping they'd soon take on frigid water and sink.

By the time Rinaldi realized what was going on and hollered, "Cease fire!" several of the junks were sinking, Chinese jumping into the freezing waters. Rinaldi's cry fell on deaf ears as another volley from other sailors found their marks in the hulls of other sampans.

Furious now, the captain snarled orders to Rinaldi to have the men cease and desist. Rinaldi, in no great hurry, climbed to where the gunfire was coming from. He yelled in a loud voice for the captain's benefit, "Men, we've no authorization to shoot to kill," but added under his breath for Giacomo to hear, "but no one said we couldn't drown a few rats." Lieutenant Rinaldi returned to the captain to report the men had put down their weapons. The captain's command to "Heave to" was drowned in the cries of the men still fighting fires. Giacomo's eyes sought Rinaldi, who could only shake his head, knowing they were trapped.

⬥

THE FOLLOWING DAY A FEW of the men were ordered to clean up the mess left by the damage of the fires. Others were given orders to paint the interior walls that had been scorched. The other men, not involved in this detail, were directed to clean their weapons. Bulldog walked alongside Gaicomo, who said, "As if these aren't clean enough."

"Keeps us busy."

When they reached the weapons cabinet, they found it open with several of the rifles and equipment already cleaned. A few rifles weren't in place. Several men took their rifles to their bunks where they stored oil cloths and rags. There would be inspection an hour later.

Above the weapons case were two old rifles, an M1882 Vetterli-Bertoldo and also an old M1890 Vetterli-Ferracciu. The Italian navy took up the Bertoldo, basically a M1870 Vetterli with a tube magazine. This ammunition storage and feeding device loaded through the top of the open action. The rifle was equipped with a cleaning rod that fit into a groove cut into the left side of the front end. By 1890 the Vetterli-Bertoldos that were left were made over into Vetterli-Ferraccius, and this new rifle had the heft and look of the old rifle's stock, utilizing a 4-round Ferracciu box magazine system, though its balance was vastly improved. This was the rifle every enlisted man aboard the *Leopardo* cleaned that day, in fact, had cleaned for the second time in a matter of days. Giacomo, peeved at having to clean his rifle yet again, said to Bulldog, "How difficult is it for the officers to understand how stupid this repeat process is?"

Chapter 15

Shuiniu

水牛

Water buffalo

THIS DRAGON'S TAIL I'VE SKETCHED in my chronicle wraps around the wayfarer's tree. And so is doubly representational of me, the quintessence of dragon, and the embodiment of my wayfaring soul.

The Boxer uprising is turning uglier and, I fear, becoming a turning point in China's history, no, perhaps even a pinnacle. There is economic adversity, and a horrid anti-foreign feeling. Many believe that this is the result of the Christian missionaries.

Has not Guo Xide tried to convert me? He tells me about the Blessed Mother; but do I not have my goddess Kuan Yin? Wo's parents gave me a porcelain statue of Kuan Yin for my birthday. They say that "less is more" so I swept clean an area on top of a medicine cabinet of every object which does not feed my soul when I gaze upon it, and there I have placed her, upon a tiny piece of red silk the pig-keeper has given me on which I embroidered her name in Nüshu. Wherever did Yang Zhugong find the cloth? He would not say, only smiled that inscrutable smile of his.

The goddess is beautiful, holding in one hand the ju-I, the Mystical Lotus, and in the other hand, a closed Lotus bud, which represents purity and divine birth; it emits good wishes and gives

*succor in an unending stream of water to sate the three dragons'
thirst. They encircle her feet, on the rock outcropping beneath her.
Each dragon's mouth opens above the other and the water empties
into them and recycles. I find this so charming and miraculous. Two
children stand on either side of the mighty dragon, a boy and a girl,
and of course, garlands of flowers.*

*How could something so benevolent, compassionate, and
beautiful be offensive to foreigners and missionaries? Most are
uncultured barbarians yet consider our beliefs heathen. I sound like
Mangen. What makes them so? Do they not worship Mary? Is our
goddess less benevolent than theirs? Why is our goddess of mercy so
repugnant to them? Yet it is widespread belief that our devotion is
superstition by the unskilled lower classes, those poor and uneducated
that have fueled this peasant rebellion.*

*Rumors have spread that the conservative dowager empress is
becoming more hostile to foreign influence, and her conservative
officials at court encourage Boxer troops to attack foreign churches
and legations. What about ships? Where is the Leopardo at this
moment? I've seen Giacomo's anger flare and cannot imagine him
being subordinate to orders not to fire back. How long can a man
keep his hands behind his back and continue to take beatings? At
some point, these troops will retaliate. He could be court-martialed.
His spirit would break in a military prison. News contains many
assaults on foreign vessels, but for the most part, these alien navies
are not retaliating, and I'm wondering: for how long will they resist
fighting back?*

*Revolt will soon reach Peking—it has already spread from
Shandong across north China. The empress's credo is that, in order
for China and the Chinese people to have a good and peaceful
life, the non-nationals, upsetting our harmony of nature, must be
eliminated. There's mention in European newspapers that the yang/
yin eunuchs that surround our empress are responsible for much
of the unsettled masses and unrest. As I write these words, I am
painfully aware of Mangen's predictions.*

*Mangen. When I told Guo Xide of Mangen's decision to leave,
he merely said it was God's will. Then he went into a tirade of
how, if I accepted things as part of God's design, my soul would be*

*comforted. Here he gave me what I now call his "Speech of Seven"—
the seven sacraments. I am loathe to tell him not to waste his breath,
since he is good and kind, and I have a roof above my head and a
safe mat on which to sleep.*

After Guo Xide held Mass the next day, we stood by the fountain.
In the pool below carp frolicked and flitted about. Since I have decided
to ignore Guo Xide's sacrament speech, I gave him news of the rebellion.

"Guo Xide, it is rumored," I told him, "not only the peasants, but
now even the gentry are beginning to accuse all foreigners of letting out
the 'Precious breath' of the mountain by mining, and destroying our
'dragon's vein' in the land by constructing railways."

He asked what this meant.

"You see, 'Precious breath' refers to something my mother often spoke
about: 'Celestial breath,' a calling to mind that souls and saints inhabit this
land and our mountains. Mother used to say, 'The height of a mountain
doesn't matter, what matters is if there are any saints residing in it; the
depth of water doesn't matter, what matters is if there are dragons below.'"

A carp did a flip and splashed his black robe. He brushed it off.
"So now with reminiscences of these spiritual ideas, these slightly-altered
expressions have captured the imagination of the people?" he asked.

I was glad he didn't say hogwash. "Guo Xide, let me break down
these expressions for you. 'Precious breath'—*lingqi, ling:* magic, precious;
qi: breath. 'Celestial breath'—*xianq, xian:* celestial, of saint; *qi:* breath.
'Dragon's vein'—*longmai:* long, dragon; *mai:* vein, especially of blood,"
and here I swept my hand in an arch for emphasis, "or mountain ridge.
Do you understand that these masses of people are uneducated and
superstitious, and they actually believe you and your kind are capable
of stealing our breath and our blood? Do you not eat Christ's flesh and
drink his blood?"

He huffed, showing annoyance. "Do you include yourself?"

"I consider myself Chinese, though I hope not ignorant." A breeze
ruffled my hair. "Gossip in the market is that the growing railway system
has destroyed the old communication system based on the Grand Canal."
I sat on the stone wall around the pond.

He sat next to me. "It would seem these unconfirmed reports gain
in strength."

"Are you certain the newspaper reports are misguided? Street propaganda and hearsay have it that whole cities have been isolated—left poverty-stricken because the railroad has bypassed them. What have you to say about that? News of this drastic proportion travels more quickly."

Mention of the poor unleashed a homily of the eight beatitudes. As soon as he finished and took a breath, I said, "I don't feel safe here anymore. In the marketplace old men grumble, spreading gossip of disaster victims of all kinds, even superstitious scholars and government functionaries—all are blaming misfortunes on foreigners."

"That's absurd. Why?"

"They've offended the spirits by preaching Christian ways and prohibiting the worship of Confucius, idols, and ancestors. Banners across the city center this morning said: *Yangguizi!* White Ghosts! Foreign devils know not our ways! Guo Xide, you preach against our gods."

"Without a doubt—"

I interrupted, reminding him that around the mission there were enough holy statues, icons, and crosses to fill the village's winter storehouse. "Are these not idols?" I asked. "What about the holy pictures you asked me to draw? You distributed them among the local villagers, and do you know what they'll do with them? Use them to stuff their shoes."

"You're like the mandarins who sermonize, urging farmers about the fruitfulness of their agriculture and toil—a necessity for the good of all, yet they themselves keep their fingernails long to ensure that no one would ever suspect them of touching a hoe."

With that he walked off in a huff, and I felt oddly smug, thinking somehow that I'd made some ground for the infidel.

THE BLIND NIGHT FELL. I slept badly. By cock's crow, the ceiling boards above still held no answers to the questions plaguing me. The newspapers were sketchy in their description of foreign ships involved in an exchange of gunfire with rebels. Were they British? Russian? Or as I feared, Italian? Why do I get this niggling feeling that Lu lied to me and that Giacomo is still alive? I went to the kitchen and made firecracker beef over noodle rice salad, the beef hot and piquant while the noodles cool the palate. My pig-keeper had mentioned this dish the day before

so difficult to rebuild. When I was about to leave him in my room in one of the still-standing buildings, he stood close to me and, as if a rehearsed and a practiced move we did daily, we bowed toward each other, our foreheads touching. Then he sat down with his tea.

I left him to rest, and took off at a runner's pace across the fields and toward the main housing of our enclave. I ran to the infirmary. A long zigzag line snaked from the door all the way around the building. Some people were on the ground in distorted positions. There was a great yammering that would seem to fade and then start in again as if a chorus of hungry children in an orphanage waited for their daily bowl of watery rice.

Then the wailing and crying began—dirt-encrusted, bleeding faces called my name.

Guo Xide hurried up to me. "Thank God you're all right. Doctor Wu is nowhere to be found. The animals smashed the scattered homes all along the hills and rice terraces."

He kept talking as his fingers jerked, unable to place the key in the lock. I took the jangling keys and opened the door. A crush of people entered behind me. Guo Xide raised his hands and yelled for them to calm down, that each would be seen in good time. As he spoke, I took a white smock down from the hook and put it on. Guo Xide opened the window and pushed out a wooden shutter so that it angled and gave shade. He used a stick to keep it in place, all the while mumbling a Latin prayer or lament. Then he escorted five people out of the room. Two strong boys lifted the first patient from a bloodied canvas sheet onto the table. It was the gardener. I told the boys to get Wo and Father Gabriele—I pointed to each as I said the name of the person to fetch so there'd be no confusion.

I washed my hands at the basin, picked up a sea sponge, and began washing the man's face to see where the blood was coming from. He had a huge, gaping gash in his head. I stuffed a wadded piece of cloth in it and told the priest to hold it there while I threaded a needle. I poured iodine into the basin and immersed the sponge, squeezed it out and poured some of the excess, and handed it to him. "Soak the wound with this."

Without warning, I began pinching the skin together and sewing the gardener's head, his eyes wide and staring at me. His face crumpled and I stopped. He inclined his head and I finished the job, calling, "Next," to the second injured person to be brought in. To the woman who assisted this farmer, I said, "Get me a bucket of clean water and get others to help you bring me a few more." She nodded and left. The farmer's wounds were superficial, and I washed them off with the same water and iodine as the gardener. "Guo Xide," I said, "there will be rampant infection if you do not bring me your store of communion wine." He looked horrified. "Now," I said as if talking to a student. He picked up his cassock and started running. On the way, I saw him grab the hand of one of the altar boys. I told the farmer to follow the priest and to help him and carry back clean sheets from the laundry room.

I had Father Gabriele go down the line of patients and bring in the gravest ones first. Amid much screaming and arguing, I kept working, patching, cleaning, bandaging, and prescribing herbal medicines whenever I could.

A screeching owl of a man retracted his ankle when I touched it lightly. He had hobbled in leaning on a sort of crosier. I told him the ankle was horribly sprained but not broken. I had him sit on the table and put his foot on a chair. I bandaged this tightly and told him to stay off it until it healed. He was not from the mission, which meant he was either here on business or had trekked up the hilly incline to get help.

"Are you able to make another staff?" I asked, "Or this?" and drew a *T* with my finger on the messy gray sheet covering the table. His crinkled smile told me he could, and I dismissed him, telling him to leave the bandage on during the day but to loose it every night and keep it elevated as much as possible.

He signaled me with his long, knobby fingers, and when I came close for him to whisper, he reached into his belt and took out an ancient coin. A long square foot spade bronze coin, possibly from the Han Dynasty. I had seen a coin like this before in my grandmother's jewelry case. Then he dug into the other side of his soft belt and came up with a Ming knife coin and pressed it into my hand.

"Oh, no, little grandfather, I cannot accept this."

Yan, a small girl with a sweet voice, who had accompanied the old one, said, "You must accept this payment. My grandfather shows respect and helps you attain what your heart so desires. You are a healer."

I thanked the old man and bowed, a long, deep, deferential bow.

Yan led the man out, but not before he turned, handed the staff to Yan, leaned upon her shoulder, and bowed once more.

I looked at the coins in my hand, a rural blessing from an ancient. I was now Doctor Zhou, a paid professional. How I wished I could share this with my father and Giacomo.

This small moment of triumph was short lived. Wo and Father Gabriele returned and I put them to work. While Father assisted a young boy, Wo brought me a mother who worked in the laundry. The woman told me her baby had been thrown out of her arms. I undressed the child quickly and felt all of her extremities. The baby smiled at me as I tickled her. If she was in pain, I explained to the upset mother, the baby would be wailing. I told the assistant laundress the baby didn't know it was being hurtled through air, as it had never happened to her before, and therefore didn't tense when she landed unhurt. I looked the baby over well, and knew its father was not Chinese, and pity enveloped me, reliving my own moments of fear with Ya Chen. The mother had an arm dangling at a weird angle. Handing the baby to Wo and I said, "Dress her." The laundress sat and looked away while I pulled her arm with great force, then released so it popped back into place.

She screamed, "That hurts," when ball bone met socket.

"No lifting heavy things for a month, or this will happen again."

I took the baby from Wo and placed it in the woman's left arm. "Always this side now."

"*Tse tse,*" she said. I asked her if the father was an Italian sailor. She said no, "Fritz is German."

Guo Xide returned with two basketsful of strips for bandages and the sacramental wine. Zhugong came to me, his arms loaded with herbs. I did not have the heart to scold him for not staying put, but sent him back to my room to sleep.

Wo's little brother suffered a concussion so I kept him with me all night. Around midnight, Cook and the head laundress came in with a pot of *yacamein* soup, thin noodles in a soy-based soup with chopped green onions, savory as I'd had in Hong Kong. It smelled delicious, awakening in my stomach a hunger I hadn't known I had till then.

DAYS LATER I FINALLY WROTE in my chronicle.

> *I received a lamp of hemp, timber, and iron—a blessing lantern, delivered by Doctor Wu. It contained this message: Doctor Zhou, I wish to extend the town's greatfulness on behalf of the fine work you did in the mission infirmary during the disgorging of the earth this past week. This unfortunate upset of the Natural Order of our lives has been caused no doubt by the influx of foreigners on our soil. Apart from that, I commend your ablity to support the rank odor of this villainous group of missionaries as you aided your people. It is with much humility and admiration that I offer you this ancient blessing, hoping you will retain your Chinese civility even whilst thrown among these alien invaders.*

How could he call it an earthquake when he knew it was a Boxer raid and water buffalo stampede? I was sure the doctor did not feel this way. Perhaps he was under duress because the note was signed in a florid Chinese script by the Mandarin of the village next to the mission.

All I could think of was the warlord, Rong Xin, who protected yet commanded our inconsequential, flimflam Mandarin Hong Lei—I knew neither of these men, but was considering making their acquaintance. When I mentioned this to Guo Xide, he counseled me otherwise. Stifled again. A woman in a man's world. Why and how had Cixi succeeded, triumphed, and gained strength over men? How had she brought it about, at such a time, and in such a backward nation as ours?

While thinking of the empress dowager, a young peasant boy from the village arrived carrying an elaborate good luck piece shaped like a birdcage of *I Ching* coins and red silk. This gift was most auspicious, because inside it lay ancient cowries, coins scattered as if by a providential hand. There was no note, only a tiny scroll. When I unrolled it and held it to the light, the Chinese calligraphy read: Doctor Zhou Bin Lian.

My hands shook, holding this, my formal graduation diploma from an unknown dean. I steadied my hand and with my pointing finger, I wrote the word *dean* at the bottom: 院长 *yuan zhang*.

Apparently outsiders were referring to this incident as an earthquake as well. This "major disgorging of the earth" was a devious plan to uproot the mission by Mangen's horde of bandits and Boxers. How sorry I was I did not succeed with Mangen. There was a backbreaking clean-up of the mission, and much discussion of the infamy of such an attack by one we considered our own. There was even talk of the famous earthquake everyone knew about from history lessons, which had devastated China's Shjensi Province in 1556. It was the worst earthquake in all of history; over eight hundred thousand people were killed. We were more fortunate. Only thirty wounded and five dead.

SEVERAL WEEKS AFTER THE STAMPEDE, Zhugong started behaving strangely. At first I thought he was seriously affected by shock. But as I began to frequent him more and more, I knew in my heart I was in for one of life's big surprises. He had closed in on himself, a morning glory after sunset. So for two days, I stayed away from Zhugong, thinking perhaps I was the cause of this disruption in harmony, the electrical shock that set off catastrophic doom.

He sent for me. His simple home and modest furnishings were restored, and as I wended my way to the pig-keeper, I picked some herbs and brought them to him. We sat once again under the canopy of the huge tree that dwarfed his abode.

"You stayed away but sent me food. Nature must always replenish itself," he said, tapping his tiny rounded belly.

"There is news of the uprising," I countered.

"News, like a bat, always flutters into the mission—it's when the sky burns red with smoke that you must worry, little starling."

"Shall I make some tea?"

He made a throaty noise, which I took to mean yes.

I cooked up a spicy, hot, almost bitter tea he was fond of, the tang of which enlivened his spirit and relaxed the grasp of disquiet that imprisoned him.

We took our tea in silence at a tiny table inside. He handed me his cup when he finished. While I washed up, he went outside, and when I was done, I followed him.

He sat with his face upturned toward heaven, the skin of his morning-glory countenance soaking in the rays of a benevolent sun.

"It is no longer safe to stay in the mission." I sat on the ground next to him, my legs beneath me.

"If you are a living being, nowhere on earth is safe, or have you forgotten our wobbling bodies at the earth's trembling weeks ago?"

"This is serious. A body of ragged troops armed with farm implements was seen skirting the marketplace."

"I will tell you a story of a cave in northern Shensi province." He cocked an eyebrow.

I blew air out of the side of my mouth in protest, as if blowing a tendril of hair out of my eyes, but he ignored this and continued.

"To be precise, Wu-tai-shan, Mountain with Five Peaks. Do not worry for your mortal carcass; it is your soul that needs nourishment."

"Are you talking about the Yun-kang Caves west of Datong?"

"You have never seen them, but you must. The stone sculptures are from the Wei dynasty about the Fifth Century."

This pig-man was so knowledgeable, I mused, but said, "I do not need to go sightseeing."

"Do not take this lightly, Lian. You are a woman unfulfilled. Your past is behind you, no matter how horrific. Even if your body was or is ravaged, you must repair your soul. Make the pilgrimage to whisper your heart's desire inside the caves. It will be granted to you, my child, I assure you."

Ravaged? "I gave up having desires when I ran away from Lu and lost Ya Chen."

He shook his head and looked at me.

"The doctor I met in Hong Kong forwards mail from Ping. I've had a letter from her."

His ferocious gaze pierced. It actually hurt me. Could he know what I wanted to say? I thought I'd given away nothing.

"Your husband is dead," he said; no inflection ruffled his tone.

"Killed in a bandit skirmish," I confirmed, wondering why hadn't he died by Giacomo's hand? I was thankful for the news that Ping had met Giacomo and that he was very much alive.

"But Lu was not the husband of your heart or Ya Chen's father."

My mouth opened, but no response was uttered. Why was I bereft with grief over this man who I had linked my fate with so long ago? Sadness engulfed me like weight upon my chest and I had trouble breathing.

"Do not grieve for him," he said.

My heart started to beat fast at the idea of knowing for sure that Giacomo lived.

"It is for the other you cannot stop the flow from your eyes. I do not know his name, but his essence. We both know that Lu does not merit grief. How your husband must have sweated and bled drop by drop upon discovering you had gone, and then finding you again in Hong Kong only to lose you once more." With those words, his eyebrow arched, the corners of his mouth became mirthful, and his eyes became mere slits in order for him to better see what had happened.

"There are emotional muscles I cannot flex with regards to Lu: compassion and pardon, but guilt is another matter."

"No wonder. You barely have sympathy for yourself, or the capacity to forgive your own past. Rid yourself of rancor. Ping's letter is a good omen, the news within better. Ties with the past are now severed. What you want is to practice medicine, but you have to heal yourself first. Look to your yearnings. They are simple. A man to love, a child to hold."

"Ah, how well you know my heart, but these are out of reach."

"Sometimes we attain our wants. Yours is doctoring, but whatever we attain can be causation for a chain of events we have no control over. What you need is love. Eventually you will see this."

"You cannot possibly want me to trek over four hundred *gongli* to whisper inside a cave."

He sat mute as the rock he perched on.

I drew my hands together like a supplicant. "I cannot—"

"You will."

"Zhugong!" I dropped my hands.

"Tell the priest you are going on a mission of mercy for your soul."

"He'll preach his Catholicism."

"Perhaps," he said, pointing to a pail of water.

I ladled him a dipperful.

A slight breeze ruffled his beard. He stroked it, and with the other hand he drank, then handed back the dipper. "It is in your horoscope. You must. You will go," he said, and wiped his mouth on his sleeve, as one of my pupils would have done.

He was so stubborn I had to think a minute before responding. "Zhugong." I pulled my knees up and encircled them with my arms.

"I am a realist, you are a dreamer. What will I use for transportation? Money? Food? Shelter?"

And with each of my questions he nodded, therefore I knew he understood the impossibility of such a voyage.

Still nodding, he said, "You will go."

"I cannot."

"Manjusri."

"What does that mean? Surely I know not."

"The God of Transcendent Wisdom. These caves—the place of this manifestation—the wall carvings are powerful. The bodhisattva Manjusri—*Wen-Shu-Shi-Ii,* according to Buddhist legend, was ordained by Gautama Buddha to turn the Wheel of Law for China's salvation."

"You have words enough for two sets of teeth, old one, but I do not understand." The wind picked up and I rubbed my arms.

"In time you will." So again he told me of the caves and said, "There are those for whom the world is never enough, but you are not one of these. Go, child, go whisper to the walls. Hear the echo respond to you. You are a child of the inner earth—as witnessed by the earth shake-up you lived through and the typhoon in Hong Kong, and you will thrive once more. You must leave here."

"I will never leave you." And there it was again, the vision of me making a funeral pyre for this much-loved ancient one. I knew as my lungs instinctively know how to breathe in air and exhale it that he would die in order for me to leave.

My eyes filled, and I rubbed them with my sleeve before they'd washed my face. He scolded me for this outburst. "You will always have me with you. How could you doubt it? I am the breeze to caress you, the honey sweetness on your tongue, the water to wash salt from your teary eyes."

"But these are spiritual things. I want you in the physical sense, I mean—"

"More physical than every sweet taste? Ah! If I were only ten years younger, I would probably have to marry you to give you pleasure," he said. A wry smile played about his lips.

"Pleasure me! Not even if you were twenty years younger, old man. I have had enough of man's pleasuring to last me a lifetime."

"You have been with the right man for such a little while. Your memory is filled with remorse. Yours is a fragile peace wrought of broken promises. Love and trust are lacking in your life. You've not been taught the art of lovemaking, have you?"

My eyebrows arched. They must have reached my hairline when I said, "I never even discussed this with Ping, the sister of my heart. Is that all men of any age think of?"

"You are a doctor. Do not look at me askance—I did say I would marry you. *Wo de tian,* my heaven! Why, even pandering for you would do, I suppose, but there are no eligible men here. Be not afraid of love, all encompassing emotional and physical, for without it, life is unbearable. You are alive; therefore, all things are possible. You must leave, Lian."

"Indeed, I am leaving—I will see you tomorrow."

"Leave the mission."

I rose and blew a kiss to the man I had surely loved in another life.

Chapter 16

Rongyu
荣誉
Honor

THE SHIP WAS ANCHORED IN a very deep bay, surrounded by a frozen shelf of water. The weather turned colder, and the ship was locked without any radio contact or another ship within shouting distance. Nowhere near a port and without a prayer the ice would break anytime soon, the men succumbed to listlessness, slow to answer commands. After dinner some of the men would play card games: *tresette, scopa,* and *briscola,* crowding around someone's bunk; others would sit in the mess hall to exchange stories.

Yi Shen was learning Italian and loved to hear the tales the men told while he and Giacomo finished cleaning the galley. Each man was responsible for his own spoon, chopsticks, and bowl. Yi Shen cleared the tables and washed the large platters and serving pieces. He gained speed and proficiency with everything related to the galley and mess.

Bulldog had just told the group how he'd fallen in love with the daughter of a *pizzataro* when he was fourteen. First her brother threatened to beat him, and then her father told him never to show up again to buy pizza from the girl, or he'd find a nice round pizza pan up his ass. Bulldog's voice and the men's laughter filtered into the galley. "Guess the color of my skin is too dark even for sunburned Neapolitans." Then he turned and said, "Let's hear something of your youth, Chef," as Giacomo sat down.

"Wait for Shen—he loves to listen."

Giacomo settled himself with a cup of steaming tea and Bulldog said, "Tell us one from when you were young and moon-eyed."

"Young, perhaps. Moon-eyed comes later." Giacomo coerced images of Lian and her words about the moon. Would he ever stop thinking about her? How could he conjure words about his youth when all he wanted was to tell the world about a doe-eyed girl he had caressed for a few nights long ago.

"Shen, hurry up and get your skinny bones out here," a stocky machinist called.

"I present," Shen said, and slid onto the bench next to Giacomo.

Giacomo sighed, and said, "Where shall I begin, my fellow fleet mates?"

I had just turned thirteen in the fall of 1882 when my older brother Neddu was sent to the Istituto Salesiano at Monreale outside of Palermo. My eldest brother, Riccardo, a redhead with a fiery temperament that matched his hair, was a renegade who'd run off and married into a Mafia family in Partinico.

I rarely got to see Neddu, but one Sunday my father took me to visit because he had business with a man in Palermo. Neddu looked strange in a seminarian's frock coat. The brothers at the school had some terrible hold over him. I wanted to ask Father what my brother had done to be locked away with the priests, but couldn't muster the courage.

At the monastery I threw a stone high over the garden wall, it hurtled straight through the sky and sailed out to sea with the ease of a gull. The smooth rock arched and then careened into the bay—beyond the valley of the Conca d'Oro, the Golden Conch.

I looked around to see if one of the other seminarians had seen me. None had, so I caught up with Neddu. Eyeing a huge fig tree, I said, "Let's pick some fruit."

"That's stealing," Neddu said.

"It isn't. This is God's house. This is His garden—it's for everyone."

Neddu shook his head. The figs were plump and ripe, the air crisp, but the sun still permitted German tourists daily swims at nearby Mondello. I shivered, not from the ocean breeze, but from the thought of Neddu's solitude—away from home and family, locked up with the brothers.

Giacomo left off his story and said, "So you see, Shen, I wasn't very trusting of the black robes either. I thought it was priests who robbed me of my brother's company."

"Do you still feel that way, Giacomo?" the machinist asked.

Giacomo faced him. "Guess I'm like the Chinese." He thought of something Lian had said about priests, and repeated, "Why go through a man to pray to God?"

◁─▷×◁─▷

THE NEXT DAY WHEN GLACIAL winds subsided, the men were called topside to run through exercises. When they were sufficiently warmed up, they did drills manning their weapons. In the late afternoon while huge kettles of soup bubbled for the evening meal, Giacomo continued telling Shen about the visit to his brother.

Neddu and I sat on an intricate wrought-iron bench, and I said, "I heard Babbo say we'll leave for home soon. Will you miss me?"

Neddu shrugged. "I can't wait for *Natale*. Christmas will be splendid after this prison."

"Do you hate Babbo, for keeping you here?"

"I'd rather be in Carini with you and Mamma."

"Hear about the shepherd boy? Babbo read in the *Corriere* the boy committed suicide."

"That's the worst sin. You go straight to hell, you know?"

"He must've been lonely in the hills tending sheep. He was my age. Do you think he repented at the last minute and God sent him to Purgatory instead of hell?"

"I'm not sure there is one. The boys here say it's an invention of a pope. People paid for indulgences to shorten time in a purgatory that never existed—that's why the Church is so rich."

"Isn't that blaspheming?"

"In a way. About the shepherd. How did he kill—" his voice quavered.

"Shot himself dead with a *lupara*. A bloody pulp when they found him, don't you think? You wouldn't do that out of loneliness, would you?" I fiddled with a twig and watched him heave a stone over the garden wall.

Neddu turned pale. "It's so lonely here sometimes. I want to kill myself. Look at this."

He showed me the red welts on his back from beatings.

"Tell Babbo." He gave me the oddest look—almost a sneer, saying, "Honor thy father."

On the way home to Carini, I pictured our meeting if the two of us had been alone. We'd have played hide and seek around the fragrant *campanella* bushes, bells all in bloom. The pure flower was the Madonna's own perfume—green, velvety leaves smooth as my mother's cheek.

What a homecoming my mother, Maria, gave us as she greeted us with her warm smile, which brightened my dark heart. Fathers are revered, and mothers loved. So it was with every generation of Sicilians, and so it would probably be with my very own children. For what is begotten, begets. Although, I could never believe it of myself.

Before dinner my father and Zu Zuffero talked in the parlor, pieces of their conversation drifted toward me, sprawled on the floor. I thought of the shepherd who'd killed himself. He wasn't Sicilian. From where? It seemed important, and I wanted to write it in the diary Zu Zuffero had given me for my Communion. The book was deep umbra leather with grained lines where I traced with my fingers, thinking. My father suggested a game of bocce after dinner. I cried out, "That's it, Bari!" grateful for the 'b' of *bocce* to recall the town of the shepherd's birth.

Mamma called us to a feast of rabbit hunter's style, and my favorite fried squash blossoms stuffed with mozzarella and anchovies. After dinner, I stretched across my bed to scribble something to the boy—though I didn't understand what 'being his father's chattel' meant. I felt his spirit and wanted to honor him in some way, and so I wrote:

Uagniun, my inner heart cries for you.
Lonely boy away from your parents and Bari,
Alone in the pastures you sing softly to calm
The sheep who bleat from fear, like you, in the dark.
Sing softly *"Il Cannochiale,"* poor boy who is
No more. You are no longer afraid of the night.
Friend, I understand why you took your life.

I blew out the kerosene lamp and adjusted the wick. I undressed, pulling on a long cotton nightshirt. Barefoot on the terrace above the lemon orchard, with *le zagare* filling the night air—the pungent sweetness was balm for my heart—I recalled the *campanella* bushes. I'd made a mistake—Our Lady's flower was the lemon blossom. I wanted to engulf the night and hugged myself breathless. I got into bed. Mamma forgot to warm the muslin sheets with the *prete.* The "priest" was a bow-shaped wooden arch, which held a pot of small live coals. Shivering, I knew why it was named *priest*—they're into your business, even between your sheets.

I looked at Shen, barely able to hold his head up, his eyes droopy. "Sunrise comes early. Off to bed with you. Pleasant dreams of Sicily."

Chapter 17

Bajitian
巴戟天
Morinda Root

BECAUSE I KNEW ZHUGONG WAS going to die, I asked him a million questions; I stayed with him late and returned early in the morning. I was insatiable to learn as much as I could about his life. After many exhausting inquisitive sessions, he said, "So, *xīnzàng*, little heart of my heart, if I tell you the story of Zhugong, will you let me die in peace?"

"How can I want your story when it's you I want to go on living? Ay, Zhugong, I want to split myself in two—be with the children to help them learn, and be here, listening to Zhugong tell me of the time he was young and in love."

"Practice bilocation. Don't look at me queerly. It is an ancient phenomenon, claimed to have been experienced—even practiced at will, by mystics, saints, monks, Yogis, and magical adepts. Choices make life interesting. Haven't you always wanted to split yourself in two? Not just now, not just because of me? Bilocation is your answer then."

"Indeed," I said, "how would you know?"

"I was taught by a Yogi—"

"You? I understand Yogis deny the body in order to feed the mind."

"Exactly. I cannot give you my life's knowledge in a matter of days, child."

"And I cannot stay for your lesson, whatever it is you are trying to teach me, but I will return to you shortly." With a slight bow, I walked away and did the only thing I could. I dismissed my class from all after-school activities until further notice, a time in the future I believed I would possess. How little we know.

I returned and saw him sitting on a chair, dozing, but not in his usual place; he was under the lintel of the door. At my approach he opened an eye. "I'm not sleeping, only resting my eyes, thinking of you, and what I said."

"Which was?"

"We spoke of love—only we ourselves can make our dreams reality—and of spontaneous, involuntary bilocation, which can presage or herald a death. But you are here and I am here. Oh, and so you do not pester me in my narrative—*para* means beyond and *Brahman,* universal life or consciousness. I was taught much, but had much to learn. I left because I was too attached to the world and had a purpose to fulfill. You are that purpose. Are you grasping what I'm saying? Have the good heart to pretend and nod your head."

I did. "Am I welcome now?" I handed him a painted fan.

"What's this?"

Since he feigned ignorance, I answered, "A fan."

"I know the object. No need for a gift."

"Consider it a loan."

I bowed and touched my forehead to his, and the action reminded me of the stampede. He recognized the gesture and the corners of his mouth turned up and he squinted and shook his head, quite pleased with something.

"Yes. No need for the fan or anything else much longer, bumpkin." And repeated, *tu baozi,* so I was sure to hear the first part, meaning rustic, and wouldn't confuse it for the last part: steamed bread!

"Bumpkin? What happened to *xīnzàng?*"

"Heart of my heart was earlier. Now you are like an arrow in my heart. Do not wear me out, or I will not have breath to begin, much less finish."

"Only if you drop the *tu.* I'll accept *baozi,* I am a steamed bun at times." He smiled. "Now then, *baozi.*"

I put down the basket I carried, dropped to a squat in front of him, and then sat, my knees up and my arms holding them close to my body.

"Are you afraid you might bilocate?" he asked, indicating my position.

I marveled at his wit and something else more akin to bravery. I knew this was in preparation of death.

"Today. This day we shall not do the usual. Take up your pretty basket and let us walk to the small rock wall and sit under the sweet gum. The light filters down so beautifully in fall, and scampers in between the leaves, all red, gold, and green."

I went inside and got his cane, but he waved it away, taking hold of my arm.

There had been a storm earlier in the day, and now everything glistened. The shining leaves, the tree bark, even the crisp air, tinged of late grass. Leaves gathered in clusters rattling and rustling. I set down a thin woven blanket I had in the basket and we sat upon it, making ourselves comfortable by leaning our backs on the wall. Between us, I positioned the picnic basket that Don Gabriele had given me with some provisions and a bottle of water. I, on the other hand, had spirited away some of the priest's altar wine.

Zhugong fanned himself, and in a singsong voice I was unfamiliar with, he began, "In a primeval woodland, I was born—"

"Where are your shoes?" I asked, pointing like an idiot. He'd come walking barefoot and I hadn't noticed.

"I felt hot," he said, beginning to fan himself. "Stop interrupting. Let me start. Green fields, tendering streams, snow-covered mountain peaks—always snow dusted right into summer. I dream still of the fog that swept in from the sea and was carried by the breezes to the foothills, sometimes a haze so milky white it sheeted everywhere, but especially where the warmed crops were moistened, refreshed, and subdued with haze into flourishing—"

"I thought this was going to be about you—"

"Patience. I am getting there."

But I felt anxious because I feared his dying. "Maybe if—"

"Maybe and perhaps—two spoonfuls to fill the philosopher's mouth." He closed his eyes and began writing in the dirt with his big toe. A bold stroke from left to right, smaller to larger. Why did I know that he was going to write the character for *love*? He continued with the lines, until almost completed, and said, "Ah, yes, the story. Where was I?"

He knew perfectly well, but still I told him, "At the very beginning, you old geezer."

"How can you be disrespectful of someone about to tell his life's story with practically the last breath he will draw?"

The shock of his imminent death had worn off and that's what he wanted. Precisely and without surprise, as natural as death is a part of life, like night following day. What had this lesson shown me? I must accept it, but I wanted the story, and not for one sesame cake was I letting him off free.

"And so?"

"Ah, yes," he took up the fan again and gave a profound sigh. "I was raised by monks. My father was an ignorant farmer and thought he must send a dowry with me, but all one needs to enter the temple to study is oneself. He left me there, and he took back with him the pitiable dowry offerings he had scratched together. Neither he nor my mother ever expressed love—not between themselves, nor for my brothers, my sisters, or me. But I felt something very akin to it that day when I watched him trudge off and down the mountain."

A blustering wind whipped some leaves off the tree, punctuating our thoughts. He shifted his position and drew part of the cover he was sitting on over his feet. "I wore a saffron robe and my head was shaved, but I was not religious and had no intention of becoming consecrated to any religion. I believed in the religion of Nature and rejoiced in all beautiful things. Nature can be tender but also cruel, as it was in a land where the body is regarded as nothing but a mere temporal dwelling until it releases the soul. Deep, deep within the hills, gullies, and foothills that lead to the mountains of the Tibetan plateau, there is a brutal and inhospitable landscape which seeps into Sichuan Province. There is where the old ways were still adhered to in the strictest sense.

"I knew a monk, intimately, whose job it was to perform—rather, let me phrase it this way, he was in charge of—how shall I say this but to tell you of one incident? On a bier a dead monk was covered with a shroud and carried to a special place. The dead man was accompanied not only by those who carried him, but also by a monk who rang a bell. Watching as the others placed the body of the deceased in a sacred clearing, the bell-ringer put down the bell and took up a wheel spinner in his right hand and proceeded to pray, spinning and marching around a Buddhist monument where the soulless body rested. Only a few of us witnessed the dispersing of a body no longer necessary to house a soul, because once a body dies, the spirit is released.

"Clusters of prayer flags, fluttering, flying on top of buildings, at the edge of rivers, on mountaintops—everywhere you look in Tibet, you find them. In a sense, they are offerings people erect to pray for good, whether it be luck, happiness, health. These streamers are colorful representations of the five basic elements of life: red for fire, blue for sky, white for clouds, yellow for earth, and green for water.

"This lean, muscular monk stopped his chanting, placed the prayer wheel into his bodice, honed and wetted his knife, then sluiced through the dead man's abdomen first—backing away for the stench was unbearable. Then he stripped the flesh off the bones, and only after he had whittled them clean of meat—

"The monk took hold of a sledgehammer with both hands, wielding it with tremendous downward strokes. Thwack! He smashed and crushed the bones into shards. Even these were carried off in the mouths of carrion creatures, such were the vultures, who hovered and milled about waiting to feed on dead flesh—buzzards and vultures swooped in catching the ruddy meat in their beaks, while the chanting of the other monks in the distance was a mournful chorus of death . . . and beyond."

I could hear their incantations, see them, as they stood in their billowing orange robes of light cotton, a winding shroud against the harsh, cold winds and drab, hoar-frosted tundra.

As the old one spoke, he shivered abruptly, cold with the telling. "These are normal undertakings for monks who believe the body is a mere shell to house the spirit."

I remembered a few days ago Zhugong's knife had slipped, ripping through his flesh at the lower portion of his thumb, though he never cried out.

"When the monk came to the head of the dead man, he scooped out the brains. The work was slow, and each handful of mush he flicked away and the birds came nearer and nearer for their treats. His hands were covered with gore, and the birds feasted upon them, pecking till the blood was no longer the dead monk's but the live one's. He saved the rounded top of the skull, the crown, for this would serve nicely as a cup for tea.

"In an hour he had finished his work, and then it was the vultures that made short shrift of an entire body. The sky burial, as it is known, is common in those parts, and though this happened before hair grew on my face, I shall never forget the shadows cast by the careering vultures, merely fulfilling a life cycle, but most impressive nevertheless."

I listened, struck dumb by Zhugong's revelation, even though I had heard that the monks use one of the three burial rites: the sky burial, cremation, or burial by water—when they cut up the dead and feed them to the fish. Yet I could not reconcile this in any way as being Zhugong's tale. Though the way he described it, with such excruciating detail, certainly made me believe he had witnessed it.

"Were you appalled by the performance of this monk in this ritual?" he asked, stretching his arms above his head.

"Not at all."

"Not even a little?" He brought his arms down and placed his hands in his lap.

"You were so young and only a witness, why should I be shocked?"

"Because, you see, I was that butchering monk."

"I cannot believe—" His look stopped me cold.

We sat for a long time. I was no longer stunned, not knowing what to say, but rather, wondered if I should say something at all, because somehow entrenched within me, I knew his story before he told it. Thoughts of Ya Chen inundated me like the rising waters that had borne her out to sea, intermingled with flashes of light shining on Giacomo's face. But without him and now Zhugong in my life, how impoverished that life will be. I kept silent and then the quiet moment was interrupted by the insistent buzzing of a bee, and I returned from that otherworldly sensation.

I asked him, "In the heart of what Universe will anyone distinguish me?"

Zhugong did not answer me, though by the look in his eyes, I knew he had no fear for me or my future. How could he be so certain?

He drank lustily, slurping as if he would never be able to slake his thirst. When he finished, he set aside the water.

"As a visitor to a Tibetan home, did you know one should pay attention to the methods of drinking various beverages? For instance, when drinking buttered tea, I would wait until the tea cooled, and then would blow away the surface oil, and sip the tea with the lips pressed close. Wanting more is indicated to the host by leaving some tea in the bowl."

"So if you drain the bowl, you have had enough?"

"Clever girl." He winked at me. "When drinking Qingke wine, keep the body erect, looking ahead, while listening to the host sing. When he is finished singing, the guest says some courteous words. The cup is held in the right hand. You dip the third finger of the left hand into the wine three times and flick the drops into the air—an offering to Buddha. Toss back the remaining wine. Sometimes the host asks you to drink a cup in three gulps. You sip twice and gulp what remains. If you do not want any more, after flipping three drops in the air, taste your finger, the host will understand. If the guest is unable to drink much, he should explain to the host. Draining several cups can get one into trouble, for there's a lack of oxygen on the lofty Tibetan Plateau. Which makes it imprudent to overindulge in alcohol, especially Qingke wine."

"Do you have this from firsthand knowledge?"

"Stop disrupting my thoughts. And so it was I returned from Tibet to my father, who made me tend the neighbor's pigs, and hence changed my name to pig-keeper. I had been exalted under heaven when a monk, and now I became the lowliest of beings. Yet I did not mind the job, or the name, for I had disobeyed my father and had displeased him for not becoming a holy monk. He was unhappy with me, and certainly not proud—even when I helped him construct two vertical-axis windmills."

"My Baba told me China is the birthplace of windmills," I said.

"Invented more than two thousand years ago by statesman Yehlu Chhu-Tshai. Before the birth of the priest's Christ."

"Zhugong, while interesting, whose story is this? Before night descends—"

"Ah," he sighed. "Then I will speak of the primary applications of these windmills—we used them for grain grinding and water pumping. Father was ingenious, though unschooled."

"And?" I said, impatience eddying in my voice.

"Windmills are scenic, marvelous spectacles besides generating windpower. Agree?"

"You are exasperating. This is sheer torture." I sipped from his bottle.

"Misery loves to share its tale, and even exaggerate and prolong it, in the hopes of alleviating unhappiness, does it not?"

"You are not miserable," I said, and handed him the bottle of water, which he refused.

"I thirst only for your company."

"I am not going anywhere." I corked the bottle.

"No, but I am."

My face grew hot with shame, and I snatched the fan from his lap and worked it as if to grow muscles. He waited and when I was done, I handed it back, said I was sorry, and in a kinder tone, asked him to please get on with the story.

He pointed to the flask. "I would like to sample that."

"Here, you old goat—but tell me the story. The true story."

He sipped, smacked his lips, and sipped again. "No wonder the priest holds Mass. It in no way tastes like blood."

Reluctance on his face, he handed it back to me. "So I went to live with my father's cousin who taught me to fish. When I learned how to fish, he in turn sent me to live with another cousin who was a carpenter. I learned to make a sampan, and when the boat was finished, he sent me to his wife's brother who was a cloth merchant, and his son taught me to make sails for the sampan, which took me to a remote island where I found a beautiful maiden who sang a sad song as she thrashed wheat.

"I took a job as a sheepherder, and every day I listened to her silken song which spun and floated on air till I breathed in quantities that overfilled my lungs, so much so I felt I was a kite with wings and climbed to the top of the mountain, calling to her with a sheep's horn. I thought surely she would come to me, but the days dragged on and my spirit grew weary and despondent.

"As I collected wood to build a fire in the cool of evening, I heard a noise on the stone path and knew she had come. We walked hand in hand till we came to a cascade. We undressed each other by moonlight and bathed in the waterfall, swimming in transparent collected pools. Our skin shone in the water. We made love under the stars, a sheepskin for our wedding bed."

He had been gazing up through the tree. Once in a while, he angled his head for a clearer view to the sky. The fading sunlight illuminated his skin till the pallor left and his cheeks radiated health as they must have in his youth. He turned his glance toward me to see what? If I were listening? If I believed him? I kept my countenance passive, a card player not wanting to give away a bluff.

He stretched his arms sideward and made lazy circles with them for a bit. "Then the moon stepped in back of a cloud, and the darkness speckled us with faint webs of light radiated from behind . . ."

He trailed off, and I offered, "A halo effect."

"The next day my true love and I went to the falls again, and again we consummated our love in the lee of the mountain. We climbed down from the mountain, then sailed away on the sampan, returning to the mainland, for it was my intention to work my way back to my father to ask his blessing and show him my respectful love—"

"What was her name?"

"Is it impolite to test the teller of tales?" He raised an eyebrow and folded his forearms into opposite wide sleeves. "And also to show Father I had acquired ambition and skills. But as fate would have it, the sea rose up and huge waves dwarfed, then smashed the boat to toothpicks, and all was lost, including my darling. All but me."

I swallowed hard. His story was not unlike mine in many ways. A lesson here, but what?

"What pictures can I draw for you of a man when he faces death? What is death? His own foremost? The understanding is the quest human beings have pursued throughout the ages. Think about this: humans are astonishing—they don't go around thinking any moment they could die, that at any one given moment it's all over, yet every day, we face death, don't we?"

"We go on, blind to the possible ending of our life histories. Are we brave or dumb?"

"We are neither. We are human."

"Did you return to your father's house? Did you ever marry?"

"Every woman's kiss thereafter held a thistle in it, or a bramble, or the pinchy thorns of nettles. Would you like that?"

In spite of myself, I smiled at the old coot.

"*Yù*," he said.

By the plaintive way he said it, I knew Jade was the name of his love, and she had been a real person and not some figment drawn of longing. We sat in silence. Starlings began to chitchat. "Hush," I wanted to say, but their rumpus broke the spell. He shook his head as if agreeing with himself or an unseen specter.

"Have you ever seen me look longingly at the velvety sky?" Not waiting for an answer he added, "The eyes of our dead light the stars."

As if on command, one of those dead ignited, flashing into oblivion out of the sky.

"Hmm," he said. I assumed he pondered the conflagration we had witnessed. "However, one can get used to even thistles as in all things, is this not so? Commitment is an altogether different matter. People need people, and if you lose someone you love, the love does not die, but goes on. You must replace the recipient of that affection, or shrivel up and also die."

I swatted a fly.

"Pay attention! Then one day, returning from a political rally—"

"You were interested in politics?"

"I had no interest in it at all, but returning, I saw a woman standing on a cliff—as though she called out to the sea. When she twisted to look at me, I knew she possessed the secrets of the oceans, the inner being of a mermaid, the heart of my departed beloved lost in the depths of the unfathomable ocean. This siren's lips held a thornless, honey-dipped kiss I knew awaited me. She was not a legendary aquatic creature having the head and upper body of a woman and the tail of a fish—a *mei ren yu*— beautiful human-being fish—no, no, but this is neither here nor there. What you must know is she came from the sea, as your great love will come to you."

I almost laughed, but he was so sweet and serious in his deliberation, and I knew his great fabrication was to enable me to see I should once again seek love. How could I? "If I lived a thousand lives—" I stopped midsentence, an image of long ago seized me in it's powerful grip, so that I closed my eyes and tilted my head upward, and the smell of jasmine and then of sandalwood filled the air with garden scents. *He was so tall, I had stood on tiptoes.*

Zhugong's words broke into my reverie, shattering it like a vial of perfume on tiles.

"Lian, Lian, you do not see. My life, honeyed yet salted, a tug and pull, gave but also took from me. You think me an old fool, inventing a tale to convince you that you must continue on your path and find true love. In time you will see you are the fool. I, too, lost the embraces of a thin-armed child, who was everything to me. He was taken away. Abducted. Worse than if he had been killed in front of me. I never knew his fate, or what that innocent endured: hurt, longing, separation. The only thing that matters is the connection between hearts." He tapped his chest with crooked fingers. "I have him here." Rooks stirred in the willows, and a many-ribboned butterfly flitted, perching on his shoulder. "The Sea Woman had hair blacker than a starless night, and though I did not love her, I respected her decision to live no longer without the child and one day, men from my village, looking down from a cliff, saw her walk into the sea."

"Ah," I said. Another life lost to water, usually life-giver. My mirth had ceased and my breath stopped, wanting to be so still. I took in air and let it out—a long, soft exhaling of breath.

"I raised bees for honey, I made *beichun* wine, I sold scuppernong at market, I spoke at funerals; I was hired to oversee weddings—a thorn in my side, surrounded by the auspicious color red, knowing for me, my own nuptials had ended in the raging sea; I was a scribe; I worked for an exporter; I was the secretary to a Mandarin; I was sequestered into the navy and fought under Lin Tse-hsü—Lin the Clear Sky because of his high sense of morality."

"You mean conscripted?" I asked, wanting to know more about the mermaid love.

He took a deep breath. "To fight in the Opium War. They say that heavy smokers die within five years, that opium is addictive, but as you and I know, Lian, the occasional pipe does the soul as well as the body enormous good. Any more wine?"

"Not a teardrop's worth until you finish—" I interrupted myself, delighted that he didn't go off on a tangent and tell me the history of Lin the Clear Sky.

"War brings out the brute in men. I watched, petrified out of my skin, when the British ship *Nemesis* destroyed a Chinese ship like a box of wooden matches. I witnessed this from one of our larger junks." His shoulders sagged. "Clear out of the water, like a harpooned fish."

"Were you friends with any of the sailors?" I asked, my heart beating faster.

"Where are those men who burned beside me? I saw troops bind a woman's thighs so she could not give birth. In dreams, I still hear her screams." He took a deep breath. "I watched cattle calve, fields of wheat destroyed by locusts, unmown grasses razed in a dust storm, iced rivers flow in spring, ripened fruit fall, trees lose leaves, dreams blow away, snow drift down to whirl around and cover earth . . . a tarpaulin of snow shrouded, and the war ended."

He smirked at me, and I knew he knew my questioning mind sought more.

"Why does a young man become a sailor voluntarily?" I asked with thoughts of my lover.

He looked at me, that wry grin on his face. "Why not? Youth is filled with curiosity for the world, and the wild, beckoning width of other worlds."

"And when they find them?"

"Most are seekers and revelers—they rarely want to settle down for fear there's something they'll miss seeing. Are these questions relevant to my story, or are they bundled into inquisitiveness for an answer you yearn to hear? One that will please you?"

"Are you hungry?" I opened the basket latch, hoping a food offering would entice him to recount more. I wanted to know if a sailor could settle down with one woman.

"You know the rest of my life anyway. I think your interest has waned with your thoughts of another time. Who was the sailor?"

I looked at him as though I'd turned deaf and dumb.

"Only the caves can reveal your future. I am not a seer—shall we not taste the trifles, my rooking girl, you smuggled into this basket? Allow us to partake and unite with this night."

"Maybe I don't want to know the future or hope for one."

"You do, and you will."

"I must excuse myself, but how is it, Zhugong, you maintain, that is, I mean to say—"

"What you want to know is why am I not feeble and incontinent?"

"I have heard that the eunuchs of the Forbidden City must wear specially layered—"

"May I remind you I am not nor have I ever been a eunuch?"

I blushed. "I beg your pardon for the reference, but I was merely comparing—"

"Do not say another word. Let me explain. With all those pigs around—do you not know I utilize the pig's bladder to steam with dry hops? I consume this as part of my diet. I thought surely you have seen me prepare it."

Had I?

"And besides, when I was in Mongolia, living in a yurt, I learned the art of self-denial in many things, especially when the descending hordes were upon us. Would you suggest something else, little doctor?"

"Let me prepare you some *bajitian.*"

"Morinda root? Never-withering-and-falling? Late for an herb to cure impotence."

"Pungent and sweet—in the warm class for your kidneys. And about the descending hordes—it is impossible to see and understand all things, and to believe half of what you say," I said, annoyance showing with arched eyebrows.

"Let me just say there are things I do not want your sensitive ears to hear. After all, would you want to know how those marauders ravaged? Or that before it happened, I was peacefully entering the name of my newborn son, writing on parchment with a quill pen, or I was scraping it onto a goatskin with a sharpened horn?"

A moment of silence.

"Finish the wine. I am going to sleep."

"No, you are running off to physical womanly needs, to cry, and to think on all I have told you."

"That too." I stood and bowed deeply.

"Morinda root, indeed," he said. "Bring some tomorrow if you think you can get me to a nearby House of Flowers." And then he chuckled.

I could not know everything he had done, or had learned, or the pattern or the fabric of his life. This saddened me, but at last I was resigned. Was this the lesson then? And his humor would not die until he did. How incredible. I meditated on every word he'd said, every nuance of his face as he uttered each syllable of his story. I felt some of the wondrous experiences in his legend had been true. But what about Zhugong's words concerning the sailor? I laughed. I wept. Since I could not sleep, I sketched a new dragon and entered the story of my pig-keeper.

When I finished writing, it was the first breath of dawn. The pages of my chronicle filled, I would make another. I packed my brushes into a tooled leather bag Liang had given me as a parting gift. I sat at the window, yawned, and looked out. There he stood. "Zhugong, how did you get here?" I opened the door and looked about, but he wasn't there. With urgency, I rushed to him. At the threshold, I looked around the room. I went back and took my bridal jacket and a tin of tea from a cupboard. I placed the leather sack with all the other articles in a big burlap bag, along with a new pair of black cotton shoes, and slung it over my shoulder.

I hastened past the schoolhouse, which was in complete darkness. Then I crossed the courtyard, dashing in front of the rectory, votive lights flickered within. I gazed at the leaden sky and walked with hurried pace. In the low lodges and dwellings I passed, lights were extinguished.

Pale and almost lifeless on his pallet, he said, "I knew you would come. I sent for you."

"You mean you came for me." I left my bag in a corner and sat with him. He pointed in the direction of the caves and patted my hands as my father had done so long ago. He smiled that crooked smile and nodded his head and summoned me closer. He took a handmade folded map from his bodice and gave it to me. I put it inside my bag.

He held out his arms. I had never held him—except for the water buffalo outbreak. Frail as a plucked, underfed chicken. He whispered in my ear, "You will go, incarnation of my love." He breathed his last and died in my arms. I held his warm body and touched the crepe skin of his cheek. I placed my lips on his as my sailor had done to me in a jasmine-scented garden and repeated what I'd said to Giacomo when he asked me not to forget him, "Never."

Why hadn't I realized his death was so imminent? I should have stayed and been vigilant to the last. This is what he wanted—not for me to see him in the throes of death's embrace.

I laid him back down and stayed with Zhugong until he grew cold.

After he died, I felt a surge of strength, as if he had breathed into my spirit. I built his pyre with wood from a pile nearby. I yanked, pulled, and carried logs until I had set up a bier in a clearing. How I wished it could be near water—a lake or a river. But there was only a miserable, little pond, and I thought, *This will have to do.* This construction of a final resting place on which I would cremate his remains was quite unlovely but practical. Then I took hold of a pitchfork from a haystack and carried several loads over to the pyre and spread it out.

I lifted his soulless body and heaved him over my shoulder, wobbling, for while he was not meaty, he was bony, and it was awkward to negotiate the rocky path. I lifted Zhugong onto his funeral pyre, covering his wrinkled and benign face with myrrh and aloe from his shack. I sat at the edge of the island of his final resting place, thinking I'd combed his hair into a queue because he had no strength of late. And yesterday, I cut his hair, a Yogi tradition, for readying oneself for the next life, but death is a shock even when one is old. Zhugong had wanted for his meal something from his youth, yet still, how could I have known it was to be his last?

I roused Guo Xide and told him what I had done. He disapproved and wanted to give Zhugong a Christian burial, but the old one was neither Christian nor wished to be buried. I welcomed him to the site. He took his scapular down from a nail and put it around his neck. He went to take holy water, but I put up my hand. This was one argument I would not lose. "There will be no need to exorcise this Buddhist, Father. He has the mandate of heaven for his final blessing." The priest had one of the little altar boys ring the bell, and soon people gathered in front of the church. We walked back to where I had left Zhugong.

I stood looking at Zhugong until the good fold of our missionary gathered. Cook touched my shoulder. His touch propelled me into action, and I lighted a pine pitch torch and set Zhugong's beard afire, and with it, his long cut queue wound around his head. I daubed his eyes with pitch; his hair burned, flashing quickly, like a hayfield after drought. I set fire to his clothes. He began to burn—his words in my ears; Destiny, like the seasons, never misses appointed days.

I witnessed the immolation and looked west where a fierce wind had begun to bluster. His ashes blew in frenzied whorls. Into the west, he was borne away on strong breezes—all of him—his heart, his mind, his monk's bones and bodily flesh; but his other self, the released spirit, remains with me, now a part of me until I shall die and pass to the other world. I must attempt to go to the caves. It's what he wanted for me.

Lulled into the feeling nothing was more important than my world, my sorrow, my loss, the official mourning of my daughter with Yang Zhugong roused me like a dragon after a long sleep. I added up bits and pieces of what Mangen had said, of what I'd read in the paper and what the priest told me of the mandarins. Troublemaking crowds of farmers had started to raid mission stores. They blamed poor crops, draught, and other natural disasters on the foreign devils—mainly the religious. Reports of secret alliances between the empress dowager and Boxers seemed less preposterous than when I learned of them weeks ago from a visiting German pastor. Frightened for myself, but not nearly as much as for the others of the mission, I warned Guo Xide of the political unrest compounding itself. I told him I was leaving to go to the caves.

The mourners were gone. When I could no longer stand close to

Zhugong's melting flesh, I moved away, inhaled deeply, and sat observing the fire from a distance. Guo Xide had left and out of kindness and gratitude for my time at the mission, came back to bring me Wang Mangen's horse, blanket, and saddle. Odd that he had not taken the horse when he left. Handing me the reins, he said, "Let me bless you, Lian, even though—"

He did not finish for he knew I'd never be counted among his converts. "Pray for me instead, dear priest." I said.

He took a piece of paper out of his cassock. "Memorize this address, in case you lose it. Go here, because I fear you'll never return." He pointed at the name of an infirmary in Tientsin, "You'll be able to use your talents for healing."

I took hold of the paper, remembering Zhugong's words. "The priest's an egotist, and like the snow leopard walking on snow all day, its paws are stiff and unyielding, but the heart is fierce and the animal attacks using speed and power. It is quick and leaps and lunges, then backs away swiftly after the damage is done and before a counterattack."

I tied the horse to a tree. "Guo Xide, leave the mission. Disband and go back to Italy. There will be bloodshed and destruction—you must heed what I'm telling you."

"I cannot abandon my flock."

"You are neither a shepherd nor Christ, and you will die for this stubbornness. Take the opportunity now and go before things turn uglier and your way will be blocked." He was determined to stay, he said, though again, I begged him to depart.

Before I could object, he made the sign of the cross over me and I bowed.

I watched his back as he moved with grace in his cassock, catching the wind, and even a part of Zhugong's ghost.

I felt a chill, and to warm myself and clear my head, I ran to the laundry and found the door locked. I jimmied and pried the window. I wrapped my jacket around my arm to smash the glass pane. I reached in and tugged at the bolt, opened the window, and hoisted myself in. I knocked over an iron warm from the coals. I stole some boy's clothing from a pile of folded garments and opened the door with my arms loaded, the jacket still flopping around my forearm.

The charred remains had dwindled down to coals, but the bier was still red hot and smoking. I could not warm myself beside it. I disrobed and tossed my clothes to burn with the last of him. I smiled at the ironic symbol of a lover and wondered if we had known each other intimately in a life before this one. Inside his humble shack, I dressed like a boy with fleeced clothes, winding up my long hair and placing it under Zhugong's coolie hat. Any wayfarer traveling alone was unsafe, but I had a knife with a bone handle from Zhugong's basket of stores. Into my belongings I put a small pot, chopsticks, a bag of rice, a bottle of peanut oil. I hefted my supplies and stepped outside under a canopy of night sky immense with fading pearlstrings of stars and a sliver of moon. Without warning, I loosed the pigs, lighted a torch with the coals from Zhugong, and threw it inside his abode. I watched his straw mat catch fire, thinking his bone fragments would cool sometime late tomorrow. I charged the cook to disperse them into the river below the mission. My vision before had been misguided; I didn't carve out a shallow grave for him, yet I would dig a kind of grave in the not-too-distant future.

Into the saddlebags I had fashioned together, I distributed my belongings. I touched the jade Buddha Zhugong had given me, hanging from a gold chain around my neck. Where had the old coot gotten the Italian gold chain? I untied the horse from the tree where Zhugong and I had spent many blissful moments. I walked the horse till I came to the spirit screen, unlatched the heavy bolt of the mission door, took hold of the rein, and left that place, never looking back.

Chapter 18

Kuli
力
Coolie

WHEN THE BRUTAL ICE FINALLY began to split and separate, the winter trials for the *Leopardo* were not over. There was a coolie outbreak of real fisticuffs in the furnace room. Giacomo and the crew got a break from boredom, taking sides and betting on which coolie would draw blood first. The furnace room was packed with hooting sailors, tossing Mexican silver into a pot.

Once that broke up, there was a riot onshore as the boat got under way. The captain ordered the men to lug out huge hoses with frigid water. These couldn't be used to put down the insurrection on shore but were directed at the accompanying junks and sampans following.

After the hoses were stacked and the ship was underway, the medic attended to two older men, while Giacomo used a needle and thread to stitch Shen's arm, dousing it with alcohol.

"Good thing I can stuff and sew a chicken or you'd be in a heap of trouble. What were you doing in the furnace room anyway?"

"Boss man Chinee send Shen wash rags. Big *kuli* say, No. Hit boss head with wok. Big trouble. All knives. Shen blood," he said, his voice ragged.

When Giacomo finished stitching Shen's arm, they went topside to watch the riot onshore as the boat got underway. The Captain ordered the men to put away the hoses once the *Leopardo* gained distance, the junks and sampans falling behind the getaway of the foreign ship.

From Hangzhou they went to Changsha and from there to Sichuan Province following the Yangtze River. The ship docked and the men were finally allowed to rest and permitted shore leave. Giacomo went to the Five Happiness Café, a place he had frequented before. He sat near the musicians and listened to a plaintive song, sung by a young girl who did not resemble Lian at all. But somehow the way she looked when she sang, and the melody of her sad song, made Giacomo think of Lian. The singer's words tore right through him, and when she was done, he stood and applauded to jeers and cheers from the clientele.

An Austrian petty officer, Fritz Munchnik, sat alone at the next table. Giacomo's and Fritz's ships were docked often in the same port, and they frequented the same taverns. Giacomo recognized Fritz immediately and observed the man with him, dressed elegantly in Western-style clothes, talking for some time over drinks. An hour later, the well-dressed man left.

Giacomo tipped his glass to the officer, who now sat by himself, and would have invited him over but for the disorderly table. He grinned, shrugged his shoulders, and opened his hands sweeping them above the messy table. The officer laughed and signaled him to come over to his own neat table. Giacomo took a bottle of good Scotch whiskey with him. They shook hands.

"Been a long time, Giacomo," the officer said in precise Italian.

"It has, Fritz." Giacomo sat down. "A drink?" Giacomo said, tilting his bottle.

"Scotch, my man, is so plebian. Join me with this gorgeous Green Fairy," Fritz said.

Giacomo looked at the bottle of greenish gold liquor. He watched Fritz trickle ice water over a sugar cube in a small slotted spoon that dipped into the glass containing the hallucinogenic and watched it turn cloudy.

"Absinthe isn't for me. I was weaned on wine, but here it all tastes like liquid poison, so I'll stick to this." Giacomo took hold of the bottle's neck and poured himself a drink.

"You should try some." He sniffed it. "Aromatic, to say the least, and it changes your outlook on the world. Nectar of gods, and artists. I heard Van Gogh cut off his ear while drunk on this drink of the gods. Oscar Wilde, and Toulouse Lautrec—"

"Friends of yours?" Giacomo said.

Fritz sniggered, the effect of the drink, Giacomo figured. "You're playing with fire. We travel in different societies—it's only because we're here in China that we're even speaking."

"Actually, my man, the alcohol effect of this makes you think better. Maybe it's the green wormwood, but you have a clearer vision of things."

A smell of fried pork wafted from the kitchen as a waiter opened the door.

"Hungry?"

Fritz shook his head.

"Me neither. Though it smells good. Been meaning to ask how you speak Italian?"

"I'm from Arnbach on the Austrian-Italian border."

"Where exactly?"

"Sud Tirol—south of Lienz, it's north of Cortina D'Ampezzo— where I skied almost all my life with my parents."

"Privileged youth. Why aren't you a commissioned officer?" There was a clattering of plates as a waiter dropped a tray.

"I'm a basic—how do you say—oh yes, *testa di cazzo*. A screwup of the first order."

"That's putting it mildly. Who's the natty little fellow you were just talking to? Looks familiar," Giacomo said.

"He says he's a banker from Shanghai, but he's an Italian priest, Father Gabriele." Fritz inhaled then sipped his drink. "Keep it under your hat."

"Have I ever met him? Why pass himself off as a banker?"

"He doesn't know behind which face lurks the enemy."

A pretty girl in a pink dress sashayed by the table. The two men appreciated her beguiling wiggle. Fritz said, "I think it's time for some entertainment, not that I don't value your company." Fritz patted Giacomo's back as he stood up from the table, "But that little tidbit is most appealing, don't you agree? Suddenly I have an appetite. Can you meet me tomorrow night at the Cottage House, say around midnight?"

THE NEXT NIGHT IN THE Cottage House of the 9th Rose, a seedy club not frequented by foreigners except conscripted ones, Giacomo met

Fritz again. "Wanted to ask last night, what're you doing here?" Fritz said.

"Yangbinguon, Sichuan—I'm on leave." Giacomo sat down at Fritz's table.

"Seems every time I see you, you're off duty. Don't you find it odd we keep meeting—whether we're near water or far from it?"

"What about you—I could say the same."

"What I find strange is why the Fates toss certain people together and tear others asunder. I'm here on behalf of the German embassy, trying to contact these missionaries. I was at a mission run by German nuns—but there was no way to convince them of danger. They decided to stay and risk—"

"I read about it in the paper. They were executed by farmers and Boxer sympathizers. Now you're here trying to do the same thing?"

"Want to come along to see the mission? I've been there before. Already spoke to the head honcho—a priest, Guo Xide." Fritz sipped some beer.

"Ah—Chinese, then maybe you could use my help. I'm getting quite proficient."

"The priest is Italian—Don Alberico Crescitelli, but his converts call him Guo Xide."

"Then you don't need me. Before last night, when's the last time I saw you?"

"Guangzhou."

"Then you met Shen?"

"Who?" Fritz looked perplexed.

"A coolie I picked up in Hong Kong. My assistant in the galley—a great little cook—teaching me Mandarin."

"Not Cantonese."

"He passes himself off as an orphan. He's not, but neither is he from Hong Kong."

"I'm impressed. You'd been talking pidgin before and had disdain for coolies, and the like. Why the change?"

"This kid—he's something special. Smart. Cunning, even. He lives by his wits."

"About this trip to the mission . . . I could use an ally to depend on, someone who might do me good. Besides the priest is one of yours. I'm surprised you aren't being sent on a task force operation of this nature.

Maybe you should tell your captain about it."

"I couldn't absent myself for so long without at least talking to Lieutenant Rinaldi."

"Let's get moving then. I'll go with you and bring the embassy commission letter. If you get Rinaldi's nod, you can borrow some of my 'civies' for the trip."

"Getting out of uniform is tempting."

With permission from the lieutenant, Giacomo and Fritz went by bicycle the next day from the village to a farm where they rented horses. They trekked up the hilly mountain pass to the mission. A light drizzle began to fall and they stopped in a dense arbor, thick, glossy, broad leaves of a plant Giacomo didn't recognize. When they started riding again, the men looked down the valley and commented on its beauty. It was as peaceful, yet greener than some of the valleys of Sicily, Giacomo thought. He remembered certain wide fields and sheathes of fertile coastal land from Mazzara del Vallo to Agrigento—land where huge caper bushes grew, and vineyards, vast lands where sheep munched the grasses to their roots. They rode on, Giacomo leaning sometimes to get a better perspective of the terraced hills.

The rain abated and they continued, once asking directions from a pretty girl, balancing a yoke with two buckets of water, pigtails undulating as she strode along the hard-packed mud road. The girl said they were close by.

They thanked her and Giacomo turned in the saddle and said, "What is your name?"

"Wo," she said, and blushed like a ripe pomegranate.

The riders entered the mission doors and rode past the spirit screen. Neither of them understood its exact meaning, but Giacomo would ask Shen about it later. They settled their horses in front of a large building with a tile roof. One rocking chair like an abandoned sweetheart sat on the porch. A small table held a lantern. A crucifix hung over the door.

Giacomo noted the pool, the shrubbery, the chapel, what looked like a cookhouse, what could possibly pass for a sickbay, and other outbuildings, and wondered if the mission could stand an attack by Boxer forces said to inhabit the foothills and surrounding lands. He looked at the high walls, the gates, and thought, if need be, the whole compound could be sealed off.

"How long would they be able to stave off continual Boxer blows? Lacking food, medical supplies, water?" He looked around. "There's a cistern way off to the left by a shed." Further to the left, he spotted a well with a canted roof. "What about weapons and ammunition? They certainly have some stores on hand, but not much, I'd bet." He considered the difficulty of getting to this outpost. "Why do you think the mission people are in imminent danger?"

"We heard they've been stampeded and have been under small attacks—those will increase. For certain."

A priest with a beard and a Chinese-style black hat, dressed in a black cassock, came forward and introduced himself in Mandarin.

"I'm Guo Xide. Welcome to our mission. What may I do to assist you? You've traveled a long way, so I imagine it's on urgent business. May I suggest some tea, after your ride?" He said this in halting Mandarin, and Giacomo noted he had more fluency than this man of the cloth.

"You may speak your native tongue, Father, we're familiar with it, more so than Chinese," Fritz said.

Giacomo winced at this.

Guo Xide said, "I wasn't sure you both spoke Italian."

Giacomo felt uncomfortable in Fritz's borrowed civilian clothes, astride a horse somewhat jittery and fearful. The priest looked at them with a cold stare. Giacomo thought, *He must know what he was about to hear wasn't going to be good news.*

Fritz dismounted and said, "I come on official business from the German embassy, though I myself am Austrian, but my *compare* here," he said pointing to Giacomo, "is Sicilian, on a voyage of mercy with me."

"What business do I have with the German embassy?" the priest asked.

"I was given orders to apprise you of the situation. A German mission was overrun and two sisters, brides of Christ, were murdered savagely and—"

"I beg your pardon, but this is old news. I've had it from a former nurse of our recent employ with us a year."

"Not more than seventy *li* from here."

The priest blanched. "This is," he hesitated, "an outrage, then I, well, it's a different missionary than the one I'd heard of, and—"

"Where was the other?" Giacomo asked. He looped his reins around a sort of hitching post and took hold of Fritz's and did the same.

"Way north of here. Many months ago," Gou Xide said, his voice weak.

"This happened south east of here," Fritz said.

"Two weeks ago," Giacomo added.

"Dear Lord." The priest put up his hands in supplication, looking toward heaven. "Please, follow me."

They followed the priest to a sitting room. Seated in front a small coal fire in a brazier, each man held a cup of tea. Father Gabriele entered in his cassock and bowed toward Guo Xide. Both Fritz and Giacomo placed their cups on a table and stood to greet this priest. Fritz, who was not surprised to see Father Gabriele, introduced Giacomo, who recognized the priest previously dressed as a banker; then the men sat and picked up their cups, steam rising from the liquid.

Guo Xide invited the men to partake of dinner and stay the night. "You'll want to freshen up before dinner. I'll show you to your room."

Inside the small dormitory off the chapel's sacristy, Fritz rolled a cigarette and took a drag. He reached for a hip flask and took a long pull, then handed it to Giacomo. "There's no convincing that priest. I've a mind to leave now, but the dangerous heights and unsure roads—too risky. I'm no martyr. I've put you in harm's way. Forgive me, friend." Fritz offered the flask to Giacomo, who set it on a small table. They took off their boots and each of them stretched out on a cot.

<hr/>

AT THE DINNER TABLE GIACOMO felt both priests' unease.

Guo Xide laid his chopsticks across his plate. "Until I'm told to abandon my post here from my order, I stay, and Father Gabriele with me."

"What about the others who aren't receiving commands from Rome? Do you accept responsibility for your behavior? They'll be killed for your stubbornness—" Giacomo said.

"Or worse. They'll abandon you. Will you then take up arms? These are indigenous paramilitary—they operate covertly in small bands—they don't just harass—they kill, rape, and pillage. Understand what I'm saying?" Fritz said with emphasis.

Making a futile gesture with his hands, Guo Xide said, "Against these neighbors, I cannot take up arms, but would rather surrender my life—"

"Oh that you will, Father, that's guaranteed." Fritz tossed his napkin on the table and stormed out.

Giacomo felt he should try to help convince the priest of his precarious situation. After Fritz calmed down and retired for the night, Giacomo left through the sacristy to walk around the mission in hopes of finding the priest. There was a light on in the cook's house. He rapped lightly on the window. Guo Xide invited Giacomo to come inside, and made gingerroot tea.

"There was a girl on the road today. Wo. Could you stand to know you caused her to be violated by an angry mob and gutted for laughs? Do you know that's what's happening?"

This sobered the priest, and he haltingly described the stampede.

"It will get uglier, I guarantee it. They'll come armed with weapons," Giacomo said, noticing dried blood on the wall, wondering why it had not been painted over. On a shelf there was a broken shard of porcelain, perhaps from a cup. "Odd souvenir," he said.

"A reminder of the fragility of spirit. The cook wouldn't throw it away or clean the blood off the wall." He pointed to the bloodstains. "We had a teacher here who once wanted to end her life." The priest pointed to another shelf. "That's a daguerreotype of her with her class."

Giacomo took hold of the frame and almost dropped it as if it were on fire. "She looks like a girl I know, but she was a nurse." He hesitated and then asked, "Is her name Lian?" Giacomo's palms sweated and he wiped them with a handkerchief. He looked again at the picture, closer this time, and his heart took an unexpected leap in his chest.

The priest nodded. "She worked here as a teacher and nurse. How do you know her?"

"Is she still here?"

"I hope my prayers helped, but she pulled from inner strength with the counsel of an old man said to have had many lives . . ." His voice trailed off.

"Lian—where is she?"

"She left, but—"

"She's back? Here? Now?" Giacomo said, the emotion in his voice unbounded.

"No. She went to—"

"Where did she go?" he asked with urgency in his question.

"What do you want with Lian?" The priest looked brooding.

"Where?" Giacomo demanded, taking a step toward the priest.

"The caves. Very far from here. She won't come back."

"Where exactly? Why did she go?"

Guo Xide explained she went to seek her destiny. "The old sage sent her before he died. She had a horse, but from the caves, she was going to Tientsin. My friend runs a clinic there."

"Dear God, I've searched all of China for her and to be so close, yet—" Giacomo's forehead glistened with sweat, and he fought to control his voice, tears gathering.

"Are you sure it's her?" Guo Xide said.

"Does a man not know his own soul? Will you give her a letter for me if she comes back? Or mail it to her if you hear from her?"

"Of course, my son. Be calm."

"Do you have paper and pen, Padre?"

THE NEXT DAY STARTED WITH snow flurries as Fritz and Giacomo said farewell to the priests. As they began the trip down the mountain, Giacomo felt the late snow pelt his eyelids and pulled the hood from his borrowed jacket down to his brow. He reflected for a silent hour, taking toll of his emotions. To have come so far and have been so close to finding Lian again was sheer torture.

He could barely sit the horse after hardly sleeping last night. He watched breath from the mouths and the nostrils of the horses in quick spurts of smoke, visibly white. Giacomo was thirsty; perspiration gathered in his armpits. "Hold up, Frtiz, we should rest the horses."

"At this rate, my man, we'll need to stop at a hostel. When do you have to get back?"

"I've got a week. But this weather is building, we may not be able to move for a while—" and Giacomo wondered just how long that would be. "I still need to report back as soon as we return. How far is that hostel we stayed at on the way up here?"

"A guess, but about three hours ride," Fritz said.

"Just curious, but how come you know these hilly roads so well?"

"I had a sweetheart once. A Chinese laundress, who worked at the mission. That's how I know Father Gabriele."

By the tone of his voice, Giacomo knew not to ask more questions, but he remembered seeing Fritz with a country girl in Guangzhou. "I knew a girl who worked at the mission too," he said, his voice wistful. Why hadn't he pressed the priest for more information of Lian?

"Really?"

"Only I didn't know till now."

"Who was she?" Fritz pulled his scarf over his head and tied a knot under his chin.

Giacomo didn't answer. He didn't have to.

Fritz stopped his horse and looked at him. "You loved her."

"Still do," he said, thinking, *If I could only follow her to those caves now.* Giacomo pulled his collar up. "Shall I ask you about the laundress?"

"Fair enough."

Chapter 19

Ma
马
Horse

THE MAP THAT ZHUGONG GAVE to the caves marked a distance of four hundred *gongli*. The trek would be impossible for a lone woman, even with a horse, yet the beginning was easy. The next morning, a little before dawn, I reached the market. The hawkers and criers set up their stalls as I walked the horse, trying to convince myself I was brave enough, hopeful enough, to attempt the journey. The horse and I passed the severed head of a steer that sat in sawdust, smoked ducks hanging from bamboo poles. Knives, hatchets, saws, kitchen utensils, basket steamers for buns, and woks abounded everywhere. Just beyond the market crush, there was a riffling, riffling, and then a profluence of egrets and ibis, cardinals, blue jays, doves, and parrots—flight and motion and swirling clouds in a limitless, refulgent sky. This heaven: chaotic, frenetic, and each species free.

I crossed the market plaza. I sniffed the air, which had changed somehow. *Danger.* I inhaled the pungent air, as if we both were alive after a catatonic sleep. Wind smacked my cheeks, baptizing me with a slight drizzle, the way Guo Xide wanted to consecrate me.

I slipped my foot into the stirrup and mounted the horse, the color of midnight. He raced with me and my heart. We galloped away from the market, away from the safety of the mission. The danger was not from the night or what it harbored, but was inside me. I felt like an unknown quantity and a danger to myself. *If I was able to leave this mission womb, cut my ties, and flee, then what other capabilities do I possess?* My heart pounded as trees and brush flew by, and I hunkered lower onto the horse's withers, at one with him and the starry night. Unbounded.

I traveled less-frequented roads and byways for the next few days, and saw Zhugong in dust squalls. In the tall grasses blowing in the wind, I saw his beard. His eyes twinkled at me at night. He would laugh knowing I had a dead man for comfort, though he rode with me as I galloped. Zhugong was with me. With me. With me. Every so often, I dismounted and led the horse to spare him and then repeated the process.

The next day was clear and windy. This animal had much racehorse in him, and he wanted to run regardless of my commands. I tethered him loosely to a tree. He shook his head, annoyed. I stood apart, admiring ducks in a pond, when from the corner of my eye, I saw he had loosed his tie and had turned to run at me. I've never seen a horse knock a person over, but I was standing and he was charging me like a bull. When a horse charges, his tendency is to swerve at the last second. I stood my ground, my knees shaking until he swerved. Furious, I told him he was a naughty boy. If only I had a mirror to see if my hair had turned white. I understood his need to romp and play. The crazy running made me recall how, with enthusiasm and joy, Ya Chen would run wild till she flopped exhaustedly among summer wheat with the sheer exhilaration of speed. Where is her spirit now? I prayed, *Zhugong, watch over her.*

Later, when the horse came to nuzzle me, seeking to make amends, I forgave him, in the same way I hoped my little girl forgave me for uprooting her from her home. To prove my forgiveness, I gave him an apple from the windfall of fruit I had squirreled away from an orchard I'd passed two days ago. From that day, I'd refer to this as the incident of the horse. Were Zhugong here, he'd ask, "What is the lesson?" Alertness and forgiveness. Even myself.

Nights before I arrived at the caves, I skirted an assembly of marauders roving the countryside. Having seen a campfire in the distance, I tethered my horse to a dilapidated fencepost near an abandoned waterwheel at the side of a broken-down stone mill.

Could there be any more of a derelict situation than this? I still had a sense of humor. Slick was the high grass from rain as I skulked along, stopping close enough to pick up the scent of roasting boar on a spit. Feeling faint, I seated myself, pulling in my knees for warmth. I counted seven unkempt men, passing around a bottle of Da Kung and playing *jiuling*, first a drinking game of finger guessing, followed by another game of animal betting. The smell of *huangjiu*—my nostrils tingled with the scent of the rice wine. Horses whinnied and moonlight spangled upon shiny stirrups and fine silver-embossed saddles. I looked back at the men, realizing their riding habits, now shabby, had once been rich brocades and fine silks, their felt boots of the best quality. Who were they? A dispatch case hanging from one of the saddles stunned me into realizing they were court couriers, traveling along hard roads with orders from the Forbidden City. A hand-embossed and carved leather quiver was strapped to each horse. These men were archers, capable of great feats of skill and at great speeds, shooting from horses at a gallop. They were the light brigade of bowmen, an illegal killing squad elected to defend the empress and slay the interloping foreigners who dared encroach upon the dragon's land.

Resting my head upon folded arms, I grew sleepy. An argument ensued among the men, and as tempers flared, I crept off in the opposite way toward the horse. I waddled, wading through rice fields, and stopped in tall grass. The horse could not get wind of me. I imagined him munching contentedly. A breeze on my neck made me turn, and I saw two men absent from the encampment speaing in hushed tones. One made a gesture with his hand silencing the other, who scanned the fields. The first man stared straight to where I'd crouched; the other man made water. They will kill me and think on it later. Could I talk to them, say I lost my way, and sit by their fire? As I envisioned this bucolic setting, my hand felt in the earth and I grabbed a stone. They turned around, and I flung the stone left with as much force as I could muster. Both men started out in a loping gait in that direction while I belly crawled away in the direction of my horse. The two separated. Squatting and shaking, I pushed my body flat out and held up some shafts of Amur wheatgrass, staying my ground until they moved away and were out of sight.

When I reached a clearing, I ran to the horse in a grassy patch. I chewed cattails, spitting out the stringy part after I'd extracted the juice. I found wild fennel and ripped off the soft, feathery tops, eating them as a delicacy. Too tired to chew more, I drifted into a deep sleep.

Faint light eased its way onto the horizon as I awoke to the horse's snorts. Between snorts, smoke billowed out his nose into the frigid air. I stripped and bathed in the rivulet that rushed down an embankment. The chilled water revived me, and I guzzled huge swallows until I gagged and water spurted out my nose. Dawn streaked pink and hazy into a gray, mauve sky. Using my clothes to dry my shivering body, I donned them again. Thunderous horses shook the ground. I yanked my horse into a thicket as the cluster of archers passed. Stepping onto a dead log, I hoisted myself into the saddle and rode to their camp, where, like a wild dog, I gnawed the leavings and cindered bones of roasted boar. I curled up by the warmth of the quasi-extinguished fire and dozed, waking with the sun full in my face.

I rode and walked all day into the heart of night, when at the periphery of a village, I saw a tavern owner closing shop. Should I chance begging for some food? If he knew I had money to pay, he might rob me. Leaving my horse in the lee of a wood, I made my way to the back of the tavern. *Remain serene,* I told myself, *and wait.* When everything was still, like the family cat, I crept in the back way and saw the hearth, whose dying coals and warmth held a soup kettle.

With the moon pouring in through a window, I took a bowl from the stack of washed utensils and dipped it into the broth. Again. One more time, I drank before the taste of chicken registered, and I saw a clay dish covered with a cloth. Someone was expected. I heaped rice from another pot into a handkerchief and stuck it into my pocket. On my way out, I grabbed the covered dish; the aroma of fried pork livers made me salivate as I closed the door quietly. Once outside, I stuck the dish into my jacket pocket, some food slid in, but the dish didn't fit, so I ran with it in front of me until I tripped on a cobblestone and it clattered and broke. I bent and crept along toward the garden, only now a dog had caught my scent. A man entered the back portal, which I had exited minutes before. The barking became uproarious, so I knew the animal was huge. There was an upheaval of crashing bowls, and the man yelled at the dog. I peered over my shoulder to see a lantern and started running as my pursuer gained on me.

Trying for the confine of the garden, I had one vision in mind: my leg being ripped to shreds in the dog's jowls. I ran less than a *li*, never making it. It wasn't the dog grasping me, but the expected guest. I ran smack into him. He had my wrists, wrenching me off the ground, my legs flailed like twigs in a typhoon. Caught. The innkeeper closed in from behind. The tavern-keeper greeted the guest, saying, "Hold on tight." I screamed. My assailant dropped one wrist, backhanded me across the face, and wrenched one arm behind me. His smelly hand covered my mouth and I bit the heel. He spun me around and knocked me down with a blow to my forehead.

Imprisoned—air gushed out of me, my neck in a stranglehold. Suffocating, I swung my legs, arms flailing like Ya Chen's in that damnable bay. Like a sack of rice, I was dropped unceremoniously and gasping to the ground. Each bone in my body felt the crash.

A boot I recognized as one of the archers crushed my chest, the man who had searched the wheat field. He laughed when he realized I was not a boy. He seized me by the wrists with one filthy paw holding them overhead, while the other smothered my mouth, silencing my screams. With his forehead, he knocked my head down repeatedly until I remembered nothing.

When I came to my senses, the monster upon me grunted, but his rutting had loosened his grip on my wrists and his hand over my mouth, so I bit down on the heel as hard as I could.

He yelped, let go my wrists, and punched me with the same hand. I tried to turn and curl into a ball, but his massive weight crushed me. Then I did the unthinkable. I looked into his face. A Chinese face. Like mine, but different. I had light eyes, unlike him, and doubted I could ever inflict such pain. He knew I was foreign and would show no mercy. The tension fissured between us, and I knew rape was not a crime of sex, but a violent crime of domination.

I breathed Giacomo's name. My attacker slapped me, harder. For he knew I'd never forget him. I was a dead woman. With this thought, driving a nail into my brain, I passed out.

❦

I HEARD THE GRUNTING, RUTTING sound again. I was pinioned, in pain, and whimpering. Two hands grabbed my ears, smashing my head like a winter melon on the ground beneath me. I revived enough to know that after both men had at me and done, they would slit my throat and dump my body down a gorge, so I pretended to be unconscious, praying to the Goddess of Mercy they wouldn't notice tears trickling from the corners of my eyes.

"Out cold," the guest said.

"More fun when she fought like a winter snow tiger," the tavern-keeper said, straightening from his bent position over me.

I squinted my eyes to see them arguing about me.

"Fool, there's no such animal." The guest tucked himself inside his pants. "Throw water in her face."

"Revive her? I'm spent. Let her sleep. I need to eat."

"When you've finished eating, we'll have another go at her, eh?"

I listerned to their retreating steps, but did not move. The dog I had feared licked the cuts on my face. One of the men whistled and the dog scampered after him.

I gasped for air till my breathing returned to normal. They tied the dog and went inside.

I opened my eyes. When I heard the door slam, I gathered my tattered clothes and scooped the dirty food into my pocket. I raced across the terraced garden to the woods to my horse. I stumbled and crawled toward the trees. A hayfork lay near a pile of hay. I thought I should take hold of it, in case my attackers followed. What folly; how could I fend them off with so little strength?

I stopped and took deep breaths, my lungs burning, my ribs aching. With the cover of the forest, I hunched like an animal and scurried in the direction of the horse. Further into the woods, I stood and ran, doubling over with cramps, which slowed my speed. The horse whinnied when he heard my approach. Mounting caused a searing pain I ignored, and half-naked I tore across a culvert, flying through brush scratching at my face. But I never halted.

Some twenty *li* distance, I slid from my horse and vomited. I slept in a bog, waking cold and damp the next morning; my ripped clothing gave little protection. I found water, stripped off my tattered rags and bathed, praying to the Goddess of Mercy. Not even the cruelest gods would let the seed of those devils make me pregnant. I sat in the water shaking, scrubbing myself with gritty dirt, pristine in comparison to the pigs who had ravished me. I rinsed off the fried pork livers from one pocket and ate them with the smashed rice from the other. I dressed in my torn garments and applied mud to my swollen face. Water chestnuts lined the muddy banks below the surface. I picked several and got my knife out of my saddle pouch, thinking with bitterness, *If only I'd had it on me last night instead of packed away.* How I wished I'd been able to stick it into the flesh of that lout's throat. Or slice his swollen member off. I sat down and peeled the brownish-black scale-like leaves off the small tulip-like bulb. I swished the chestnuts in the water and nibbled the tiny tuber, so white, sweet tasting, and crunchy.

I was overjoyed to find my horse munching on some cress. I hacked at several clumps and swished them in the running water and ate avidly. When I was done, I washed again and changed to the clothing in my saddle pack. I bundled some cress and chestnuts in the ripped clothes in case I didn't find anything when next I stopped, but my body was too ravaged to sit a horse. I rested all day and night, trying to rid my heart of hatred and self-recrimination.

As the horizon brightened, I removed my bottom clothing so that I could urinate in the water, and the act wouldn't burn or sting so much. Then I gathered moss, dried weeds and grass, and strips of cloth from my ripped garments to wattle into padding to cushion my sore and oozing privates. I hoped the crotch protection would buffer the jostling I was about to undertake on the day's ride. I moved upstream and drank a great quantity of water before filling a goatskin, part of the horse's equipment that Guo Xide had given me. I could not help but think Mangen's lips had once touched it.

I spent the afternoon riding several hours, passing a village with the loveliest gardens. Women cleaned yards, raking old leaves and debris. The daffodils were already starting to bloom. Riding by one thatched cottage where an old woman was working in her garden, I asked if she'd be kind enough to give me a drink of water.

Everything was rain-washed clean and clear. Even the spiced air sparkled. I dismounted and winced, still in pain as I walked to a barrel of water near the house with a small garden in front of it. I caught my haggard reflection when I leaned over.

The owner of the house had just discovered purple crocuses were opening, and she told me in a sad voice these were the only crocuses the rabbits had not gotten.

I was famished and considered eating some of the crocuses, but they're only good for squirrels and rabbits—they'd kill a human.

After I drank the water, I let my horse also drink from the trough at the back of the dwelling. She left me to prune the roses and rake some grape hyacinths.

"With more raking they will breathe easier and see the sun," she said. "If we tend them well, our gardens flourish. They give us food to feed us, color and perfume to please us."

I dropped onto a step and could have sat all day long on the tiles warmed by the sun in front of her door, watching her prune roses and clean out the hollyhock bed.

"Soon I will have other flowers: red azaleas, blue asters, pink camellia," she said, pride in her voice. "Right now everything still looks brown and bare."

All I could do was watch in amazement at the energetic movements of this old woman, and wonder if I could eat some other flowers.

"You come from far away. Are you injured? Are you part of this peasant revolution we are hearing so much of lately? You do not look dangerous, or like a fighter."

I pulled off my hat and let her see my hair. It produced the effect I wanted.

"Ah," she said. "Let the sunshine warm you as you rest."

She took pity on me, for when she came out after her lunch break, she knew she would find me still—a firmly rooted weed in her garden.

"I am poor," she said, "but I can spare some rice and wild greens with rice vinegar."

"Celestial bounty," I said, ate three spoonfuls, and fainted.

THE AROMA OF DEEP FRIED fish, shallots, and garlic awakened my senses. How long had I slept? I was clean from head to toe, tucked underneath a warm quilt in someone's sleeping attire.

"Have I died?" I asked the little woman peering at me.

"Not yet, but you will if you do not feed your body. You did not get those bruises falling from a horse." She made a sweeping gesture over my ravaged body.

"You are very kind, little grandmother, but I cannot repay your hospitality."

"Do you like yellow river carp?"

"Does a dog not like to gnaw and worry a bone?"

A man's voice called to her through the open window. She answered him but didn't budge, and instead turned toward me. She sat on a wooden bench below the window and began to sing in *Nüshu,* so he wouldn't understand. Her voice was melodious in our secret language, but how did she know I knew it as well, me with big feet?

I sat bolt upright. By my astonished face, she knew what I was thinking, stopped singing, and smiled. Then she waved the man away and took up her song, crooning to me of how she had undressed and washed me as a mother would a child, and in my clothing she found a handkerchief with our writing on it. Her refrain, "Who is the sworn sister of your heart, if not Ping?" Her name called to mind so many memories that I cried.

"In your sleep-talk of Ping I gather you owe no more tears," she sang. "Consider how you shall pay the debt of Ya Chen's death. You begged for your strong body to be thrashed into the sea to drown, as replacement for her lithe ghost that swims, reels, and twirls awash in fathomless water— soon she'll touch shore on the foam of a wave. From water a new old love will arrive."

I cried at the beauty of the words chosen for her song and thought of my sailor. If I had been obsessed by the fact that I had allowed Lu to touch me, I was immeasurably more consumed by the violation of those men. What damage to my psyche.

Her voice, so like my mother's, interrupted the pitiless and vicious images. The mention of my special friend's name, a sweet and piquant recall, but the allusion to my little one was a calescent arrow straight to my gut.

Before her song ended, she sang, "Seek forgiveness for the violence you endured but could not have prevented; go forward with your life. You owe this much to your great love, who will pardon any violation and more. I have had days to prepare this song for you. You have traveled with ghosts in tempest-tossed dreams."

"I am grateful for your song," I said.

Her shy smile lit up her eyes. "I am the only one in this village who knows *Nüshu* because I come from far away and had to learn the language of my husband. I have tried to teach others our women's language but with no success for my humble efforts. With no daughter or daughter-in-law—now you are both, so you must eat for them."

What had she sung to me about a love from water? Water. I washed away the seed of those vermin who raped me. Could I love such a child conceived in such aggression?

She served me a bowl of rice with carp, and I told her the herbs to gather along with marigold, *dong quai,* and angelica, to make infusions for her arthritic hands. She had nourished my body and renewed my spirit. "I wonder if you will pay the debt in twelve moons? But unlike *Heng-O,* the mother of the twelve moons, I fear you will not wash your children."

In all this time, neither prayer nor magical imaginings afforded me the whimsy of payment, and although I didn't understand her cryptic, arcane jargon, it brought relief in the knowledge that the life I owed would be paid. And so I slept, weightless, winding in space, buoyed on the tail of a dragon. When I next awoke, she had covered me in a second quilt—warm and smelling of violets. Rested, I looked at the hearth, flames shooting sparks as if the wood contained salts from the sea. How had it come inland so far? How had I voyaged here?

My unsettled mind brimmed. In what manner could I say good-bye to this gentle grandmother who had nursed me, knowing I could not repay her kindness? Even if I passed this way again, her ancient body would no longer be making shadows on this earth. With a stick I scraped the charcoal from the bottom of her cook pot, and I drew a picture of her garden on the back of the map Zhugong had given me—I had studied it so long that I knew it by heart. On top of the pallet where she nursed me, I placed it, humble thanks written in the feathery strokes of our hidden language in columns from top to bottom on the side of the artwork.

I RODE TWO DAYS, SLEEPING at intervals, but always on the move, thanks to the food stores from the ancient one. On the village outskirts I saw a burned hovel. A man in a thick hemp necktie hung from a tree, clad in priest's robes, his body desiccated. A rosary of woven string beads and a wooden cross encircled his neck and rested on his chest. Scavengers had been at him. The sight of him frightened me, and his spirit was unhappy. I quit the place fast as I could. This was what the old woman warned me of—this hanging had Boxers all but written on it.

◄►►∢₩∢◄►

ON THE THIRD DAY, I fell asleep in the saddle in a wheat field where the happy horse stuffed himself like a pillow. I was out of food, wilting like a cut flower in a vase, when a day later, I arrived at the caves. My horse grazed and watered in a shallow stream, me alongside of him.

I tied him in the shade in a spot where he could forage. I loosed the saddle and propped it against a tree and rested, leaning on it until I had the strength to enter the mouth of one of the caves. I deduced there were many caves, but I knew the one I was supposed to cross the threshold, instinct told me, just as surely as if Zhugong had said, *Enter here, Lian.*

Chapter 20

Wing Chun
詠春
Spring chant

AFTER A MORNING WORKOUT OF martial arts, Giacomo sat aft of the ship. He could not stop thinking of Lian and when he thought he couldn't take it any longer because his head felt like it was about to split open like a smashed watermelon, he went to the galley and sat down with pen, ink, and paper and began to write.

My dearest Lian,
    I will send this letter to Guo Xide at the mission in hopes that he will forward it to you wherever you will go next and contact me. I am praying you return and the priest gives you my note. I am writing you in hopes that this letter will find its way to you somehow. I am writing you because if I don't, I think I'll go insane with remembering when I came to you in Peking when your father had gone away for two days. Forgetting time and place, and without knowledge of what was in store for me, when you opened the door, I was ensnared forever by your beauty. You cast a spell over me as I felt you melt into my embrace. You had to stand on tiptoes for my kiss. I can still feel my hand reach to touch your face. I caressed your cheek, and there was an invitation in your eyes. Do you recall? You leaned

forward to welcome a second kiss.

You said, "I'm not used to kissing foreigners—my father doesn't count because he is my father and Chinese by desire—and I kissed a sailor in a palatial garden and then many times in the embassy. Do you remember?"

I kissed you again and the kiss was beguiling.

We didn't speak after that. You donned a jacket and we went for a walk. You guided me along dark lanes and narrow passages telling me the history of the neighborhood. We walked for a while, passing an alley with a full clothesline, the materials stiff with the cold, like ghosts with frigid wings sailing in back of them. You stopped and said, "I never kissed a mustache before."

"You didn't, you kissed my lips."

"But I felt the hair above your mouth."

"Your lips grazed my mustache."

"Why did you grow it? Lucky I recognized you."

We returned to her house and I asked, "How'd you like it?"

"It was . . . strange. It tickles somewhat, but I was afraid to laugh and break the spell."

You cooked me dinner. And then, and then, and then. Need I remind you, my little Lian, of what happened then?

I think you would be proud of me. I have now become very proficient in the art of *Wing Chun* 咏春拳 Singing Spring Fist, but most call it Spring Chant 詠春 which I like better. The important thing I wish to communicate is now I can trounce any adversary easily if I concentrate. I only wish I could give you a demonstration. I have heard many and varied stories of how *Wing Chun,* the martial art I now practice, came into being. The legend that intrigues and fascinates me most, although probably only myth, has been passed down through the years as oral history. It is the tale of the Buddhist nun, the Abbess Ng Mui. Do you know the story? Have you heard of her? They say there is no evidence that the nun really lived. But I believe her spirit is very much alive in you and the *Wing Chun* I've been taught and now am teaching to others. It is said that in the seventeeth century during the reign of the Emperor Kangxi, she escaped from the Fukian Shaolin Monastary when it was overrun by

Qing forces. She was one of few who survived, and she fled to the distant mountains of Daliang on the border between Yunnan and Sichuan.

Alone one day, she observed two animals—a snake and a crane—in a bitter fight for survival. Ng Mui studied their carefully articulated movements, and these observations led her to incorporate them into the Shaolin *kung fu* she already knew. In this way, she created a new style from the examples she learned viewing the ferocious battle between these animals. By uniting the studied movements with her own lessons of Shaolin *kung fu,* she created a new method of fighting. There is no written proof that this occurred.

The story continues. Ng Mui bought her bean curd at the tofu shop of Yim Yee who had a daughter named Yim Wing Chun, whom a local warlord was trying to force into an unwanted marriage. Ng Mui took the girl under her wing and taught her the new fighting style. Wing Chun used it to fend off the warlord once and for all. Can you imagine the disgrace of a warlord being beaten by a girl? Wing Chun eventually married the man she loved, Leung Bok-Chao, to whom she taught the fighting techniques that Ng Mui had passed on to her. Husband and wife in turn passed the new style on to others. Her kind husband named the new art *Wing Chun* after her.

For some reason this fighting brings me back to when I was a boy in Sicily. While I was on an outing one day among the high cliffs above Carini, I became lost quite by accident. I climbed a hill and there was a secluded farmhouse in disrepair. I was delighted to find the hidden old house and scaled a wall to see if I could find someone to give me directions home. Instead, as I approached a broken window on the side of a cliff, I heard voices. I peered in and saw a group of men seated around a stone table. *Luparas* were slung from the backs of their chairs. Several carafes of wine and glasses were on the table along with a burning candle. I knew instinctively that these men, too well dressed for farmers or hunters, were part of the Cosa Nostra. I hunched, near afraid of moving for fear of divulging my hiding place. What I happened to see and overhear was the initiation of an aspirant to become a Mafioso. The young man was seated at the table. In front of him was a *capo* that I recognized as being a friend of Ciccio, a man who sometimes worked for my father. This man took hold of a thorny branch and pricked the young man's finger till it bled. The *capo* caught the blood on what looked like the image of a saint—a holy card of Santa Rosalia—like the nuns always give my mother for donations, or perhaps the Virgin Mother. The *capo* took the picture with the dripping blood and placed it over the candle to set it on fire. As it burned, the card was quickly passed from the hands of one man to another until it was delivered back to the man who was being initiated—this novice then took an oath of loyalty to that Mafia family, becoming a "man of honor."

Why is it that blood oaths are the most fierce? What is it about blood? I'm guessing it is a liquid form of *chi*. Here in China I have learned that the deer's velvet antler can be divided into sections, each of which is ground and used for different medical purposes in traditional Chinese medicine. But when the growth of the antler is of its potential full size, between fifty-five and sixty-five days of growth, before any significant calcification occurs they are sheared from the animal, and the blood is collected so that people can drink it to improve their health and vigor.

Blood. It is a binding force. I beg of you to forgive me for taking your virginal blood, but now you are forever mine.

With all my love. I am your,

贾科莫 Giacomo.

Chapter 21

Dòngxué
洞穴
Caves

THE INSIDE OF THE CAVE stopped my breath—a vault in a gothic cathedral in one of my father's books. Stalactite icicles grew from the arched ceiling and stalagmites spiraled up from the floor. My eyes beheld cave pearls, curtains, and columns in wonderful profusion. I had been so hungry for so long I didn't know if it was the effect of starvation or a true vision. I spoke of my desires for Giacomo, to find him and once more love and be loved, and again to suckle a child at my breast. Inside that cool cave, rubicund and ruvid, my body took another form. I ascended as if raised on clouds close to the zenith. The moment my faith wavered, I began a quick descent. I screeched—a defenseless animal caught in the teeth of a jaguar, or perhaps the giant dog of days ago. Elevated upward again, I soared toward the summit, my heart palpitating with wild frenzy for fear of crashing through the barrier of the cave's apex. I yelled her name. His name. "Giacomo. Ya Chen, Ya Chen. Giacomo. Zhugong, Zhugong!" I heard laughter and his words: *"Faith is a narrow gate, slip through it."* Reaching for the outstretched arms of Ya Chen, I levitated. Unafraid of these ghosts—two real, one a figment of my past. The chamber's echoes reverberated every breath, each whisper, sounds amplified like yelling through cupped hands.

Voices of my dead ones floated around me.

Zhugong spoke softly. "Go on with life, my *bazoi*."

Ya Chen declared, "You are blameless. Be spiritual."

Wai Po expressed a blessing for my hands to heal.

Ma said she loved me and to be happy.

Baba uttered the final words. "Find him if you can."

Only Lu's mouth seemed gagged and what he tried to say was too muffled to comprehend. Zhugong had forbidden him to speak.

My arms were feathered wings, fluttering in rhythm, and I laughed a caw, understanding I always possessed the capability of flying, and came to roost on a plateau where I slept the sleep of the dead. I tread like a ghost in the netherworld and did not wake until shafts of moonlight draped me. There was an aperture at the top of the cave. I was beyond thought, hunger, or thirst. Before scaling down to the cave's floor, I asked, *Will I ever find love again? Will I find Giacomo?* Questions. I want to be a healer but could not save my father, Zhugong, Ya Chen. I cannot heal everyone, least of all myself. I tried to control my fate. I rid my body of a baby to take possession of my destiny, only to lose the child I had. "Heal me so that I may heal others."

"Cave, tell me. No one gets to choose the vital details of life—what happens to us is the will of nature and the gods. Illness. Old age. Death. Blindly thinking I could be in command of all that would befall me." I glissaded downward at a steady pace to an outcropping.

Starlight flashed like a thousand fireflies, bursting stars flickered close enough to touch, not allowing me to rest. Sleep—I craved a senseless, drugged state, not within my grasp. On the ledge of that cave, I wanted to die. To join Zhugong. To leave the cares of mortal life. But the constant brightness, a twinkling wink before my eyes, would not allow me to fall into the unconscious. A wink. His wink. Giacomo's. Whose? I wept for wanting to sleep. I felt as though I were floating again, no, swimming—a tadpole diving and fighting currents making its way upstream. Diving yet ascending. I must eat. Eat or die. I was half-crazed.

My hand groped along to the side and picked a tuft of moss and stuck it in my mouth and chewed. A feeling of nausea overcame me. Squiggly. A worm or bug shared my moss, but now saliva breaking down protein as I bit in and chewed viscous material. I swallowed, wanting to regurgitate, but worried about choking on my own vomit. Now on my knees, digging moss, stuffing earth into my mouth with saliva enough to swallow. Other crawlies invaded my mouth, teeth clamping down on any fugitive trying for escape. I thirsted and my thirst was gargantuan like the cave itself, which brought me to my senses. I heard a trickle of water nearby. My hand cupped water and brought it to my mouth. Water. Moss. Worms. I must have passed out. Upon waking, I spewed forth the last of what was in my mouth. I hugged the cave wall like a man on a wedding night. I licked the rough rampart, sucking up the tiny waterfall seeping down because I finally decided that to couple with this cave was propitious, wonderful, and sane.

Who, who, who? Came back to me the insistent hoot of an owl rhetorically answering. Had I dreamt? So real was the man in the blue uniform, he might have been a saintly vision. Whatever he was, he was tall, an occidental personification of the love I desired. Memory caused my blood to rush faster, coursing in and out of my heart, and I passed out of my own skin.

The lilt of his laughter reverberated in my ears, while a night of joyous rapture played itself in my mind—a thousand spectator stars exploded in a shower of fireworks.

I slept again, this time dreamlessly. After sleep I tried to walk, but kept falling backward, not physically, but mentally, back and back more into befuddlement. My brain refused to make the passage into the waking world. The contextual sense of everyday matter seemed illogical, the inertia of my movements, the shadows of the cave, the hardness of the ground, and the rigidity of the wall I leaned upon.

I remember nothing of how I climbed down and made my way to the cave entrance. It seemed like an eternity before I could summon the energy to exit back into the living world, but the cave's message resounded in my ears: the lesson is forgiveness so you can be redeemeded.

I MUST HAVE FAINTED AT the entryway for after what seemed like release in a long sleep, I awoke.

I heard voices and knew if they came from marauders, I would not live. Zhugong was with me, for the people of the caravan that stopped were joyous country people camping by the river that flowed near the cave. A boy tended my horse. He rubbed its ankles with a salve. I was grateful but could not express it. I must have been prostrate, for they all seemed to be giants above me. I did not understand their dialect or their ways but remembered what Zhugong had taught me when with strangers and I was grateful.

I mimicked everything these people did to make myself welcome among them. I felt great joy at the warmth of blessed monthly bleeding as I was carried along by women, who took turns bathing me with fragrant oils and shampooing my hair with liriope—a tufted herb, grass-like evergreen foliage that grew all around in clusters of dark-mauve grapelike flowers.

A few women rinsed me with the frigid ever-running stream, the same water used for their cook pots. No one person dictated the care of me; it was a communal effort. They dried me with tufted cloth turned inside out. I balked when they tried to dress and swaddle me but had no energy to fight them off, despite the refreshing bath.

They would have none of my protests and donned me in their warm, sturdy quilted travel clothes. I tried to eat but had no strength. They fed me like a baby. I watched how they took their wine so later I could drink with them. My eyes followed every nuance, each appropriate step of their ritual, and laughed with joy, understanding as I watched an elder clansman flick three drops to the air for Buddha. I slept near the fire with them, yet grasped only a few words of their language and harsh dialect. I'd master it if I stayed with them, but knew I could not.

For days afterward, I asked Zhugong how had I been so fortunate to meet this band of nomads, traveling at the speed of aimless clouds, directing me toward my destiny. I had my answer when an old man offered me his pipe.

❦

WEEKS LATER I REALIZED THAT this traveling horde thought me a saint, ecstatic, or hermit. This is why I was treated with reverence, the reason I was not molested, or touched in any way by the men. One elderly woman had been brought to this traveler when she was little. She remembered some *Nüshu*. I explained I was just an ordinary person found starving by the cave.

I had nothing to give them to repay their goodness. I told the chieftain to take my horse, but he refused. This kind, high-cheeked, brindled traveler had given me back the life I thought ended at the mouth of the cave. He had treated me with respect that I did not deserve and had ensured my safety and comfort. The chief, whose name I never learned, wore leather larrigans that fascinated me and were made by the woman who had first bathed me. Perhaps because he was always in the saddle or on a horse, they protected his calves from chaffing. Using signs, I asked the stocky chief, calling him "great huntsman," for his knife, and he unsheathed it, handing it to me by the hilt. Before anyone could object, I cut my waist-length hair from where it was bound with a thong at the nape of my neck. Along with his knife I gave him the hank of hair to barter or sell. The women cried. The men blushed. If I ever understood what sacrifice was, it was in that frozen moment, in their faces. Maybe not sacrifice, but love.

In awe of such humanity, I bowed. He touched me on the shoulder with a quirt. This was a command to stay, to wait. He rummaged through his saddlebag and took out a pair of brand-new, beautifully designed larrigans with laces and chamois fringe and handed them to me. What could I do in the face of such generosity? I clutched them to my breast, hoping he knew that this sojourn with his people would remain in my thoughts and heart until these leather leg coverings and I had turned to dust. Parting was bitter, and remembrances swept over me like the swirling snow that had begun to fall, draping everything it touched. Snow birthed a winter sun, white, weak, and young, and then a flange of light circled me. Zhugong taught me, we meet people along our paths, like the chief, and they facilitate our way. All we can do is be grateful.

⟡

WHY DID I LEAVE SPRINGTIME and the old lady with the garden and these travelers to climb these mountains and plateaus back into the cold climes and wintry snows?

Riding along, I felt a drop in temperature. Glacial winds moaned through trees, and branches creaked and rattled—forlorn cries of ghosts. The snow and mist formed diaphanous puffs in shafted rays of sunlight beneath centennial trees—they were charming, mysterious, and magical, although they spooked my horse. I nudged him over to one glittering bubble, edging him into it, making him walk through so he'd see there was nothing to fear. Instantly he calmed down, feeling snow familiar and wet on his coat, a thing recognized. Maybe he thought as I did that snow phantoms appearing here and there were harmless after all, and because we were lonely, we welcomed these apparitions. Snowfall settled and steadied itself into a snowstorm.

Ah, the feeling—unsafe and lost in blowing snow. Naturally our tracks covered over rapidly, so I had no fear of being followed by unwanted guests, though I had to dismount to cover the horse's eyes with a ripped shirt. On we trekked. How long had I been a solitary rider, parted from the chief? How much farther must we travel, this steadfast animal and me?

As the day wore on, the going became more difficult, the snowdrifts deep, and I had to seek shelter. The ribbon of sky was opaque—no more sun to guide me. We came to a swale and then a rise and finally to a hollow between two hills.

I trudged along on foot, leading the horse. I followed the crest of the lower hill until I saw a field and in the middle distance a copse of trees. Since it was late for snow, the trees had all their leaves. Here we took cover for the night. In a dense grove with plenty of overhead cover, I tethered and hobbled the horse, unhitched the saddle, leaving one of his blankets on him. I loosened his bandana so he could see what I was up to and then spoke sweet words. "Black horse, stay calm while I work. We must make it through this snow squall to continue our journey. Did you know you're the color of midnight in this waning light?"

The horse whinnied, showing his sense of approval. He nickered and I nuzzled him to show my fondness, patted his withers, and said, "You are a brave and noble beast, but I'm not so sure of your intelligence allowing me to tire you out in snow-lion weather." I took hold of his bridle with one hand and held his snout down with the other and then blew my breath into his nostrils. He snorted and whickered.

I dug a trench with my hands and smoothed and flattened it by stomping on the loose earth with my feet. I piled snow high all around to make a wall, which I then packed. The exertion warmed me. I gathered and used felled branches with leaves over my snow shelter, and thought to cover it with more snow, but decided that it might melt and drip on me if the weather warmed, which I knew was wishful thinking. I lined the inside of my refuge with evergreen boughs and then threw in my belongings with the saddle and the rolled blanket I had tied to the back of it. Then I unfolded the horse's blanket, spread it over his back and fastened it at his chest by making holes in it, sewing and tying it with fresh twig lanyards in several spots, and twisting them closed. "Do not shake off this cover," I said, my voice calm, belying my fear. He looked at me with unhappy eyes, but I couldn't build a haven for both of us. My legs refused to move and my back ached as though I'd pushed out a baby. If my heat source warmed the inside too much, I would need an escape hatch. For the door I used more branches, my pack, and some clothing. I fit the bandana shirt over the horse's eyes once again.

I clambered into my snow grave, leaned against the saddle, and covered myself with the blanket. *Ah, Zhugong,* I thought—*you and your analogies to the snow leopard, rarely sighted thriving so high in the Asian mountaintops.* How I'd love to hunt one now to use its fur for warmth. Buried alive. A beaver, a trapper caught in an avalanche. Exhausted, I slept. At sunrise I crawled out of my snow room, greeted my horse, and complimented him on how smart and brave he was. I knocked off fresh snow from his back and relieved myself.

In the woods, I searched the forest for old stumps. When around pine trees, Zhugong had told me, look for fallen or toppled rotting trees, or big limbs that have plunged down and decayed in a solid central part. I scraped this inner core to see if the heart was a tough honey color. I struck gold. The scent was fresh pinesap, which wasn't at all decomposed. I knew that even a more rotted knot or stump held this treasure—the best fire substance —flammable gold. I tore and split off wood splinters to help me start a fire. I took extra pieces for my pack, so I'd have it easy at my next respite. Zhugong had cautioned me that survival techniques and gear were important in the elements. I had never considered just how essential equipment and skills were before, though I did try to quiet my mind and shut it down as he instructed me to do. Meditation, he had said a thousand times over, is the key to freeing the body. But for now the sun was shining, the air brisk, and the snow, which had all but stopped, swept by in small eddies and flurries. There was no sound, except the tinkling of ice like fine crystal in the trees, and the crunch of snow beneath my feet. My legs, protected by larrigans, made my body in harmony with nature. I navigated a wintry world, but my soul and mind were at peace.

After giving my horse a handful of oats, I cleared an area and banked it with rocks. Into it, I placed tinder and dried leaves, criss-crossing larger pieces of wood, adding resin, to flare as though alcohol had been poured on it. It burned for quite some time but put off a good deal of sooty smoke, the color of eggplant, until the fire caught the wood chips and the pitch burned off.

I heated snow to melt to boiling and then cooled it and drank a great quantity of it, remembering my father's words that snow is unclean, even though as a youngster I wanted to eat it. I sipped hot tea, reliving vicariously the encounters during my travels and travails. Zhugong was with me. My mind voyaged with him in the netherworld till I grew sleepy. With the warm cup in my hand, I reentered the snow house and slumbered in a landscape of dreams.

Toward midday, I watered the horse, now called Snowflake because he'd try to catch the falling snow with his tongue. Sad, I thought, to give him a name now that we would be parting. I wondered if he would think of me in the future, the way I knew I'd remember him. We rode down from that entombed place.

Chapter 22

Yangguizi
洋鬼子
Foreign devil

THE SHIP'S LOUDSPEAKER SQUAWKED AND then blared, a loud voice giving an announcement that the *Leopardo* would arrive in Shanghai before dawn. The ship was docked for hours and by noon onshore at the port, there were cries of "Support the *Ch'ing!* Destroy the *yangguizi!* Kill the *dabizi!* Take the heads of the *huangmao!*"

The shouts could be heard in a thunderous chorus, and hundreds of fighters in strange garb, mostly blue, waved white or red banners with the same words written on them. They wore long red scarves entwined around their heads and wide red belts wrapped their waists. As the rebels moved closer to the dock, even the material of the red shin-guard coverings could be discerned. Linen, cotton, or silk. Too close for comfort, Giacomo felt. The crowd made an immense, chaotic racket, bursting eardrums with bells, gongs, drums, flutes, and other instruments along with heinous cries and screams. A sea of men, moving in one long foaming, fomenting wave, entered the bund and approached the wharf where the *Leopardo* anchored.

Every man aboard ship knew what *yangguizi* meant: white ghost or foreign devil, but several asked Giacomo what *dabizi* meant.

"Big nose," he said, sliding a finger down his Roman nose.

"And *huangmao?*"

"Yellow hair." He grinned, and raked his fingers through his dark hair.

The captain gave the order to cut the anchor lines. The command was relayed over in a series, until it reached the men with axes ready to sever the ropes. The delay in getting the command down the ranks was time enough for the Boxers to start firing, and the men of the *Leopardo* manned their stations and guns, waiting to fire back. The captain deferred, "We will not start this fight."

"They already started the fight, they're firing at us!" Giacomo shouted back, his words lost in wind and distance.

Every manned position—arms and men— seemed to move as one in unison, turning in the direction of the captain. Each and every sailor had eyes trained on him.

"He's out of his fucking mind!" yelled Bulldog to Giacomo, who stood behind a steel bulwark above him.

"Waiting to see our blood spill before he gives the command to fire."

Bulldog took aim, "My blood ain't trickling for this cause—"

"Hold it," Giacomo said, "a gunner's been hit."

From out of nowhere, Shen appeared at Giacomo's side. "What the hell?"

"I jump ship. They kill all."

"Don't—"

"Good-bye, my friend. We meet war over."

"Kill you too—for aiding us. That's an angry mob. Think, Shen. No time to abandon ship. You're a dead man if you do."

"Boxers—"

"Last week, remember Bulldog on the radio? It was scuttlebutt— hearsay— from a Russian trawler. Some Manchu leaders have colluded— aided the Boxers—you've heard this. It's true, I'm afraid."

"Giacomo, what all mean real life?"

"In simple terms, high government officials have sanctioned—that is to say, backed-up the raids and chaos caused by the Boxers against foreigners and Christians—and even those Chinese converts to Christianity."

There was a cry to man weapons and load guns. It resounded throughout the ship. Giacomo nudged Shen to come along, but the boy stayed put. There wasn't much Giacomo could do, and he was pushed forward to his gunnery position. Giacomo peered over his shoulder several times, hoping the boy would be behind him.

The ramparts, walls, and fortifications were now a seething wave of humanity. Men were jumping into the water and swimming toward the ship. No longer hundreds, there seemed to be thousands.

Abruptly Shen stood near the gangway, which was in closed position. He climbed up on top of it and waved, crying out to Giacomo, saying, "I little important. No-man life on ship. Only for you. I Chinese. Belong murder crowd, my people. I see you next life."

Bulldog restrained Giacomo, though it wasn't necessary as he understood it was futile to attempt to reach Shen.

Shen, among others, dove into the water and swam to the jetty and then to the quay, where a bunch of hoodlum warriors awaited the incautious boy. He was hoisted with others out of the water, and Giacomo thought he saw Shen being flayed raw with flashing knives before he had time to dry his face. If Giacomo could have trained his gun on this carnivorous crowd, these flesh-devouring monsters, he would have. Before Giacomo could even raise his rifle, before he could draw a bead on one of the men slicing at Shen and his comrades, Rinaldi, a dense shadow and impressive presence, stood beside Giacomo. Rinaldi's hand lowered the barrel of Giacomo's rifle.

Chapter 23

Gaobie
告别
Farewell

A FEW HOURS BEFORE DUSK, Snowflake and I reached a glen. A valley spread unctuous and green beneath us, verdant due to heavy snow melt and springtime rains—everything seemed polished and alive enough to pick and eat. My eyes feasted on variegated shades of green. All around new birth and energy spread before me. It really was spring and had been even though I had relived winter in the high mountain altitude.

⋙✦⋘

TWO WEEKS AFTER I'D FOUND spring greening once more, I rode into the mission, and just before consigning my horse to Guo Xide, I kissed the horse's snout and thanked him for all he had done for me and especially for being the companion of the heart, who had safeguarded me the two months I'd been traveling. I gave him two apples—such paltry payment.

Guo Xide was happy to see me, but even more so relieved. Things had become even more difficult, and the mission suffered the consequences. He mentioned an Italian sailor out of uniform and a German military man coming to see him. These men had urged Guo Xide to quit the mission. I could have cursed I was so perturbed at this priest's conviction to stay and die—such stupid stubbornness. But then another thought occurred to me. *A sailor out of uniform.* What an improbable, impossible quirk of fate to have missed seeing him again. But, of course, it wasn't him. A happenstance such as this would never, could never really happen in life—it is the stuff of fiction, like the books I read when I was a girl. What was the one Father gave me when I was fourteen? Oh yes, *Pride and Prejudice.* For sure, my sailor had left China months ago.

We sat in the kitchen while I sipped soup. He asked me many questions. He fussed with plates and then sat down and from his cassock, pulled out a crumbled piece of paper. As I reached for it, I knew it had been written by my sailor, my love. In disbelief and silence, I read of his search for me. He had left me word in every embassy of every city he'd traveled to. My wet eyes could barely discern the last words: *Never forget me. You are written in my heart. I will see you again before I die.*

I read the note over and over until I had his words memorized.

❦

GUO XIDE CAME BACK INTO the room. I'd been so preoccupied with Giacomo's letter that I didn't even know the priest had gone. He placed a cup of tea in front of me.

"Foreign embassies are being besieged—the situation has worsened," he said.

"What are you going to do?" I put down my porcelain cup.

"Stay put. My obligation and duty is to—"

"What about the obligation to yourself? What if the mission is blockaded by these sympathizers? On the way to the caves I saw a priest hanged, his body desecrated—I can assure you it was not a sight for human eyes."

"I thought you would go to Shensi Province—to my friend, the Jesuit, Bruno Giordano. That was your plan."

"Did you not hear what I said? You, priest, are in danger. Here. Now."

I looked down at the newspaper and read an article about missionaries and diplomats being slaughtered. Many in small hill towns and villages surrounding Peking and Shanghai had been killed. But from the reports, those who had died swiftly had been the lucky ones—a merciful deed. What had happened to the others was unmentionable.

He pointed to an insert in the newspaper that stated insurrection would not be tolerated by the eight treaty powers, and in order to assure civilian safety, they were sending in troops from all nations. "To subdue the uprising," he said.

"More fuel for the fire. I'm afraid—"

"Before long," he said, his voice somber, "they'll occupy Peking. Soon troops will loot and pillage even the grand palaces and private residences, as well as large villages." He raised his head—a lamb's looking toward the slaying hand. His voice changed to a mournful one. "What can eunuchs do? Only some—very few, from what I've read, are skilled as warriors, the others are corrupt bloodsuckers who use influence to obtain power with the dowager."

"Who lavishes it on the court, instead of her armed forces."

"The parents of Hang Wo requested to be informed if you came back. They want to see you. Will you stay for some time?"

"Tonight only, and pay my respects to them in the morning."

"Good. It's settled. I'll write a note to Father Giordano for you to give to him. The dispensary where you will meet him is the Dragon Chasing Rainbow Infirmary. Donations, food rations as well as silver taels, medicine, drugs, bandages and supplies, alms, and other monetary support come from Father Giordano's family and others. Can you enlist your father's friend Piero Milano to send supplies or funds?"

"The owner of the apothecary in Hong Kong could not even help me."

"At his behest some wealthy German, French, and Swiss bankers might. They can make charitable contributions to the men fighting for them."

"I've thought so many times of Piero and Hong Kong." How odd the man could be so generous for countless strangers, but could not help one friendless woman?

"Supplies are dwindling, along with hope. Please write him." Guo Xide handed me a piece of paper from a child's ruled notebook. "What about Doctor Casetellano?"

"Ah, the good doctor. How can I ask for more than he has already done for me?"

The cook came in to greet me, and Father Gabriele and a few of the children that remained. By the time they left, I felt weary and wished I'd not returned. Good-byes should be fast and truncated. I left once, why did I come back? I took Giacomo's note from my shirt and knew this was the reason. A gilt thread of hope to sustain me. Oh, caves, blessed caves.

"Finished eating? I'll have your old room made up and you can rest."

I nodded and watched him walk out the door. For such a young man, he seemed stooped by age, or perhaps defeat, and yet I sensed his difficult days and his battle were not even begun.

"Wait. Have you any news of Wang Mangen?"

He turned, sorrow flooding his usually placid face. Shaking his head, he cried.

◆━━◆

THE NEXT DAY, BEFORE I paid a call on the Hang household, Guo Xide gave me the horse to bring to them. Wang Mangen had no use for it now, wandering in the land of spirits. Guo Xide wished me Godspeed and safe journey, but this time instead of the sign of the cross over my head, the man put his hands in his sleeves and bowed, a low bow, which I returned.

The Hang family had prepared a sumptuous breakfast of rice porridge and soy-bean milk soup and strong black tea. After polite exchanges, the old parents gave me a red envelope, a money pouch, and a fistful of train ticket transfers to Tientsin. My face flushed. I bowed, looking down at my hands holding this small treasure. Surely, it must be from the priest. I gave Wo my larrigans and thanked them. Wo, who had grown in grace, slender and a head taller than her father, offered me transportation to the train station on Snowflake. She rode in back of me with her parting gifts of a parcel of loose tea, a burlap bag of rice, and *gan si,* shredded dried tofu, translated "dry silk."

At the station a paradoxical meaning came to me. Tofu: *gan* means to dry or to do, and city folk attribute *si* as the word fuck. The humor of this would never have been lost on Zhugong, and so I smiled and readied myself for change, adopting a spirit of survival that this voyage had taught me. I felt a surge of strength when Wo, astride her horse, called to me, "Farewell, Lian."

Behind the window, I waved and repeated, *"Gào bié.* Farewell."

Chapter 24

Meihao shiguang
美好时光
Life is beautiful

1899 SHENSI PROVINCE, CHINA

THE UPRISINGS AND RIOTS CAUSED by the *I'ho Ch'üan,* the Righteous and Harmonious Fists, were becoming more audacious and, with the sanction of the governor of Shensi Province, were enlisted to create havoc and unrest against foreigners. The Boxer anarchists changed the name to *I'ho t'uan,* the Righteous and Harmonious Militia, which made the vicious task force sound more officious. This more authoritative title and the fact that by now almost everyone believed the cause was supported by the empress dowager, gave the insurgents even more power, causing chaos. There were so many riots that the Mission of Repose in Shensi Province was forced to close. A few of the dedicated missionaries stayed on, working with the poor and the occasional foreigner who had become embroiled in some mishap, but one by one the foreign missionaries were leaving China.

From the sea up the Peihao River, *Il Leopardo* reached Tientsin. Giacomo had been ill for the nearly one-hundred-and-thirty-kilometer trip from Peking to Tientsin. His fever broke when the ship docked up at the wharf. He and Bulldog walked the kilometer distance of the wharf, which housed an arsenal, a commercial depot, cotton mills, rice and salt markets. The city teemed with life, commerce, and foreign concessions along its abundant, crowded streets.

"Are you still weak?" Bulldog asked.

"I'm up to any carousing you can invent." Giacomo pretended to sip a drink.

"Let's go. I pulled leave time, did you?" Bulldog said.

"Twenty-four hours."

They walked quayside. Bulldog said to Giacomo, "Your high fever caused delirium and you called out Lian's name a hundred times or more."

"Someday I'll find her. She's part of my destiny. I wonder if she'll ever forgive me for taking advantage of her innocence."

"Sure, if she loves you, does she? Could she still?"

Giacomo raised a fist as if to punch him.

The two companions had seen nothing of the city, and Bulldog wanted to go to a good place to drink and stir up trouble with other seamen. They scoured the area close to port, looking for the infirmary that Guo Xide had mentioned to Giacomo. After searching for hours, Giacomo relented, saying, "There's always tomorrow. Maybe it's better to look in daylight." They went in and out of bars in search of sailors from other foreign ships till they found just the right place for a first stop. Music, a singer, a brothel, and a cherrywood bar five meters long.

Bulldog and Giacomo drank and played cards till their pockets were empty. They found themselves, along with three American sailors, in a back alley behind a whorehouse they'd been bounced out of. They thought they'd meet up with a gang of rowdy Frenchmen. Instead it was a gang of Boxers who ensnared them. The two men of *Il Leopardo,* outnumbered and separated from the Americans, hoped to outrun the opposition, but they made a wrong turn, one that cost them dearly. It was a cul-de-sac, lined on both sides with old, shambling buildings, smelly garbage, and a hoard of rats. They tried to scale the wooden-fenced wall at the end of the lane, but it was too high. Each of them picked up whatever was handy as a bat or weapon. The rebels were armed with knives and clubs, but Giacomo and Bulldog managed to disarm two of them, though Chinese-reined fists and blows knocked the Italian sailors down until they lay unconscious and seriously bruised. A shot rang out and the assailants dispersed.

"Was that you who fired the shot, *Padre?"* Giacomo asked, lying in a pile of swill.

The black-robed priest patted his breast and nodded. "I recognized your uniforms—I, too, am Italian."

"How many of them were there? Where were you?"

"I hid myself in a shadowy doorway. I conferred Last Rites on a dying woman and was leaving. I thought it was a group of drunks fighting, but I saw Boxers and then knife flashes in the moonlight, so I fired a shot in the air. The Boxers fled and so did three American sailors."

Giacomo read pity in the priest's face. The priest helped them to their feet. When they stood, Bulldog said he felt some ribs crack.

The priest and Giacomo all but carried Bulldog, who was in terrible pain. The sailors were filthy and the priest pulled a face. "Offer it up for sins, Father," Giacomo said, and added, "we've got to get back to the ship tonight or we're AWOL. Can you help us?"

"I can go as far as the dispensary where I assist the sick and the dying. Maybe you, my son, can return aboard ship tonight, but this man," he indicated Bulldog, "needs medical attention and we must be quick."

"How far?" Giacomo asked.

"About two *li,*" the man robed in black answered.

"A kilometer," Giacomo said, unable to disguise surprise in his voice. "He'll never make it, *Padre.*" Giacomo nudged his head toward Bulldog. "He's pretty broken up."

"He has to, there's no other way. There's a nurse there who can take care of him."

Suddenly Giacomo thrust all of Bulldog's weight onto the priest. "I'm dizzy, hold up. I'm going to be sick," he said, leaned a hand against the wall, and threw up. When he finished, he zigzagged toward the priest, sagging under Bulldog's weight.

The priest said to Giacomo, "You may have a concussion."

"You've got to see a doctor," Bulldog said, taking short breaths in between his words.

"I just need a good night's sleep." Giacomo wiped his mouth with his tunic sleeve.

The priest shook his head. "We're going to the infirmary—it's nearby. You've got a head injury. Too dangerous. You could die in your sleep."

This sobering news made Giacomo acquiesce. *Infirmary. What was the name Guo Xide had told him?*

They limped along; Giacomo kept trying not to shift all of Bulldog's weight onto the priest, but was feeling progressively weaker and was grateful when the priest said, "Almost there."

Dressed in a white doctor's long coat, a medic stood with her back to the sailors when she spoke to the priest in Italian. Giacomo's head jerked up. He knew her voice. She turned slightly and said something in German to another patient. Then she looked at the priest.

The priest said, "These men are Italian serviceman. One is hurt badly."

She glanced at their uniforms. "I'll be with you in a minute, Father."

Bulldog asked, "Are you the medic?"

But as she took hold of the register, Giacomo was on his feet, saying "Lian. Lian?"

"Yes. How did you know my—" Her head was down, hair covering her face, writing something on a chart. "Some call me Doctor, but I'm merely a healer with particular skills—" She looked up, a hank of hair flying backward to reveal her face and green eyes. She dropped the register and stood up straighter, the color draining from her face.

She stammered the words, "You? Is it really you?" She began to cry, and her hand flew to her mouth, and she hid her face behind her hands.

He reached for both her hands and drew her near, then brought them to his lips, to his cheeks, to his lips again. "I was losing hope I'd see you again."

She tugged her hands away gently. "I have lived a thousand lives just to see you once more in this life."

He stepped back from her and opened his arms, palms heavenward. That one gesture spoke everything that needed to be said between them, and she fell into his waiting embrace, her face nuzzled into his chest.

He held her tightly and after a long silence said, "Do you remember my friend Bulldog?"

She nodded. "I do indeed."

"Lian? My God, Giacomo, it's her," Bulldog said.

Lian pulled away from him and busied herself, attending first to Bulldog, settling him on a cot in an alcove.

"I'm afraid there isn't much to do for the ribs. I bound him loosely, but those bones will need six weeks to heal," she said to the priest. He thanked her and stood next to Giacomo in the tiny corridor that served as a waiting room.

The priest said, "In all of China, it's impossible you know each other. Life is beautiful. I wish you Godspeed."

Giacomo said, "Many a sailor is thankful to the Jesuits for forecasting the weather and relaying it to us."

The priest raised his hand and made the sign of the cross over him. "Be well, sailor."

"Father, please go out the back way. It'll be safer for you," Lian said.

The priest started to walk toward the rear entrance.

"Oh, Don Bruno, find more secular garb." She pointed to his cassock. "You're inviting trouble in that."

"Don Bruno? Friend of Guo Xide?" Giacomo asked, seeing shock register on the priest's face when he heard the name.

"You know him?" Don Bruno asked.

Giacomo nodded. "I was at the mission—"

"Bless you both, my children. I'll be back tomorrow," Don Bruno said, and opened the door to leave.

"Thank you, Father, you have bought me a precious gift." She closed the door and said, "Where did you go? I looked for you everywhere before I read the letter you left for me at the mission."

"I searched everywhere for you, wherever my travels took me. I never ceased. Did you get any of my other letters?"

"None." Lian's shoulders sagged.

He leaned on a table near the cot. The nearness of her overwhelmed him, and he tried to control his hands from shaking.

"Giacomo, there's so much I want to say to you, to tell you, but I see you're not well," she said, turning toward him, her training asserting itself. "Please get on the cot for observation." She poured water from a pitcher into a bowl and added something fragrant. The air was filled with the sweetness of honeysuckle. She dipped in a cloth. Giacomo's shaking stopped and he flashed a grin when she washed his face. She blushed. She still cared for him. Against all possible hope, here she stood in front of him. What were the odds of his ever finding her? How he blessed the uprising and the Boxers who had beaten him. How much more his body would've endured for this meeting.

"Bulldog should stay the night, but you only have a nasty bump on the back of your head and superficial wounds—though you smell like a dog. Were you in a fight?"

He nodded.

"Other sailors?"

"Boxers."

"Lucky you both are alive." She placed the wet cloth in front of a small statue of Kwan Yin underneath a painting of the Immaculate Heart of Mary . His eyes followed her every movement.

"What does the priest think about Kwan Yin and Mary in the same room?" He pointed.

"You know Kwan Yin?

"She's the Chinese version of Mary, isn't she?"

Lian smiled. "So you don't consider us heathens?" She looked at him, took his chin in her hand and moved his head side to side. "Did you throw up?"

"Yes," he said, the feel of her hand on his face seemed like ecstasy. How impossibly wonderful this moment was—he never wanted it to end.

She held up her hand. "How many fingers?"

"Three. I had a lot to drink."

"Follow my finger. Good. Now this one. How do you feel?" She didn't wait for an answer. "Close your eyes. Open. What do you see?"

"A spring blossom."

Lian covered her mouth to suppress a smile. "Quite poetic. Sure you're not Chinese? Are you seeing double?"

"I wish I did see two of you—that'd be heaven." His look turned serious and he said, "I'm so sorry about your father."

Lian straightened. "He no longer walks this earth, and I miss him so."

"*Condoglianze,*" Giacomo said. "I remember our talks—he was so knowledgeable about the sea and tides."

A moment of awkward silence ensued before she said, "What else do you remember?"

"Everything. I've lived every minute we shared all this time."

"Me too."

"What can you do for Bulldog? He needs to make ship with me tonight."

"I bound his ribs—not tightly, and I gave him some morphia from opium for the pain. He'll be able to walk but will have to lean on you."

"Will he need more painkiller?"

"I'll give you some to dispense to him, but be careful. It's habit-forming, although I must confess I shared a pipe with the sage Zhugong. My father used to collect the milky juice of the unripe poppy. Am I babbling?"

"I knew you were an angel of mercy the minute I saw you." Giacomo shook his head as if to wake from a dream.

"This," she said, pointing to Kuan Yin, "is the Goddess of Mercy."

Giacomo noted Lian's smile as she stoppered an ampoule of morphia and wrapped it in a piece of green and gold material.

He touched the package. "It's beautiful, what is it?"

"Silk brocade. It's made here. I have nothing else," she said, sounding apologetic.

"I have to see you again soon, when?" He stepped in closer and clutched at her hands, but she pulled away.

"I want to see you too," she said, her hands shaking, "but I have work."

"You're afraid, aren't you?" He reached for her arms and yanked her to him and pressed against her.

She wiggled away. "I cannot begin to think what would become of me if I lost you again."

"You won't, and besides," he said, foundering for words, "I'd like to find out more about this material for my mother."

She smiled, her dimples showing. "Is that all? I work the night shift again tomorrow, from six to midnight. Come by before I go off duty so I can redress your wound."

How he longed once again to engulf her in his arms.

A thought flashed and Giacomo knew it wasn't the wound she wanted to undress and redress. With a broad smile, he tried to pay her with some coppers he had in his pocket, but she refused. He took out Mexican silver.

She shook her head. "Bring me some medical supplies from your ship."

"What kind?" He leaned into her and brushed his lips against her neck.

She leaned away. "Anything at all."

"You're asking me to steal?"

"No, I'm telling you how I wish to be paid. It's difficult to get foreign supplies now. Ships are blockaded by renegade Boxers."

"I'll try. Thanks for everything." He heaved Bulldog to his feet. "You will be here tomorrow night? Swear—promise me. I cannot lose you again," Giacomo said, his look and voice imploring.

"I looked for you in every place I've been. Promise enough?" She took a paper from her bodice and waved the letter he had left with Guo Xide.

THE FOLLOWING NIGHT GIACOMO CAME to the dispensary a little tipsy. Lian, all in white, stood by the door of the infirmary. He blinked and rubbed his eyes to make sure she was not a vision. In moon shadow, he approached her.

"I've dealt with both Chinese and foreigners taken with drink, but never expected to see you inebriated." She spoke to him in a low voice. "I am on duty until midnight when I am free to re-bandage your head."

She tapped his watch but his vision was bleary.

"It's only ten thirty. I have many others to attend to now."

"Why are you outside then?"

"I heard a noise and came to investigate." She hesitated. "What's that you're holding?"

"Last night's payment. Here," he gave her a package enveloped in a work shirt.

She took it and said, "You should rest on one of the cots in the back. If you go out, you'll only drink more and won't make it back. I hate to be kept waiting and need to talk to you. Understand?"

He nodded. *"Grazie."*

She placed the package by Kuan Yin and led Giacomo, like a willful child, shrugging his shoulders every time she took him by the elbow. There was a cot, where she made him sit down. His head wasn't on the pillow more than a minute when he fell asleep.

She covered him with the shirt. "The wonders of drink." She kissed his forehead and then brushed a forelock out of his eyes, whispering, "Gorgeous earth-colored eyes."

IT WAS MIDNIGHT WHEN SHE woke him and washed and disinfected his cut. She unwrapped bandages he'd brought and read the label on a brown bottle: *il perossido di idrogeno.*

"Ouch." He winced as she poured. *"Acqua ossigenata!"*

"Peroxide doesn't burn. You're overreacting." She dressed the cut with one of the bandages. Now you've got to leave. I can't talk to you like this."

Lian took his arm gently and escorted him out by a different door. She dropped his arm and continued into the courtyard. He pulled her to him and lifted her into his arms and kissed her over and over till she shrieked.

"Tomorrow we will make a picnic on a windy hill. Come early. I have much to say to you, and my heart is bursting."

❦

PAST DAWN THEY STARTED OUT. Into the basket of food Giacomo carried with their provisions, Lian had placed a present for him covered in a cloth, saying, "Don't look at it yet." They walked the narrow footpath leading from the river. The area was thick with bamboo, but then as it widened, it came to a small copse, surrounded by dense foliage and more bamboo.

"Must have taken years for that bamboo to grow so big."

She laughed. "A few hours more likely. Grows as fast as wildfire spreads."

A lantern boat sailed passed. Two men on two bamboo rafts followed. The fishermen, dressed in black with coolie hats, had lashed together four long bamboo poles to make the raft. Each little barge carried a lantern front and aft and two cormorants each. As they glided past, Lian said, "In Guilin we have the same pacific scenes, except there, mist covers the water and majestic hills loom in the foreground. The saying, 'Guilin's mountain and water scenery is the best under heaven,' comes to mind. It is so true. I have not heard from my friend, Ping, and wonder how she is faring and if Guilin endures the mayhem caused by the Boxers."

"I met her in Guilin. She told me the child is mine. When do I get to meet her?"

"Ping wrote me when Lu died." Passing the field, they walked by a patch purpled with cabbages and then came upon a flagstone path. Wildflowers grew amid nettle. Kites were flying, skating through clouds like wings with tails. Leaves skittered hither and yon. The trees, decorated in green, gave the hillside a holiday air though it was summery hot with more than a hint of a breeze. "I am reticent and deeply troubled to answer you about the child. Please be patient."

Giacomo started a fire of pinecones and small branches encircled by stones. *All in due time,* he thought.

"In my travels, I made a fire with pine pitch to melt snow for the horse, Snowflake."

"Were you afraid?"

"Sometimes."

He wondered about what his heart longed to know, when she'd reveal the child to him.

The wind soughed through the trees. Scattering leaves and acorns brought the pungent fragrance of pine and the acrid smell of twigs and sap from the fire.

Giacomo said, "Listen carefully when the wind blows, you can hear God whisper." He was squatting on his heels by the fire.

"How Chinese," she said. "Our fierce wind is called *ty-fung.*"

"Ah, typhoon."

"God's wrath." Her dreamy look was unsure, as if floating in uncharted waters. "A life typhoon whipped my rice-paper heart above a fire, curled with burnt edges. Smoldering still hurts. Scars can be seen as black snakes twisting at the borders."

"What are you saying?" He touched her hand, wanting to encourage her.

"I have hidden secrets."

"You need fear nothing from me."

"Perhaps." She adjusted her skirt and worried a crease in the garment.

"What is it, Lian?"

"You know about Lu and how I escaped to Hong Kong with my, our daughter," she said, her voice forlorn.

"When will I see her?"

"My little Zin-Zin—that's what I called her before we left for Hong Kong—Ya Chen, Precious Pearl, was killed in just such a wind. *Tai feng.* I ran away to Hong Kong. I was a coward to run from Lu. Maybe I should have left her with my husband, but my heart unhinged merely at the thought. I took her from her natal home, selfishly wanting her, a part of you, to come with me. Though, it was her karma."

Giacomo's eyebrows arched.

Horses frolicked in a meadow nearby. Two mares and two colts.

"I left him after I lost a second child. His." She raised her hand to silence his next question. "No, I didn't lose the child, I aborted—the punishment for this was intolerable, costing me Zin-Zin. I thought the gods were appeased. I need and want your baby. The child will never replace Ya Chen, but—"

Giacomo covered his face, his shoulders wracked by torents of sobs. He stopped, wiped his face with his sleeve, took hold of her hands, and bent his head into her lap.

"We're both damaged. I killed a man in Sicily, not in war, and you killed a baby. And a life is a life is a life. And forgiving ourselves comes at a high price. The past never goes away. From what you've told me, you've atoned for your sins."

"Without your forgiveness there is no redemption. You see, I only married Lu because I was pregnant with your baby. Ya Chen was our love child."

"Our child," he repeated as if the words conjured magic.

"I left messages for you at the embassy in Peking."

"I received no message."

"I went to the Summer Palace to see the big eunuch with the medallion, hoping he would give you my letter."

Giacomo shook his head. "What of me? Seems to me, I haven't searched hard enough for pardon. I don't know how to seek the path of redemption. I need—maybe we can heal each other through our love. Our lost child . . ."

Buttercups bloomed in profusion a touch away. Lian picked one. "I wonder if this is how forgiveness flowers, amid a field blasted with regret and cannon shot, a frank admission, an epiphany, a willingness to try to love anew. But when does the pain that gathers itself in the solar plexus leave finally and for good? Will it, one day, wad itself into a huge sigh and exit the body with a breath, unnoticed?"

"Our stories, our histories are ugly, aren't they? We're lucky to love, it's one of life's greatest gifts—but there are other beauties," he said, indicating the horses. One of the mares was cream beige, the other roan. The colts mirrored their mothers. The darker of the two pranced and ran—a dashing splendor to behold. Lured by cowbells, he courted the grazing calves with curious attention and then spirited away back to his mother's waiting teats.

They were quiet for a long time. Then she took something out of the basket but stuffed it back into the basket and laid the cloth.

"What are you hiding?" he asked, his question encased in two folds.

"Haven't I hidden enough? Oh, dear. Something I made for you, but I shan't give it to you, unless you promise to wear it."

"I must know what it is first," he said.

"Promise me, sight unseen." While he was still exaggeratedly shaking his head, she said, "A vest." She unraveled it, and he let out a low whistle. "You must swear that if you engage in battle; you will wear it on top of your tunic."

"Nonsense—I'd be killed for desertion."

"You arrogant fool. You'll be killed if you don't." She pulled it out all the way, and Giacomo's jaw droped a bit.

"What?" She handed it to him. "At least underneath your tunic."

He took it in both hands. "Beautiful material. The dragons are incredible—like those you draw . . . and the blue is . . . is indescribable. How could you afford it?" Giacomo held it in one hand, running his other over it the way his palm slid along her thigh not long ago.

"I made it from my wedding jacket. It's a family heirloom, but wasn't meant to be a wedding jacket."

"I have no words." He walked over to her, trying it on.

"Fits you well," she said.

He held up her chin and he kissed her. *"Tse-tse."*

She pulled away from him and bowed and he returned the bow. Then she stood straight up and looked at him for a long time. He spun around for her with his arms outstretched so she could even see the fit under his arms. She nodded approvingly. "Now take it off so you will not muss it up before you need to wear it. But remember you promised: you will wear this in battle. It is your protective shield. I hold you to your word," she said, realizing he never gave it. "Say the words of promise."

He hedged. "If there is a call to arms, do you really think I'll have time to search for it? And then leisurely put it on?"

She turned toward the open basket. "Then promise me if there is time, you will."

"I—" he let out an exasperated breath, "I will."

She placed it in the basket and closed the lid.

Gazing at the horses, Lian said, "And where is my beautiful horse Snowflake now?"

"Was he unkind?"

"My husband? His parents beat me, you see. He owned me. I was chattel, and he made me slave. This is China." She hesitated a moment, and then said, "I craved freedom like a marsh heron. I wanted to be a healer—I had the skills, but he wouldn't hear of it. Then in Hong Kong, I worked for an apothecary, but my talents were wasted. I was nothing more than a stock girl."

"There's so much I don't know—I want to know everything about you. What was our baby like?" He toyed with his mustache.

At the gesture, she said, "I adore when you do that. You can't get inside my skin—you'll never know everything about any one. Before Zhugong died I asked him to tell me his life's story."

"Zhugong?"

"My Yogi, my friend, my teacher, my inspiration for growth. His death gave me the strength to mourn our daughter and go on with my life. I believe we knew each other in another life."

Giacomo was quiet for a moment. "Do you remember me from another life? I ruined your reputation and I want to continue to ruin it."

She laughed a small laugh. *"Ayii!* And what reputation would that be exactly? Now that I have slept with you and intend on sleeping with you and have confessed to abortion, it is I who may ruin your reputation."

"You're a sailor's wench. What if we can never marry?"

"I'll never leave China. It doesn't matter. Don't you see? You have no control of it. Love's first feeling rises up like a small wind. It's as though you lose yourself in clouds. The skin prickles. Every pore is aware you are no longer yourself, but a part of something else, something universal. The physical *you* drifts into someone else, dragging your soul, until you become bigger, better than you are, a part of what you see through one square centimeter of space. Close one eye; now squint the other eye shut partway and what do you see?"

"Like looking through a lens? A telescope reporting back."

"Your senses see that tree, this field, those horses. Your mind filters what you observe, trying not to succumb, but everything in nature overwhelms—that bee's buzz, the ocean's fog wafting to these cliff tops, my breath clouding the air between us." She blew out for emphasis.

"Like playing with dice, wishing the toss will make you a winner, when you realize it's not up to you—the toss is governed by fate. You cannot know the outcome until you gamble. Fall where they must. Everything takes its proper place and order is restored from chaos. You know—" he started, but she placed her fingertips on his lips.

"What are your orders?" She took her hand away from his mouth.

"Floods from the melting winter snows made the river wide and deep this spring. Anytime. The ship can leave anytime. I may be going on a mission soon, but now that I have found you, I will never lose you again," he said, and brushed stray tendrils away from her face. He raised her chin.

"What we want and what the Fates have deigned for us do not always coincide. Look what has already happened to us. *Chúan yào ting ma?*" she asked. "Don't answer—I really do not want to know how long your ship will remain. I shall make a prayer scroll for your safekeeping as you travel the river. There are many dangers. The sandbars, the floods, the bandits."

She handed him a package of steamed rice wrapped in a lotus leaf. With a small pair of sewing scissors, she cut across the top and opened it, perfuming the air with the pungency of lotus. "The leaves are more fragrant than the flowers," she said, indicating the lotus leaf.

"The statue of Kuan Yin in the dispensary—she's holding a lotus leaf."

"For that you deserve a thousand kisses."

"Come here and pay up."

She laughed. "The Moon Festival is coming."

"When?"

"Tomorrow. The fifteenth day of the eighth lunar month. We will eat moon cakes to celebrate the Mid-Autumn Festival."

"Like Harvest Moon."

"Not like, it is." She gave him a porcelain spoon for the steamed rice.

He took the lotus leaf like a plate and began to eat. He passed her the empty leaf but held on to his spoon. "I doubt I can be with you tomorrow. What will you write on the scroll?"

"I shall write this for certain, the same way that Zhugong, my sage, did a lifetime ago, only he used his toe to scratch it into the earth." Lian picked up a stick. "Like this . . ." and wrote in the sand: 爱 *love*.

"*Ai?* Love? And your grandmother's *feng shui?*" He pointed to the basket.

She put away the used leaf and gave him another, repeating the cutting process, saying, "Ah, so you recall my grandmother's story." The wind had picked up. She brushed hair from her eyes. "Let's hear it, then. Good *feng shui* is like—"

"Chinese enchantment."

"Not magic. Literally it means: wind-water, and it makes sense to keep energy flowing and all in harmony."

He leaned in toward her and kissed her. She licked her lips, sticky from his rice, looking around quickly to see if there were onlookers. She bit her bottom lip, and he kissed her again but held her head fast so that she couldn't look around. She shook her head, acquiescing to his silent request.

"Tell me about the New Year's holiday coming up."

"Oh, no. The Moon Festival is not our New Year's. That's *Yuan tan,* and is celebrated on the second moon of the winter solstice. Every nook and cranny of the house is cleaned, but we never sweep on New Year's lest all the good luck is swept away."

"Don't you clean any other time?" He finished the rice and gave her the leaf and spoon.

"You are so bold. Naturally, we do. But this is hysterical kind of cleaning."

"Go on." He wiped his mouth with his handkerchief.

"A week before the holiday the kitchen god, who watches over the family, is fed sweets. Families even give him honey to make his mouth stick so that when he is burnt and goes to heaven, he'll not say bad things about the family.

"The day before New Year's is reserved for cooking, because no sharp objects can be used on the actual day, for fear that all the good luck will be cut out, and neither can hair be washed on that day—"

"For fear that all the good luck will be washed away?"

"Exactly!"

"On the night before *Yuan tan,* the children wait for New Year, and after midnight the family greets each other, generally saying, 'Kung-shi,' which means 'I humbly wish you joy.' Then they all go to sleep."

"That's it? No noisemakers? No parties? I've always been onboard ship."

"The next day, the children get gifts of red packets with money inside. This reminds me of my last meeting with Hang Wo's parents, for they, too, had given me a red envelope with money inside as thanks for all I did for my student, their prized daughter, and of course, to thank me for the horse. Ah, horse, I miss you. Wo's father had pronounced the words, *zhu ni duguo meihao de yi tian,* thanks a million, with such reverence that it had sounded like a prayer."

They'd been silent for a time. "Red," he said, his tenor and manner reflective.

"Our good-luck color. When a boy is born, we even have red eggs—a son is most propitious. Lu wanted a son. Do you care if it's a boy or girl this time?"

"Most Italian men want sons, but I like girls—if you promise she'll look like you. Did Ya Chen?"

Lian was quiet for a minute. "Ya Chen had much of her father. Her eyes—your eyes. It broke my heart to look at her at times. The daughter of a sailor but could not swim. Lu would not teach her."

He sighed. "Nothing more for the children on New Year's?"

"Of course, mm, let me think. Oh, if flowers open on that day, then it is special good luck. All debts are paid so the debtor saves face."

"Ah yes, one must save face."

"You're making fun. I was going to tell you of the parades for fifteen days, including the lion dance. But you're cruel, and I refuse."

He laughed and pulled her to him. "Here, let me show you a lion dance."

She giggled and struggled free.

"Wait a second, what about the god that got burned? Who watches over the family?"

"Ah, so you were listening? The father."

"The father becomes the god?"

"Foolish man. The father replaces the god, drawn with bright colors on a piece of rice paper, to the shelf that has stayed empty for seven days."

A man passed them, wearing a quilted coat and peasant hat, carrying a yoke with two big wooden buckets full of water.

"*Ku li,*" she said, pointing to the man sloshing water as he stumbled on a rock.

"I heard some American sailors use the word 'coolie,' but it sounds like a term to belittle—not at all how you said it. What does it mean?"

"Bonded labor, hence, bonded laborer. But not all Chinese who left for America were laborers. My father told me theirs was a huge exodus—they went during the gold rush in California and ended up working in gangs on the railroads, or doing laundry, but some made fortunes."

"Listen, I've almost forgotten, I have something for you too." He pulled a tiny packet out of his tunic. "For you. The color of your eyes."

She took the box, opened it, and exclaimed, "Oh, oh, oh."

He took out the emerald ring and put it on her finger. Then she cried in his arms.

LATER THAT AFTERNOON AT HER flat, Giacomo asked about fleeing from her husband.

"I escaped Lu's home, but he came to Hong Kong and told me you died. Our actions are not without repercussions, for the gods speak in whispers but their breath can be fury. A *tai feng*, a big wind—you call it a typhoon—took my precious baby's life. Your baby, Giacomo. Afterward I didn't care if I lived or died. I lived only for her and the idea we'd be reunited as a family. Can you ever forgive me?"

Giacomo looked surprised. "You bear guilt for something you shouldn't."

She sipped her tea, motioning if he cared for more. "I left Hong Kong for Yangbinguan, Sichuan, and lived in the Catholic mission till I came here to Tientsin and you. I have been traveling toward you, all my life—even my vision in the cave of a man in blue uniform. I asked if it was you."

"Tell me about my little girl," Giacomo said, and saw in his mind's lens a baby girl with quick intelligence from both races in Lian's face before him, plus beauty beyond measure—witty and courageous despite sadness. He held her eyes till there was recognition of each other's soul.

"Zin-Zin loved dolls and stories. She ran free because I did not bind her feet—she was too young, but I never would have."

"Was she as pretty as you?" He took hold of her hand.

"Hers was an innocent beauty from within."

"Do you have a picture of her?"

"Look in the mirror. Only her hair was straight."

"Talk to me about your life without me."

"I keep a chronicle like my father, but wrote in it for you since the moment I met you. I left it for safekeeping with Cook at the mission before my travels to the caves. One of the reasons I went back. How fortuitous. I never would've known you were still alive and searching for me." She told him that her husband and family were murdered by marauding hordes in a brutal peasant revolt of Boxers, even though Lu was one. "Maybe because he was landed gentry."

"I thought he was still alive. Then are you free to marry me?"

"You've had several beers, and I need air. Let's walk."

Outside he said, "Ah, thank God for the bright moon."

They walked, not speaking for a few minutes.

He stood in a doorway but wouldn't budge. Lian stepped in front of him. She turned, bathed in light, and he knew for sure he'd found his someone special. She was not yet another girl in another port. For the first time his head warned: *Remember, this isn't home, this is China.*

She motioned him to follow her, but his feet were glued. She retreated a few steps and took hold of both his hands.

A shattering roar of silence filled the night air, and he wondered if she noticed it too. In their eyes, each saw the other in miniature. "You're not as drunk as I imagined."

They walked for a long time without speaking, but the closeness was enough for both of them. She took a tiny purse from her bodice, opened it, and extracted a key. "This is my humble abode," she said, opening the door.

"May I come in?"

"You are already in." She shook her head, closed her eyes, and pursed her lips. Giacomo obliged, kissing her gently, not passionately, so he wouldn't frighten her.

She faked a yawn. "However, now I must ask you to leave. It's late and the cock crows early—"

"A regiment of Boxers couldn't tear me away from you tonight." He closed the door behind him.

THAT NIGHT IN A SMALL loft room with wooden rafters, Lian stood before him. She took the silky lapel of her dressing robe and slipped it off her shoulder, opening it to reveal her breast, cloud white against the sky blue of her gown. She whispered, "Touch me," and sighed.

Giacomo heard that sigh and understood its daring. She wanted him to caress her, to hold her, but more than this, she wanted to be wanted.

"Touch me here," she repeated, indicating her naked breast with a downward brushstroke of fingers across her raised nipple.

He reached out his hand, looking at her puzzled face. "What?" he begged. "What is it?" he asked, perplexed.

"It's that I want to say—"

"Yes?" he prompted, frightened he'd spoil the mood and disturb her beatific look, a Madonna bathed in shimmering moonlight peering though the wavy panes of a small window.

He felt he knew everything about her. That maybe this wasn't real but a dream, like all the others, and it was his memory continuing to create the scene.

"I want to say," she said, lowering her gaze, "love me. Love me now. Love me forever." She raised her head. "There is nothing else in life but love and the surety of death."

❧❁❧

ALL THE THINGS GIACOMO HAD wanted to know about her, he finally asked in the days that followed. While she was talking, he whispered that she was breathtaking, thinking he had never known a Eurasian before or after meeting her, though he was familiar with Chinese "dolls." He found her changed from the inexperienced girl he'd fallen in love with; yet he didn't understand why and this surprised him. Hadn't he changed?

❧❁❧

A FEW NIGHTS LATER, LIAN made green tea in the back room of the dispensary, and told him the details of her marriage and her escape to Hong Kong and her work in the mission.

He asked her about traveling to and from the caves, and she explained she'd experienced life-altering growth. She added the part that included coming to the Shensi Mission, meeting the priest who had brought Giacomo to her the night of the fight, and opening up the infirmary.

The following night Giacomo jumped ship to see Lian in a garden close to the infirmary.

As they strolled through an archway and into the garden, Lian said, "There's a great resemblance to another garden when we stood by a pool of water, don't you think?"

He stopped and kissed her. Then he asked if she were sorry they had consummated their love and she bore his baby.

Haloed in light, she faced him and said, "Never," first in Italian and then repeated it in Chinese, *"Chüeh mei yu."*

He took hold of her shoulders. "I still can't believe—it can't be, but, it's really you. "Are you happy?" Disbelief and excitement crossed his face like shadows from different casts of light. "I never stopped dreaming of the girl I kissed in the Summer Palace."

"How long have I yearned to hear these words, sailor? The experience of loving is not unlike the beauty of 'lotus petals,' tiny bound feet Chinese men find irresistible, the unbinding of which is excruciating."

Chapter 25

Wǒ bùdǒng
我不懂
I don't understand

A FEW EVENINGS LATER, GIACOMO and I walked to a market and made small purchases. Back in my lodgings, I cooked a meal of rice, braised pork, and vegetables.

"You look so pensive, what are you thinking?" he asked.

He looked into my eyes, and then he kissed my shoulder as I leaned into him.

"You must know I tried to break with Lu, but I was expecting our baby. What was I to do? My lovely father cautioned me to tell Lu about you so as not to begin the marriage in deceit. What I did not tell him was the man who made me conceive wasn't Chinese. That was a huge mistake—a shock when Ya Chen was born and he couldn't claim the child as his. I have longed for you, but dreaded this time when I would speak of our loss."

"Don't you believe in the will of the gods? Losing our child was written in our karma. Tell me about Lu. Was it unbearable to stay in his protection while you raised our child? The thought of someone else touching you, kissing you, revolts me beyond reason." His look became a mask of molten iron.

"How can you even ask? I stayed for Ya Chen's sake. As for his lovemaking, if you can call it that, it was physical torment I endured. He never kissed me. Ever. Think of it, my lips are as virginal as when you first took me."

"Forgive me," he said and hung his head. "*Wǒ bùdǒng.* I don't understand, or can't possibly know your trials with Lu if you don't speak of them."

"Know this then." I pointed to my eyes. "These gave me away. They also betrayed our daughter. My mother-in-law knew her "granddaughter" was not hers at all and hated our child and me. And Lu? I was an impertinent rock in his garden."

"We won't speak of this any more." He uncrossed his legs and moved from the small table to a roomier place on the floor. He leaned back against the wall, extended his long legs, and looked around. "But tell me something. Anything. I care little to hear what you say. All I want is your voice in my ear. I want to hold you in my arms, chest to chest as one beating heart. Come here to me."

The room held calligraphy on the opposite wall and cut flowers cascaded from a painted porcelain vase on top of the windowsill. A silk brocade green and gold coverlet adorned the pallet bed just two feet from where he sat. I settled close to him. "My mother was in her ninth month of expectancy and died in a horrible accident—I couldn't save her. She was run over by a cart in the street right in front of me. I am haunted by the memory—even now, after all these years. I suffered her screams in nightmares until I lost Ya Chen. Now my screams for my child will be with me forever." I put a pillow behind his back. He took my arm and kissed my wrist.

"At dusk when shadows fall and day recedes into darkness, I'm reminded of that time alone. Though there are things I forgot today, this morning, I have a clear vision of my father finishing an experiment, holding up a vial in his laboratory, and saying, '*C'e lo fatta!*' I did it."

"Did your father—"

"Never remarried. He remained faithful to the memory of my mother until he died."

"And the infirmary?"

"Guo Xide gave me the name of the priest you met—his friend Bruno Giordano. Odd, I met a stranger in Hong Kong who became a guardian angel of sorts, Doctor Castellano, who gave me Guo Xide's name and location. Destiny. I had much help opening the Dragon Chasing Rainbow Dispensary. I had been tutored well and speak French and German."

"You're lucky your father taught you medicine to such a degree—"

A breeze from the window made me shudder.

"He said I matched his doctoring skills. This was untrue, but I wished to heal."

"You're unaware of your beauty, aren't you?" he said, stroking my cheek. "Your eyes sometimes remind me of upturned olive leaves."

I crossed the room and closed the window.

He stood in back of me and whispered, "You're enchanting when you speak—tiny gestures to emphasize your words."

I shrugged away. "Shall I prepare more tea, Giacomo? Such a lovely name, and how I love saying it, but I refrain from using it often, like a magic potion."

He shook his head. "I'll make tea for you. Sit."

WHEN I SAW GIACOMO NEXT, it was at the infirmary, and he said, "I feel feverish and unbalanced."

"Stick out your tongue. Now close your mouth."

"Ah, did I pass the test?" He adjusted himself on the seat. He appeared nervous.

"Calm down and open your mouth, but this time when you stick out your tongue, open your mouth wide. A little wider. Mmm."

"Well?"

"I didn't say to speak—just hold your tongue out." I probed and pressed. After a few seconds, I said, "Close."

"Thanks. I was gagging. Is it bad?"

"Let's say, not good. You Westerners believe the tongue is an inside organ, but to us it is outside because air touches it. This body part explains much of your internal organs. Now give me your hands—please, not to hold—I need to take your pulses."

"Pulse." He pulled one hand away.

"Give me both—we use both, and we take the pulse at more than just one spot. Are you trying my patience? Don't be difficult."

"Yes, ma'am," he said, then grinned. "What ailment do I have?"

"*Ai.* I think what you need is—bed rest. Definitely. And with me."

Chapter 26

Cha
茶
Tea

A WESTERNER IN MANDARIN DRESS sat with a man sipping beer. At first Giacomo didn't recognize the man with Bulldog because he was in Chinese garb. The Jesuit priest again.

"Giacomo, this is Don Bruno Giordano," Bulldog said. "We meet finally, formally, and I'm sober enough to recognize him."

Shaking hands with Bulldog and then the priest, Giacomo said, "A reverse name of the pantheist martyr Giordano Bruno? Ironic. As a Jesuit do you think like the monk?" He extended his hand to the priest, who shook it as if he were wringing a dishrag. Giacomo winced.

"There's much truth in his philosophy, and I revere nature," Father Giordano said.

"Where does that leave God?" Bulldog asked, his tone mocking. "And with that, gentlemen, I take my leave." Bulldog gave a fake salute and did an about-face.

"Goodnight, Bulldog," they said in unison.

There was an awkward moment of silence. Giacomo looked at his hands as if they'd give him an idea of what to say next. After he cleared his throat he said, "'And the greatness of His Kingdom made manifest; He is glorified not in one, but in countless suns; not in a single earth, a single world, but in a thousand, thousand, I say an infinity of worlds.'"

"On the infinite universe and the Infinity of Worlds. 1584. You are well read, well versed, indeed, Giacomo."

"For a sailor. Haven't I seen you someplace before?"

"You have. I took you to the infirmary the night the Boxers beat you to a bloody pulp and almost slit your neck."

"I mean someplace else?" He didn't wait for an answer. "How well do you know Lian?"

"She's a dear friend, another missionary friend—Father Alberico Crescitelli—sent her to me after she left his mission. Guo Xide. You said you knew him."

"Personally. Met him with an Austrian friend who was trying to convince him to vacate the mission. Stubborn son of a—so you're the priest who helps her with the dispensary."

"When I saw you two together there—you know each other from another time, but I couldn't help think—I doubt she'd be interested in the likes of you," the priest said, and plunged on. "Remember, 'Nature is none other than God in things. Whence all of God is in all things. Think thus of the sun in the crocus, in the narcissus, in the heliotrope, in the rooster in the lion.' This philosophy of the monk is lovely."

"But the sun is in Lian too—she's lovelier, lovelier than all the flowers. She's serious and intelligent and I'm in love with her and she with me."

"I don't believe it, but for now it's enough if you think she is. I would hate to see her get hurt again. She's been though a great deal of loss."

Giacomo said, "I know."

"Everything?"

Giacomo nodded. "But perhaps you don't. The child lost in the typhoon was mine."

Surprise registered on Don Bruno's face, and seeking composure he said, "However, 'All things in the universe and the universe in all things: we in it, and it in us, and in this way: everything harmonizes in perfect unity.'"

"Here's perfect unity—you, me, and this bottle of Scotch, and hours to while away. I don't have to be back onboard till sundown tomorrow, so you tell me your story, and I'll tell you mine." He uncorked the bottle.

"Nothing much to tell really. Born the seventh of ten children in Roma in '52, consecrated in '77 and came to China in '87."

"Why a priest and why a Jesuit?" Giacomo poured himself a drink.

"I sought a life of self-examination. I'm in constant search for the state of my soul. I contemplate, maintain, and seek to die well. At death the soul will be judged—there'll be a resurrection and my eternal condition will be—"

"Your dwelling will be determined?" Giacomo picked up his glass and sniffed it.

Father Bruno Giordano inclined his head.

"What about the sin of intellectual pride you Jesuits—"

"I admit in Rome my life was taken up with books and learning. Here things are different. I feel closer to God, and my self-examination is doing battle for the Church."

Giacomo poured a drink for the priest. "Now you no longer meditate because you're casting about for souls?"

"I have colloquies with God every day." The priest picked up his glass, tasted it, and then poured in some water from a glass pitcher. "And you?"

"Oh, I have a much longer tale than yours, and no way in hell am I searching for death or to live a holy life on this earth."

"We have all night."

Giacomo poured more Scotch. "What I remember clearly is this," he said, but a loud commotion interrupted what he was about to say.

Fritz stood in front of Giacomo and the priest. "Giacomo, you must be dry, twisting this Mandarin's ear off—and in Italian too—but he's too pale to be a Mandarin."

"Father, this is Fritz, the Austrian I went to the mission with," Giacomo said.

"We've met before. Here, Father, let me pour you a drink," Fritz said.

"Giacomo just did. I'm here for conversation, not to get drunk," Don Bruno said.

"Then I'll have one." Fritz reached for an empty glass.

The men clinked glasses and sipped, then sat silent for a few minutes. The noise of the barroom brought them back to the present.

"Life. Each of us has a story, eh?" Fritz said. He turned toward Giacomo. "Tell me why you joined up."

"I'm not noble, and I'm not patriotic." Giacomo ran his fingers through his hair and let out a deep breath. "I'm here because I killed a man."

"Now that's a story I want to hear," Fritz said.

"It's late. We'll talk again soon." Giacomo smoothed his mustache with two fingers.

The two men stood, shook hands, and Giacomo paid the check in Mexican silver.

"Peace go with you both," Don Bruno said, and walked toward the door.

"Be careful, my friend. This is a dangerous city," Fritz said.

Don Bruno turned. "That goes for both of you too."

Giacomo wasn't tired and decided to walk to the infirmary to see his pretty nurse. Maybe she'd take some time to be with him. He had another day's leave.

Crossing boulevards and thoroughfares, he trotted off, toward the outskirts of Lian's district. He would go some distance before cutting inside the quarter again, seeing in periphery fires from some of the neighboring outlying villages smoking from the hills. Boxers had raided, ransacked, and destroyed for loot and the booty sold to purchase weapons where they were available. Giacomo picked up his pace, slinking beneath small awnings and staying close to shops for slight protection from the mizzling rain. He pulled his collar up and buttoned it, looking over his shoulder, but felt it was even too late for Boxers to be roaming. Even they needed sleep and so did he. However, he was wrong because at the next corner, passing a tavern, he heard the innkeeper say to a group of Boxer women, one of whom identified herself as a member of the Society of the Red Lantern, "No Christians here, leave us in peace."

Another woman said, "We'll go on our business then," which Giacomo learned the next morning was the destruction of a Catholic chapel nearby.

He knocked on the back window of the infirmary and Lian peered out. She opened the door and fell into his arms. "I'm exhausted. The last patient has just left. It's so late. What are you doing here?"

"Wondering if you can take a pitiful sailor in for the night, or better still, maybe you can sneak away from work for a day with me?"

She shook her head. "Spend the night. Tomorrow I can meet you at a teahouse."

"Not quite the romantic interlude I imagined, but all right."

THE NEXT DAY HE STAYED late in her rooms until close to the appointed hour. He would be meeting her for tea. He felt his pulse increase as though he'd been running. A fierce gust of wind blew his hat off, and he ran to retrieve it in the gutter-filled runoff. He squeezed out the excess and put it in back on his head. He didn't want to be caught out of uniform, which meant his hat on his head. He thought, *What if she doesn't come because of the inclement weather?* Just when he needed cooperation from heaven and had prayed for a sunny day, it poured. Of course he only prayed when he needed something, not like when he was a child, pious and pure.

He zigzagged the quieter streets of the quarter and crossed the park diagonally, remembering being with Lian only weeks ago to listen to musicians with odd instruments: the *yang qin,* a hammered dulcimer. Giacomo particularly liked the *yue qin,* or moon guitar, with its circular body and four strings which reminded him of his boyhood: the hills with the sheep, and the shepherds coming to Carini at Christmastime to play the *zampogna*—the Italian bagpipe with two drones and two conical chanters, all in one stock.

He took off his hat and shoved it in his peacoat the minute he walked inside the inn. It wasn't quite a booth, but an end table attached to walls on two sides. Lian was already seated. He inclined his head. His tousled hair, his warm eyes crinkling at the corners, his mouth in a capricious smile, he said, "Warm and comfortable enough?"

"You've lived so many more life experiences. How could I be?"

He took off his jacket and hung it on a peg on the wall.

Giacomo ordered tea. "My thoughts seem jumbled—won't come to me straight. I want to apologize for last night. I was too rough, but I hunger for you."

"I feel the same way." She looked at him, smiling. "My eyes should be lowered—but they disobey and I want to devour you with my glance."

Her smile warmed him as if he'd put both hands on the steaming teapot, which had just been placed on the table. It was blue and white with a wicker handle and came with tiny porcelain cups.

Lian took off her quilted jacket and the blue of her silk dress was the exact color of the cups. He was going to comment about it, but she inclined her head and the instant was lost. He was about to pour the tea, but she stayed his hand.

"Let it draw a moment longer," she said in a voice honeyed enough to sweeten the tea. He wanted to take her hands in his, but knew she would withdraw them, embarrassed for the show of affection in public. Then she breathed in deeply the steam above the teapot. After a minute longer, she poured the tea for both of them. She held the cup in two hands and, after inhaling, placed it on a bamboo mat, and raised the palm of her hand signifying that he, too, should take in the steam. "Inhaling breath is taking in life, perking up one's ego, like a fat pigeon's breast inflating as he prances, calling attention in a mating dance."

"And exhaling?" Giacomo went to place his hand over hers, but moved his cup instead.

"Ah. Exhalation can be one's dying breath."

"And if a person is not dying?"

"Then as the breath dies and words are spoken, meaning is born into them. And with the last of the breath, even more meaning is given to them."

"I had hoped for a better icebreaker than death."

She smiled. "'Icebreaker.' How apt an expression."

Jasmine. The fragrance came to him pungent, pregnant with scent, the way her words perfumed the air. There was a *spifero d'aria*—a little current, wheezing through the fixtures of the window, and Giacomo felt the draft. "Sad sound that little whistle, isn't it?" The lace curtains fluttered, and the slight movement caught his eye. He lifted a corner of the cloth. Giacomo saw what he wished not to encounter. A mob of Boxers led by the Golden Turtle owner's son marching by. "Keep on going," he muttered.

He put the cup down and reached across the table and covered her delicate hands with his huge ones. She whispered it would be better to be more covert in public, and he withdrew his hands, the hurt he felt surprising. His first instinct had been right, and he knew better than to touch her in public.

"Back home in Carini there's a café where my mother sometimes takes cappuccino in the afternoon with her friends. They serve large round cookies with jam in the middle—raspberry or apricot, and they're called *occhio di bue*—cow's eye."

"A funny name."

"Here," he said, and, taking a small carpenter's lead pencil from his pocket, drew a circle within a circle for her on a napkin, "that's what it looks like."

"The circle is the sign for eternal," she said.

"And blue—the cups, teapot—your jacket?"

"Heavenly things. The sky, a majestic sea on sunny days." She poured more tea.

"Not today with all this rain." He moved the curtains and pulled a face.

"What's wrong?" she sipped her tea.

"Boxers on the march again."

"I've heard rumors that the owner's son is one of them."

"He is. If they don't come in, we will leave immediately after they've passed. If they get any nearer, we'll leave by that door." He pointed in back of her. "Put on your jacket." He called the waiter and paid.

Outside they skirted the park. "We missed them, but you're still upset. Why?" she said.

"I lost my temper and almost hit one of the coolies in the galley. It wasn't my watch—I had no business being there, and I made the lieutenant lose face."

"'If you are patient in one moment of anger, you will escape a hundred days of sorrow.' Chinese proverb. Why are you so hostile? Volatile? Have you ever considered this?"

"I don't think. I act. Maybe react. Oh, he wears an earring."

"Who does?"

"The coolie. Why does he?"

"He has a name, I'm sure he'd rather you use it."

Shame colored Giacomo's face. "It's Bohai."

"It means: elder brother sea. Earrings and Spirits," she said, her tone wistful. "Girl babies wear two, boys one. You see," she said in earnest, "Evil Spirits cannot bother themselves about little girls, and so boys are made to wear a female adornment."

"Aha! The idea being the Evil Spirits see the earring and do not bother the creature because they think the child is female."

"My, my, you are clever," she said, derision in every syllable.

"You're teasing me," he said, wanting to kiss her.

"Only a little."

They made their way to the Shadow of Seven Swallows Inn—the rain had stopped and now the moon shimmered on the tops of maple trees, wind threshing through them, a tiara of light crowned the willows. Soon cicadas chirred a wild rhythm.

"Isn't it late in the season for them to mate?" Giacomo asked.

"For some things, there is no season."

They entered and rented a small room where they were served dinner and he could think of nothing else through the meal except undressing her. Since he couldn't do it there and then, he did it in his head.

"You are so quiet," she said.

"I have a lot on my mind. You."

"Can I guess?"

"Shall we go?"

The scent of fall dwindling, edging itself to winter's precipice was increased by the washed evening air. He stopped for a moment to inhale the drenched, loamy smell, harbinger of death and decay. Giacomo glanced over his shoulder. He took his hands out of his pockets and had an urge to dash across the park from where they came. He took Lian's hand, though she objected, and all but dragged her into a labyrinth of small alleyways and crooked lanes.

She let go of his hand as soon as they stood in an overhanging, unlit doorway. "Is there something wrong?"

"When we turned the corner, I saw some hell-raisers. I didn't want the pleasure of meeting up with them. They're armed and wearing bandanas with script on them. Their eyes are fierce—out for blood—and I'm not a willing martyr. I'm afraid they'd attack you too—"

"Not just for being with you—one look at my eyes—I'm foreign too."

His gait slowed when they reached the town limits. They meandered through the streets. He remembered how the dim light slanted across her face as they ate dinner, her face as she smiled first with her eyes, then letting mirth take possession of her pert mouth, her crinkled nose.

They had touched shoulders stepping from the door's threshold onto the cobblestone street. He'd put his hand in the small of her back as if to guide her through the entranceway. She had looked up furtively as if they'd been seen by someone spying on them, and the inappropriate gesture unsettled her. They passed a small gate and ambled through a narrow passageway, and as he ushered her though, his hand climbed to her shoulder.

He said, "Sorry," but didn't mean it.

She inclined her head.

"Can I walk you the rest of the way home?"

"I'd rather not. It's late and you have to get back to your ship. You must be careful."

He took her hand and brought it to his lips and kissed it. "Small like a child's but so capable of strong deeds and kind acts." He turned her hand over and kissed her wrist, the pulse made him grow hard. "Till next time—" he broke off, turned, and loped away.

Walking back to the wharf, he recalled her touch and felt melancholy, wondering if that was a malady of youth and of the lovesick. He had felt her blood coursing through her veins. It had become a part of him.

GIACOMO HAD BEEN ON MANEUVERS for a week. When he returned, Lian and Giacomo skirted the Bell Tower. They walked through the same park as the previous week, but toward a different teahouse— *Xiaotaoyuan*, Small Peach Garden Teahouse. The air smelled of snow, and the temperature was dropping.

"I want to tell you my dream," she said, stopping to look at him. "Here's what happened." Her forlorn voice caught his attention.

"Wait," Giacomo said. "Let's sit here under this pomegranate." Where were the beautiful leaves of russet and red? He guided her to a bench that really was just a wood plank settled upon two large rocks.

"I was strolling along the Li River with my grandmother. You know how it is in dreams when you just know where you are? I carried a basket that held sheaves of rice paper, a paintbrush, and a black ink stone. A huge attacking bird, not a vulture, and not black, but a sickly white/gray/beige animal with enormous wings attacked my basket and I dropped it, scattering the contents. I beat off the bird and Grandmother helped me. I then collected the contents of the basket and replaced them. We turned around and started to walk in the opposite direction toward a house perched above a body of water. The windows were open. A breeze stirred the curtains. A woman long dead from my grandmother's hometown of Hunan was there but did not speak."

"Was she a ghost?" Giacomo asked.

"No, she was alive and stood in back of my grandmother, who was no longer with me."

"But you said—"

"Patience. Please do not interrupt. Just let me ramble. I must tell you in the correct sequence. Grandmother's friend, dressed in a gray dress—a *cheongsam*—was there still, though she refused to speak to me. I felt my grandmother and my mother's presence, yet I was apart from them. They showed me a piece of paper upon which was *Nüshu,* which I have never read or seen. Strange that I recognized it, don't you think?"

"What's *Nüshu* again? A recipe?" Giacomo asked.

"You are mocking me."

"It's a kind of script."

"Not just script. Weren't you listening when I told you it is a secret language of women and started in Jiangyong county of Hunan province, where Grandmother was born? She taught Mother when women were not allowed to read or write—"

Giacomo started to speak, but Lian held up her hand in protest. "Hush. Please. I think the realm of possibility of things we do not understand in this life, especially from the dreamworld or unexplainable, is infinite. Do you agree?" She smiled at him, realizing he had something to say, but she had silenced him.

"What's the difference between *Nüshu* and Chinese?"

"Our written Chinese is 'boxy' whereas *Nüshu* is cursive and leaner, longer. Feathery. The words are written from top to bottom in long columns and then read from right to left."

"The writing in your book."

"Book?"

"Diary. Journal."

"Oh," she said, nodding her head. "Precisely."

"Tell me more about the dream," he said, thinking of his superstitious mother.

"I asked all three women a question: will our love last? I cannot for the love of jasmine tea remember the answer. They were young and happy. Yet I never saw Grandmother joyful. Were they happy for me?"

Lian's voice was almost disembodied, washing over Giacomo, smooth as a river stone.

"Then I realized I had lost something from the basket and knew I must search for it. But I awoke." She raised her palms in a futile gesture.

Giacomo hesitated and like a schoolboy, raised his hand for permission to speak. "What does the dream mean to you?" he asked.

"Perhaps my loved ones want me with them, or are sending me a message. Perhaps they want me to be happy and to love again. Perhaps I must write a prayer scroll and honor my ancestors. Perhaps. Perhaps." Lian pulled her collar tighter around her neck. Her cheeks were colorless.

"Or perhaps I should write a prayer scroll for you."

"What would you say in it?"

"I would say I wish for you happiness times three."

"No, you wouldn't. What would you write for me?"

She thought a minute.

"Well? What—"

"I face the moon. In every morsel of sky, constellations attest my love. May each shooting star descend, fishtailing into oblivion; every comet burst into nothingness to light your path. I wish you a night of dazzling wonderment, the strength of a dragon's heart, fear and awe to ignite your eyes."

Giacomo turned to face her and put his hands on her shoulders and drew her close. "I don't know what to say. Lian—"

He was about to kiss her, but she shrugged her shoulders. "Please," she said, just above a whisper. "Please," she said again, and lowered her head. And he released her.

The serried ranks of clouds overhead had dispersed; the sky had turned dull pewter, reminding Giacomo of a drinking tankard. "Let's go now. We'll have some tea and warm ourselves indoors. You look so pale and cold."

WHEN THEY SIPPED THE LAST of the tea, he remembered the timbre of her whisper. It contained the tiniest bit of grit in a pile of scree. He pulled her to her feet and in back of a six-part screen decorated with fishermen and mountains in mother-of-pearl drew her tightly to him, and this time she didn't resist. He kissed and kissed and kissed her till they were breathless and panting. She pushed back from him and shook her head, adjusting the hair at the nape of her neck, then put out a hand of protest to forestall another reckless episode of passion. He grasped her scarf, which he gently draped about his neck.

BEFORE DUSK FELL, GIACOMO WAS back onboard. He couldn't
settle in for the night because he knew sleep wouldn't come. He would
dream awake her profile, her silhouette, her shadow on the ceiling overhead.

He went up to the bridge and stood for a long time gazing out. In the
bright moonlight, he sighted water buffalo, geese, and ducks in the tall
grassy wedges of sedge along the riverfront. On the bridge, a cold breeze
whipped his cheeks, and for a moment he closed his eyes. He felt as
though he were falling into the water he was gazing into. Falling. Falling
off the deck into deep water, or was it that he realized he was falling more
in love with Lian than he could ever have imagined?

He recalled her sitting on the bench, feeling cold in the infirmary
garden, before they went to the teahouse, how he'd wanted to put his
arm around her, and then later the way she'd blown a speck out of his
eye when they left the teahouse. So close. Her warm breath jasmine
scented. She'd said, "This is how I met my husband. Not an auspicious
beginning." When she gently tugged his top eyelid to cover the bottom,
he automatically closed his other eye. But the irritated one began to tear,
and she daubed it with a clean hanky. She teased him, saying, "Now
what's the big sailorman crying about? Has your girl left you for another?"

Giacomo hadn't paused a second after that, but opened his eye and
pulled her into his muscular arms. "You're my girl now, aren't you? And
you're not going anywhere."

Lian tensed, and he saw fright fill her eyes, so he relaxed his grip.
"Unless, of course, you want to go."

On impulse, he felt it was the right thing to say. He didn't want her to
feel as though he were coercing her. By giving her the choice, he relinquished
power over her, and in so doing he hoped she'd succumb voluntarily. He was
relieved to see she trusted him. Her guileless face seemed to acquiesce. He'd
gambled, and almost felt arrogant with the win, yet in a sense conniving,
and this was something he didn't like about himself.

But as her slender arms climbed upward from his chest to encircle
his neck, his center was shaken and his balance rocked, for he knew he
wouldn't go a step further unless she truly wanted him. Did she want him?

A sputtering remembrance of what Lian had told him about her violent husband made him apprehensive—the thought that he might be forcing her made Giacomo step back, but as he moved away, Lian leaned into him, caught a little off balance but compliant.

He braced her tipsy position and instantly understood that her yielding was shy but needy. Once more she stood on tiptoe for his kiss. His mouth had thirsted for hers, but he didn't want to frighten her and so his kiss was gentle. He was not sated. She caught her balance; she pressed into him slightly. She wanted his kiss. As their lips pressed deeper and deeper into each other's, he lifted her into his arms, and holding her breathless and suspended, he covered her face and neck with real kisses he'd only dreamed of minutes before. He carried her inside where they made sweet love.

Now, alone on the top deck, the breeze fluttering his bell-bottoms, he felt bereft. He returned to his bunk but couldn't sleep. Fighting covers, listening to the snores and coughs of his bunkmates didn't help. Before long he was up on the bridge again. A gibbous moon smiled on high, but it didn't lighten his heart.

THE NEXT DAY, GIACOMO WALKED passed the machine guns and onto the bridge, where a magnetic compass hung on the wall next to the brass voice tubes. Charts rested on a rectangular wood table bordered with a five-centimeter protective edge that kept things from sliding off like the mess tables. In back, against the starboard wall a locked arms chest rested, signal flags above it. Aft of the cubicle was a ladder to the flying bridge.

Bulldog was at the wheel.

"What's the speed? Feels like eight knots," Giacomo said.

"Close. Seven," Bulldog said.

Captain Morante stepped through the porthole. The men stood at attention.

"At ease. Where are we, Rotari?" the captain asked Bulldog.

"Pulling out of the channel, sir," he answered.

THAT WEEK DRAGGED, BUT BY the weekend they were back in port and most of Giacomo's ship had liberty. Bulldog accompanied Giacomo to the dispensary on Friday night. They smoked a cigarette together and then Bulldog said, "Okay, mate, I'm going to shove off."

"Non bere troppo," Giacomo said, pretending to toss back a shot.

Bulldog trotted away, calling over his shoulder, "Have fun, lover boy."

Giacomo waited for the better part of an hour, pacing up and down the street. Lian said good night to a colleague and closed and locked the door. Giacomo appeared, and Lian jumped, putting a hand to her chest.

"I didn't mean to scare you. Can we go someplace for dinner?" He put his hands in his pockets not trusting them not to pull her into his grasp.

"Let me think." She opened her tiny embroidered purse.

"What is it?"

"Making sure I have my key. We could go to the Shanghai Star." She put the purse in the bodice of her dress.

❦

A WEEK LATER GIACOMO RUSHED to see his love awaiting him in the little set of comfortable rooms he'd come to cherish. He took the key from the lintel and opened the door. The room was dark except for one candle burning on top of a bottle of beer. Lian sprawled on the bed, leaning on an elbow. He undressed, dropping his clothes on a chair, and walked over to the bed to be next to her, resting on the opposite elbow. He leaned over to kiss her. She pulled her head and shoulders back and looked into his eyes. He inched forward again, trying to kiss her, but she tugged her upper body away from him. She looked at him. He knew he wore dismay on his face, and a look of sorrow and misunderstanding dwelled in his eyes. "Are you angry?" he asked.

"Only teasing." Then in one swift, catlike move, she rolled on top of him, her open kimono a deep V to her waist, where it flared out over him covering them both. She kissed him slowly, and then again. She repeated and repeated these little kisses, until one instant of complete possession of his mouth, his arms around her, his hands open and pulling her onto him.

❦

A FEW DAYS LATER GIACOMO was once again aboard the *Leopardo* traveling the Chen River. Along the riverfronts the tragedy of the Boxer Rebellion could be noted in the devastation of towns and Christian missions. From northern China reports came in and were repeated over the loudspeaker every day. Several hundred foreigners, mostly missionaries living in small towns or in the countryside, were being massacred monthly. *Murder* was a frequently heard word bandied about in cafes, bars, nightclubs, tearooms, restaurants, whorehouses, and on ships. Scuttlebutt flowed like the Yangtze herself about the rebellion, and most especially on Giacomo's gunboat. Rumors had it that more than fifty thousand Chinese Christians had been killed.

The ship made repairs, took on water and supplies at Hangkow, and was ready to get underway to Panchen. When the last men left shore to return shipside, they spotted riots on the quay. They scurried into launches to make it back shipside. Caught up in the chaos, two men were injured by enemy fire and two more through their own clumsiness. Captain Morante ordered the hoses out and guns manned, though no one was to fire unless fired upon and only after receiving the captain's order. Giacomo and Bulldog had rifles trained on the seditious gang. Bulldog asked which one Giacomo would kill first because he didn't want to waste a shot on the same man. Giacomo turned left and trained his gun sights on a youth at the front of the crowd, waving a saber and shouting orders.

"The loud mouth with the sword—no shirt and wearing a long red bandana."

The men were itching to engage in combat but nothing untoward occurred and all launches made it back safely. Audible grunts and groans could be heard when they were told to stand down and lower their weapons and prepare to depart. After repairs, the *Leopardo* traveled the Hanpu River to the Mother River of Shanghai and a mooring rendezvous at Shanghai, on the opposite side and not far from the Bund. When they reached Shanghai, Captain Morante was entertained by Italian diplomats.

◆━▶✖◀━◆

GIACOMO WAS TIGHT-WIRED LIKE A copper spool when three more weeks passed and the gunboat patrolled as far inland as it could.

Bulldog was on his bunk reading aloud from a book on China his mother had sent him about the wonderful sights in Pechino: the Great Wall, the Forbidden City, the Summer Palace, Tian An Men Square, the Temple of Heaven. But these sights would remain unseen by the sailors aboard the *Leopardo,* except for him and a few others who had made up an honor guard when Giacomo had met Lian.

Giacomo interrupted and told the men about the exquisite beauty of the Summer Palace, reminiscing all the while about his sweetheart.

There was an announcement over the loudspeaker, and the men herded to the main deck. Lieutenant Rinaldi called attention and announced Captain Morante, who gave a five-minute speech, the outcome of which was that he was sending a small detail to accompany the officers to scout the situation outside of Shanghai where riots were taking place and there was much burning and looting. But the real mission was to safeguard the officers directed to the Italian embassy as a control unit, if necessary.

Lieutenant Rinaldi then informed the men that they were on alert and were in constant communication with some of the other international naval gunboats.

Giacomo and Bulldog headed out for shore patrol duty. Sartori volunteered to go with them. Giacomo was at the helm ready to shove off, when he said to Sartori, "Hey, you may get to see something after all."

"Bet your ass, if there's a way, you know I sure as hell will." Bulldog threw a kiss to the men leaning over the top rail waving and whistling good-bye.

Giacomo tied the boat. *"Va bene.* Check your watches. 21:57 hours. Rendezvous at 23:45. Detail leaves at 24:00. No shots fired. If you have to kill, use your hands or knife."

Bulldog drew his hand across his throat. "Just don't get caught."

Sartori seemed nervous and checked his watch again. The men worked their way toward shore, expecting to see rioters surging down the streets toward them.

Four of the men were back onboard, all but Bulldog; Giacomo kept stalling at the helm of the tender. He glanced at his watch and saw it was 23:57.

"Shove off, Scimenti, he ain't coming. He's a goner," Sartori said.

Giacomo thought, *You little prick.* "Wait, you brass ass-kisser," he said and revved the motors.

"I saw him go down," Sartori barked. "Take off or you'll get us all killed."

Giacomo tossed him an ice-pick look. "Three minutes. What if it were your miserable hide out there?" Again Giacomo craned to look back toward the encroaching mob. Now that he'd found Lian, he prayed he wouldn't end up dead tonight.

"What's the time?" another sailor asked.

"*Cristo,* you just asked. It's 24:03. Release the ropes," Giacomo said, maneuvering the tender in the direction of the *Leopardo.* Untethered, they bobbed in the water. Giacomo pushed the levers forward and started gaining momentum. Over the hum of the engine he thought he heard something and threw it into neutral. *"Merda."*

"Go! Scimenti, or I'll—" Sartori shouted but was thrown off balance with the rocking.

As Giacomo gunned the motors to take off, Bulldog leapt from the dock into the boat. "Thought I heard you squawking!" Giacomo shouted.

"Cazzo!" Bulldog yelped. "Since when are you so punctual?"

"Welcome aboard, sailor." Giacomo grinned. "Why so late? Hardly a scythe's breath of a moon. Figured in the dark your face would pass unnoticed."

Bulldog settled down and caught his breath. "I was jostled and spun in the opposite direction in a crush of foreign servicemen. Knocked about again, I looked upward to see a man dressed in long overcoat, leggings, and soft boots." He told them his Bulldog eyes focused over the heads of the mass and scanning right and left, he faced a bevy of archers strategically placed on other rooftops. Realizing what was about to happen, he started yelling for the men to push forward quickly. There was no room for a zigzag run. He'd been separated from his crewmates and dashed into the fray.

The captain had marshaled the men to their battle stations when the alarm had sounded at the beginning of the shore siege. As soon as the crew of the shore detail boarded and the skiff was in place, the captain gave the order to sail.

Bulldog, with no time to clean up for his report, and Giacomo by his side, stood at attention in front of Lieutenant Rinaldi.

"At ease, men. Scimenti, Rotari."

"Yes, sir," they said simultaneously.

"Rotari, your take of the events?" the captain said.

"I got surrounded by armed Sikhs, part of the Eighteenth Bengal Lancers—they had been stationed in Peking as a relief expedition before arriving here. They clubbed a mob of unruly Chinese Boxers, insurgents, armed with farm tools, axes and knives, a few guns. They attacked the Lancers while they escorted English, German, Russian, and other Italian servicemen to their launches by the wharf. On the roofs of the outbuildings of the compound, hooded archers stood with bows.

"There wouldn't have been any need for the escort, sir, except for this one sharpshooting archer, who, at the sound of a gong, got everyone's attention. He brought the string of his bow backward—touched the arrow tip to fire—it was like watching something in slowed time. He yelled something—havoc erupted and the crowd started running helter-skelter. When the archer released his arrow, it hit its mark. A British sailor went down and was trampled. Then other archers swarmed the rooftops. Arrows flew from up high in all directions. Even Sikh intervention couldn't allay the mayhem."

Captain Morante entered and the men stood at attention.

"At ease, gentlemen. How do you assess the riot, Lieutenant?"

"From what Seaman Rotari says, sir, things were out of control due to a handful of zealot archers. Definitely Boxers."

"Then it's true the empress dowager allows them to attack members of the alliance forces. Anyone hurt, Rotari?" the captain asked.

"Scrapes and bruises, sir," Bulldog said. "Our men had already cleared the launch; I'd been cut off and caught in the crossfire, but managed in my bulldog way, pardon the expression, sir, to haul ass and jump clear just as the anchor lines were released."

"Anything to add, Scimenti?"

"No, sir."

"Well, then, gentlemen, there'll be a little R and R after we head back and pull into the harbor of Tientsin." He coughed his usual cough to give him time to make sure he would say what he meant. "We'll come into port in a few days, and in turns, all will get leave. Dismissed."

Under his breath to Bulldog, Giacomo said, "We're literally playing Chinese hopscotch."

Out of earshot, Bulldog whispered back, "If Sartori rats you out about the delay, I'll chop him into minestrone."

Chapter 27

Shangdi baoyou ni
上帝保佑你
God Bless You

IT WAS EARLY AFTERNOON. GIACOMO and I sat on a swing on a small porch on the terrace overlooking a courtyard at the back of the infirmary.

"I see our story as steps toward a collision—I'm riding for a fall, put more bluntly, a mouse going blindly along the parapet, always in your direction. Thinking logically, how could I possibly desire you?" I took my hand from his.

"Perhaps the differences between us?" He draped his arm over my shoulders.

"You are opposite of everything Lu was. I am finally free of the binds to him and his parents. What legal authority can prevent it? I am a foreigner here too."

"There's a guy—a shipmate named Manetti who wants to marry a Chinese girl, but the head honchos are holding up all his papers. They discourage any fraternization—but how can they keep these guys from shore leave?"

"You mean to find the exotic?"

"Maybe even the real thing?"

"This is the first time I've ever heard you speak seriously of the issue."

TOWARD EVENING WE STROLLED ALONG the jetty. A kite to the right of us billowed, and we watched its flight till our eyes found onshore an old man, the little kite launcher, and a child guiding it. The child took the string and ran with it, and the old man followed along with a clumsy gait. Soon the kite was behind clouds, as though it had been borne away to a faraway land, tucked between the fantasy cols and valleys of every child's mind, every lover's, too, where all things are possible. Before we reached his ship, I turned and left as darkness eased in to cover us. He mounted the gangplank, and I looked back once to see his shape recede into the bowels of the ship.

HE RETURNED TO ME LATE the next day. I wore his blue work shirt that had swathed the medicines he brought me. He handed me another package, this one wrapped in butcher paper.

I took the pork and served it fried with eggplant he loved, infused with a fistful of garlic and ginger to keep away any ghost or revenant. I had to turn my head and hold a handkerchief over my mouth and nose. "I'm a little seasick, sailor. Sorry, but this cooking smell is killing me." I opened the window and sat down.

Giacomo's chopsticks, holding a piece of pork, froze midair. "Just when were you going to tell me?"

"I didn't want to worry or anger you. You are angry, aren't you?"

"I'm jumping through hoops of happiness. Angry? How could I be?" He put down his chopsticks and stood, walked to where I sat by the open window, pulled me to my feet, and embraced me. "Our baby. We've been given another chance. You will have the baby?"

"You want—I don't give you responsibility, but it's my heart's desire," I said softly into his broad chest. He lifted my chin and kissed me gently. He knelt down and whispered to my belly, then sang our baby a Sicilian folksong, *"Ciuri, Ciuri."*

"What's it mean?" I asked.

"It's dialect for flower and it's an endearment."

"You are not displeased then?" I asked.

"Light of my life, how could I be?"

WINTER SNOW-DRIFTED BY. LATE in the evening I thought, *It will fade soon; like the dying light from the window.* What could be borne of this alteration of light and night? Snow swirled in gusts of wind, little dervishes, piling themselves into huge heaps. As I listened to Giacomo's breathing in a deep sleep, thoughts of Yogis and Zhugong came to me. I picked up a page of *mao-bian,* a rich golden paper handmade of bamboo fibers according to centuries-old methods. *This soft consistency will augment the composition,* I thought, *for it is perfect for any ink and all my watercolors.* I wrote *mao*—rough, and *bian*—edge. Together their meaning was "roughly made paper out of dry straw," or "some dry stems from a rice paddy field." Chinese. Perfect sense.

I began to scrawl:

> *Giacomo calls my name so sweetly that I feel baptized. Guo Xide wanted to douse me with sacramental water, but his ablutions couldn't wash the sins of this housewife, who abandoned the conjugal roof and ran off with her child, only to see her pulled away into a watery grave.*
>
> *He sleeps late. I draw on the dao-cao fibrous rice straw, soft, absorbent paper, durable and suits my watercolor and brush painting. I paint the dragon with hunter's eyes, deep brown, like forest duff, wide as a river, oval eyes, shipwrecked pressed-glass beads. Giacomo's eyes. He is leaving me again. Each separation is the grappling of a thousand clinging souls forced into the netherworld for eternity.*

On my windowsill sat a green pear. I picked it up and sniffed its gentle perfume, wanting to bite and taste its delectable flesh, but had bought it for Giacomo and so replaced it. The fruit reminded me of an old tale, *The Magic Pear Tree.* Outside the cold iron-gray sky was flecked with meaningful milk clouds. Snow, heavier now, all-encompassing and determined to blight. Soon a blizzard's winter white would silence, blind and bury everything. So late in the season. A fleeting thought of my snow house and the horse came to me. *Where is the beauty now?*

Giacomo stirred.

"Finally, you wake. What were you dreaming?"

"Come here and I'll show you."

LATE THE NEXT DAY, I took up again the wet ink stone and brush.

I cannot finish drawing my dragon. The hour grows late and still he does not come. Waiting. I do it best. I look at the clock and my father's pocket watch till I hypnotize myself. How long must I wait?

I am taken up with clocks and time, and the memory of Giacomo's face and the sweet, almondy taste of his tongue when he kissed me good-bye. Good-bye, yes he had said that, not good night, or farewell till tomorrow. Time is my enemy; it keeps him away from me. I should be working to occupy my brain, and not ponder timepieces and time passage. My grandmother used an hourglass to time eggs. For me, time has stopped, circumnavigated itself, the mechanisms unwinding and finally standing still.

Here I sit writing this in order to fribble away my time, or else I will become frenzied by thought. It was only after I gave Giacomo my father's watch that I remembered: never ever give a clock as a gift. The Chinese sound for clock is 鐘' *zhong. One should never give it as a present because the pronunciation of giving a clock* ' 送鐘' *sung zhong to a person is the same as* '送終' *sung zhong, which means to bid farewell or attending to a dying relative on the deathbed. What would Guo Xide say to that? I'm so superstitious.*

Perchance he's in danger. He could have fallen into the river, or may not have been given shore leave and jumped ship. This I told him would not please, but rather vex me. How can I remain calm when the object of my love absents himself? He is such a gambling fool, and I am such a fool for loving him. What can I possibly expect from this except a broken heart? But I am happy in the moment. I live for his company. The times when I am without him are unbearable. I sewed a fob at the waistline of his blue uniform pants, to house this watch I gave him, like my father, on those rare occasions whenever he wore Western dress. Why did Giacomo leave the watch behind? Did he forget it, or is this the way to tell me he will never return? He wears a wristwatch—two golden rigid bracelet bands on the side of the watch hollow in between where I tug at the tufts of the hair at his wrist. Giacomo is very hairy. Like a monkey. Like my father. Chinese men's bodies are hairless. I love the soft down that covers his body. I am driving myself over the precipice of sanity. I am in a time warp from which I must escape. I will close this writing now to pace. What else can I do?

Time will not go forward. Why did I refuse to work today? Oh, foolish, foolish, lovesick woman. I paced and counted the steps and then timed myself. How many steps in thirty seconds, forty? I held the timepiece and counted as the little hand made its upsweep. I stopped. This is no good. I must occupy my time with some useful task. But what?

I have not been writing much, but did a little each day, and I accomplished some task or goal I'd set for myself. On a sheet of sky-blue cataloguing paper I scribble words crooked as the winding path that leads you to me. I've eaten nothing since Sunday last, imparting a dizzying vortex, senselessness to all I attempt—the cookstove still unlit, the wok empty, the vegetables uncut in disarray upon the tabletop. A blind sympathizer to others in wait. My hearing has become acute. So sharpened. I listen now for the sound of your step on the stair, joy in my pain as I twist and curl and uncurl my hair with my index finger, seemingly serene, the palms of my hands moist, while moons form under my arms staining my silk blouse. Dominated by a humble display of love, desire of the beloved's presence. It has been months now that I am overwhelmed by nausea. My constant fear is that I will lose his baby. I lie upon unchanged sheets that hold your cologne, and the sweep of my long hair on the pillow reminds me of my wedding night and what I lost so long ago in the past, before I could even claim it as mine. How many things have I lost in my life before you came to me, oh, savior of my soul, my life, my heart, my all?

You're late. Perhaps you'll never come again; my despair widens like ice fronds in the windows' corners, shadows on a deserted ghost ship—daunted, discordant— even the mirrorless dresser mocks me.

My brush marks skittered. I jumped when I heard his voice call to me, so lost in thought had I been.

IN THE IMPROVISED CLOSET, AN alcove with a curtain draped across a wooden pole Giacomo hung for me, were his boots, salt encrusted, curled leather toes from the wet of rivers, rain, and ocean— misshapen, unlovely, but how I loved them. I picked them up and held them to my breasts, caressing them the way a mother does a child. Even when the world thinks it ugly, a mother always will find it beautiful. All the relatives say this child has special charms and will be lucky. But the mother isn't fooled by the compliments and wards off the evil in ways she knows will work.

I took the boots on the way to the infirmary and dropped them off at the cobbler's. He said he'd do what he could with them, but not to expect a miracle. Later on my way home, I was happy to pay him for indeed he'd tonsured and resculpted, transformed the boots, now blacked and shining beyond recognition—such ugly twins altered magically into sprites.

Icicles hung from the slanted eaves and a smattering of snow covered me as I walked, admiring the precision of snowflakes, each a different crystal wheel or lace doily. I stuck out my tongue and caught one, like the horse, Snowflake, feeling at once silly yet sublime,.

WINTER DAYS TURNED TO SPRING and rain washed away the remaining soiled snow. I was glad to see it go. Pristine snow falling from the sky seemed so magical, but the remaining muddy slush somehow reminded me of Hong Kong. Flowers bloomed and I was radiant with love. We were together as often as time would allow. But before I adjusted to the lush green of spring, Giacomo visited me with bad news. On May 28 and 29, Boxers had burned railroad stations between Peking and Paotingfu, including a huge railroad junction at Fengtai. The legations in Peking, afraid they were going to be isolated, telegraphed for help. The instant reply was the deployment of sailors and marines from foreign ships off China's coast. On May 31, US Marines reached the Chinese capital of Peking to defend the Legation Quarter from the Boxers.

Giacomo was sure he'd be dispatched there again soon and was furious at the stupidity of his captain for leaving Peking in the first place, but then Giacomo knew the captain's orders were from someone higher up. In which case, Giacomo wouldn't have been able to spend all this time with me. There were riots right here in Tientsin, where Boxers marched in the city with the heads of murdered missionaries on spikes.

⟡

BEFORE HE HAD COME TO me he'd been on maneuvers for the weeks of June. I had heard a rumor his ship fast approached the city harbor. When his ship docked, I was there, pacing, waiting, watching from shore, accosted by bugs and French sailors along the quay.

When he finally got off, we managed to hail a rickshaw and rode on it to the edge of town and there found a horse and cart to take us outside the city for what we hoped would be a weekend of leisure.

We stopped at a guest cottage with a thatched roof. He told me he and some of his comrades had been engaged in a skirmish and his arm was grazed. It was superficial, but I washed and wrapped it. It became chilly in the evening and Giacomo set a fire. I slipped under his arm and rested my chin on his chest. We made love by the fire. He caressed my belly and spoke to the child in a delicate singsong. Then we shared a meal of rice, garlic scapes, green onions, and eggs in a tiny respite hall.

Giacomo had wanted to buy some meat but found nothing available along the way. I was not interested in food to fuel the body, but the taste of him to feed and nourish my heart.

We walked in a garden after dinner. Giacomo said, "The choices Captain Morante is dealing with are career-making decisions, and he's fouling up. Personally, I don't care one way or another for his advancement, and want to stay out of the fray, but the men are itching to fight."

"I am afraid for you all the time. One day you will not return to me."

"I will always come back."

"Soon it will be full summer. Fireflies are swarming." I dredged up a memory of how I had helped Ya Chen capture these bugs, always promising to set them free at the end of playtime. I was accosted by dust squalls. "How I long to be quit of the city and on the outskirts just to breathe fresh air and take a bath in the river like that weekend at the cottage. Do you remember? Where has the time gone?"

We returned to our quarters and spoke of a future life together. A dream. Giacomo fell asleep, and reality descended upon me. How could we carve out a life together? Impossible.

◆━┿┽┿━◆

AFTER OUR BLISSFUL WEEKEND, HE was gone again. My habitual morning actions seemed bogged down by the heat. I sent word with a courier—a neighbor boy who was fleet as mercury on his two-wheeler—to the infirmary I would not go to work as usual because I was unwell. When I was not at the dispensary, I whiled away the morning reading, heated some soup for lunch, and took a nap, so out of character; I reproached myself for the waste of time. I took up the brush, and when I finished painting a dragon's claws, his heart, his flame-throwing mouth along the border of the page, I refreshed the ink and wrote in my chronicle.

> *Telling Giacomo when I first fell in love with him surprised even me. I said to him, "If you ask me if I love you, I have to tell you that I barricaded my heart from you, but despite it, I fell—a starling pierced by a hunter's arrow." I said to love someone you must divest yourself of yourself completely, for you become a part of the other, and therefore his fate is mixed with yours, and yours with his. Love is, after all, the giving of oneself gift-wrapped with the expectation of being opened. Something in the way he calls my name makes me know I mean the world to him. Something in the way he looks at me with his intense eyes, but is that love? Without his love, the center of the world will not hold for me, the planets will not orbit, the gravitational pull will not exist, and I will fly off somewhere into space. But so different now. Blame no longer rests within me for leaving Lu. What I did, I did to survive, but never would I have gone to Hong Kong if I knew it would mean the loss of my daughter. Never. Never would I have left Lu, no matter what sacrifice to myself, had I known it would have cost me the loss of my precious Ya Chen. I went . . . blindly thinking I could control my fate, but in the caves I learned the truth. Nothing happens by accident. The important aspects of life—sickness, aging, and the surety of death—cannot be dominated by will.*
> *Copulating with Lu was an obligation, and he wielded his*

dominance over me by crushing my strength of will, making me subservient to his desires. He didn't desire me at all as a lover, but as a vessel in which to deposit his frustration and need for supremacy. At times, I despise myself for renouncing Lu, for being a coward and fleeing, but when I remember the harshness of his tone, the tight-lipped commands, the impatient movements of his lustful body crushing mine, seeking release from his own devils, then I wish hell had taken him before my darling little girl. Perhaps she'd still be alive, and together we would be in celestial Guilin, with its hills and cliffs and miraculous mauve mist.

Giacomo. I even love his name. Love to say it. Love to look upon him, and see the muscular strength of his arms as they encircle me, and the powerful shoulders through his middy. Different in so many ways. I look at Giacomo's mustache and know his huge grin of snowy teeth hides beneath. Sometimes in sleep, his eyelids twitter like a bird's wings before flight. I can almost see goodness and kindness behind his lids, his eyes, warm and brown like deep-plowed earth drenched with sunlight.

On a piece of wrapping paper I had saved from Giacomo's last supply package, I cut and folded three papers, and wrote these words: *sunlight, starlight, moonlight*—all the lights in his eyes. I felt somewhat better. I took the papers with me and walked to what I now thought of as "sickbay," a term Giacomo used. There, I hung the papers from the wayfarer tree in the infirmary's garden as if I wanted the wind and rain and all of nature to temper them. *The wayfarer's tree*, I mused, *a hobblebush*. Hobbled. Yes, Zhugong. To Giacomo. A prayer escaped my lips, "May these ripe purple berries mixed with red bring luck."

I left the garden and walked to a neighboring teahouse, where already the night lanterns glowed. I had an appointment to meet Don Bruno there, and went often to this House of Cha for a cup of Dragon Well Tea after my duties were finished. I ordered a pot of tea. Settling myself, I watched the tall priest dressed in Chinese garb enter and bow his head under the lintel. When he was seated, I began to perspire.

I fanned myself and was quiet for a time. Without preamble, I said, "My visions are a wayfarer's dream. How can I hope for a future with Giacomo? He'll leave me and once again, I'll have to fend for myself. I've been alone so long, no wonder I grab at any straw of affection—wouldn't a dog turn his head if you scratched behind his ears?"

"He's not tossing a bone to a dog. You're beautiful and you're wrong if you think like that. I've heard his deepest desires, though I will not speak of them."

"Blind faith, a blind man's Seeing Eye dog then."

Don Bruno shook his head.

I felt warm and removed my silk jacket as the tea arrived. The little servant boy in black cotton bowed and backed away.

"Father, I see him at the oddest times—in the grain of the wood of my trunk, in cloud formations as I gaze toward the Man of Heaven. I see him as the wild fury of the sea, unbridled in his passions; he is as lush as the green leaves of summer, sometimes harsh like a stormy wind. He's fate and mystery in one. Giacomo is an entity beyond hope or magic—all I desire."

"Oh, God bless you, my child, you are bewitched by him. I will—"

I poured the tea. "What? Pray for me? I'm beyond prayer, good priest. I'm possessed. I am losing myself in him. He's everything I've ever wanted, everything I wished to have had with Lu." My words a whisper tinted with surprise, I said, "Absolutely everything."

My mind painted him as my soul, a dragon in sailor's cap, and I smiled, the image so ludicrous. Don Bruno patted my hand to bring me back from my reverie.

"I'll be all right. Please don't worry about me. And heaven forbid! Don't write Guo Xide to tell him I've fallen hopelessly in love with a sailor."

"Then you haven't heard."

"Heard?" My eyes drifted and caught sight of a hand-painted scroll.

"Lian, you must be more cautious. The mission was destroyed and Guo Xide . . ."

"Tell me."

"There's no other way to—he was hacked to pieces. Lord have mercy on his soul."

"Oh no, oh no, that can't be true." I felt my heart race and my stomach churn.

"His suffering, his body are all mortal, his soul is in celestial realms now." He took a newspaper from his pocket and slid it across the table. It was dated June 2, 1900. A month old. Aloud I read, "Alberico Crescitelli, known to his parishoners as Guo Xide, was removed from the mission in the Shensi Province near the Han River and then transferred to Ningqiang. Arrested on May 20, 1900, during the current anti-Western Boxer Rebellion, he was tortured and murdered. One of the seventeen PIME missionary priests (Pontifical Institute for Foreign Missions), the Roman Catholic Church is now referring to as martyrs."

I wanted to write him a letter. Why had I postponed? If my mind was not preoccupied with Giacomo, I would have. Thinking of Guo Xide in terms of deceased, how impossible. Confused, I finished reading the brutal commentary of the details.

"They beheaded him." After a moment, I said through tears, "An act of mercy, you know? And Don Gabriele?"

"He had already returned to Italy. You're so pale, my child."

I clutched my stomach. "I feel sick. Won't you please help me outside for some air?"

Don Bruno tossed some coppers on the table. "I'll see you home." He stood, put the paper back in his pocket, and reached for my jacket, which he placed over my shoulders and helped me from the chair.

Chapter 28

Xingfu
幸福
Happiness

GIACOMO WAS LATE. EVERYTHING WAS shut down in the closed market or the streets of her now-familiar warren. Approaching Lian's street he'd seen a rag woman on the corner who sold chickens, hens, and eggs. She was almost blind and held out her last two brown eggs as she heard his footfalls. Thrilled to see them, he offered to pay her, but instead the woman wanted something else. She asked him to bend near so she could stroke his cheek. "You are not Chinese, but one of those foreign devils. Let me judge for myself if you are dangerous." Her fingers grazed his mustache. She patted his smooth cheek, her bent fingers climbed to his thick eyebrows. He closed his eyes as she ran her finger along his eyelid feeling his long, curled lashes.

"Mmm. Delicious to make broth." She let her fingers outline his Roman nose and skim the bushy mustache covering his lips. She smiled. "Perhaps too thin for soup. No fat?"

"Here, little grandmother," he said, guiding her hand across his chest down to his belly. "Lean as a stringbean."

Unguided, she patted his shoulder. "Eat the eggs, devil. They'll make you strong." She chortled, and gave her most-winning toothless grin.

"*Tse-tse.* May I share them with my lady-love?"

"Ah, so you've stolen the heart of one of our girls?"

"Not really. She has robbed me." He wanted to say "of my soul," but didn't know how.

"Will you kill us in our beds?"

"We have orders not to shoot anyone—are you armed?"

From beneath her quilted jacket she drew a dull paring knife, brandishing it like a sword. "You see, I am."

"Then please let me slip away for my own safety," he said, eyeing a whiskered man in a gray cotton frock close his shop. Giacomo recognized the man who had tattooed Bulldog's arm.

She cackled again.

He bowed, though he knew she couldn't see well, and was surprised by the touch of her hands on his head.

"Wait," she said. "I was given this fish for ten hen's eggs. Is it fresh?"

"I think so."

"How do you know?"

"The eyes are clear, not filmy, and—" he sniffed. "It smells fresh of the sea. The scales are moist and—"

"You are not as foreign as you make out. Your Chinese is good. *Ni de zhongwen shuo de hao,*" she repeated. "Where did you learn to speak, foreigner?"

"I'm a sailor and work as a cook. I had a—" He started to say coolie, but caught himself and said, "a Chinese mate assisting me."

Mulling this over, she asked, "Do I know this girl you court?"

"She lives just down the lane." He pointed in the direction.

She squinted hard. "The doctor?"

"Nurse. Healer."

"You may have the fish." She bowed her head.

"But what if the other is not as fresh as this one? You keep it."

"Here. Look." She reached inside a pliable straw bag and showed him another fish. "Take them both. They are very small."

He shook his head. "I don't want to break your rice bowl—"

"I insist. I don't eat much anymore." She started packing up her wares.

"How can I thank you?"

"You already have. The girl will do well to have you look after her in these treacherous times. Besides the fish isn't for you but for the doctor who eats for two."

He laughed, bamboozled by this old woman's kindness and sharp tongue. He tried to put a copper in her hand, but she gave it back, bowing deeply. Giacomo had an urge to pinch her cheek, but instead bowed even more deeply.

Before Lian prepared the soup or steamed the fish, he brushed aside her robe to expose her shoulder. The soft silk swept her collarbones, falling like a curtain, sliding across her breasts. His warm mouth upon her skin and the scratchy stubble of his cheeks, were all too familiar. He rested his head on her belly and made a circle of kisses. "Both mine," he said. He cupped and released her breasts with both hands, moved his lips over them, repeatedly, bringing her to maddening heights. Her wet, sensitive nipples responded and she held back no longer.

"Why did I let you near me before dinner?" Before she could push away, or have another thought, she was in his embrace. "I've ached for this—what I've only had in daydreams during the time you were gone."

They rolled on top of the quilt in front of the brazier, the firelight in her eyes telling him far better than words how much she loved him, and how much the tiny image of himself reflected in those eyes said he wanted and needed her love.

"Will you love the baby too?" she asked.

"How could I not? He is you and me."

"Now will you cook for the three of us?"

Giacomo prepared the fish steamed with ham, ginger, scallions, and hot pepper. He offered her some. She declined saying the old woman had really meant it for him, and she wasn't hungry. She brought Giacomo a Ha'erbin Beer. "My appetite of late isn't very good."

"Please?"

She shook her head. "I have soup and some rice. It's enough."

"Cin-cin." He raised the bottle in a toast. "When did the Russians start making beer?"

"The factory opened this year."

"Thought their specialty was vodka."

They ate the meal in silence. She was pensive and he intent on not swallowing a bone.

When Giacomo finished cleaning and eating one side of the fish, he was about to flip it to start in on he other side.

"No!" Lian cried. "Don't flip it. You must clean it the way it lies on your plate."

"But why? It's so much easier to debone the other way."

"Do you want your ship to flip over?"

Giacomo stifled a laugh. He was just about to place the chopsticks down by crossing them, when Lian snatched them up and shook her head.

"And never drop them. Use care." She was about to hand back the chopsticks when she let out a little "Oh."

"What is it?"

"One is shorter. I can't imagine how that happened. Not on purpose I swear to you."

"Why are you taking on so? Who cares if they're uneven. I'm just happy to be here with you and eating this luscious fish."

"You don't understand. Now you will miss your boat."

"Of course I won't. I have shore leave for two days. The boat won't leave without me. Don't fret. Now may I have them back so I can finish?"

Lian got up from their makeshift table and brought back another pair of chopsticks. She measured them before handing them to him.

After the meal Giacomo sipped tea and slipped off his chair to the floor and knelt beside her. He unbuttoned his work shirt, a soft blue in the dim light of candles. "Don't worry."

"Say you forgive me."

"You didn't do anything."

Tears brimmed her eyes.

"Va bene, va bene. Ti perdono, amore. Come here. Let me hold you in my arms."

They fell asleep. He woke from the nap when she stirred and tried to get up. He caressed her curving stomach, and murmured, "Do you think he minds if I ravage his mother?"

"I'll make some tea."

He reached for her wrist and pulled her down to him. "Tell me you desire me—the way a sailor wants savory Shanghai pancakes after a long trip—the way I want a steady diet of you."

"Are you saying that we are *yin* and *yang?*"

He nodded.

"You are a rich and plenty soup. I am a plump dumpling floating in it. Am I everything fat your lean body desires?" She laughed. "Here take hold of my simple steamed buns and taste—"

"Which ones, these?" he asked, taking hold of her breasts swollen with pregnancy. "Or these?" he said, giving her rump a two-fisted squeeze. "Let me fill you the way you should be filled, my dumpling," he said, his voice husky.

"Are you chopped greens and tofu? What need of you to complete me?" She pushed him away, and swiped at a tear.

"What's this? It was silly food banter nothing more. I thought you were happy."

"I am. It's just a drop of memory," she said, "and this is so different from that, perhaps it's a bead of moisture, a dewdrop to slake the thirst of a bud in bloom and nothing more." Then in a low voice, and bending very close to his ear, she whispered, "I don't want the gods and heavenly powers to know of this fleeting happiness." In a loud voice she said, "Is this what you call lovemaking? Our talk of greens and tofu, when it is hot liquid I need? Pooh, pooh—I say, it is like little pigs oinking."

Giacomo's roar of laughter filled the room, pouring out the windows into the courtyard. "Did you hear that, gods?" he yelled. He pulled her into his arms, picked her up, her body draping his, while his lips dusted every part of her, his hands molding her as if she were clay. Her arms entwined about his neck, she burrowed her face in the crook of it, then leaned back, still perched on his lap.

"Stop. Please," she said. And he did. "I crave sweet affection and intimacy. With Lu everything was mechanical, rushed, and inconsistent. You are my man." She kissed him with tenderness, a brush of lips.

He waited and she was thankful for his patience until she readied herself—she loved him even more for this.

ON THE MORNING HE WAS to report back, a peg of sun crept in the window from behind stout clouds marbled with haze until it cleaved the space on the bed between them. She snuggled warm in his arms, and sleepily said, "Why do I let you near me? You jeopardize my psyche and I am a slave to your embrace. I have no force to push away from you. You cannot jump ship again. Bulldog warned me." She squirmed and stretched. But in spite of themselves they made love again and he almost missed the boat and thought of her chopstick superstition on the gangway.

THERE WAS NO SCHEDULED LEAVE for Giacomo so he jumped ship again, making his way in the center of a cache of men who had consent to go ashore. Once on land, he headed to see Lian. He walked passed a dusty storefront window and saw a scrawny man tattooing a shipmate. He was about to wave, but saw it was Sartori, and kept on walking.

When he got to her flat, Giacomo reached above the lintel and found the key to the door. She stood up from her painting table and crossed the floor to him. She smiled. "I heard you fly up the stairs."

It took him by surprise how changed she was. How could this happen overnight? Her face was puffed, her breasts full to overflowing with milk for his child, her slim hips were now voluptuous and curvy, and her abdomen, round as a ball.

He was afraid to squeeze this doll too tightly or she might break. He kissed her gently and accompanied her back to her table. She sat down and Giacomo pushed aside her paints and sat on the corner of the table, leaned over, and kissed her again. He saw her depiction of a dragon on a page in her journal. She blew on the wet image, then looked up. "If I could give you a diamond, I would," she said, starting to put away her pigments and brushes.

"Why?"

"It's a forever gift." She closed the lid of her cake of ink.

"I don't need one."

About to close her chronicle, he said, "Wait." He pointed. "Draw that dragon on my forearm, I'll have it tattooed. Maybe it'll quench—"

"Do you have such need to stake out my identity upon you?"

"A living record of my time with you. It will die when I do. I'll always be reminded of you no matter what happens to us."

"You are going away now?"

"Not now, but soon."

"I will never go away. You can always come back to me."

He started to speak but instead picked up a thin brush and handed it to her. He rolled up his sleeve. When she finished the dragon, she wrote *Lian* in *Nüshu* beneath it. In her heart, she would always be Chinese first. He blew on his forearm, plopped his hat on askance, and yanked her out of the chair, whisking her out the door and into the road to the tattoo shop.

She tugged at his sleeve, and whispered, "This is no place for me in my condition." She patted her bulging midsection. "I'll wait outside."

"Uh-uh, you're needed right here—for courage—" he hesitated. "What's wrong?"

Tears fell down her cheeks. "I can't. Please . . ."

"Tell me what." He released her hand.

"There are spies all over my neighborhood. Things are becoming difficult. Not everyone is amiable like the fish vendor."

"I'll take you home then."

"No. Please. I'll go myself. It's better. In fact, I will go to the dispensary for a few hours. The dyes are poison, you know."

"Wait for me later. Even if this takes a couple of hours."

"If it takes forever." She crossed her heart.

HE WAITED FOR HER WITH his new, bleeding tattoo when she got back. She washed and bandaged his arm with light gauze. "Now look what you've done. No clouds and rain for us."

"Huh? No lovemaking? I only need one hand."

"I have a better idea. Tonight we eat dinner first. Afterward I may be too tired to cook.

"I'll help. Remember, I'm chief chef onboard my ship. I know a thing or two."

AFTER DINNER AND AN ATTEMPT at some romance, they walked toward the wharf. Approaching it, they saw above the harbor brightness appearing sleepily; the skylight playing hide-and-seek after a night on the town. A white-gold orb appeared tranquil and benign, making a majestic entry into the sky. As the light became stronger, she retrieved her arm from his. They had agreed to meet later that day, if he could make it to shore.

"That," she said pointing at his ship, "is my biggest enemy. Worse than a concubine."

"I surely don't love her as much as I do you."

Chapter 29

Wo ai ni
我爱你
I love you

I MET GIACOMO EVERY SPARE minute I could while he was in Tientsin, every night except when his ship was on maneuvers. We became so intimate one knew what the other was thinking. He'd start a sentence and I would finish it. We shared a platonic love as well as an emotional and physical one. So close in thought, he said we were like brothers.

"You mean brother and sister." I started to say, "My only wish is that—"

"What is it?"

"I thought I was over this, but I sometimes still desire golden lilies to offer you." She pointed to her feet. "Bound feet are ugly, not beautiful."

"But they produce a certain walk like the willow switches undulating in wind—"

"Your walk is lovely."

"It can't produce the erotic effect when you look at those with golden lilies." Giacomo laughed.

"You do not know why the feet are bound?" I asked.

"Custom. Tradition."

"That yes, but the forced walk produces many folds of the vagina giving deep pleasure to husband as well as wife."

"It does? Let's bind them fast."

"Now it is my turn to laugh. Do you know how many euphemisms we have for them?" I said.

"Name some besides golden lilies and lotuses."

"Winter cherries, and some call them dragons playing with a pearl. My father never wanted me to be subservient to a man, but I often wondered if he did not adore my mother's tiny feet."

THE FOLLOWING EVENING A DOOR slammed. Footsteps in the vestibule below. Someone was coming up the stairs, rushing, running. A man's heavy footfalls. Now slowing, stopped outside the door. Before the runner knocked, I opened the door, my heart racing as if I had been doing the running.

"Oh," I said to Bulldog, "I thought it was Giacomo come—"

"I'm so sorry. He pulled duty and couldn't make it. He wanted me to give you this."

I took the note, looked at it as if it might speak, then held it to my breast and slipped it into my robe. "I thank you, but you and he are both lying. Will you come in?"

He hesitated, and I said, "Let me make you tea."

Bulldog entered and I saw by his flushed face that he had been running a long while, not just up the steps.

"Why did you rush so?" She helped him with his peacoat and indicated a small bench.

"You were waiting."

"I seem to do a lot of that lately."

When I brought the tea, Bulldog withdrew a flask of brandy from his coat pocket, opened it, and poured in a healthy dose. He raised the flask, as if to say, "Want some?"

I shook my head, nauseated by the smell. "Tell me the truth."

Bulldog took a pull on the flask. "Ratted out."

"You have rats onboard?"

Bulldog shook his head. "That, too. It means someone squealed on him—told the brass Giacomo was going over the side. He didn't get leave."

"How long has this been going on?"

"You don't want to know. But the rat did him a favor. If Giacomo gets caught doing it, they'll toss him in the brig and the key overboard."

"Prison? Are you here legally?"

"Yes." He blew on the tea.

"Stay here. Sleep till dawn. It's safer then," she said, preparing a pallet for him.

"We just heard the railroad between here and Peking has been severed."

"From here . . . about 120 kilometers from Peking," I said, supporting my belly as I bent forward to cover a pillow. "What does this mean?"

"The radio news was that a contingency of Australian troops are trying to repair the railroad and move forward overland. Word onboard is we'll probably sail the Pei-Ho River, toward Tong-Tcheou."

"How far is that to Peking?" Weary of the bad news, I sat on the trunk that served as a table.

"About twenty-five kilometers."

"When will you leave?"

"Can't say for sure, but soon."

TWO DAYS LATER GIACOMO CAME to the dispensary laden with arms full of flowers and a mouthful of apologies. He then told me that an edict was issued from the court—the ultimatum stated all foreigners were ordered to leave Peking. On June twentieth, Baron Von Kettler, the German Minister, was killed.

My face was stony. Fear rose in the back of my throat. I would lose him because he'd be killed or because he'll leave me at the end of this revolt. But still I could not help being angry for the chances he took coming to me. I crossed my arms and fumed. "You have duties and can't be with me every minute. Promise, never come to me without permission or you will not share my bed. I have my work too. Consider that. Shall we eat?"

There was a noise and loud voices in the front of the building.

"It's all right. My assistant will tend to it."

I placed the flowers in a vase filled with water and washed my hands. He followed me to the small kitchen at back.

After I drank the tea, he cleared away and cleaned the kitchen; we sat by the window and I told him garlic can scare away ghosts.

"When Grandmother died, I did not watch the sealing of her coffin because it is bad luck. Yellow and white holy papers were pasted on the coffin to protect the body within from bad spirits. The pallbearers—there are always many who offer to carry because a blessing of the deceased is given to them—brought her outside head first and set her coffin down on a side road and prayed over her. Then we continued on to the cemetery, which was on a hillside, insuring good *feng shui*.

"When Wai Po's funeral party came to a river and we had to cross it, I told my dead grandmother it was necessary—the dead must be informed or they cannot cross the water. At the burial site, I threw a handful of dirt into the grave, and when I got back to the house, I burned my clothes. I mourned her for one hundred days, as custom requires, and during this period I attached a blue piece of cloth—blue because I am a granddaughter—tied to my arm.

"Seven days after her burial, her soul returned to me, and to our house, and to make sure she didn't get lost, I put a red plaque up outside the house, a welcoming gesture to guide her to the right place. I stayed in my room all day, as is the custom. Before retiring, I scattered flour and talcum powder, dusting the floor entrance and hallway in hopes of detecting her visit."

"Footprints?" Giacomo asked.

"*Wo de tian!* Not actual footprints, the white dusting had been brushed away as if by the hem of a skirt."

"Or a gentle breeze." He smiled.

Thinking he'd avoid meeting Boxers abroad, Giacomo left me a little after 11 p.m. Later I found out he was mistaken. When next we met, he said that when he crossed the main road leading out of my district, he saw them, drunk and smashing windows, and not just those shops known to trade or barter with foreigners.

He skirted them and ducked into a passageway, scaled a small fence, and came to a wall, which he shinnied up and climbed over, tearing his pants. He jumped to safety and sprinted, zigzagging along to freedom. He handed me his pants to mend and left me after I sewed them. He had to buy fresh produce and supplies for the galley but was back by midnight.

❦

THE LATE SPRING MONTHS HAD been wet and the roadways muddy. But now in full-blown summer the streets were hot and dusty, and before long I was great with child. Giacomo thought I would be ashamed, but instead I was overjoyed. I told him that when he left China, I would always have him with me in the child, and I prayed for a boy. He met me after work and we went into the secluded courtyard where he blurted out, "Russian troops have been dispatched for Port Arthur. I've been thinking about deserting."

"I—"

"Wait. Don't speak just yet. If I jumped ship now, there's a good chance they'd come for me and find me, but if I did it when they're leaving for home, I mean Italy, well then, there's a likelihood that they'd just keep on going. But what could I do here? How would I support you?" We sat on a courtyard bench, talking till the sun set. Packing up some of his belongings, he said, "If the ship goes back it's one thing, but if we move to assist other ships already involved in battle—"

"You will not desert. It is cowardice."

"I'd rather die than have my parents know I was branded a coward—a worm of a man like the one who shot my friend Enrico in the back. And—I'm saddened to leave you, of leaving China," he said. "Impossible for me to accept."

Yet I knew when the fighting was over, he would leave, maybe even before the last skirmish. It would inexorably reach a conclusion. There would be no way I could follow him.

We spoke mostly of the child-to-be, instead of rehashing the theme of departure.

"And what of a name for the child?" I asked.

"And what of a life for us?" Giacomo answered, desolation in his voice.

"If a boy, what shall we call him?"

"Enrico, after my friend."

"If a girl, I'll name her Caterina after my paternal grandmother."

"Why not name her Lian?"

My face must have changed, eyes hooded with grief. We moved to a patch of lawn. I sat in a wicker chair.

"I'm sorry. Caterina is a lovely choice." Sprawled on the grass, he rolled over and picked at some weeds.

"Lian is not a Christian name."

"Oh," he said, "but it's beautiful and I don't care."

"Thank you." I thought about Fate and how it imposes its way with us mortals any which way, reversing at whim. "Caterina's a good, strong name. Shall we go? I will make you dumplings."

"A lovely name, though not lovelier than your name, Lian."

I colored at that. "Tell me about your friend Enrico."

"We have all night. I'm starved."

"You always are—but we will eat after I get comfortable."

We walked to my flat and ate the dumplings. He sat on the floor, extended his legs, and leaned on the trunk, a pillow tucked behind his neck. I sat next to him and he put his arm around me as he rendered the story of Enrico's murder.

We talked to the last of the darker side of dawn.

In the morning, I borrowed a neighbor's clothes and insisted that Giacomo wear them so we could attend the *jeitouju,* a street theater.

"I'll be shot for a deserter if I'm caught," he said, picking up a shirt.

"And I'll shoot you if you don't put them on."

"Way too small—my arms will stick out."

"Better your arms than your heart torn out and head cut off and stuck on a stake."

AS WE RETURNED FROM THE theater, Giacomo spoke softly and close to my ear, saying all the things he enjoyed about the street theater. He saw a cart full of fruit and bought two. "Wild peaches. Sweet and soft, like you," he said.

A sailor, whom I did not recognize at first because he was not in uniform either, approached Giacomo and whispered. I leaned in closer to overhear their conversation.

The sailor said, "It's the beginning of the end. Peking foreign legations are under siege; Chinese military and rebels have cordoned them off and are firing on the embassies."

"Who's in charge of the compound? The Australians?"

"British Minister MacDonald."

"Who are the defending forces? Brits only?"

"All the blockaded legations—everyone—staff, safety personnel, anyone who can hold a handgun. The compound's armed with one old muzzle-loaded cannon."

"Are you serious?"

"No, mate, they've got what they call the 'International Gun.' The barrel's British, the carriage is ours, the shells are Russian, and the crew manning is a bunch of Yanks."

Giacomo tapped the sailor's shoulder, murmured something, and steered me home.

Still standing in the doorway, I said, "Come change. You look like a scarecrow. And I have something for you."

He called after me, "No more playing dress-up, I hope."

I came back to him, flushed and happy, and handed him a small silk brocade pouch. "We never did talk about the material for your mother. I can show you where to purchase some."

Giacomo opened up the tiny sack and took out a carved jade Buddha.

"I guess this means you're not becoming Christian any time soon?" He laughed.

"It can't hurt. We call it the heavenly stone."

A little gasp escaped my mouth as he attached the charm next to the cross on his chain. He caught me as I swooned and carried me to the pallet on the floor.

"I've been bleeding a little all day, but now I think I'm hemorrhaging. I am afraid I may lose the baby. How cruel a fate, my love?"

"Why didn't you tell me sooner?" Giacomo laid his head on my breasts and caressed my belly. He whispered, "I am your father. I love you," and repeated, *"Wŏ ài nǐ."*

"Your Lian begs you to go to the dispensary. In the white cabinet near the statue of Kuan Yin, you will find a vial of snake venom and a hypodermic needle with which to inject it. Bring these to me." In his face, I read he was afraid to leave me. I assured him I'd be all right, but needed the medicine to stop the bleeding.

"Don't run, please take a rickshaw and make the driver wait for the return trip. And don't be surprised if when you give him a coin, he bites to test it."

"I know, my love."

WHEN HE RETURNED, I EXPLAINED how to sterilize and prepare the injection, which I self-administered. Giacomo pleaded with me to let him stay, but, after an hour when the flow diminished, I insisted he leave, lest he be caught absent without leave and have to face a court-martial. "Till tomorrow," he said, sounding forlorn.

"I promise, we will be here."

Chapter 30

Tianzuo zhihe
天作之合
Heaven-made match

WHEN GIACOMO RETURNED TO THE ship, he found a letter from his mother. He had received few letters from her, and he always wrote back when one arrived. The last time he wrote his father to beg forgiveness, lest he die in a foreign land without the opportunity to make peace. Don Stefano didn't write back, so Giacomo asked his mother to intercede for him.

Terrible dreams plagued Giacomo. Only that morning, he had awakened in a sweat, a sense of foreboding so great, he couldn't shake it till afternoon.

That night he dreamt of his mother, and although it was not a bad dream, it filled him with dread. His mother handed him a prickly pear and said, "The fruit is sweet, but beware, the spines sting." She wasn't talking about the fruit—what did it mean?

In the morning, his ship was readied for active combat since skirmishes had escalated in the surrounding areas. Daily news reports came through, and he was afraid he'd have to ship out without seeing Lian. But the gods were with him. The *Leopardo* had engine trouble although nobody could go ashore. Extra guards were on duty so no one would go over the side.

Giacomo stood right next to Bulldog as he signaled Fritz for parts, and in that way, a message got out for Lian that Giacomo couldn't get leave.

DAYS LATER, WHEN CALM WAS restored, some of the crew were
given a five-hour pass. Giacomo got off the ship at noon. The promenade
of the bund, an embanked quay, was lined with lepers, soldiers of fortune,
and vagabonds.

Descending the gangway, he saw a drove of pigs ready for transport
that blocked his path and had to skirt them. Men making wheelbarrows
were lined up in rows, toy salesmen cried out to would-be customers, and
clothes-makers were crowded by pedestrians and shoppers. It was rare
now that nuns, clergymen, and foreign devils meandered about. If they
dared show their faces, they were usually seen only in or near the foreign
concessions. Outside of these areas, they were often stoned or spat upon,
due to claims that these religious fanatics collected the eyeballs of Chinese
children and ate them as a delicacy. Giacomo read that this gossip had
begun in foreign legations kitchens where pickled onions were seen in jars
and served at table by grounds workers and staff.

He found Lian recovered and told her his dream. They purchased
green fabric—a silk brocade with a raised, overall silver pattern for his
mother. While shopping, Lian insisted they see Master Li, a fortune-
teller who cast horoscopes.

The city was a maze of skinny streets and almost impassable alleyways.
Banners and streamers hung everywhere at busy intersections and along
crowded thoroughfares. There was a profusion of beggars, merchants,
children, barbers, carpenters, and vendors. Messengers flew by on bicycles,
almost overturning sedan chairs. Winnowers bagged tribute rice.

Giacomo asked, "How did you come to know Master Li?"

She said, "On my way to and from the clinic, I'd often stop to chat
with the herbal doctor. I purchase remedies from several, but in particular
Master Li. He had also helped Don Bruno."

When they had almost reached their destination, Giacomo said,
"How can you believe in casting fortunes? Old wives' tales."

Lian and Giacomo climbed the stairs to see the man who read the stars.

Master Li, a withered, old man with a thin mustache, long beard,
and a queue, bowed profusely upon their entrance.

He asked Lian to leave the room, but she refused and said she
would translate if needed instead. After a few perfunctory questions, Li

put into words all the many things Giacomo feared but wouldn't admit, even to himself.

"You," he said to Giacomo with a bony finger pointing toward him, "will leave China shortly and all you love behind."

Lian didn't flinch. It was exactly what she'd tried to talk to him about, he realized but he wouldn't hear of it. Lian had told Giacomo after the hemorrhage that her pregnancy was not going well. She had very little energy but refused to stop working at the dispensary. In tears, she told him that there was a strong chance she'd lose the baby. All of that conjecture did not prepare him for what he was about to hear.

Master Li pointed at Lian with the same bony finger. "This woman," he said, as Lian translated simultaneously, "will bear you a son, but she will not enjoy other fruits of her womb."

Giacomo grabbed the little man by his collar and lifted him off the ground, "What are you saying?"

"Giacomo, please," she said, "it's not his fault." She tried to pull his hand off Master Li, but Giacomo's strength defeated her. "I beg you, please, let go of him."

"He's wishing us bad luck saying we will only have one child."

"He's telling you what he knows is true, my love—he's terribly frightened."

With that Giacomo released him and turned to face her, tears streaming down his face. "You'll be fine. I'll come back for you. I promise, if I have to leave you, I'll be back for you and the boy and we'll have other children."

"Yes, you will try to return," she said.

With that Giacomo knocked over the table, got up, and dragged Lian to her feet, while he screamed, "Nonsense, he's a charlatan!" He flung a handful of Mexican silver at the man who stood shaking.

Lian wrenched free of him, bowing in Master Li's direction. The old man bowed with exaggerated reverence. She picked up each coin and placed them on the table after she righted it.

Giacomo stood outside the door, his face buried in his hands. He caught a few words of pardon as she spoke to Master Li.

She sat again at the table and beckoned Giacomo to come back. Almost in a whisper, she said, "Master Li only reads what he sees. You cannot alter destiny, nor deny karma."

He thought of his mother's words, *What will be, will be.*

"Wasted tears, no matter how much you rebel or rail against Fate," Master Li said, and Lian again translated, though she knew she didn't have to.

Giacomo looked at her serene face. "You knew this, didn't you? You couldn't tell me because you knew I wouldn't believe it. I still don't." He threw more money on the table and stormed toward the door, where he turned to ask her if she was coming or staying. He saw that Master Li wore a bewildered expression, Lian one of hurt. She got up, bowed, and followed Giacomo out into a day so bright with sun that it dispelled all his trepidation. They walked past a temple and he asked her if it was a Buddhist shrine.

It was, and on an impulse he pulled her into the fenced-in atrium.

She squirmed free of his grasp, imploring him to stop a minute. He did, and seeing she took off her shoes, he removed his also. He doffed his cap and hooked it in his pants' waist.

A bald monk in a dirty saffron robe greeted them. Lian purchased joss sticks and incense and a sheaf of paper with gold foil on it.

Giacomo watched, fascinated as she removed the gold and attached it on a benign-looking, fat Buddha. She penetrated the heart of the shrine where she lit the joss sticks and incense and placed them in a huge earthen font full of sand.

She removed three lacquered wooden sticks from her tiny purse, jiggled them, and tossed them on the cold floor. All he could think to say was, "Why you little heathen, just what kind of Buddhism do you practice?"

She looked happy and felt as if a summer cloudburst had instantly ceased, and in its place blew sultry breezes. He wanted to kiss her right there, but the monk was peering in at them.

She said, "I like to cover my bets, it's a very Chinese thing to do."

He remembered the gambling houses he'd been in and the dangerous games played there. Again, he shuddered with fear. "Lian, let's go. I need to be alone with you."

On the return home, she was chilled. He heated broth for her, adding a spoonful of rice.

"You don't eat enough, that's your trouble."

In the penumbra light of dusk, he was struck again by her frail beauty and knew he must have a photograph of her in case they must part.

She ate the soup and then recited an ancient poem for him called "Winter Night."

He asked her to repeat it and she did three more times. But by the time he got back to the ship he could only remember snatches of it.

◆─▶✖◀─◆

THE NEXT DAY HE HAD a picture taken for her and she posed for one to give him. As he walked her back to the dispensary, he asked her to repeat the poem.

"I've an idea. Be patient."

When they reached their destination, Lian handed Giacomo a piece of rice paper she removed from a writing desk in the small waiting room. She dictated the poem, and he wrote down the words:

> My bed is so empty that I keep on waking up:
> As the cold increases the night-wind begins to blow.
> It rustles the curtains, making a noise like the sea:
> Oh that those were waves which would carry me back to you!

"So simple, but marvelous."

"And poignant."

"Who wrote it?"

"Emperor Chien Wen-Tiî, only a few years ago in the 1500s."

Giacomo smiled. "Only a few?"

Lian laughed and handed him a pencil. Giacomo wrote the poet's name after the lines scrawled on the coarse filament paper.

"Some things do last past the grave," she said.

"Name me one thing other than some men's talent for music, painting, and literature."

Without hesitation, she said, "A great love. A love like ours, heaven made."

◆─▶✖◀─◆

BEFORE RETURNING TO HIS SHIP late afternoon, the couple walked separately to a nearby park lit by paper lanterns where musicians gathered to play. One was a renowned *qin* or Chinese lute player, which was really a zither. After some time, Lian got up from a wooden bench and left without so much as a wave, going in the opposite direction Giacomo took. He detested this, but she insisted she was perfectly safe and he must comply with rules of propriety now that danger and violence were everywhere. She'd be safer without him. He shook with anger and fear.

◆━◆◆◆━◆

A DAY AFTER THEIR JAUNT in the park to listen to the music, Lian went into labor at the dispensary. Giacomo was with her purely by accident to tell her they received orders and were pulling out for so-called maneuvers, but he believed it was to engage in combat. Bulldog was with him. Protector. Brother. Friend.

Lian's face was drawn. Giacomo saw fright upon her face, not for the ordeal she was facing, but for sorrow at his departure. "How much I love you," he said. "Now more than ever."

"I am not alone. My assistant Yin is a trained midwife and even washes her hands," she joked. But her forced lightheartedness fell on deaf ears.

Giacomo saw her suffering. He paced and prayed aloud, "In heaven's name, dear God, take the child if You must, but spare my wife!" The supplication was like a dip in a frigid mountain stream and was quickly followed by the thought, *We're not married.*

"Lian, would you marry me if we could?"

"You cannot bargain with heaven. No pacts with your God. We are one, believe me."

Giacomo disconsolately knelt by the cot, burying his face in his hands. "Forgive me," he said in a muted voice.

"We shall marry, if you like, sailor. It is about time you made an honest woman of me."

Her anguish seemed to dissipate with her teasing. He didn't wait, but intoned the words, "In the sight of God and our witness Shona Bulldog Rotari, I take you Lian for my wife."

She gave him a small smile and said, "I take you, Giacomo, son of Stefano and your forebears, for my cherished husband, till death parts us."

He checked his watch for the third time and then buried his head in her shoulder and his tears mingled with hers.

"How cruel is Fate that I have to leave now," he said, hoping she would implore him to stay. But she did not. Instead she puckered her lips for his kiss, and said, "Be kind to the one I love, won't you, *anima mia*? Funny, there's no expression for my soul, in Mandarin. I'll have word sent to you in Shanghi or Peking through your friend Fritz."

"Fritz's ship pulled out yesterday," Bulldog blurted. "I could rip my tongue out."

"No matter. I will get word to you somehow—we Chinese are ingenious. Now go, but tell me something sweet for your son Enrico."

"When he takes his first breath, let him hear this: 'I will love you both all the days of my life.'" He kissed both her cheeks and then her lips. He looked into her sea-green eyes and was struck by the fact she had tiny golden freckles in them. "I love you."

"Be safe."

Bulldog kissed Lian on the forehead and wished her luck.

Giacomo waved from beneath the lintel of the door, then bolted.

In the street he cried, and ran like a wounded buck until he collapsed near the port. Sampans glided across the black waters of the bay. The moonlight silvered a path toward his ship. Boxer snipers, patrolling the outer reaches of docks had stolen munitions, and at night small groups would ambush sailors trying to gain entry to their ships. The whizzing sound of fired shots in close proximity. This was a battle zone and danger lurked, cloaked in black behind the pings of bullets hitting metal, ricocheting off Red Cross medical supplies, burying into flat strips of balled cotton. Giacomo stumbled across an inert body with a slit throat while making his way shipward. Bulldog leaped over the corpse, following at a fast pace.

THE *LEOPARDO* ENGAGED IN SEVERAL battles during the Siege of Peking, where many foreign legations were attacked. Forty battle-starved sailors were finally satiated, but the exhilaration of fighting soon wore off. This was real, no longer just preparation using scare tactics. Di Luise, Manetti, and Sartori were killed, five men injured, and one gun lost. On the way back to Tientsin, the fallen sailors were given a water burial.

News of Lian never reached Giacomo until weeks later when his ship returned and docked. Even in Tientsin, imminent danger lurked everywhere. Fritz waited at the bottom of the gangway to greet Giacomo and then sent him by rickshaw to the dispensary.

There at the back he found the Jesuit Don Bruno, who jumped up from the porch swing and greeted Giacomo with the words that came like a bullet out of nowhere, "It was her choice. The baby or her. She wanted the baby to know his father." He hesitated and coughed. "But in the end the infant suffered too much trauma to live. I'm sorry to say . . . he died with his mother." Don Bruno could not meet Giacomo's eyes.

"Was he born? Did she hold him? At least once?" Giacomo's voice broke, and he wrapped his arms around a wooden stanchion support.

"She held him, I assure you. I baptized him Enrico."

"Master Li," Giacomo said, as if that were all the explanation the priest would need to fully understand. "But he never said the child would die. He said she'd never have other children—or was it that she'd never live to see him grow, nor to raise him?"

"Here," said the priest, and handed Giacomo a piece of paper. "She wrote this and told me to give it to you with these volumes of her life chronicle. Her brushes, ink stone, and paints."

Giacomo unfolded the paper and read: "Time to write an end to the chapter called life—time to close the book, but you are near to me, for I feel your breath upon me. My mind now travels in realms unimagined. I have no more use for this body. Seek my essence in your dreams. I will not disappoint you."

"Did you see to the burial, Father?"

"She was cremated. That was her wish. I scattered her ashes on a hill near a field of bamboo and cabbages."

"And the baby? Was he with her?"

The priest nodded and turned away.

"And her ring, Father? Nothing was folded in the paper you gave me."

The priest cleared his throat, and Giacomo thought, *Is this from emotion, or is he just gaining time?* Where were the provisions he'd left for the child?

"What ring?" The priest looked around in haste.

"The one she promised never to take off."

The priest shook his head and raised his palms skyward.

Giacomo slumped to the floor. "I thought I might be killed, but this? I will not emerge from Lian's death unscathed. The scar on my heart and mind will remain with me the rest of my life. If only the baby had been spared. Why is God so cruel?"

"Who are we to question?" the priest said as he helped Giacomo to his feet. "You are young and strong. You will love again."

Giacomo didn't feel strong and cared nothing for life.

He jumped ship often and came back drunk. After he again saw the priest in Shanghai, his drinking was out of control and many of his friends onboard covered for him in the galley. The ship docked for little more than a month, and after two solid weeks of this behavior, he finally sobered up and stopped drinking before they shipped out for a rescue mission to Pechino.

Not a day went by that he didn't look at her picture or touch the Buddha dangling on his chain. But it didn't matter where he was, or whom he was with, he suffered an acute case of introspection, hanging over him like a dark cloud, a shroud around his shoulders. He recited Lian's poems and words like a mantra. Some days he couldn't think of them, not one word, not a turn of phrase, nor even part of a sentence came to him, and he became distraught and morose.

He had known complete bliss for such a little time, and now he despaired almost always. He felt doomed to live without love. He took up praying, yet demanded of God to know the why of what happened.

Bulldog tried to comfort him and bring him out of himself and back to life again.

In mess hall one day, Bulldog yelled for Giacomo's attention. "Resuscitate, man! You're not the one who died, for Christ's sake."

It was the first time he got a rise out of Giacomo, who picked the stocky fellow up by his shirtfront, whisking him off the floor, holding him aloft.

Before anyone could say anything, Giacomo was surrounded.

A gruff voice commanded him from behind. "Ease him down, sailor, and remember where you are," Lieutenant Rinaldi said. Then the two mates involved took their places, and the lieutenant and Ensign Bartolo, who had just been passing through, walked off. Everyone took a hint from the officer. They acted as though nothing had happened. No reprimand followed.

The episode was closed but gave Giacomo much to think about during wakeful hours in his bunk. Why wasn't he punished or thrown in

the brig? Later he learned Bulldog had explained Giacomo's loss and grief
to the upper echelon, requesting they give him some leeway and time to
get over Lian's death. The ranking officers complied, and nobody knew
why, least of all Bulldog, but guessed it was because Giacomo had filed
the application to marry Lian.

It was this incident that brought Giacomo out of his profound
depression. Seamen talked of nothing else for two weeks straight, the
miracle of how Scimenti got off free. No swabbing the latrines, no time
in solitary.

Lying in his bunk one night, Giacomo asked Bulldog how he'd
convinced the men with decorated sleeves to look the other way.

"I don't really know. I just saw you frittering your life away, pining
for her. I didn't know if you'd ever snap out of it." After a while Bulldog
said softly, "She's gone. And nothing can bring her back. Let her go. It's
what she would've wanted."

Giacomo realized that Bulldog was careful not to mention her name.
Giacomo cried, burying his face in the crook of his elbow, and wiped
tears away with the heels of his hands, then grabbed his feather pillow to
muffle his crying, almost stuffing it in his mouth. His body racked with
uncontrollable sobs. When he'd brought himself under control, he said,
"Thank you, my friend."

"Come drinking with me next leave?"

"Afraid not, my liver's about to explode with all I've guzzled lately.
But if there's a concert in a park somewhere, I'd love to hear some music."

"Why wait?" Bulldog said, and pulled out a small concertina.

Giacomo fell asleep to a plaintive melody and slept the night through
for the first time since news of Lian. As Giacomo's ship left the China Sea,
he was convinced his child's ashes had been scattered with his mother's.
Yet somehow he felt the Jesuit had lied.

ON AUGUST FOURTH, LIEUTENANT RINALDI'S voice came
over the loudspeaker and made the report that US Marines in an
International Relief Force marched out of Tientsin to boost the siege of
Pechino. Several days later the ships' loudspeaker announced the heroism
of US Private Dan Daly, who won the first Medal of Honor.

The troops of the *Leopardo* cheered riotously, waiting their turn to be heroes.

Giacomo's gunboat, a backup to ships involved in the siege of Peking, headed north.

❦

LESS THAN THREE MONTHS LATER Giacomo and his shipmates were on their way home. The only danger they'd encountered was a blockade of sampans and junks that had bottlenecked an entryway to a river. Giacomo had time to locate the vest that Lian had made him, and as homage to her, and his love and promise, he put it on. He and a handful of other marines had jumped on a sampan and while his mates were engaged in hand-to-hand combat, he hacked at thick hemp ropes that blocked passage. Boxers and their compatriots were shooting, and when they ran out of ammunition, they bordered the sampan Giacomo and Bulldog were on, trying to sever the ties.

A Boxer stole behind them and was about to hack Giacomo to pieces, despite the colorful vest he wore, but the second Giacomo turned to face him, a coolie stepped between Giacomo and his would-be assassin. A moment too long. The Boxer's hatchet dug deep into the back of his little assistant. The Boxer went down with a single shot, and then Giacomo yelled not to shoot waving his arms wildly, but was impotent in saving the boy. "Shen," he said, as he caught the boy's body riddled with bullet holes. "I'm so sorry. I thought you were dead."

"Now end of story?"

"Yes, my friend." Giacomo kept speaking in a low voice until he felt Shen's life force ebb away.

❦

GIACOMO SENT A TELEGRAM TO his parents from Rome. The ship stopped in Naples for repairs and dropped off Bulldog and some other Neapolitans. Giacomo and Bulldog did not drag out their parting. Neither man promised to write the other, though they exchanged addresses, handshakes, and a firm embrace.

On the gangway, Bulldog turned and shouted above the din. "Who knows, friend Giacomo, what the future holds for us? Never lose faith."

Giacomo waved. Then he shouted back, *"Tante belle cose."*

"Many beautiful things to you too."

The ship then coasted the Mediterranean Sea till he could see Messina across the straights. The smell of the air was so distinctly different, he wondered how come he'd never noticed it in China, where he had felt so much at home and at ease in his skin, in his body, and on this earth. They made a three-day stop in Messina to pick up new recruits. It seemed like an eternity before they set sail for Palermo. Finally the *Leopardo* sailed from Messina. Giacomo stood on the main deck and faced the east, strewing the petals of a chrysanthemum to the wind. He placed his hands, joined by the thumbs, in front of his face and made a deep bow.

Epilogue

Qing Dynasty
Ghost Festival the 15th day of the 7th lunar month
15 July, 1900

It is in Nüshu, the secret language of women, I brushstroke these final words into my chronicle with a sense of urgency. This writing is second skin to me, having learned it as a child. It has been a source of both comfort and pain all my life, like my parents' decision not to bind my feet. My father said I was a child of two worlds. My body has never been at peace with itself, the Western side wanting to claim my father's lineage and knowledge for his medicine, but the dragon in me, my Chinese side, has fought to belong, seeking an herbal path, that alas, is no longer any use to me.

There are things I want pardon for in my life, a life of self-wrought afflictions. Looking back on the words that spill over these pages, I realize I began my life in search of love, but end it hoping for forgiveness for actions I regret, for those wreaked upon me through karma. Fear, however, does not grip me since my sage Zhugong comforts me, chanting a mantra in soft tones as he awaits me.

Who will translate these pages for my beloved? This, I cannot know. Still it is for him that I write. You, my warrior sailor, will find someone to explain the contents within so you may understand my heart and mind. Yes, it is for you, Giacomo, all three of my luminaries, my sun, my moon, and my stars, that I write so you can explain to the one who will never know his mother's milk that he was conceived in love.

My little ones hover near me—like bees in a blossoming magnolia. I feel the souls of Ya Chen, and the sacrificed, unnamed one before he knew the light and warmth of the sun. May they forgive me before I cross the threshold and behold them again.

The wind is now ceaseless and a storm rages, heralding a typhoon outside the confines of this small infirmary room. The candles flicker, casting grotesque shadows on the wall, cavorting like the Monkey King on the coverlet of this gurney, transforming himself into seventy-two different images. My feet are cold.

The ink smudges, my characters blotch, or is it that my eyes are bleary? Ah, the wavering candlelight. The book is heavy for these weak arms. How strong when we embraced.

Light. Time. Memory. The topography of my spirit is what I, a wayfarer, have taken with me. I have been traveling to lose myself, and yet all of my losses, everything that is me in this voyage of renewal has deposited me here contemplating you. The greatest tragedy in my life is not having had enough time to be worthy of you, for it is in awe and ecstasy I treasure you and our love.

This room still holds the essence of you, Giacomo. I see you through a veil of pungent smoke, an airy wisp of burnt rubber, peculiar to opium. I am no longer in pain, but my thoughts run away like I did on the train from Guilin. I thought you would be the one to leave me one day forever, but it is I who must depart, and I have no wish to leave you. Your sweet eyes sweep across my body. Those eyes, the depths of the universe, understand me; you are telling me to sleep and will awaken me with your tongue. Now as my light and my pipe extinguish, I dwell on this—time cannot choose time, nor bequeath or relegate it. Time has no time to choose, nor have I.

Our baby has a healthy wail. Love him enough for both of us, and do not blame anyone for my choice to save him, to birth him and give him life.

I am so tired and await the priest's return . . .

~𝕷ian
蓮

Finis

ACKNOWLEDGEMENTS

THERE ARE MANY PEOPLE I want to thank for bringing this novel to life, but first and foremost is my friend and mentor, John Dufresne, who showed me the inner workings of the novel writing process and how best to accomplish this—he believes that what matters most is the learning progression involved in the writing, and I agree.

I wish to thank everyone at FIU, especially Lynne Barrett, who taught me to draw a plot; and Campbell McGrath, who showed me how to hone in on the energy of a poem, which somehow translated into writing stronger prose; and Meri-Jane Rochelson, who taught me to read on different levels.

I'd like to express sincere appreciation to all the readers and writers who had "hands on" with this novel: Marni Graff, Lauren Small, Melissa Westemeier, Mariana Damon, Mona Birch, Guo Liang, Dawn Li, Rosalie Muskatt, Chris Edwards, Stephanie Beard, Elizabeth Sullivan.

Special thanks to Barbara Wood and to Turner Publishing.

There are people whose feet no longer tread this earth, but roam in ethereal realms—thanks and grateful prayers to my wonderful parents: Marie, my first reader, John, who told me to write a novel; my grandparents—especially my maternal grandfather, Stefano Scimone, a sailor who fought in the Boxer Rebellion. Thanks most of all, to my brother Buddy, whose belief in my writing sustains me still in the dark, doubtful hours. I hope you finally get to read the published version of my book in Paradise.

This novel and its author owe a debt of immense gratitude to Lian's "adopted auntie," devoted reader, and chief rain dancer, Jane Brownley.

WAYFARER TRILOGY
BOOK TWO

Lemon
Blossoms

A NOVEL

NINA ROMANO

AVAILABLE FEBRUARY 2016

FROM

TURNER

PUBLISHING COMPANY